THE MARK OF DREAMS AND DARKNESS

ARABELLA K. FEDERICO

THE MARK OF DREAMS AND DARKNESS

For those whose darkness sometimes
overpowers their light, I see you.

THE ELENDRIL CRYSTALS

MAGIC	RINGER MAGIC
ANTIMATTER	MENTAL MANIPULATION
GRAVITY MANIPULATION	HEALING
REANIMATE THE DEAD	DREAM WALKER
RENGENERATION	MEMORY MANIPULATION
BODY MANIPULATION	VISUAL MANIPULATION
ELEMENTAL CONTROL	SENSORY MANIPULATION

PROLOGUE

Are we still a family, when all we have in common are the masks we wear and the smiles we fake? As the resentments mount, they threaten to consume us alive, gradually transforming us into strangers. Perhaps it's a higher form of insanity . . . trying to love those who deem this soul unworthy.

Now, it is time to do what I've been taught—play the role. Wear the mask. Adorn a smile. Be a good brother, even when I am not one. Being cordial and impassive is the only way I can assure my devious sister does not catch wind of what I'm doing here on Earth. The Starseeds are now at risk by her mere presence in the Aurora System. My Karalevine more so, knowing that Selenyte delights in destroying the very things I care about. I will not allow it. Not when I'm this close to getting her heart for real.

This sector of the Azurite is freezing, even for me. Not much separates this area from the harshness of outer space. Naresteé and I walk down an empty hallway, passing several circular archways by the time we reach our destination. Against the black walls of my preferred home, the orange lights bounce off Naresteé's decorated horns as she stops beside me. The entrance before us is made of clear glass and indestructible tempered nano-plastic, a red caution symbol etched across the entire length of the door flashing brightly in our faces. The SSPARROW soldier standing at his post bows deeply.

"Sir, the airlock is stabilizing the atmosphere, and the incoming ships will be safe to disembark once the system gives the all clear. The princess can exit her craft momentarily. Do you wish to take the elevator down to the cargo bay and meet her outside her ship? I personally assured the princess no one else would be docking at this time. Only her brigade is permitted entry. Your privacy is ensured."

I don't have to think long. "We will wait here." Instead of meeting her, I can simply find the eject button and blast those ships into the unruly darkness of space. The chamber beyond this door is a vast landing strip, vessels entering and exiting constantly. Disposing of the princess would be as simple as a critical failure of the decompression or atmospheric generator systems, sucking my sweet, manipulative sister back into the depths from whence she came. See how she'll play her three-dimensional chess then, when she's floating out into the vacuum of space as nothing but a bewitched ice statue.

Who am I kidding? She's already made of ice.

Besides, there's no way I'll be free of the curse of my baby sister that easily.

"I can feel your crystal surging," Naresteé says as she stands to my right, my personal SSPARROW guards clanking their way up behind us. I don't answer her. I don't need another to confirm that my rage is as palpable as the sun's roaring winds. My sister's presence always riles me. "You may want to tone it down. The Dawsons are scheduled to arrive right after your sister."

Fuck the Dawsons.

Fuck my sister, too.

She didn't travel thousands of light-years for the view of these galactic boondocks, that's for certain. Nor was it to visit me, as she so stated. She shouldn't be here. Earth is mine, its people mine. She gave it to me. Now she's coming in a pathetic attempt to pilfer it out from under me. My speculation, at least. No doubt she has more nefarious plans hiding up those wicked sleeves of hers.

A hiss of air blasts around the seal of the access point, the pressure and atmosphere both acclimatizing to suit the carbon-based, oxygen-breathing bodies exiting into the sweeping chamber beyond. The red lights on the door cease flashing.

The door opens slowly, mist spreading out into the black hallway.

"Here we go . . ." Narestée braces beside me, voice feigning excitement.

I do not step back to permit room, and my personal SSPARROW guards awkwardly shift to allow the entourage within the confinements of the hallway.

I hold up my chin high and maintain the glare that glides down my nose at her. Preserve a straight-backed, impassive expression; don't let her see an ounce of me. Do not allow her to see any vulnerability she can exploit. Be applicable. Be cordial. Be what a sibling should be.

She has no such compunction.

At the head rank of all her insufferable cohorts, my baby sister stands like a queen in the making. As if every hard angle of my sleek, sophisticated Azurite is all hers.

Our frigid blood and glacier skin are essentially the end of our physical similarities. Where I take after my father's darker features, my only sibling, Selenyte, takes after our mother. Thanks to the Silent Breath, not one wrinkle scars her porcelain face, despite her being nearly two centuries old. Her dark-blue lips are full, the smile she wears as wicked as the bejeweled crown atop her head and the metal accents of her immaculate gown. Like our mother, her hair is stark white. Yet, we share one more feature that we both got from our father, which happens to be his inky-black eyes. They're large and open, similar to Mother's, but the judgment that's glaring back at me is all our father's disappointment and malice.

"Oh, big brother . . . whatever happened to your face?" Selenyte chuckles as we come to stand face-to-face after all these years.

"Mother and Father will absolutely have a fright at the sight of that scar. Don't you have people to fix mishaps such as that?"

Karalevine's rage-filled expression flashes through my mind the moment before she slashed my face. My fists clench tightly.

Do not slip, not in front of her.

"Sister," I say as a way of greeting, "you're looking as spurious as ever, I see. Leaning a bit heavily on the Silent Breath serum again?"

"Perhaps you should consign yourself to the Silent Breath a bit more heavily, big brother? You're looking rather haggard. Certainly, you're not attempting what Mother had all those decades ago with the serum? She almost died over her principles and passivity. You're not as foolish."

No, Mother doesn't push back an ounce on anyone or anything. Father beat that tenacity out of her centuries ago.

The crowd of bodies surrounding us delivers a heaviness to the air that not even the windows to my right can dispel. The expansiveness of outer space resides directly beside us, yet we cannot help but feel choked by each other.

"Aren't you going to hug your baby sister and welcome her to your home?" Selenyte holds her arms out wide, canines fully visible.

We've never hugged. Not since we were forced to as children. Conspicuous.

What is her play? Why is she here?

It takes all of my composure to embrace her cold frame. I am left shivering; it has nothing to do with her body temperature or the frigidness of the space.

Selenyte studies me, her eyes attempting to unlock my secrets through mere force alone. Instead of lurking in those voids she calls her eyes, I scan the large group of mercenaries skulking behind her. For a royal princess's guard, they aren't many; however, what they lack in numbers they make up for in pure savagery. Exactly how my sister likes it.

"I see Marett is still planted firmly up your backside, dear sister." I smile my own devilish grin. Her main guard is dressed all in black and is a massive shadowy figure. He hasn't changed much in the

last decades since I've seen him. The long tendrils of his hair have grown down to his thighs, however. "I know you've been obsessed with little Selly since we were all children, but I'll give you three million Cato credits to toss her into the chamber's landing dock once the atmosphere gets sucked back out. What do you say?"

The constant shadow at my sister's back says nothing, the glower around his face a practical insult, as if he didn't hear a word from his future king. He's trained well, far too well.

Laughing, Selenyte slaps my chest, but I can tell how much it isn't playful by the strength of her "love tap." "Oh, Mal. It isn't like you to tell jokes."

She's right. I wasn't joking.

The docking chamber begins beeping once more, its red lights flashing. A ship is approaching the Azurite. The attending workers must park my sister's fleet and make room for the next. A constant shuffling, a perpetual coming and going.

My package has arrived.

"Are you expecting someone else?" My sister asks, genuinely surprised I may have more to do this day than cater to her every whim.

"I am, sister." Thank the stars. "Your usual room awaits you. I took the liberty of preparing your typical accommodations in anticipation of your arrival. I hope they hold up to your exquisite standards."

For a moment, she almost looks grateful. "How sweet of you, brother. Do let me know how I can thank you. I would hate for my sudden arrival to impose on your duties here. I'm sure I can find my way around the fleet. I do not need you breathing down my neck when you've got such important work to be done, I'm sure."

My sister often says one thing and means another. She's also a parasite for my attention, so if she desires to be left alone, I find that suspicious. Does she already suspect something? Could she know of Karalevine?

"We'll see you at dinner, Selenyte," Naresteé dismisses casually, something we both know my sister loathes. Naresteé always knows when and how hard to bite.

Selenyte's smile falls quicker than she likely intends it to, her façade beginning to crack. It's only a matter of time before she reveals why she's truly here. Can I keep Karalevine safe from her in the meantime, or is my darling little rebel already in my sister's crosshairs? Regardless of why my sister has come. I have no doubt our crowns will be clashing sooner rather than later.

Let the games begin.

CHAPTER I

THE FOLLOWING CITIZENS ARE OFFICIALLY WANTED BY THE ARIANYTE EMPIRE FOR REBEL ACTIVITY: KARALEVINE RUZZ, ARDELLE DAWSON, SYLO TORRES, JANCE GALLIVAN, SARIS SATO, AHREN JOHNSON, AND TRINITY MONTEREY.

KARALEVINE RUZZ

Grief wreaks havoc. It barrels within, infects your heart, and eats away at the soul until you're nothing but a vessel for its darkness. It's like the Grim Reaper in a way, ever watchful, always waiting. You can't keep it at bay, can't stop it from seeping into your bones in the middle of the night, when you wake in a cold sweat, realizing you're just a human in a finite world. And one day, you'll be gone, too. So tragically ironic. Grief makes you care too much yet also not at all. You're concerned about doing good on this planet, but all you seem to do is burn it all down due to the anguish latched onto your heart.

Whatever happens to me, let it. I don't care. All I want to do is feel something other than the grief and pain and hatred that's all consuming. Consequences be damned.

That hollow ache of uncaring only grows as I wander the streets of Zarmenia City. The thunder cracks violently against the downtown buildings, its alien-built structures trembling with the rolling booms. Lightning bounces off the slick, metallic buildings, spring rain walloping the apartment structures in an endless assault. The eerie night sky ravages this metropolis, taking no prisoners and no shit—much like me.

Dampness settles into the clothing beneath my hooded jacket. This is what I get for not having Pacey here to recommend the proper coat for the occasion. No longer do I dress for the citizens' peering eyes. I'm not their tyrant's champion anymore.

I'm something else entirely.

Pouring rain taps on metallic bodies as they approach from around the block, the clink of metal against metal reverberating as their marching forms draw closer. They think they've caught me. How cute.

But I've chosen my mouse trap effectively, drawing a Nest of SSPARROWs into a dark and hidden alleyway, an animated Arianyte Empire propaganda sign flashing close by. The amount of water cascading over my lashes doesn't block the sight of the dozen soldiers coming into view. Removing my soaked hood, I feel them closing in. This time, they are the prey, and I am the predator. Now, I will go after them with full force. After I've been hunting Nests for the last two months, *they* are the ones who should be afraid.

"H-Hands up!" a voice calls, half drowned out by the storm, half distorted by the suit's tech. "Turn around, now!"

I turn away from them.

"Your disruptor is trembling, Nest leader," I call back, voice neutral yet taunting as I side-glance the solitary red SSPARROW in a sea of cyan soldiers.

The air smells of earth and rain and the promise of death.

"Put your hands up where we can see them! We will attack if provoked."

I finally deign a glance over my shoulder at them. With a devilish smirk on my face, of course.

I do what the Nest leader instructs, slowly lifting my arms, but then reach for my sword. The twang of my ancient weapon sliding from its sheath causes the SSPARROWs behind me to go rigid, their tense bodies raising their long alien rifles directly at my back. *Do it. I dare you to shoot me. Split me open so I feel something—anything.*

Bam! A shot fires.

I swing my sword and body in one full, graceful swoop and slice the stunner bullet in half before it hits me. The two pieces clank to either side of me as I face my opponents. The alien occupation's police force, the SSPARROW soldiers, stand in front of me. Since the Titan Games finale events, where Geonni was murdered and Gavrielle's death was finally confirmed, there's been no room for fear. Only the ever-present grief.

My body flies through the rainstorm on the cusp of the thunder's roiling boom. The sword slices the closest soldier like they're nothing but air. Whatever the SSPARROW suits are made of is no match for the alien metal of my dark blade. I do my best not to kill them, even if it means I must hold back the rage within me. But I have no qualms about kicking the shit out of these squid-humping asswipes.

When that soldier falls, two others take their place, and I smile wickedly as adrenaline rushes my heart faster and faster. I'm a machine. No longer do I hide my lethal skills. No longer does the fear of my power keep me leashed; the Elendril crystal swimming within my heart peeks its head up in anticipatory delight.

Play with me, it purrs, desperate for me to set it loose. But I make it wait because I want to have my fun first. I covet the moment I get to lose myself in the chaos of battles and blades.

My punches yield little effect on the metal bodies, but I pour anger and pain into my kicks, the source of my strength leveling out an alien ass licker twice my size, before immediately cutting down another with my sword.

Don't kill them, I hastily remind myself, removing my sword from the chest of a soldier.

Every point of impact eases the pain inside me a little more.

My sword and I are one, gracefully dancing like a deadly ballerina. Puddles at my feet become plashes of blood.

As one soldier falls, I raise my blade to take on another. One more soldier comes out from a blind spot in the mass of metal limbs and decks me right in my face. An angry grunt escapes my lips as my cheekbone roars with hot pain.

The group freezes and goes eerily silent, sensing the danger. The only sound is the booming of thunder, the smacking of rain, and the cries of the wounded.

I do not feel good about myself, but in this wild, frenzied battle, at least I'm feeling something.

My crystal mark lights up, purple illuminating my face in what I assume is a mask of pure evil. I'm not, though . . . at least I don't think I'm evil. I'm heartbroken, and *my* pain must become *their* pain. They work for the enemy, so they are my enemy.

Malakyte Ardeen is my enemy.

He won't order his little birdy squads to kill me. He's too obsessed with me—too deranged in the head—to risk having me killed. What he didn't anticipate was that I'd come after him, sending a clear message that I am not afraid and will not stop until I get one thing.

"Where is Pacey Dawson?" I seethe, teeth bared.

The glow of my star-shaped mark on my chest lights up all that fury and rage on my face.

I've said these words so many times in countless similar situations. I have beaten and slashed and hacked away at those metal bodies, week after week. All in a drowned-out effort to find where Pacey is being kept against her will. No matter what, I will be the hero that girl deserves because she's my friend, and I don't leave friends behind anymore.

"Where is she?"

"Shut up, bitch!" a soldier yells from somewhere behind several others, lifting his rifle among the tight bodies surrounding him and landing a stunner bullet right on to my shoulder.

It hurts even more than it typically does since I'm wet, and with a roar, I rip the claws out of my skin and chuck it to the ground.

Fine. That's just fine. They can have it their way. This Nest has recently raided an apartment building full of low-income refugees. Several were detained on chumped-up charges of being suspected rebels. Stars know how many more would have been taken away if I hadn't lured the soldiers to this alleyway. They deserve every ounce of pain I'm delivering and then some.

It's been almost six months since losing Pacey, of dealing with this endless pain. Here, I have a shot at finding her, at least. The passivity of the others has been driving me mad. If I must do this alone to get results, then I will. I won't lose another person I love to Arianyte.

Another shot from a disruptor pistol fractures the air around me, and even though I manage to dodge it, I feel like I've still been struck with it.

Zeroing in on the soldier who fired at me, I find that he's holding the exact model of disruptor Malakyte used that night at the Titan Games finale. The disruptor Malakyte used to blow out the brains of the rebel leader—my mentor. I'm immediately pulled into the moment of Geonni's murder. Now, it's like I've returned to that room again. Utterly helpless to save him. The terror of that moment floods in, the memories an unstoppable tsunami. The pool of blood, my mentor's brain matter, splattered across the floor . . . A cold sweat breaks out onto my body, and I'm trembling from more than adrenaline. I need to destroy this soldier so the grief inside doesn't destroy me.

I don't hesitate. Pouncing on the SSPARROW, I jump and wrap my legs around the man's waist as I latch onto him like some kind of monkey. He's not big, tall, or broad—thank the stars—and my momentum takes him down easier than I expect. We fall, and I land on top. He screams as my sword slices into his hand, forcing him to release the disruptor and cry out in pain. I punch him over and over in the face, knowing he's got a metal helmet on, and at most, I'm merely jostling him. He's lucky in that regard.

"Didn't anyone tell you that it's rude to shoot at a young lady?"

I knock him out with the butt end of my sword before he can respond.

But I'm distracted, and I don't see when another soldier comes from behind and knocks me to the puddled pavement. I splash into it, pivoting and swinging my sword in a semicircle, slicing the soldier's ankles in the gap between the armor.

Her screams are already bleeding into the others' as I move onto the next.

The soldiers press in on me, but I continue to fight them. One comes at me as I'm thrown against a giant dumpster, the smell reeking of rotting things. I dodge a punch, slide out from under him, then jump to reach the back of his helmet to slam his face into the lip of the container. The metal on metal makes a hilarious ringing sound as I imagine the soldier inside jostling around like some cartoon character getting hit by a colossal bell. I pounce onto the next, moving far too quickly for any of them to catch me in those stocky uniforms. My body is beginning to tire, and they're gaining on me with every jab to my ribs, every knee to the gut. I need to find the red Nest leader—soon. If anyone knows where Pacey is being kept, it'll be him.

Gasping, I lose my balance as my feet trip over a fallen soldier. I'm falling backwards. Fear flashes through my body like lightning.

Now! I hear that familiar voice call out. And this time, I do not stop it.

My mark spikes, pure elation barreling into me like the best drug. Nothing else matters. No pain exists here, and I can lose myself in the ecstasy that my crystal allows me. The magic takes control and blooms from my body like spider's legs. Each arm of my antimatter energy finds its target without my conscious effort.

That's one of the many new benefits of trusting the crystal instead of hating and fearing it. We've completely merged.

With one fell swoop, every SSPARROW soldier collapses in a heaping pile of black metal and agony. The power I hit them with was minuscule, let alone enough to fry them to a crisp, like they truly deserve.

It all happens before my back whacks the asphalt, the bloody puddle splashing around me as my lungs burn from the air's violent exit.

Lying there, I stare into the sky, rain battering my face. Lightning dances across my vision, following another earth-shattering boom of thunder. If the sky could judge a person, it would pass its judgment upon me. Just like the judgment of the people waiting for me to return home.

With a painful huff, I rise and look around at the carnage I've so viciously delivered. Stars. But I'm not the monster they perceive me to be. No . . . Malakyte has kidnapped an innocent girl and refuses to return her. Emily and Richard Dawson, Pacey and Ardelle's parents, had quickly aligned themselves with the occupation when they realized how close we were to finding Pacey. Since then, she's been a ghost.

Walking past moaning metal soldiers, I find the red Nest leader and snatch him up. I rip his faceless helmet off and throw it down the darkened alleyway. I'm surprised by how average his face is. For some reason, I've always imagined the people underneath these uniforms as sadistic, evil aliens. There's something truly shocking about seeing a typical Terran beneath this oppressive uniform.

The man trembles as I pull the scruff of his undershirt up toward my face and whisper, "Where is Pacey Dawson?"

Thunder claps on the tip of my tongue, reinforcing all that I'm willing to do to find her. Save her. Protect her. Do for her what nobody did for me. *For Gav.*

The soldier trembles, head shaking in protest. *Don't kill me,* his eyes beg me.

The Nest leader doesn't speak, squeezing his lips into a tight, determined line. I shake and push him, but he refuses to budge. His gaze darts as he refuses to look at me, the damned coward. His gaze is solely focused on the sky behind my head. But wait . . . there! I spot something in his glare. A widening of his eyes, a slight narrowing of his pupils, a flash of fear or recognition, perhaps both. But there's nothing above us but the sky. My neck aches as I crank it around to see what he could possibly be looking at, and that's when a pit as wide and deep as a black hole opens inside of me. I glare back at him with shock written on my face.

I see it.

Above us, lights penetrating the thick storm clouds, floats the Azurite Fleet. The Arianyte mothership is the most guarded and highly sought-after location in all the Aurora System.

That's where she is . . . that's why she's all but disappeared like a ghost. Pacey is on the stars damned Azurite.

The Nest leader knows I've spotted his slipup. He knows I've seen what's floating above us. "N-No . . ." He's backpedaling. "I-I didn't say anything. I didn't say anything! If he finds out I told you, I'll be screwed. He'll kill me. He'll kill my family. Please, please . . . I have children."

The SPPARROW's face is twisted in horror as his fate becomes more sealed by the second. This is the hardest part for me. When I feel the pain of my enemy . . . I wish it was as simple as good versus evil, but it's never that straightforward in real life.

"You shouldn't have put all your eggs in the basket of a madman." I drop him. My work here is finally done. "Arianyte will always do what's best for them and not for us. That's why I won't stop until Malakyte is dead. For your sake, I hope I get to him before he gets to you."

After grabbing my sword, I use the rainwater to wipe off blood and slide it back into its sheath. The pain within me is finally satiated. For now.

Flipping the soaked hood back over my head, a large looming figure at the dark dead-end of the alleyway catches my gaze. He's tall, seemingly made of complete darkness, long hair blowing in the wet and wild wind.

Lightning flashes across the sky, illuminating the figure to reveal his large pointed ears and muscles that could easily break me in two. Despite the jagged light dancing above him, he's nothing but a dense shadow, lurking there like he's darkness incarnate.

The man is far too massive to be Malakyte. Plus, the prince is far too obsessed with me to simply stand there and watch.

So, then, who is this person? Why are they simply watching me? The thunder follows in the lightning's wake, and I can't help but feel a spike of fear as the sound booms so loud even the buildings quake.

When lightning strikes again, the figure is gone.

The smartest thing for me to do is get the fuck out of here.

I walk over the fallen SSPARROW soldiers and into the city's unforgivable streets. The SSPARROW sirens follow me home, hoping that's the only thing following me.

I'm not even a block from the alleyway when I'm stunned to see a sloppy, albeit distinct version of my star mark spray-painted on the building in the shade Grape Juice. At least, I think it's mine. The two triangles, one right side up and the other upside down, are obvious.

I can't help but smirk that it's there. My performance at the Titan Games really did inspire some people, it seems.

The SSPARROWs may see this and feel fear, but when the people of this city witness the star, I yearn for them to comprehend what it truly means—hope.

As I continue keeping close to the shadows, I can't help but think of one thing on repeat: it feels pretty damn good going after the bad guys.

Chapter 2

AN EXCERPT FROM GEONNI'S *A REBEL'S GUIDEBOOK TO MISCHIEF*:

INTRODUCTION: A REBEL HAS ONLY ONE OBJECTIVE AND WITHOUT IT THEY ARE NOTHING: FREEDOM NO MATTER THE COST; EVEN IF IT MEANS THEY SACRIFICE THE LAST BAG OF CHEESY PUFFS.

Even though it hurts like hell to walk, I circle the surface entrance to the undersewers three times before slinking through the abandoned church doorway.

There's no way I am going to chance that shadowy figure having followed me down here, and I've made enough turns, hopped enough walls and rooftops, to feel confident there wasn't anyone on my tail.

The streets in this area are dark, desolate, deserted. Go figure. Ever since the Reptilians overran these blocks, no one besides SSPARROW are dumb enough to enter here.

I walk up the steps of what used to be a place of worship that now sits skeletal, pieces of its long-ago architecture hanging on by a mere thread as chunks of its gray stone crumble under the weight of time and neglect. Nobody worships this religion anymore. They put their faith in a different tormentor instead.

It's even darker inside, the rows upon rows of pews left covered in inches of dust and fallen debris from the collapsed ceiling. I head straight down the center aisle, taking one last cautious look behind me to assure I'm not being followed, and I disappear through the hanging tapestry that portrays a cross and a flying dove.

The darkness practically chokes me.

The temptation to stir my crystal to life for the comfort of some light tickles my mind, the same way it does every time I come through the pitch-black passageway. Although, I know the guard at the end of the way will get touchy about it, so I hold back.

Once I feel the floor begin to descend and get steeper, my hand keeps firm contact with the cold stone wall as I go deeper underground. The air transforms from stuffy to cool, becoming earthy and moist. Then I see a flicker of firelight twinkle into view as it mimics the fireflies that used to buzz around at the orphanage. Every time I see the light, I reflect on the time I had there. I think of *him*. It's taken roughly two dozen trips up and down to not get claustrophobic in here, but it's the memory of Gavrielle that truly squeezes me to my limit more than any walls ever could.

"Wassup, ugly?" I announce myself sweetly to the guard on duty, who bares his sharp needle teeth at me the moment he sees me come into view. Although, I bet he's seen me coming a lot sooner than I saw him. Dudley's long scaly snout glistens, the slits of his vertical pupils thin as he sits in front of the firelight. He's casual for a giant lizard, legs spread open to allow the warmth of the fire to envelop him. It is cold down here, even for the Reptilians.

Dudley sniffs me with a gag of exaggerated disgust. "On the rag, little girl, or did you just get your ass kicked? Again."

"Suck it," I spit back. "You overgrown, sexist lizard."

We don't really get along, Dudley and me. I shake my head and continue on the lit path. Living with these savages is the sacrifice we make to stay within the city. There's no other place that Malakyte Ardeen can't reach, and here I sleep directly under his pompous nose. Knowing that makes it entirely worth putting up with Dudley and all the Reptilians.

The earthy tunnels eventually give way to stone, an entire catacomb hub expanding layer upon layer underneath Zarmenia. Its large city with walls and openings and hallways at least ten feet high to accommodate the largest Reptilians. Once I reach the central hub, where it bustles with levels above and below the supporting structure like slices of an orange, I head downwards to our small area we currently call home.

I get my typical growls and sneers from the Reptilians, who dislike our presence in their space. By the time I reach the lower quadrant, the lights are dimmer and the air is thicker and quieter. Every archway is a rounded half circle. The exposed brick along the walls is chipped and flaking off. There's no decor down here, no art or plants or spark of life in this dreadful place.

I enter the metal door that leads to the quarters I share with Jance, and this is where I am met with a wall of incessant glares. Looks like I'm fighting two battles tonight, and I know this one isn't going to make me feel good in any way. I must convince them that what I'm doing does work. Make them see the value by sharing the precious information that I gained this evening.

"Aren't you all supposed to be in your own rooms?" I say awkwardly as I close the squeaky door behind me, trying to ease the tension as it grows by the second. Sadie approaches me, and the dog wags her tail as if I've been gone for weeks. At least someone is excited to see me.

I then notice Trinity. The new leader of the Resistance is quite busy these days. Not sure why she's slumming it with us, even if she did negotiate our place here with the Reptilian leaders. "Girl, you're looking a hot mess." Trinity's voice is as skeptical and judgmental as each pair of eyes that assault me with their disapproval. *Here we go again . . .*

Except, this time, I've got proof that what I'm doing actually does work.

The apartment is tiny, which is why only Jance and I live in it. As far as square footage goes, it's somewhere in the realm of five hundred, and that includes the tiny kitchen that leads right off the entryway and into the living room. Two even smaller bedrooms are on each side of the trivial living room, where everyone is seated closely together on the uncomfortable couch that's in the color Pea Soup Green. These quarters weren't built for the Reptilians themselves. That much is crystal clear. The lighting consists of several lamps instead of one overhead light. Ardelle and Ahren sleep in a similar apartment to our right, Sylo and Saris to our left. And Pacey . . . there's a room for her, but it remains as bereft of life as a graveyard.

My eyes immediately find Ardelle's, as he's my second softest place to fall, and I know the man who holds the first spot will be looking back at me with disapproval in his gaze. Ardelle's handsome face is a touch sad, but there's more. There's *always* more.

"What you're doing is assault and murder," Sylo booms as the silence becomes awkward, dark brows knitted tightly and fists even tighter. Those Seafoam-Green eyes are darkened by anger—for me.

I turn towards him, ripping off my soaked and bloodied jacket. "I haven't killed anyone. I'm in control. All I'm trying to do is get some answers to bring our teammate home. She's the light of this family for all of us, not just for me. We all want her back. She brings us together. I'm doing this for all of us and for her."

I realize in this moment how little Sylo realizes that I'm doing all this for him, too.

"That's bullshit. You just want to go out there to piss him off."

Everyone in this room knows who he's talking about. *Malakyte.*

"Well, maybe I do? Maybe it feels good to get back at that asshole for once," I say, leaving out the fact that I'm doing it to ease my pain. But they can't know that. "Maybe I'll go out there and do it over and over again until Malakyte himself shows up and I can hack up the other side of his face?"

Trinity interrupts. "It is a bit selfish, girl." Is this why they brought her over here? To preach at me with her moral high ground? Or are they using her because, out of everyone, she's known me the longest and knows how to deal with me? This is starting to feel a lot like an intervention . . .

"I'm trying to get Pacey back," I say, chucking the coat into the corner of the kitchen as it lands with a wet flop. "It's more than any of you are doing. And for your information," I say with rude indignation, "I got something this time. Something big."

Well, that shuts everyone up real fast.

I hobble over to the small refrigerator, which is outdated and barely hanging onto life, seize a cold bottle of water, and begin to chug it down just to keep the "I told you so" grin off my face. I have to play this right. Get them to see that what I'm doing is working. That it's better than what they've done—which isn't nothing.

It's an odd experience, to feel so utterly alone in a room full of people. My eyes bounce quickly to Jance, but like a coward, I look away immediately when I see the fire burning over there. They're all upset with me—clearly. I get that. I get that they want me to stop going after the Nests. But the risk was worth it this time.

"One of the SSPARROW soldiers let it slip that Pacey is on the Azurite."

Silence. Because, like me, they're all realizing how hard of a rescue that's going to be.

Sylo doesn't seem as impressed as I'd hoped. "And we can trust this information? You're beating them up to the point that they can't even defend themselves, and you think the information they give you is accurate? I doubt that."

"You weren't there," I argue. "The man was delirious and fearful that Malakyte would kill him for letting it slip. It's accurate information. And it's far more than you've gotten by begging your daddy for information."

"Leave him out of this," Sylo seethes, and for a moment, I think he's going to get up and start fighting me with the anger in his eyes. "He lost his position because of you."

I laugh incredulously. "Because of me?"

"Listen, we all want the same thing," Ahren interrupts, his voice as calm and steady as ever. I don't think I've ever heard him raise it. "We can come up with a plan to secure Pacey's return. But we need to work together as a team to do that."

Sylo crosses his arms as he leans back on the couch with a huff. "Tell her that, not me."

I roll my eyes.

Then I hear that gravelly voice finally come out to play.

"Throwing your life away or getting yourself captured by Malakyte isn't going to help Pacey one bit, and you know it. This isn't going to continue."

There it is . . . he finally speaks.

Jance stands, Saris sitting beside him and rubbing his forearm affectionately, as he eyes me down with the strength of ten armies. He's pissed. I can see it all in his expression, and I can't hold his stare for long. His body is as strong and ripped with muscle as ever, his black hair and stubble grown out more than usual. Each day, I've wondered if this man I call my Ringer is also someone I can call my father. I've said nothing of Malakyte's proclamation from the Titan Games to him—or anyone—except Ardelle. Jance is tall, his skin tanned, eyes so dark they're practically black; we look nothing alike. Yet, there're small things, like how our feet are so similar, our exact same Raven Feather hair, the feeling of home and safety and connection . . . but until I'm sure, I cannot bring this up to him. If it turns out that we aren't related, then . . . Well, that'll be terribly awkward—and it'll destroy me.

"Everyone, get out." Jance isn't asking, and the boom in his voice is enough that nobody questions him as they consecutively get up to leave. Ardelle stops by me briefly as the others file out and bends down to whisper in my ear.

"I'll come by later." Then he's gone.

Jance and I are left alone.

Without speaking, he disappears into the bathroom. After some rummaging, he returns with a first aid kit, motioning for me to sit on the couch. I must look pretty rough if he's busting the kit out. If my injuries are still bothering me tomorrow, I'll ask Ahren to heal them.

I sit down in the center of the couch, avoiding eye contact as neither of us speak, only the sound of him ripping open bandages and snapping on gloves between us.

I wince as he dabs an alcohol-drenched cotton ball onto my cheek, and I curse when he places it where the stunner bullet latched its hooks into my shoulder. It tore some of my tattooed ink, which I'm not happy about. I'll have to fix that later, but it's a tough spot to tattoo yourself. It's not like Geonni is alive anymore to do it for me, and I'm crushed all over again by the fact he's truly gone. It's like I have to lose him and Gav on repeat. Every single time, I remember I'll never see their faces again.

"You're being reckless," Jance finally says, his tone more relaxed but still stern. "I understand that you want to get Pacey back home. We all want her back, but what you're doing, Kara, is so damned dangerous."

I open my mouth to give my retort, but I stop myself, knowing I've said it all before. Dozens and dozens of times. He's sick of it. They're all sick of it.

Sick of me.

I guess it doesn't matter that I got the information we need. At least not to Jance. So much for me sticking it to them.

Jance continues. "If Malakyte gets a hold of you, there's no telling what he'll do, especially after all that happened at the Titan Games. You scarred his face. You humiliated him. You turned the Terrans against him. Not to mention he's got your face plastered over every SSPARROW wanted list, news feeds, and the Network, and that's only the public avenues he's taken to find you. Any Nest can be outfitted with new weapons, new technology, and they can be the ones ambushing *you* next time. Especially if he gleans the information you've collected tonight. Whether you believe it or not, your luck will run out, and you will be caught. And where does that leave all of us? Where does that leave me? I'm your Ringer, and I can't watch you risk your life so recklessly any longer. What happened at the games happened, and I'm sorry for it. I'm sorry your tattoo mentor was killed and that your young friend, Gavrielle, had also been killed. It wasn't your fault. It was Malakyte's. And Pacey wasn't your fault, either. You can't protect everyone, kid, but you can protect yourself. Start there. You're no good to Pacey captured, injured or dead. You're certainly no good to any of us that way, either. There are ways you engage with a team, Kara, and that doesn't include going off and doing whatever the hell you want, when you want, because you want. That isn't the way we do things here. The rules we all abide by are there to keep every one of us safe. When you break those rules, none of us are safe. It defeats your entire purpose for fighting so hard in the first place."

"But I got the information that we needed. I did what I had to do to get results. If I hadn't, we wouldn't know—"

"I don't care about that." He interrupts me, eyes burning into mine like scolding coals.

The pain in his voice almost brings me to tears, and I still can't look at him. He's right. I'm being selfish. I'm not thinking of the group. He doesn't understand that I don't know what it's like to be a part of a team in the first place, let alone how to be good to one.

"I'm sorry," I whisper, looking down at my soggy boots. I'm ashamed and angry at myself but also torn because it did work. They weren't doing enough, so I stepped up and got it done.

His gloved hand rests upon my chin and gently raises my face so he can meet my eyes, and my chest pings with a blooming pain as I see the hurt there. "Promise me you're done with all this. Please don't make me take drastic actions solely to keep you safe. I can't lose you, too."

I know what he means by that—his family, his wife having been killed and the daughter he believes died with her. He sees me as someone just as important. Even without knowing I could share his own blood. And I'm throwing this relationship away by being stupid.

"I have to find her, Jance," I say, voice weak. His brows immediately crease, and he releases my face with a heavy sigh of disapproval. "Within the Resistance, Geonni created something he called 'The Rebel's Song.' It was like the anthem of the rebels.

It's what he lived by for so many years, what drew so many people to serve under him. Basically, what it means is that it's our duty as rebels to protect the people, to keep them safe and fight for those who cannot fight for themselves. Nobody came and fought for me. Nobody was there to be *my* hero. I don't want anyone, let alone Pacey, to experience what that feels like. And it's also even more than that . . . it's Malakyte, too. I'll never be free unless I stop him. None of us will be free. You, Ardelle, and all the others are trapped because of his obsession with me."

I search Jance's rich, emotional eyes. He sees me in such a raw, exposed way, there's no hiding from him. The way he observes me has always gotten under my skin.

"I'll stop attacking the SSPARROW Nests, okay? But we've got to stop sitting on our asses and come up with an actual plan that'll work this time. You all have your moral reasons, but I also have mine, too. I'm sorry they don't align as perfectly as you'd like them to."

"We will do more but pragmatically. We need to work as a team and follow the rules so we all stay out of Malakyte's clutches."

My grunt is full of annoyance. This is where we aren't agreeing. "If I didn't break your damned rules, we never would have found out where Pacey is! Hello!" I almost laugh out of pure frustration with him.

"You got lucky. The chances of it happening again on this course of action is unlikely."

"Stop putting me before the mission," I protest.

Jance looks at me like I've struck him. His eyes, however, are all fire. "To me, you come first. I will always put you before any of them. I've told you this. I wish Pacey had her Ringer here to put her first because she's a doll, and she deserves it just as much as you do, but I can't protect both her and you at the same time."

"Then, fine. I'll go back out there until I find her because somebody has to do something." And beyond that, I just want to fight and lose myself again and again till I don't feel this way anymore.

Jance doesn't back down. "You said you'd stop going out there and ambushing the Nests. Do not go back on your word to me."

"You're not my father," I spit, standing up and charging for my bedroom. "Stop acting like it."

The slamming of my bedroom door is followed immediately by my tears. Tears of frustration, of anger, of feeling useless and hopeless and depressed and confined all at once. I kick the dresser, and it hobbles a few times. I could really punch something right now, but if I break one more piece of the Reptilian's property, they've threatened to kick us out.

Sliding my back against the door, I can hear Jance walking up to it. "Go away!" I yell through the flimsy piece of wood that separates us, wiping away my tears with the back of my hand, only for more to follow in their place. Why am I acting this way? Why am I pushing him away? I hate myself. I hate that I can't be perfect and that I'm constantly messing up. It's no wonder they're so annoyed with me. I'm annoyed with me. Can't I just tell him what Malakyte said? What would he do? Would he be happy? Excited? Embarrassed of me? Ashamed that this out-of-control girl is *his* daughter? Or would he feel insulted because he knows his daughter is dead—at least that's what he believes—and he may see this as some sick plea for attention or something? Living in foster care taught me you never know how people will take things—big shit or small shit, they're unpredictable. Jance cares, I can see that, but when it comes to his family, he could change. Or he could be happy about it and then we can find out it's not true. Another lie from the mouth of a monster. Then all of that hope and delight was for absolutely nothing. And I'd still be a parentless orphan whose parents didn't want or love me enough to stick around—much like everyone else. There's no filling those shoes if they don't actually fit. Blood is different. Blood is everything.

Jance's footsteps drift away, as do my tears, and I'm left feeling numb as I stare blankly at the dinky bedroom. It's got a twin bed with a shitty mattress, the dresser I had kicked, a small television, and a hole-in-the-wall for a closet. Jance and I share the only bathroom.

After a few minutes pass, I hear Jance leave the apartment, and I breathe a sigh of relief as I allow the tension to seep off of me. Taking the opportunity, I decide to strip and take a shower. The rain soaks into my bones and chills me deeper than any cold could. It seeps into the cracks of my soul, widening those fissures and bleeding them until they are raw and red and festering things. The water does little to warm me or change any self-hatred I may be feeling.

As I exit the shower, I gasp when I see Ardelle sitting on the couch, waiting for me. So much so I almost drop my towel.

"I told you I'd come back," Ardelle says, eyeing me with a smile as he spots me in my towel. He still gets his kicks out of making me squirm.

Jerk.

Ardelle taps his pants pocket. "There's something I want to talk to you about."

I have no idea what he's referring to in that pocket of his. Hopefully, it's something fun and not yet another lecture or tongue thrashing. I've had enough of that for one night. And right now, the distraction of Ardelle is one I don't merely want—it's one I need.

Even if it's hard to trust him completely, I still feel for him. And that's yet another gray area I've been living in lately, as if my entire world has been tattooed in the colorless ink of Iron Gray. I fear that if I don't get a handle on my feelings and how to cope with them, I'm going to be seeing the world in the shade of Bloodred instead.

CHAPTER 3

After changing into some nightwear, I let Ardelle into my bedroom, assuring to shut the door behind him.

"Where did everyone putter off to?" I ask solemnly, shoving some clothes into my raggedy drawer. I miss Jance's house.

"Jance is with Saris, likely . . . doing whatever it is they do," he tells me as he sits on the edge of my bed. "Sylo and I were supposed to hang out, but I ditched him for you. You should be honored."

"That you chose me over a sky-rat-loving traitor? Yeah, I'm delighted." The mattress squeaks as I sit beside him, his cinnamon and sage scent hugging me in an embrace I need more than I can express.

Ardelle leans in, his lips tickling the tip of my pointed ear. "Don't be mean, Thumbelina."

His fingers brush my half dried hair behind my ear, and he leans in even closer, gently kissing the pointed tip, and it sends a spike of shivers down my spine.

It also lights something up, warming that coldness from deep inside. He shouldn't be allowed to do this to me . . . He betrayed me, almost had me killed by Deimos. How could I ever let him into my heart again?

Harder still, how can I ever keep him out?

I turn my head, and we face each other. It's been months since we've been this close. I've been keeping him at a distance, too, holding everyone at arm's length should they dare try to hurt me again. Fearing closeness yet yearning deeply for it, terrified they'll eventually be taken from me. What I can't tell them is that I do want them to keep fighting their way in. Until I finally break under the proof of their love for me. It's the only way I can fully trust them.

"Are you okay?" he asks me, eyes tender as he looks upon my scraped and bruised body. The back of his knuckles barely touches my cheekbone, where a nasty welt has formed in a purple bruise.

I want to tell him how defeated I feel. Now that I've promised Jance I wouldn't go hunting Nests anymore, I don't know how I'm going to deal with my pain. How that fact causes more anxiety in my bones than it should. I want to tell Ardelle how badly I want to rip down the wall between me and everyone else, but my shame is holding me back from it all. But I'm done talking, thinking, or being consumed with this. I must escape it. I need to know something besides the boiling in my blood and all my anger and fear and pain.

"I will be if you promise not to talk about it anymore." My eyes plead with him, begging him silently to leave all our baggage at the door, where we can forget about all that's haunting us. Simply be two young people who damn all the consequences.

My eyes drift down to his mouth, his jawline strong and defined, and I curl my toes as the desire flares up within me and the thought of what he'd do with that mouth if I let him. His own gaze falls to my lips, and like magnets, we drift closer, unable to stay apart.

His tattooed hand moves to gently clasp around my neck, his fingers curling into the hair at my nape. "Are you sure?" he asks, and I need no clarification as to what he's asking me. *Are you sure you want to cross this line? Because, if we do, we cannot come back. You have to trust me again, and I have to trust you.*

Can I trust him again? Can he trust me? We've both damaged this relationship, yet neither of us can manage to let it go. We tried.

I arch my head backwards, revealing my neck for him as my yes to his question.

When Ardelle's lips kiss my neck, a soft moan escapes mine.

Both our hands glide and claw against the other's body. He's as eager to touch every part of me as mine are for him. He picks me up and plops my back onto the squeaking mattress. Wrapping my legs around his waist, I trail my fingers underneath his shirt to the peaks and valleys of his abs and chest.

It's unholy for his body to be this well defined.

Breaking his kiss on my neck, Ardelle quickly rips his shirt off, and my eyes are instantly given access to all the beautiful ink tattooed on his chest, stomach, and arms. I smile despite myself, knowing that I've left my mark on him with the tattoo on his back and perhaps the one on his heart, too.

"Thumbelina . . ." His voice is a low growl in my ear as he slips further down to my neck, where his lips lightly kiss the sensitive skin of my collarbone. It's everything I've been missing these last months. His taste, his hands, his strong arms around me. The way I completely melt into him makes me realize how truly lonely I've been and how badly I wished to be held and made to feel safe.

He's like the darkest of nights, threatening to never seek dawn because, with the break of the sun comes the harsh, stark truth: the trust has been broken between us, and neither of us knows how to mend the chasm it caused.

Yet, the tension in my body craves him like a drug, yearns for his every touch. Every moment I'm around him, I've been inexplicably pulled in. My body responds to what feels like an endless desire for him, for those arms to wrap around me and never let me go. To feel his lips on mine again. Now that he touches me in ways that are better than any fantasy I've explored, I need more. More and more and more, so I can't think of anything else. He gives me the rush that hunting SSPARROWs does, and I'm instantly hooked. I want him to take all of me and drown me in the current of my heart, the adrenaline in my blood, and the beautiful distraction that he is.

Reaching for his hands, I place them at the hem of my shirt. He stops kissing my body and looks up at me.

Undress me, I say with my eyes. If I open my mouth, I may beg for it.

Eyes glossed over with desire, Ardelle is debating, combing through the consequences of our choices here tonight. We both know this is dangerous, but touching is one thing. What comes after going further than we've gone before? Does it bring us closer or rip us apart?

We're supposed to hate each other, to not want this—feel *this*. My eyes glance to his Elendril mark, and I think of his past-life self, Erodis, how much I felt Zariya's love for him. Maybe it's the fact our souls loved each other once before that's got us all messed up like this, but being mere inches from Ardelle's face tells me he's been feeling it, too, and it's driving him wild.

"Ardelle..." My weak voice cracks slightly as I bring myself to say his name while also keeping my dignity. "It's okay. I want you to."

There's a slight flush on his chest, and I feel exactly how much he desires me by the tightening of his jeans. His hesitation isn't because he doesn't want to—it's something else.

Shiny blond hair falls into his eyes as he leans over me, coming in so close I feel the soft caress of his breath on my lips. "So, you want me to take you all the way? You want me to satiate your desire over and over until you can't take it one moment longer? And you're ready for that step? With me? Right now?"

I swallow, heat rising within me. I pull him closer to me with my legs.

"Yes," I pant, an uncertain declaration—but I won't flinch first. If he wants to take me all the way, I'll let him. If it means I don't have to think about all my problems. I need him to kiss me after so much time has passed since our lips last met. I want him to rip my clothes off and ravish me till I can no longer handle it.

Ardelle kisses my forehead. My trembling legs squeeze his waist at the tender act, and my hands glide down his powerful arms. "I don't want to rush this," he whispers, and it's hard not to dissolve before him with disappointment. "Plus, I know you want me to always be honest, and I think it would be best if we stopped here. You're hurting. I can see that. Let me be here for you, Thumbelina, in the way that'll help rather than hurt in the long run."

Unwrapping my legs from him, I raise up on my elbows, and he follows, sitting up in all his beautiful glory. Stars, he's gorgeous, and even bigger and buffer than when we first met. His body is a machine. Guess I don't get to explore it—at least not tonight, anyway. He's doing the right thing, and I can't be mad at him for it. I've been enough of a brat today to add being angry with him to the list.

"Let me hold you," he says, lifting his arm up so I can snuggle underneath. "I know I've hurt you in the past, but at some point, you've got to let me in again. Otherwise, this'll never work."

I don't know how to respond to that, how to tell him he's right.

He shifts and lies longways on the bed, and he beckons me to lay with him. I lay down with my back to him and let Ardelle wrap his arms around me. Bring me in close to his chest, intertwining his legs with mine.

It takes a bit of soft coaxing from him, but ultimately, I relax into this overwhelming sense of warmth and safety. We lie like this for a while, our breaths becoming calm and steady, hearts no longer racing, and eyes clear and free of the wild frenzy of yearning for each other. Ardelle gently runs his fingers through my hair. He did this when I was injured from Deimos's Elendril dagger, and I remember how he promised me in those early days of my recovery that he'd never let anyone hurt me like that again and how I believed him. Ardelle is flawed—we all are—but I trust his intentions are pure. I suppose he wants what's best for me, and tonight is proof of that. If he wanted to use me in the way I wanted to use him, he'd have taken the opportunity, and we'd be doing something far different right now. I'm glad he stopped us. Because he's given me what I didn't realize I needed. It's silly how simply being held by someone who cares for you can make the pain inside slither to deeper, darker places. At least, for the moment.

"Thank you," I whisper to him. Neither of us need to say more.

He holds me for what seems like hours before he finally speaks again.

"While you were talking with Jance, Trinity mentioned she may have a way up onto the Azurite," Ardelle says softly, rising me from the edge of sleep. I blink my heavy eyelids in response, clearing my throat. "She said one of her members is a pilot and can fly us up. She went back to the rebels to come up with a plan and told me to tell you that she'd be back tomorrow so you can be involved. She wants to help us. She wants to bring Arianyte down and free the Tributes and Hijacked."

This wakes me completely.

I raise on my elbows and crank my neck to look at Ardelle.

"When did Trinity become the leader?" I say, not sure if I'm joking or being serious.

He gives me that judgmental, disapproving look he must've gotten from his parents, and I roll my eyes at the implication. Fine, enough said.

"We put together a timeline. We're going to get my sister back in a couple of days."

Hell yes.

"How?" I ask. "Even I'm afraid of trying to get onto the Azurite."

"Apparently, Trinity is confident in her pilot. Getting in, however, is going to be tricky. It's the riskiest thing we've attempted so far."

That's putting it lightly.

"At least we're doing something, stars. About time."

Ardelle agrees with a relaxed *mmhhmm* sound in his throat, peppering the back of my neck with an innocent, soft kiss.

"Do you think she's okay?" Ardelle asks me vulnerably, his voice almost trembling with what I know is outrageous thoughts of what's possibly happening to his sister.

"Malakyte will keep her alive. She's too important to harm. Plus, if your parents are involved in handing her over to him, like we suspect by their presence at his press conferences lately, then I doubt they'd hand her over to be harmed. They're not that depraved to do that to their own daughter. So, likely, she's all right. Physically, anyway."

It's that last bit I think he's worried about the most. Pacey's past history of self-harming herself weighs heavily on both our minds.

"She was a wreck when I was there to support her. Now—well, now I'm not there for her at all. She probably hates me. I let them take her. I should have done more to save her back at the stadium."

He sounds so defeated, so sad.

"Bullshit," I say defiantly. "She knows you're coming for her. If I were in her shoes, and it really came down to it, I know you'd come for me. You're an honorable person, Ardelle, even though you've made mistakes. You've always been there for everyone on this team. Way more than I ever have. It'd probably be only you and Jance coming to rescue me, but still. I'd know you were coming, and she knows, too."

I place one hand on my heart and the other on his. This is why I fight, why I'm out there hitting Nest after Nest, because Ardelle deserves the peace of having his sister back. Seeing him in this much pain is heartbreaking.

He's quiet for a while but finally says, "Thank you." Another pause, even longer than before. Turns out, both of us gave the other something we didn't know we needed tonight.

For the first time in days—weeks, possibly—I smile. Maybe things aren't as bad as I feel they are? Perhaps I let this tiny ray of light illuminate the most elusive prize of all—hope.

"Have you talked to Jance about what Malakyte said? About him possibly being your father?" Ardelle just had to change the subject to that, *didn't he?*

I groan, leaning my body back into him.

"You've got to talk to him, Thumbelina."

Of course he's right, but I just . . . *can't.*

"Until I know it's true, I've got to keep it to myself." It's a stalling tactic. He knows it, I know it.

I feel Ardelle shuffling, and I peer over to see him fishing for something in his pocket. It's a little box, all crumbled up from being in his pants for stars know how long, but I realize what it is instantly.

Ardelle reads the box out loud.

"Paternity test. The results are ninety-nine point nine percent accurate. Test can be used on saliva, hair, blood, skin cells, and can manifest results within five minutes." Pausing to wait for my reaction, I give him an unenthusiastic grunt. "Let's get a piece of his hair from his comb and finally put this to bed. You don't have to tell him tonight, but you'll be able to stop going back and forth in your mind. You'll know."

Stars. I'm not sure if I'm ready to know.

"You'll stay with me? Till the answer comes?"

Ardelle smiles at me, seeming to know more of what I need than I do. "I'll always stay with you, Thumbelina. Always."

Always.

"I can't look. You got to look for me."

Ardelle and I cram ourselves into the extremely tiny bathroom, the two of us basically touching, as I stand with my back to the Sky-Blue tiled walls, and he leans against the single vanity sink with the grime-covered mirror above it. The lighting is harsh and far too bright. It hurts my eyes. The jingle of the paternity test chimes as the result arrives. It sits on the sink's ledge. Neither Ardelle nor I go to pick it up.

My heart is thrashing.

Stars . . .

I can't look. I can't.

Turning away, I face the wall, wishing to disappear inside it.

Ardelle, on the other hand, chuckles at me.

"It's not funny!" I whine, even though I know he's teasing me because I'm being a little dramatic about it.

"Just wait until the day you need to take a pregnancy test. That's way more anxiety inducing, if you ask me."

Redness floods my cheeks despite myself, and I'm suddenly glad my face is currently pressed up against the dull tiled wall instead of facing Ardelle.

I finally find the courage to look over my shoulder at him. Ardelle's face is expressionless as he looks down at the test. It's a small circular piece of plastic that's cheap and flimsy and so unsubstantial for what it's about to tell me. What do I want it to say?

Ever since Malakyte told me about Jance possibly being my father, I've bounced back and forth about whether I'd like that information to be true or not. And knowing I'm mere seconds away from getting this life-changing answer, I'm terrified.

I want it to be true. I want him to be my father.

So much so—I'm trembling.

Paternity either is or it isn't. How much analyzing does it take? Ardelle's Sapphire Jewel eyes finally glance over to mine. His face reveals nothing.

"Well?" I press, unable to take the silence one second longer. "What's it say?"

"Malakyte wasn't lying for once," he says, and I feel my body instantly fill with an overwhelming feeling of joy that I let go of my breath in a wave of glorious relief, becoming instantly dizzy. "He's actually your dad."

My dad?

My body tingles with pure bliss at that single assertion. I never thought my parents existed, didn't think they wanted me or cared. And even though I have so many questions, they can wait. For now, I know that I'm not alone in this world anymore, and for an orphan, that's worth more than gold.

Although fear instantly sets in.

"What am I supposed to do now?" I whisper, still staring down at the test.

I feel Ardelle's fingers gently caressing my cheek, drawing my eyes up to his. "What do you mean?"

A bitter scoff, soft and twinging with a touch of heartache, escapes my lips unintentionally. It's scary to admit this, to be so open with him after what he's done, but I've got nobody else to talk to about this. And I want to trust Ardelle—or try to, at least.

"I never thought too much about my father," I begin, looking past Ardelle's eyes to the paint chipping on the bathroom wall. "Truthfully, I always imagined him as some stumbling down drunk who knocked my mother up during a one-night stand. It made it easier to hate him for not being there for me, for leaving me to the mercy of the occupation and foster parents who could never take care of me like he could. Don't even ask what I thought of my mother. You don't want to know. So, when Malakyte told me that Jance . . ." Stars, I can't even say it out loud. Forcing myself, I continue. "That Jance was my father, I just couldn't believe him. Malakyte's lied so much I thought it was a ploy to get me to go with him while in the arena all those months ago. I never actually considered or let myself hope that it could be true. I couldn't because, if it wasn't true, it would have broken my heart."

Ardelle waits patiently for me to continue, softly playing with the curls of my hair. Not pushing, not prying, just listening.

"So, now that I know, I don't know what to do. I've never had a parent, let alone a father like Jance who's . . . well, he's Jance. You know how intense he is. But he's a good man. He's present and asks questions and requires a level of being that I don't know how to meet. I don't think I know *how* to be a good daughter, Ardelle. And that terrifies me. I don't want to disappoint him. After he finds out, if he even accepts it—accepts me—I don't know if I'm enough to make him proud."

Instead of replying with words, Ardelle steps up to envelop me into his arms. It's impossible not to hug him back, and he rests his chin on the top of my head and says, "I don't think Jance would ever reject you, Thumbelina. He's a man who respects authority and whose own principles guide him on a fundamental level. He was told that a complete stranger was his responsibility and that, as a Ringer, he was to care for you. He went above and beyond what either Saris or Ahren did. That's because of who he is at his core. You could burn the world down, and he'd still love you. He'd be pissed, but he'd never turn his back on you."

I really wish I could believe that. They're beautiful words, but I don't. Ardelle doesn't know how many people assured they'd never leave me, yet they still did. Geonni and Trinity left me when they promised they wouldn't. Not to mention every single foster family did, too. And even though I got Trinity back by default, our relationship is strained because of it.

"Thank you," I say to Ardelle, holding onto him tighter. I didn't want to do this. I resisted it for months, but thanks to him pushing me, I feel a small broken piece of me seal up just a tiny bit. Another pinprick of hope peeks in through the darkness.

That's what Ardelle has done. He's given me hope to battle the pain inside.

CHAPTER 4

Trinity sits with the entire group in the apartment Jance and I share, him and me barely speaking all morning after last night. Truthfully, I can't look at him the same since I took the paternity test. That's my father. Stars . . .

Focus, dammit. Trinity is walking us through the plan to rescue Pacey, and I need to pay attention to that, not on my father, who . . . Fucking hell, I'm doing it again.

"Kara?" Trinity barks, and my back straightens instantly.

"Yes! Sounds like a great idea. Let's do it."

Sylo starts laughing.

Trinity's hands rest on her hips, as thick and curvy as they are. "You were all gung ho last night and have been begging us to do something for months. Now that we're finally devising the plan you so desperately wanted, you're not even listening."

"I am." I'm not.

"Girl . . ." She shakes her head in frustration, pinching the bridge of her freckled nose.

I flip my wrists out to either side of me. "I'm listening!"

We're all scrunched onto the couch, using every chair, bucket, and armrest to sit in a tight circle around each other, and I feel their eyes on me. The tension in the room is rising, and Ardelle's hand comes across my low back and caress it as a silent show of support.

I clear my throat, cheeks heating with embarrassment. "You were talking about how we've got to sneak into the Arianyte airfield, where they transport goods to and from the Azurite, that the cargo bay is our best way into the mothership. And we have to go super late at night during the shift change. See, I'm paying attention."

Trinity's Honeypot eyes glare at me, her glossy lips pursing in the way I know means she's displeased. We're like sisters, her and I. Our relationship is complicated, but we still love each other, even if, half of the time, we'd thoroughly enjoy biting the other's head off. I can't exactly tell her that my father is alive while hers is dead, and that's why I'm having trouble focusing. So, I suppose she's just going to have to be upset with me.

"I'm taking lead on this," she says sternly. "It makes the most sense. It's my people who are doing a lot of the work, and they don't know you guys. I think the whole thing will work smoother if I take the lead."

"No fucking way," I pounce. "We only got here because of *me*."

"I agree with Trinity." Sylo throws his hand up in the air like this is some kind of democracy. But when I look around for support, I can tell mostly everyone else agrees.

Crossing my arms, I don't say another word. Fine.

We continue to go through the plan, and I force myself to listen and not zone out about Jance. It's a solid strategy, and we have a real chance of rescuing Pacey. But if we're going to pull this off, we'll need a lot of luck, tenacity, and a prayer or two to something divine.

A few nights after our detailed planning session, the transportation dock is deserted before us. Only SSPARROW and pilots pepper around the massive hangers that hold the transport ships, whose sole purpose is to fly to and from the Azurite Fleet. At three in the morning, there's a chilly bite in the air.

According to the contact within the Resistance, a shift change is about to occur.

The other Starseeds and I are dressed for battle, our Ringers by our sides as we hide behind a few large freight boxes to the right of one of the hangars.

Trinity has two of her most loyal Resistance members in tow, people I've only met in passing. How they elevated themselves to her side after Geonni's death, I don't know. If Trinity trusts them, then, that's good enough. Although, I've never gotten the warm and fuzzy vibes from them. They're both young, but years on the streets and fighting Arianyte has aged them emotionally and physically. You can see the ever-present exhaustion in their eyes, the roughness of their hands, a type of tiredness I had forgotten about living posh in Jance's mansion. Until we got kicked out— that is, and life back on the streets and the undersewers reminded me of how terrible it is.

The rebel girl named Shante is dark-skinned like Trinity. Except her head is buzzed clean to the scalp, tribal tattoos from her culture gliding along the side of her skull in a gorgeous pattern I would have been thrilled to ink myself. I wonder if Geonni had done the work? It looks like his hand and style. I'm too heartbroken to ask if he had or not. The boy, the one who has yet to utter a single word or greeting to any of us, is an average-looking dude with brunette hair tied in a greasy man bun at the back of his head. He's built tough and seems to have an aptitude for pistols. And, from what I remember of Terryn, he's a damn good shot. Shante and Terryn keep close to Trinity, while my Starseed family stays close to me.

"When are they going to switch out?" Sylo asks impatiently, bobbing on his feet and continuously checking his Elendril rifle. He misses Pacey, and I know how much he loves her and wants her back. We simply don't agree on the how most of the time, but I hope he knows I'm doing what I do for everyone, including him.

Trinity glares at him, not so used to being questioned these days. "The new patrols and pilots will be coming any minute. Calm down. You're not the only person who has someone up there to rescue."

I'm about to bring up who Trinity is referring to when we hear laughter from up ahead. Peeking around the boxes, I see what has to be the pilot for the cargo ship we're planning to commandeer.

"We all loaded up and ready to fly, boys?" the pilot says to the several young Terrans, who are red-eyed and ready to go home to murder their pillows after a long night's work of loading the massive transport spaceships. It's all alien technology, the ships silver and sleek and propelled with antigravity tech that's similar to what makes the hovers fly. After a few minutes of chit-chat, the men finally scuttle off and out of sight.

"We go now, before anyone else decides to show up and talk more bullshit about the upcoming Titan trials. Let's go," Trinity barks, and I'm a little irritated she's the one giving orders. Both of us fought for the coveted spot that Geonni held up until his death, and it turns out blood won out in the end. Maybe I'm still jealous about that for multiple reasons. But how jealous can I be when her father is dead and mine is alive?

Crouching low, we move as a group across the shadows and into the opening of the hangar.

I'll just have to grin and bear it, letting Trinity take the lead. *Be a good team member, Kara, remember?*

The pilot is whistling some tune that's way too cheery for this ungodly hour when Terryn leaps on him before any of us even decided what we were going to do. A minute later, the pilot's head is slumped in the crook of Terryn's arm, fast asleep like a little baby.

These Resistance members are sure taking charge tonight.

And they're also idiots.

"Hey," I hiss angrily. "We need him to give the passwords so we can take off and get onto the ship. How are we supposed to do that when he's taking a nap?"

Trinity specifically said nobody goes anywhere from this port without their daily passwords given to workers upon the start of their shifts. See, I was paying attention, and it should have been me leading this operation. If I were, this wouldn't have happened.

Terryn looks back at Trinity, realizing his mistake. She growls in disapproval.

"Just get him on board." Trinity's voice betrays her anger.

With no other choice, we all file onto the craft. It's already mounted on some giant launch mechanism that's holding the ship at a forty-five-degree angle pointed towards the sky. Even walking up to the cockpit alone is a challenge. Cargo pallets are strapped firmly in the ship's center, so we use those to assist our trek up to the front of the vessel.

"You sure you know how to fly this thing?" Ardelle asks as Shante begins pressing buttons and flipping switches. It sure looks like she knows what she's doing.

A voice comes over the speaker in the cockpit, indicating some procedural go-ahead or something. That's probably the password we're supposed to give for takeoff.

I shake the pilot violently, but he barely mumbles some incoherent gibberish. "Wakey, wakey."

Nothing.

"Ardelle," I say urgently, "a dude is supposed to be flying this thing. Make something up."

Ardelle looks to Ahren and then back to me, unsure of what to say. Leaning in, he clears his throat and says into the comms device in a comically low voice, "Affirmative, Jasper-Rabbit. We're good to go."

The entire group of us holds our breaths, certain this is not going to work. What did Ardelle just say?

Stars help us . . .

The voice on the other line gives a long pause. "You sure have one sense of humor, Boston. Roger that, Mr. Rabbit. Wow. Don't pull that stuff upstairs, or we'll all be knee-deep in interrogation for weeks. Clear for takeoff."

The tension leaves my body in the form of a nervous laugh. "Jasper-Rabbit?"

He bashfully rustles his hair, blushing. "Isn't that flight speak or something?"

"Dude, no . . ." Sylo answers for me.

"We're lucky they believed the pilot was simply joking around," Jance says, and he's right. That luck won't be there a second time.

However, commandeering the transport craft and flying out of Earth's orbit was never meant to be the hard part of this mission. The tension has always been about getting onto the Azurite. As the ship begins to vibrate intensely, we all brace ourselves for takeoff to the most guarded place in the entire Aurora System.

And pray we don't get killed in the process.

CHAPTER 5

REBEL RAPPORT:

FIRST THINGS FIRST, FOLKS. BUILD THAT CAMARADERIE. STICK TOGETHER LIKE A PACK OF WILD COYOTES ON THE PROWL. THE BOND BETWEEN REBELS IS STRONGER THAN STEEL. TRUST IS YOUR AMMO, TRUST YOUR LADY, AND TRUST YOUR FELLOW BROTHERS AND SISTERS. UNITY IS YOUR FIREPOWER.

My stomach is body-slammed down to the soles of my feet as the vessel blasts out of orbit. Most of us go a bit green around the edges, having never been into space before. Ardelle takes my hand in his as the spaceship trembles and quakes, making us feel like we're inside a snow globe being shaken by a toddler.

I curl into Ardelle's chest, both of us on the ground with our backs against the wall. This is a cargo ship. There're no seats or belts to keep our bones from jolting with the force it takes to blast out of Earth's orbit.

Then, suddenly, it's complete, utter silence and stillness.

As if we've jumped into another dimension.

"Thumbelina," Ardelle breathes, looking at me with awe. He reaches up to my face, and I'm not sure what he's doing until he curls his fingers around my ponytail—as it floats.

"We're in space," I say, a bit dumbfounded.

After we all get our bearings, I look towards the cockpit and see the bright lights of the Azurite Fleet shining before us in all its glory.

It's humongous.

And terrifying.

Beautiful and intimidating and expansive.

I can't look away.

Rising to my feet, it feels like I weigh ten pounds as my body begins to hover in the air. Taking my hands, Jance helps stabilize me as we float towards the cockpit where we can get a full view of the alien mothership.

It's made of a metallic black material, the lights that illuminate from it varying from shades Banana, Snow Cone Blue, and Orchid Purple, but the colors on the exterior of the ship itself are Tangerine Orange. It's twenty times longer than it is wide, clearly meant for traveling in outer space. There are tons of different levels and areas and attachments that seem to exist, perhaps even added on over time. Many smaller crafts float nearby like loyal worker bees buzzing around their hive to serve only their queen or—in this case—their prince. The familiarity of this ginormous fleet continues to pull at me. The desire to go inside and explore its countless shadowy hallways is overwhelming. Isn't this where Zariya, the person I was in my past life, lived at one point? Or was it another spaceship? Is that why I'm feeling such a strong draw towards it?

"You know where to dock this thing?" I ask our pseudo pilot as she glides us ever closer to the Azurite. Shante finally takes a moment out of her day and bothers to glance my way, gives me a once-over, and then looks forward again. My glare turns to Trinity as I curl my lips together in a disapproving frown.

"She knows where to go," Trinity claims, but I'm skeptical after their performance with the pilot.

All of Trinity's braids are floating around her shoulders, and they slither like snakes each time she moves her head. Sensing my disapproval, she says, "My mother is up there somewhere, being forced to work as their slave. So, trust me, I'm not here for a good time, Kara. This rescue mission is as important to me as it is to you."

She's right. Trinity wants her mother out of Arianyte's clutches as badly as we want Pacey back in ours.

As our transport ship glides closer, Shante finally speaks. "We need to get past the security measures before we can dock."

Ardelle's voice pipes up from behind me. "You say that like it isn't going to be an easy thing."

"It won't be," she confirms, eyes forward and fingers tapping against buttons and knobs. Her focus reminds me of Pacey when she's in the middle of hacking something. "Someone better wake that pilot up—and fast."

It takes us almost ten minutes, but after shaking, slapping, and yelling in the pilot's ear, he finally opens his eyes for us. For a moment, the man doesn't understand what's happened and why we're all standing above him with impatient expressions on our faces.

When his eyes go wide, it finally dawns on him. "P-Please don't hurt me."

"We won't hurt you," Jance says first, taking the lead as his booming voice is demanding, stern yet calm. "All we want is to get into the Azurite. The only thing you have to do for us is do what you do every single day. Give the password, we sneak aboard, do your job like normal, and take us back without the occupation ever knowing a thing."

The man considers his options as he sits there, mouth gaped. He looks at each of our faces, trying to find an ally, perhaps. I don't know.

"And if I don't?" he barely manages to stutter out, and I look to Jance.

"We make sure Arianyte knows you let us on board in exchange for a lot of credits," I say before my Ringer can. And even though

I can tell he isn't particularly happy with what I said, he doesn't contradict me in front of the pilot.

The pilot's mind seems to tinker away at his predicament, but we don't have the time for this.

"Yes or no?" I demand, seeing the Azurite docking station approaching our sights.

"Okay. I mean, yes. Yes, ma'am. Whatever you want me to do." The pilot nervously nods to the others, and we float him over to the cockpit just in time as our craft approaches the loading dock. Moments later, a voice comes onto the intercom system, asking for a code so we can latch on.

With shaking hands and wild, shifty eyes, the pilot clears his throat and says into the intercom uncertainly, "He who rides the dark will never kiss the dawn."

Ardelle and I lock gazes, the two of us finding that phrase a little odd but say nothing.

"Over," the voice on the other end says.

We wait and wait and wait.

"What's taking them so long?" I push the pilot, who flinches at my words. He's awfully jumpy for a guy who hasn't even been struck once into compliance. Yet, he's acting like we're holding a disruptor to his head or something. Eyes bopping around again, he speaks hastily into the intercom, but I noticed he forgot to press the button that actually sends his voice through the literal space between us.

No, he didn't forget a thing.

Fuck.

"We need to get out of here, now," I stammer out. "He's screwed us."

"What?" Trinity scoffs, the faces of the others just as confused. "Not after all this. We're not backing out."

The pilot looks aloof, and he's playing his role quite well. My mouth opens to argue with Trinity when alarms begin blaring, stopping me in a frozen vise of anxiety.

"Shit," Shante hisses, "we've been locked on to."

"Locked on to?" Ardelle reels. "Locked on to by what?"

Shante shakes her perfectly shaped head as she begins pushing and flipping buttons wildly. "What else? The mothership is about to blow us into outer space. Literally."

Knowing time is of the essence, I grab the pilot by the scruff of his shirt. "You little weasel, what did you do?"

"Arianyte strong!" he says between clenched teeth. "Our saviors will not succumb to devils like yourselves. I'll die for them before I let that happen. I recognize you criminals from the wanted posters. I know what you did to our leader."

Jance curses under his breath, and the back of my skull thuds with fear and the blaring of alarms.

This is bad.

These "Arianyte strong" religious nutbags are obsessed with Arianyte, with Malakyte, and the other higher-ups. They see them as practical gods. They're infatuated with them, worshipping them like deities.

This is bad.

"Hold on to something!" I hear Shante shout, but I'm too far from any handholds, and there's nothing for me to latch onto as the ship tilts a full ninety degrees and I go flying.

"Thumbelina!" Ardelle shouts, and others follow. Me and the pilot both go flying, and I slam into a pallet of supplies face-first. The pilot, to my amusement, missed the pallet and is now rolling about the cabin like he's a ping-pong ball.

"I've got it!" I shout at them. I'm good. I don't need help.

"Just stay there, hold on to it!" I hear Jance yell back to me, and I dig my nails into the securely wrapped cellophane pallet and hope to the stars it's enough to keep me latched on. Press-on nails hardly have the staying power of acrylics, but when you're on the run, it's the best you can get.

Trinity is up by the cockpit, holding onto the seatbelt of the pilot chair, when she curses. "These assholes are legit trying to kill us. Get us out of here, Shante, *now.*"

"Told you so!" I yell up there, just because.

 48

"We know, Kara! You're always right!"

I smirk at Trinity, despite the danger. Now even she knows I should've been the one to lead this team.

"Shit, watch out!" Sylo shouts, and even I can see the giant burst of orange light that's blasting straight for us.

Is this it? Is this the end for us?

Fear whips its way around my mind, slashing my hopes and dreams to bloody heaps of frayed ribbon. The ship cranks upwards so fast, so violently, my entire stomach drops to my ass, my grip slipping.

"That missile barely missed us." Shante's voice isn't calm, cool, and collected any longer. She's sweating. We all are.

I hear something above me, but I'm far too late to react to the pilot crawling atop the pallet I'm clinging to. This motherfucker actually bends down and yanks a fist full of my hair, and my shriek draws the attention of everyone except for Shante.

Shouts and protests erupt, but they can't help me from where they are.

If I let go, we go flying, but if I don't, I can't defend myself in any substantial matter. My crystal is useless here. One spark could blow us all to high hell just as easily as the missiles chasing us can.

The pilot is dragging me up onto the top of the supply pallet, and stupidly, he wrenches my hands from the wrapping. And for his efforts, he gets a hard punch to the face.

"That's what you get."

As the ship veers hard, the two of us shift, and he lands on top of me, anxiety immediately flowing through my blood, causing it to roar with panicked fury. *No, any position but this one.*

He begins wailing on me.

Punching and slapping and scratching, with no technique whatsoever, but he's emotionally savage, and all I can do is hold my arms up to block him from hitting my face.

"You won't destroy this empire! It's the only thing keeping humans and Earth alive!"

The two of us are floating in midair atop the pallet, and it's almost impossible for me to maneuver with enough strength to get him off. I just have to wait for another shift in direction, then I'll throw him off me. I *need* him off me.

He's in a frenzy, his adoration for Arianyte propelling him to madness, as if he believes he's to be the martyr that'll save the entire empire from its ruthless, evil foe. Me.

Realizing my arms are taking the majority of the impact, he moves to my stomach and sides. I try to lift my legs up to protect me, but his body is in the way.

"Kara!" someone shouts.

"I got him!" I yell again, refusing assistance for this goober.

Ardelle's frustrated voice flies through the ship. "Stop being so stubborn. Let me help you."

"I don't need anybody's help!"

Stars, I can't get him off! This zero-gravity shit is throwing me completely off balance, literally and figuratively. I can't use my speed, my quick reflexes—anything. I'm just a blob floating in the air, and I hate myself for how useless I feel. I don't want help, but I might *need* it.

I hear my father's voice in my head. *Use your size to your advantage. Catch your opponent off guard.*

Pushing myself higher into the air, I wrap my legs around the pilot's waist and thrust us both into a tailspin.

My forearm cuts off his windpipe as he pulls my hair. We both spin and spin, inertia throwing us faster and faster into a barrel roll. Like I hoped, his hands stop their assault on me and try to rip my arm from his throat. That's when I finally manage to unhook and toss him off me, back towards the front end of the ship. And just in time, too, because it veers hard, and I go flying once again.

It's hard to see exactly what happens to the pilot, as I'm still bouncing around the cabin of this ship. But I see Ardelle's hair flash by as he throws himself into the fray. All right, let him deal with the pilot. He's better qualified to fight in zero gravity than I am.

By the time I manage to hook back onto the pallet again, I see the pilot's body limply floating around, terribly whacking into walls and floors as the ship veers through space and dances alongside missiles. The pilot has been knocked out cold. That didn't take long.

Ardelle doesn't hesitate as he nabs me up and floats us both back up to the front of the cabin, using his own gravity magic to keep us steady as Shante flies us wildly through the stars. When the red glow finally fades from his eyes, I'm safely holding onto one of the bars that's built into the top portion of the ship's sidewalls.

Ardelle takes his thumb and wipes off a small trickle of blood from my temple. I didn't even realize I was bleeding. His touch is soft and gentle, and I scoot just a bit closer to him.

"You should have just let me help you," he says, fidgeting with me.

I shake my head. "I had it under control."

Our spaceship flies smoothly for the next ten minutes, and I begin to feel it shudder as we enter back through Earth's atmosphere.

"Are we in the clear?" I ask nobody in particular.

No one speaks, as if doing so will cause a barrage of Arianyte ships to come chasing us down till we're nothing but burning embers flying through the atmosphere. Trinity finally breaks the tense silence. "Looks like we made it out. I don't think they're sending ships after us. We're not going to be able to land back at the hangars. They'll be expecting that. We'll touch down in the outer fields."

"What do we do with Mr. Hero over there?" Sylo asks, face solemn. "It's not like we can just leave him. He'll tell Arianyte who we are. Malakyte will know it was us. He'll know we're coming for Pacey. He could retaliate against her because of this."

Just like I told you he would, Sylo wants to say but doesn't.

"We'll wake him, and I'll adjust his memories of this event, fuzzy them up as best I can." Jance's voice is confident but sad. The only time he's used his Ringer powers was when I was injured. For someone with such a wicked, horrifying ability, he truly does use it responsibly.

Nobody argues with the plan, and thank the stars we land in the fields without incident. No fighter jets pursued us, and I count that alone as a major win.

A dark blob catches my eye in the orange sky of the rising sun, sticking out like a sore thumb. There's some large platform being constructed nearby, and I wonder what it's for. Despite it being thousands of feet high and huge, I hadn't noticed it until now. Too much time underground, apparently.

"Damn, you hit this bastard hard. Look at that goose egg." Sylo picks the pilot up by the scruff of his uniform, a giant bump on the guy's forehead already purple and swollen over his right eyebrow. That only happens so quickly when you're hit very, very hard.

Trinity approaches, then looks at me, to Ardelle, and back to the pilot. "Damn, archer boy, don't come at me like that the next time I flip your girl some shit. I'm far too pretty for a shiner like that."

"I'd never hit a woman in that way," Ardelle says, running his fingers through his hair shyly. That wasn't really her point, but the blush on Ardelle's cheeks says he knows that. He nailed this guy so hard for one obvious reason—me.

Ardelle comes and stands beside me as Ahren shines a light in the sleeping pilot's eye. When Ardelle's arms squeeze firmly around my waist, he whispers confidently in my ear, "Anyone touches you, and they die."

My toes curl despite myself, biting my lip at the feral, primal edge in his voice.

Stars . . . damn it all.

I lean against him, feeling safe in my protector's arms. I can trust him . . . I can allow my heart to trust him again.

Eventually, the pilot opens his eyes long enough for Jance to connect his Ringer magic, doing his thing. Before I know it, we're walking back towards our hover just as the sun is beginning to rise.

Nobody says it, but we're all thinking it.

What the fuck do we do now?

CHAPTER 6

MALAKYTE ARDEEN

"What do you mean the Dawson girl is missing from her cell?" I fume, a practical shadow forming around me. "Again?"

Naresteé looks unnaturally disheveled.

"She used her toilet water to form an ice spike, and she cut the guard as they brought in her dinner. She's been out for the last twenty minutes. Cameras caught her in the eastern sector, still far from the public. We'll find her. The guards are on alert."

I bare my teeth at my second-in-command. "I thought you calmed her down enough to convince her fleeing is untenable. This childish behavior of hers will have consequences. I've had enough of it."

For all her indifference, Naresteé looks unhappy at my words.

The two of us swiftly travel down the hallways heading to the eastern sector of my Azurite, the windows to my right paint a stunning portrait of Earth as it floats in orbit beside us. Ships come and go beyond this glass, coming and going from here to the planet below. It wouldn't be inconceivable for Miss Dawson to find a way off this vessel if she is resourceful enough. The fact she's escaped twice now has proven to me that she is, indeed, clever. Especially being so close to a point of entry near the loading docks, I mustn't underestimate her.

"The girl is merely afraid," Naresteé says as we walk briskly down the halls, my cape continually hitting her.

"It is unlike you to be empathetic, Naresteé."

She huffs, horns shaking. "I've been in her position before, is all. She's . . . she's not a bad person, Malakyte. She's a child. Let me talk with her one more time."

Keeping my eyes straight ahead, I hesitate to be as forgiving as I previously have been. "I do not have the patience or time for this nonsense. Glean from her the information we need and let us be done with her. The parents want her back as soon as possible. As do I. They're grinding on my last nerve."

My second snarls softly, and as we arrive at the sector entrance, cries await us.

"Get off!" The young voice echoes off the sleek black walls of the fleet, and as we turn the corner, Miss Dawson's face falls flat at the sight of us.

"Miss Dawson, here we are once again," I say, attempting to keep calm. The girl has an ice pick—a sharp one, I might add—gripped tightly in her hand. Blood drips from it, stippling my black floors in dots and smears of deep red. Three of my SSPARROWs lie knocked out on the ground, a fourth limping in my direction. Had we not arrived at this precise moment, she likely would have made it to the cargo bay, where the ships from Earth dock. She easily could've escaped, and as I glance towards Naresteé, she realizes how close Miss Dawson has come to freedom as well.

"Pacey," Naresteé hisses, taking a step closer to the girl. "Your arm. You've been cutting again, haven't you?"

Miss Dawson instantly covers the bleeding slashes on her forearm, large eyes averting ours. I hadn't even noticed, but the blood dripping on to the icicle isn't all theirs, apparently.

Naresteé continues pressing the girl. "You promised you wouldn't do that anymore."

I find it entirely odd that my second-in-command even cares. If the girl is going to harm herself, let her. As long as she doesn't go too far, that is. But Naresteé seems to disagree. I can tell by

the softness in her voice and the warmness on her face. She's concerned for this Terran girl—deeply.

"Don't act like you care about me," Miss Dawson says. "Let me go! I'm not going to give you any information on Kara, no matter what you do to me. I'll die first."

"There's no need for such theatrics," Naresteé says sweetly, using the tone of her voice to calm the young Terran into a false sense of security. "We do not wish to harm you and certainly do not wish to kill you. All we want is a little bit of information on Karalevine, and you can go home to your parents. Until then, we must keep you here, Pacey. Make this easy on yourself and simply tell us what we wish to hear. You don't need to hurt yourself over this."

Naresteé is far superior in these types of situations than I am, so I back off, allowing her to take the lead. They've built a close rapport.

"I won't," she swears, and by the stars, I believe her. Which is why this is pointless. "They'll come for me. I know they will. My brother won't abandon me here."

Naresteé chuckles cynically.

Miss Dawson goes to retort but stops short.

"Nobody has tried to rescue you, Pacey. Not once." Naresteé's voice slices through the girl like any skillfully placed blade would. Right into the heart. "See that window behind me? See all those ships coming and going? There's been no reports of suspicious activity or anyone trying to board this ship without permission. It's as quiet as ever up here on the Azurite. And you've been gone for such a long while they've given up on you. It's been almost six months, Pacey. They would have at tried to rescue you at least once. So, why do you continue to protect them? Protect her? Karalevine has one weakness, one thing that'll hurt her the most. All we want is that information, and in return, you can go home."

The girl's face falls as the words sink in, and I smile. Naresteé is good at what she does.

A spark from within the stygian void beyond the Azurite draws my attention. One of our missiles was launched mere moments ago, now exploding within the silence of space. It appears it's just me who notices, but I'm concerned. Only someone trying to board this fleet unauthorized gets the missiles. Miss Dawson cannot be allowed to see this. Hope will be nothing but a detriment to her because the only way she's getting off this ship is when I allow her to disembark.

Without a word or warning, I step in front of the girl, and she cowers before me. I seize the ice from her hand and smash it to the floor. How she's able to use her crystal with my collar around her neck is something I must look into.

I grab her slender body, turn her from the windows, and walk her the long way back to the cells, if only to avoid the windows. Her bare feet make the solitary sound as they slap against the floor.

If only Karalevine would be so submissive, she wouldn't be such a glaring pain in my ass.

That being said, she likely wouldn't be so attractive, either.

CHAPTER 7

ANNUALLY, ARIANYTE WILL HOST THE TITAN GAMES,
AN ARENA BATTLE COMPETITION OPEN TO BOTH
TERRAN AND EXTRATERRESTRIAL COMPETITORS, AS
A SHOW OF SOLIDARITY TO ARIANYTE AND EARTH'S
CONTINUED COOPERATION.

KARALEVINE RUZZ

We failed.

Miserably.

I slam my fists against the coffee table in the small undersewers apartment, and Sadie jumps.

"Sorry, girl." I slouch deeper into the cushions and pat my thigh. She jumps onto the couch and snuggles into a ball by my side. "What do I do, Sades?" She looks up at me curiously, her mismatched eyes silently asking me why I'm upset. Her panting breath fills the small space.

How do we get Pacey back now?

The door flies open, and Trinity is there, breathing heavily, as if she's run several miles without stopping.

"We've got a huge problem."

"What's happened?" I sit up straight, bumping into Sadie's jingling collar.

Trinity falls on the couch beside me. She's wearing all black. The somberness of it isn't her typical style. Her long braids of intertwining blonde, black, and light-brown hair almost reach her backside.

My chest tightens as she stares at me with those Honeycomb Haven-colored eyes. Trinity finally catches her breath and says, "So, you know I've got somewhat of a backdoor into Arianyte, right? Sometimes, certain SSPARROWs like to yack their jaws once they're bribed with contraband or they get a little liquor in them."

"Right." Trinity has always been able to swindle a SSPARROW like a professional.

"Well," she continues, "after our screwup last night, I put some feelers down through my whisper network. Turns out, when I confirmed Pacey's location before the mission, I found something else out. I didn't mention it because I wanted to confirm it, which I only just have. We know that Pacey's being held deep in the ship's confinement cells, but it's worse than that. According to a SSPARROW, who's friends with someone up on the mothership, she's up there for one specific reason. Her parents have been convinced there's a way to remove her crystal by performing a special high-tech surgery that can only be performed up there. They're going to do it in the next couple of weeks."

I stare at Trinity, not believing the absurdity of what I just heard. "That'll kill her," I whisper.

"I know."

I feel tears brim my eyes, and Trinity has known me for so long that there's no point in trying to hide my vulnerabilities from her. Despite everything we've gone through together, she's the closest thing to a sister I've ever had. Trinity's brows furrow, and she gives me a sad smile.

"I've failed her. Just like I failed Gav . . . I'm exactly like I was back at the orphanage. I'm just a scared, useless, stupid girl."

And all I want to do is hack and slash and fight my way out of this feeling. My pulse pounds in my ears like a taunting anthem of my failures.

Trinity takes my hands, and for the first time since before we went to kidnap Naresteé all those months ago, we connect like the sisters we are.

"Pacey isn't gone yet, Kara. There still might be a way to save her, but it's insane. I only mention it because, if anyone can do it, you can."

Tell me, I beg her with my eyes. *Just tell me what I've got to do in order not to be a useless piece of shit who lets my friends die.*

"The Titan Games."

I blink the wetness from my eyes. "Huh?"

"If you win the Titan Games, you get a guaranteed ride up to the Azurite." She beams, as if it's the perfect plan.

Contingency after contingency floods into my mind. How could we guarantee we'd win? Would Malakyte recognize us before we even had the chance? Would jumping through their hoops just waste what little time Pacey has left? "I have questions," I say, letting the shock of her suggestion wear off as I wipe my tears from my cheeks roughly.

She smiles, her ebony skin practically glowing with excitement. "I'd consider you daft if you didn't. But I have a plan for this if you're down. A plan that'll turn you into what Arianyte fears most."

"Which is?"

"The symbol of their downfall."

CHAPTER 8

AN EXCERPT FROM GEONNI'S *A REBEL'S
GUIDEBOOK TO MISCHIEF*:

UNLIKELY ALLIES:

THE ENEMY OF MY ENEMY, RIGHT? FIND THOSE EXTRAS
WITH A CONSCIENCE, REBELS. THOSE TIRED OF THEIR
OWN TYRANNICAL BUDDIES. FLIP THEM, MAKE THEM
SEE THE LIGHT, AND WATCH THEM HELP US TAKE DOWN
ARIANYTE FROM WITHIN.

The first hurdle I must face to even consider this insane plan of Trinity's is to become a Titan competitor. Unfortunately, not just anyone can waltz up to the ticket booth and participate in the games. I've got to earn it by surviving a grueling tryout process. And, like it or not, we only have one viable option to get me through those tryouts without being spotted.

Together, Trinity and I risk the upper streets of Zarmenia until we make it to one of the rebel hideouts disguised as an apartment building. The outside looks run-down, its paint dull and chipped, the hinges on every door squealing like poorly oiled brakes on the hovers, and the smell of musky mold is cause for serious health concerns. However, once we pass through a dimly lit hallway and enter the courtyard, it turns into a miniature paradise.

A grassy field spans most of the length of the courtyard, a few tiny hills here and there. Large thick trees stand firmly planted and freshly sprouted for spring, their limbs fat and full. It's tranquil. Tons of people pass us by, many of them saluting Trinity and ogling me like I'm a celebrity. Almost ten times the number of rebels have joined since Geonni's death, and a lot of them have been moved into this building specifically. If this is merely one of the Resistance's hideouts, and it's packed with rebels, I can only imagine how much they've grown. Perhaps something good came of Geonni being murdered, after all.

"I'll let you two speak privately." Trinity winks as she clicks her tongue, turning to walk away from me. "Would hate to interrupt this glorious reunion."

I cross a small bridge that traverses over a tiny river within the compound. The tiny overpass is completely unnecessary. However, it's my favorite feature of this place because it's quaint and unique.

Shortly after I cross the bridge, I'm standing before the man who tried to kill me.

Deimos sits in a meditative trance under a giant maple tree, with closed eyes and legs crossed. His Terran apparel of cropped tan pants and a baggy shirt are completely human and utterly at odds with his alien appearance. He's missing that dreadful scowl I had grown accustomed to, though traces of it remain permanently etched into his brow. He looks nothing of the terrifying extraterrestrial that hunted and almost killed me not so long ago. It's as if, in some corner of his blackened heart, he found a tiny ounce of peace. I can't help my hands begin to shake as I see him there. His Elendril dagger is attached to his hip, and I practically feel the phantom pain and terror from that night he drove that blade into me.

"Geez, kiddo, if I didn't feel your incredulous glare on me, I'd think you'd be happy to see me." Deimos's eyes pop open, and that scowl returns in earnest. Amazing how this guy was Zariya's father. I can hardly imagine being raised by him.

Placing my hands on my hips, I deadpan. "Nobody is ever happy to see you, Deimos. We need to talk."

"So I've gathered. How can I be of assistance to *the Star*?" His extenuation of that ridiculous title is as sarcastic as his feigned pizzazz.

"I'm sure you've heard Malakyte took Pacey during the fiasco at the games, in league with their parents. I have an idea to get her back."

"I don't care about the Dawson girl." Deimos shrugs half-heartedly, his voice flat.

Crossing my arms, I tilt my head sideways at him. I need him, so he needs to be convinced helping me and entering the Titan Games is in his best interest. "But you care about killing Malakyte, right?"

Now his gaze flickers back up to me, eyes slightly more alight. I continue, hoping to keep my momentum. "We got intelligence that tells us Pacey is on the Azurite. We tried getting up there, but we couldn't get in."

Deimos scoffs. "No shit. Not even I can get up there, so before you even ask, no. I'm never setting foot upon that wretched ship ever again."

The scowl on Deimos's face is as real as the agony within me. Looks like we're both avoiding our pain in our own special, fucked-up ways.

"I'm not asking you to go up there. I'm asking you to join the Titan Games with me."

In classic Deimos fashion, he cackles right in my face. "You've lost your mind, kiddo."

"No, it's a solid plan. The winner gets a trip up to the Azurite. If one of us can win and get up there, we have a solid chance of freeing Pacey. And just think of how great of a laugh you'll be able to have knowing you beat him at his own game."

"You're as smart as you are tall, kiddo. This plan isn't going to work. Malakyte won't let you on board the fleet if you win the games ten times in a row. You won't be able to free the girl and then you'll become another captive. It's an idiotic plan."

"Then, help me come up with one that'll work." My voice cracks, but it's my eyes that plead with him. "We can't leave her up there with them. In a matter of weeks, they've scheduled some bullshit surgery that's going to attempt a crystal removal on her. And we both know that'll kill her. Not only that, but it'll also give Malakyte even more power to fight us off. Imagine what Malakyte could do with the power to control all the elements combined with his crystal's ability to bring him back from the dead. You must care about him being unstoppable, don't you? Don't abandon Pacey and this world to such a terrible fate, Deimos. Zariya wouldn't."

Deimos lunges at me, sharp canines bared and snarling with a growl so deep in his throat the hairs on the back of my neck rise. I take several steps away, and Trinity yells from across the courtyard at Deimos to back the hell off. I do my best to stand my ground, to not fear him. If I didn't absolutely need him, I'd leave right now.

"Don't you say her name," he sneers, hands balled into fists and the vein in his forehead bulging so big I think it might pop his head right off.

Dampening down my fear, I manage to say, "She wouldn't leave another team member to suffer and die, and you know it. She'd do whatever it took to help, even if the plan wasn't the smartest or safest. Sometimes, an idiotic plan is the only plan you can come up with and hope the stars are on our side."

"In this harsh world, kiddo, hope alone can't accomplish jack shit."

"You can't actually believe that, though?" I counter, not knowing how I became the positive person in the bunch. That's Pacey's fault, and someday, I'm going to get her for that.

The only response I get is a squinting of his eyes, and even that feels like more than he wants to give.

"I'm guessing you need me and my magic to get your little ass in as an official contestant? Why else would you come begging for my help? What about your little entourage? Can't they help you?"

I look away, cheeks heating.

Laughing at me once more, Deimos switches his demeanor back to his sarcastic, cynical side. "Oh, kiddo. You haven't told them, have you? You're going to enter the games without letting them know? Fat chance, especially with that Ringer of yours. He's like a dog with a bone, that one."

He's right, of course. "I was hoping you'd agree to join with me, help convince the others this is the only way to save Pacey and stop Malakyte and then get me through the tryouts."

After today, I'm going to hear Deimos's cackle in my dreams, no doubt. "You're a dolt if you think I'm going to simply hop on board with this little plan of yours. Go find someone else."

"There is no one else," I shout as he turns his back on me. "It has to be you. You're the only one who can get me through the tryout undetected. I need you." Stars, I hate admitting it. It tastes like ash on my tongue, but if it gets me to Pacey and possibly saves her life, I'll swallow burning embers if I must. "If Malakyte gets her crystal, I won't be able to stop him, and neither will you."

He turns back and glares at me incessantly for an uncomfortably long time. "Does Malakyte know you know about the girl being on the fleet? Or that you're aware of this so-called surgery?" Deimos asks.

I think about that for a second. "No. He knows we're searching for her, but I'm pretty sure he has no clue that we know she's actually up there or what her parents are planning."

Deimos smiles for the first time since I arrived, the sun lighting up the thin wisps of his white hair to the point where it looks like glowing moonlight. "Fabulous." Deimos's face stiffens in concentration as he taps his pointed finger on his lips. "I believe we may be able to use this to our advantage. If done properly, we may have a chance at getting Malakyte's head for real. And I want it on a spike after what he did to my Zariya. If I help you, can you give me that?"

"I can't promise anything, but I want him dead as badly as you do. What are you thinking?" I ask, heart puttering in excitement.

Deimos taps his chin with a finger. "The girl being held captive is good at hacking, right?"

I nod.

Deimos taps a pointed nail on the hilt of his dagger. "Good. That's good. If we can rescue her, we, likewise, can get her to

hack their entire communications hub up there. Listen, up on the Azurite there's a giant computer system, an artificial intelligence, and it controls everything. And I mean everything. From Earth to the colony bases to the SSPARROW schedules and Nest locations and deployments—everything. Let's say we get the Dawson girl to funky up all those systems, and conveniently, at the exact same time, Trinity and the rebels launch a full-scale, planet-wide attack. With Arianyte's communications literally cut off at the knees, they won't be able to mobilize the SSPARROWs at all, let alone organize quick enough to stop us from taking them all out. We can then take the Azurite from within, kill Malakyte, and end it all right there and then."

I'm silent. It's genius.

"I'm in," I say, and Deimos's grin is both wicked and shrewd. "Are you?"

"Fine, yes, whatever you want. But I'm only coming on board if we do this my way. I'm not risking everything just for the girl. I want the whole meal, not just a small snack."

I snort but whatever. Let him gorge himself for all I care. "We'll have Malakyte's head roasting on spit in a matter of weeks."

He flashes those long canines once again. "Perhaps your moronic plan isn't so doomed after all, kiddo, but be prepared for one hell of a fight. Especially when it's time to tell that Ringer of yours you're about to jump headfirst into the fight of your life."

"What the hell is *he* doing here?" Ardelle barks, standing up from the lumpy green couch as Trinity, Deimos, and I stand in the doorway to mine and Jance's apartment in the undersewers. The living room is much darker than usual, illuminated by the light above the stove, the old television turned on to the news feeds of the most recent Zarmenia protests.

Jance and Sylo rise as well, bodies tense. I throw my hands up and stand in front of Deimos.

"He's with us. He's cool. Deimos is here to help us with Pacey."

Ardelle roughly rustles his hand through his hair. "Help us how? What's going on? When we came back, you were gone. We thought you were hunting SSPARROWs again."

They have such little trust in me . . .

"She wasn't," Trinity says in my defense. "She's been with me. I need to fill you guys in on some important information I gathered between last night's rescue attempt and today."

The three of us fully enter the apartment, but Deimos lurks in the corner next to the door, trying to keep Sadie off him. Even with all the Starseeds and Ringers present and cramped into this small room, it still feels empty without Pacey. Trinity fills everyone in on what her whisper network has told her, and I watch as Ardelle's face goes paler and paler. When she's finally finished, Ardelle is as white as a ghost.

I take his hand in mine as I sit on the couch's arm, lacing our fingers together. "Hey, she's going to be okay. We're going to stop them."

He's looking forward, eyes completely unfocused. I look to Ahren, who's also eyeing Ardelle with his evaluating gaze.

"Son? It looks like you're about to faint."

Ardelle doesn't answer, and Ahren leans across the space between them and grips his free hand.

Jance and Saris glance at each other worriedly, the latter swirling her wine glass slowly.

I shake him, but he's nonresponsive.

"Wake up, pretty boy, and get it together, or else your sweet little sister is going to be killed."

I instantly throw daggers at Deimos with my eyes. Stars, I told him to keep his mouth shut before we got here.

"I have to go to my parents'." Ardelle's voice is haunted and cold. "I have to put a stop to this. I won't let them do this to her."

"You can't, Ardelle. Malakyte will not let you get anywhere near her. We have a plan . . ." I say, brushing his inked arm soothingly.

Jance clears his throat, and I look at him; he's silently fuming.

Sylo finally speaks up. "What plan? You said we only have a couple of weeks to stop this procedure. If we can't get on board through a spaceship, how are we going to get to her?" Stopping, he takes a breath, then points at Deimos. "He literally stabbed you and has said on multiple occasions he wants your crystal. If anything, this squid is going to make it all worse."

How is *squid* supposed to help anything?

Ardelle stands up, practically knocking me off the couch's arm. "I have to go. I have to go home and make my parents listen to reason. I'm sorry, Thumbelina."

He doesn't even look at me, just charges towards the door. Deimos, however, moves to block his path.

"Now, now, pretty boy. Take a breath. We've got a better plan than whatever's bouncing around in that head of yours. Trust me, you're not a master strategist. Leave the scheming to those who are decent at it."

"Move."

"Ardelle." I dash over to him and take his arm. "Please, just relax and listen. Trinity came up with an idea that might be our best shot at saving her. And not only saving her life and saving her crystal from falling into Malakyte's hands but also saving all of Earth. This can be our one and only shot to take the empire down. I know Pacey comes first, and you don't care about the rest of it right now. I get that, but listen to us, please."

"Yeah, I don't like the sound of this . . ." Sylo mumbles. He and Saris look at each other with skepticism in their eyes.

Ignoring him, I look at Ardelle. Behind the quiet rage, his eyes twitch, wild with fear.

"Trust me," I say, "I know you're scared for her, but don't sacrifice yourself without thinking first."

This, out of everything I've tried, seems to get through to him. We sit back down on the couch. I hope this means he can trust me again, too.

Trinity speaks to the room as she leans against the kitchen island. "We concluded there is one way to save Pacey from her gruesome fate." She turns to me, everyone else following her gaze. She's going to make me say it, isn't she? I suppose it's like ripping off a Band-Aid.

"Winning the Titan Games."

The silence is deafening. I try again. "Let me expla—"

"Absolutely not." Jance is the first to speak about the idea, and by the look on his face, he's not happy.

"Just listen, please," I beg. They must understand. "The winner gets a ticket up to the Azurite, and Malakyte's under too much political pressure to back out of that agreement. He's on the Network feeds nearly every day, begging for us Terrans not to go to war. He won't risk the political backlash."

"So, you think he'll simply let you waltz on up there and bring Pacey back with you? That's ridiculous." Jance's argument is sound, but I've already thought of all this.

"Obviously not." I lean towards Jance as I wipe the sweat off my palms and onto my pants. "That's where you guys come in. You sneak onto the transport ship while I'm brought up to the fleet. Pacey is also crucial to this plan." I tell them about Deimos's idea to have Pacey hack the Arianyte mainframe. "Once we launch the full-scale attack and destroy every one of their communications and systems, we get Pacey out. Trinity's mom, too. We'd be able to hit Arianyte like we never have before. With the rebels at our back, we can take them down. We'll never get this chance again."

"But only contingent on you winning the game," Ahren says.

I take a deep breath. "Look, I can win. The only people who join the games are average Terrans. People with Unnatural Abilities don't enter because they're too afraid of Arianyte. And extras rarely have abilities that can match mine. It's not like I'm going to be competing against other magic users. I'm strong. I can beat them."

Jance's eyes are dark as they barrel into mine. "People die in those games, kid. You're not going."

I challenge Jance with my own stone resolve. "I can win."

I need Jance to agree to this. Otherwise, I don't know if I can do this without risking our relationship. My Ringer's head shakes.

He's not convinced. "This is too dangerous. Malakyte can wrench you away and then you're a prisoner, too."

"I really don't think he'd do that," Trinity interrupts.

Even I look over at her with skepticism. How would she know that?

"If there's a big enough spotlight on Kara, Malakyte can't do anything to her." Trinity's face goes still, her mind tinkering away at the plan, just like Geonni used to.

"If this is played right, she can be the voice of the Terran Resistance, playing inside the occupation's games. This could play very well with public opinion if Kara acts like she's Arianyte's villain and Earth's hero. I have enough sway within the Resistance to push this on the Network feeds, and soon enough, our little rebel will go viral. We'll set her up as the one who can save us all. People will eat it up. Forget the Rebel's Song—she'll be the whole damned anthem."

Pressing his fingers against his brow, Jance practically growls with frustration. "This is insane. It puts you in jeopardy. Doing this is a slap in the prince's face, and he will not be happy about it."

"My life will always be in jeopardy," I counter. "With Malakyte alive, I'm at risk. Anything and everything I do will set him off. It's a lose-lose situation. He's never going to let me go, no matter what. I want to free Pacey and honor the Rebel's Song. The Hijacked and Tributes and Terrans deserve their freedom and their autonomy. I can't let what happened to Gavrielle happen to Pacey and all of you. Let me take the risk so you don't have to."

Yet, there's one other reason I want to do this, and it's an entirely selfish one. These games will be the perfect distraction I need. Distraction from imagining all the ways Gav was murdered. Distraction from hearing the disruptor shot that blew Geonni's head off. Distraction from it all. And I know that's terrible, but it's just for now . . . until we get Pacey back. Then I'll deal with my shit.

"More reason not to walk you over to him on a silver platter," Jance scowls.

We battle each other through our eyes, and I'm begging him to see this my way. I guess I got his stubbornness as well.

"I'm doing this," I tell him, voice defiant.

Jance doesn't blink. "You're not."

"You can't stop me."

Then he does what I'd never expected him to do. He stands from his spot next to Saris and begins to stalk out of the apartment. "I'm done. I'm not doing this."

He's done? I'm stunned by it . . . frozen in astonishment that he'd actually *leave me.* He promised me—*promised*—he'd never desert me.

Saris gets up and chases after him. "Kara, he's just upset." She knows. She was there when he made that promise. Both she and Ahren were. How could Jance do this to me?

The entire apartment goes silent for an extensive period of time. The tension climbs the longer Jance and Saris are outside.

"What if I enter, too?" Ardelle chimes in. His eyes are still averted onto the carpet between his widespread legs in his usual man slouch, but there is a hint of optimism in his voice.

My heart sinks.

"Having another one of us in there gives us a better chance of winning. Plus, we can look out for each other. The public knows we're his old elite team. Malakyte won't risk doing anything to us outside the games. Especially if we play it the way Trinity suggests. He's been in hot water since Kara blew the whistle about the Hijacked. Malakyte barely skated by with his excuses, and where he's relaxed with protocols and rules, he's tight with others. There's plenty of tyrannical behavior we can use to sway the public to our side. I think it's brilliant. And if it's the only way to save Pacey's life, I'll risk mine."

I don't have the heart to ask him not to fight for his sister. So, I don't.

"These are a lot of assumptions, son." Ahren's voice is skeptical at best, and I get why. He doesn't want his Starseed going in, either.

Ardelle's eyes finally look up to meet his Ringer's, and they're clear and full of fiery determination to save his sister's life. "I need to get my sister back, and I don't care how dangerous it is. She's up there, likely terrified and wondering why we haven't rescued her yet. Even if the procedure did have a chance of working, Malakyte wouldn't allow her to survive. He just wants her crystal, and my parents are desperate to be rid of it."

"And kiddo makes a point that, if he were to obtain that crystal, he'll likely become unstoppable," Deimos chimes in.

"Why are you here?" Sylo asks, half genuinely curious, half condescending.

Deimos snorts. "To assure kiddo here gets through the tryouts without being spotted, of course. That, and someone needs to be the brains of this operation. Stars knows it isn't going to be you people."

"You're such a dickhead, you know that? SSPARROW-killing squid." Sylo's voice is venomous.

"Traitorous sky-rat."

"Enough, both of you," I bark, still staring at the door my father had just exited.

Sylo isn't in the mood to stop, however. "You really think he won't try to kill you again, Kara? Take your crystal and go full psycho on us? If Malakyte can play us like fools, the squid sure can."

"Do not compare me to that bastard, kid, or I'll make you shut that mouth of yours in a very unpleasant way." Deimos's voice dips into that lower octave. But Sylo does make a good point about Deimos's loyalty. I sure hope I'm right about him not wanting to kill me anymore. Otherwise, I'm a dead girl.

And dead girls don't rescue their friends.

Or stop tyrants.

Or liberate planets.

Or do much of anything.

After what seems like forever, the door to our apartment opens again, and my father walks back inside with Saris on his heels.

"You and I need to talk. Privately. Right now."

CHAPTER 9

I don't know what Jance wants to say to me, but I doubt I'll like it. I'm prepared to fight him over this if necessary, and I fear that he's going to walk away from me again.

Jance and I don't speak as we leave the stuffy air and artificial lighting of the Reptilian undersewers for the late afternoon air. We walk down the deserted street not even looking at each other, yet the tension between us is thick. I take Sadie as emotional support. She roams freely around us, sniffing dried weeds as they break through cracks in the sidewalks, which are desperate for sunlight as they prove their defiance to this concrete jungle.

Jance's gaze slides past each building we walk by. Structure after structure is completely overrun by foliage, trees, vines, and weeds. It's endless. Those deep, dark eyes search the cloudless skies for drones, people, or SSPARROWs on patrol. I have no clue why we're risking it by coming up to the streets or why we couldn't just talk back in the undersewers. I follow his gaze, also checking for any signs of Arianyte's spy tech. I don't expect to see much of anything but then a blur of shadow against the sunset catches my peripheral. It seems like a giant black mass, a shadow from the depths of Hell, but the moment my eyesight shifts to look at it straight on, there's nothing there. I swear I saw a flash of movement, as if it leaped out of my sight right in the nick of time. Or maybe I'm seeing things? I keep my eyes peeled for any other signs of a figure, but I see none and neither does Jance. I assume mentioning what I saw would be a bad idea, not when he's so upset.

Is doing this Titan Games mission worth losing him if it comes to it? I am willing to fight for it, but am I willing to lose Jance over it?

Finally, Jance takes me off the streets and in through an abandoned building, its doors hanging off their hinges with poorly drawn graffiti on all sides faded from years of sun exposure. The art here was once brilliant, saturated in color, and fresh. Now, it's sad and dull.

We hike straight through the building and out the back door, where an overgrown field expands across the corner lot. My eyes widen when I notice it's a cemetery. It's from before Arianyte arrived here. I know from the age of the gravestones and statues as we walk by them, time and nature overtaking them with vines and the eroded letters of the dead.

I'd expect a place like this to smell like death and decay, but instead, there're only hints of primrose and lilac, the smell of woods from back home. The ache in my heart at the longing to return to Jance's house punches through my chest. The aching for *home*. A desperate desire to not let it slip through my fingers.

I let him walk ahead of me, giving him the space I'm sure he'll appreciate. The plot of land is small, and we can both see each other through the tall grass and weeds, the dog prancing around like this is the best day ever. I wish I could also feel so free, so careless of where we are, of my own mortality. Knowing that the promise of death will one day come for me and for everyone I love.

To the left of the cemetery is a patch of wildflowers, newly emerged from winter, coming back to life in such a dead, quiet place. Here, I find the source of the smells, several types of flowers blooming out along the side of the lot. Birds chirp as I pick a bunch of the best blossoms; then I see one, bobbing in the gentle sway of the breeze. A dandelion. Where is he buried, I wonder? Does Gavrielle even have a grave? Or did Arianyte simply incinerate his body as if he never existed? Silently, I pick the dandelion and add it to my makeshift memorial bouquet, then slowly walk towards my Ringer.

My father.

If he wants to talk, let's talk.

His back is to me, his black coat and dark hair making him look like a shadowed statue. He's still, unnaturally so. My mouth is dry, the dead grass crunching under my feet as I come to stand beside him.

I'm surprised to see him staring down two gravestones as I approach him, one for his late wife and daughter.

"Her name was Astoria," Jance finally says, the gravelly texture in his voice accentuated by his pain and grief. The gravestone reveals it's been nearly two decades since she died, and still, it breaks his heart in two. Does grief ever go away, or do you simply live with its weight until you yourself are dead and gone and someone else holds up that torch in your absence?

"We met so young. I joined what was the United States Marines, and my unit was working on tactical advancements against the newly arrived extraterrestrials that were floating out in orbit at the time. Many other extras arrived within that time, claiming peace and their desire to help humans with what we later found out was Arianyte. That time was chaotic, at best. People thought the world was going to end in a mighty war for control of the planet. Hell, it almost had. But Astoria was from a star system named Surius, and she was the most beautiful thing I've ever seen. She looked practically human; however, there were clear signs she was from off-world. Her eyes. They were almost comically large, yet, somehow, they fit her face. Her ears were abnormally pointed, like some elf or something I thought at the time. Straight from Tolkien."

Jance snickers softly, that anger from earlier seeping away into something else, something much more melancholic. He seems like the man I've always known, all that terrible tension plaguing us seemingly gone as fast as a spring storm.

My Ringer continues, and I listen. "She was a tiny little thing, hardly up to here on me." He raises his hand mid-chest, then laughs, but it's so sad. "Astonishingly, the woman was unnaturally strong, her race super-human. And stars was she the feistiest woman I've ever met. So demanding, so pushy and bossy that I couldn't stand her when we first met. Looking back, however, I knew I loved her from the very first moment I laid eyes on her. She had this absurd accent. And when she got heated, I could barely understand a word she was saying."

His eyes glisten with a memory, and it must be a happy one because there's a hint of a smile somewhere in all that misery. I take his hand, holding the wildflowers in the other. He's been there so much for me I can do the same in return. I can take this one step to being a good daughter to him, even if I don't know what I'm doing. Squeezing my hand back, he reassures me that he appreciates the gesture.

Blinking out misty eyes, he says, "We married quickly. I was twenty, ready to climb the ranks in the military, and Astoria was working with governmental leaders to keep war from breaking out between Arianyte and the humans. She was good at her job, and if it wasn't for her, Earth would've gone to war much sooner. She was a pioneer, an angel for the humans who shunned and feared her. She was an alien, and aliens were the enemy back then. Several months after we married, somehow, our biology was similar enough, and she became pregnant. Neither of us expected it. I certainly didn't know how to be a father, not at that age. The military doctors urged us to terminate, claiming all the unknown complications of an interspecies child would be infinite to both mother and child. But she would not hear it. Soon, it became dangerous for her to continue working. I left her in the care of my parents. She was out of the city limits. She was safe. I couldn't get out of duty, and one of my biggest regrets was not being there for her as much as I should have been. We found out we'd be having a girl. Which, at first, disappointed me. I wanted a strapping young man I could teach to fight and shoot guns and how to be a man. That quickly changed, however, when it dawned on me. I was having a little girl whom I was supposed to look after and protect and scare away any little punk attempting to steal her heart. I grew up because of her. Everything I do is because of her, because of them both."

I'm locked in like a moth to flame. This story so pertinent to my past that the urge to shout out what Malakyte had told me is overwhelming. Although, I don't dare interrupt. It's not my time to talk.

He struggles to find the words. "Astoria wanted to be closer to me, as she was well beyond her ninth month. So, against my protests, she came to live where I was stationed, which, ultimately, became Zarmenia. I should have said no. I should have forced her to stay where she was safe." Regret fills his voice, and his shoulders hunch down in shame. "On a late night in December, I got a frantic call from my mother. Astoria hadn't returned home from shopping. I left my post against orders, scoured the streets for her. It wasn't until long after midnight that we got word from the local police. That's when I found out she was murdered. Both were."

His last words are barely an audible whisper on the wind. He can hardly bear to speak.

"I'm so sorry, Jance," I finally say.

What other words are there? Nothing makes grief better; nothing takes away the hole in your heart. I study the grave beside his wife's. It's smaller, with the name Rivara Gallivan etched into stone along with the phrase, *Beloved daughter, taken too soon.*

Pain blooms in my chest at the realization. A grave means a body . . . so how could that baby girl be me? Hating to ask but needing to know, I let the words tumble out of me. "You buried them separately?"

Swallowing his pain, he holds the sorrow so eloquently at bay I didn't even know it was there. "No," he says plainly. "I knew Astoria would've wanted to be buried with her daughter. I created the gravestone to give Rivara something that was hers, to tell the world that she was a life and a person and her own, beautiful spirit."

It's these words that finally break me, and a single tear falls onto my cheek. "It's beautiful," I manage to squeeze out of a tightened throat. Letting go of Jance's hand, I kneel and place the flowers between the two gravestones. I look at the dates of death, approximately eighteen years ago. My birthday—or what I assume is my birthday—was last December. That's around the time this woman, Astoria, died, and from how he describes her, she sounds a hell of a lot like me. This has to be my mother. Her appearance, paired with my unnatural strength and pointed ears. The dates and everything all match up. I seriously doubt Jance was with another woman at the same time. Not with the way he speaks of her. He *loved* her.

It sounds like this is her, and she's gone . . . I'll never meet her, never get to ask her if she thought of me or loved me.

Standing, I lean in to hug him. He's all I've got left.

Jance looks down at me, his usual strength and sturdy demeanor returning, although his eyes harden, and that tension from earlier returns in full. "Understand how much I recognize what you're going through right now. I know what it's like to want to burn the entire world down to get justice, to right a terrible wrong. To be so hot with rage and fury that you don't care if you burn your own soul to cinders if you can find the person responsible for your pain and make them feel it tenfold. But I don't want you to make the mistakes I made. I don't want to see your past trauma ruin your future. The only way Malakyte will win is if you slip up. And when you let that pain, rage, and the avoidance of it all lead the way, you *will* slip. I promise you, kid, it'll happen. And when it does, I don't know if I can be there to protect you from yourself."

He isn't wrong, but it still hurts to hear. "I'm trying," I say, not defensive or angry, just honest. "I wish I could be different. I wish all these shit things never happened to me so I could just be a normal person with a normal mind who isn't so messed up all the time."

"Don't be anyone other than who you are, kid. That's not what I'm saying." Jance looks across the small cemetery, as if he's seeing it for the first time. "Just don't lose yourself in a maze of your own red-eyed fury. It's always harder to come back from rock bottom than it is to plummet down to it. Trust me."

I nod, not knowing how to respond to that. It's hard for me to imagine Jance as a person who's burning so hot with rage that he's out of control. Perhaps that's a part of him I did get. If he could grow out of it, maybe I could, too?

"If you want my blessing to do the games, I need you to convince me that you've heard what I'm telling you here. That you're not going to self-sabotage or let your emotions take control. I've lost my child already, and I can't lose you, too. You understand? You're mine, remember?"

But you walked out on me. You said you were done with me . . . I want to tell him—I just don't know how. Why did he leave me back at the apartment? Would he do it again? I can't tell him I'm his daughter, not after that . . . I just—I *can't.* Even after all he told me about our past, I'm simply too afraid. I'm a damned coward.

"I'll keep a level head, Jance, I promise. And I won't let what I'm dealing with personally or my desire to get revenge on Malakyte cloud my judgment. Ardelle said he'll join the games with me, so he'll be there to make sure I don't lose control. I know that'll make you feel a little better, right?"

"Slightly," he grumbles, but I can tell he still isn't completely sold on the idea. "I want you to promise me you'll do everything I say. I'll make sure we can communicate the entire time and that you'll listen to me without being difficult."

"I'm not difficult."

Jance laughs softly at me.

Okay, fine.

"I'll do whatever you say," I promise. "Please, let me make right what I couldn't for Gav. He haunts me . . . and it's like, if I can save Pacey, I can save him, in a way. At least make up for not being able to save him."

"I know, kid. I just don't want to lose you or see you hurt again."

"You won't."

"You can't promise me that. And these damned games, they're full of bloodlust, booby traps, people who will take pleasure in hurting you, and none of that has anything to do with all the risks we're taking with Malakyte. If he gets you, kid, he'll never let you go. I'll never see you again."

My blood goes cold at the reality of what I'm asking him to let me do. The true risks. Is Pacey worth it? Is the chance to bring Malakyte and the entire empire down worth this gamble? Is temporarily satiating my pain worth it? I was sure before now, but Jance is painting quite a grim picture.

"I promise I'll come back, Jance. Just don't walk out on me again . . ."

His eyes turn soft at that.

"I'm sorry for that, kid. I shouldn't have walked out and said what I did. I was frustrated at the situation. But I meant it when I told you I'd never leave you, no matter what. I'll *never* be done with you." He says that, but the broken little girl within reminds me that I can't trust words. And Jance walking out on me today shook my faith in him some.

He dives into his coat pocket, and I see a flash of silver. It's a dark black ring—a man's ring—on a chain of silver. He takes my hand and places it there; it's warm against my palm.

"My wedding ring," he says. "I stopped wearing it a few years ago, decided to put it on a chain and wear it that way. It means a lot to me, more than I could ever express. Because, no matter what other woman comes into my life romantically, Astoria will always be the love of my life. This ring is a symbol of the love we share and the life we made together. To assure you that I mean what I say, I'm giving it to you. I'll never part from this ring, and I'll never leave you. Keep it until you come back safe and sound."

I stare at the smooth black metal. The ring is simple, elegant and stylish, yet strong. It's perfect for him. And I suppose it's a step in the right direction. We'll see.

"I'll make sure we both come back," I say, holding myself up as confidently as possible.

Jance smiles, although it's full of apprehension. "Then, you can join the Titan Games. Just don't die on me, kid."

CHAPTER 10

ALL ANIMALS WILL BE LIBERATED FROM CAPTIVITY WHERE POSSIBLE AND RELOCATED TO NONDISPLAY PERMANENT SANCTUARIES. THIS WILL INCLUDE ALL AQUATIC MAMMALS.

"Don't cut your hair," Ardelle pleads, the words aching on his tongue as the two of us squeeze into the miniature bathroom hundreds of feet underground. "It's too beautiful. We can disguise you some other way for the tryouts tomorrow."

To help us help Deimos, he demanded we disguise ourselves to avoid detection. "I'm talking to you, kiddo," Deimos had said, voice taunting. "I'm not a miracle worker. Change your look, or I'll ditch this absurd plan."

I really hate him sometimes.

But he's right.

Now, Ardelle and I are on a mission to change our looks, but he doesn't seem to like my suggestion of chopping all my hair off.

My brow arches skyward. "Since you're now my stylist, how do you suggest we disguise me? I'm pretty sure it was the other Dawson sibling that was good at this stuff."

We laugh for a moment until we remember her absence, the ticking clock attached to her life, and silence is the only thing left in the wake of her vacancy. Brushing his fingers through his own hair nervously, Ardelle shimmies past me and stands behind me as we both stare into the small mirror before us. The bathroom sink doesn't hold much aside from the two toothbrushes, some soap, and a hand towel. As I gaze into Ardelle's reflection, I can see so much mischief dancing there. A tiny battle is waged, one for power and control and desire and the aching need for each other.

Picking up my teal ends and tickling my nose with them, he leans in and kisses my cheek. "What if we make it a different color on the ends?" Ardelle suggests, letting go of our silent battle and focusing on the clear problem at hand—disguising ourselves from all those prying eyes tomorrow.

A painful twang hits my heart at his suggestion, though. Ardelle couldn't know that the color of my hair corresponds to the color of the flowers Gavrielle had transformed for me the night he was taken away. The night I failed him. Doomed him.

Killed him.

Does holding onto this color keep his memory alive, or does it continue to keep me chained to my mistakes and the trauma that bloomed from them?

"Well," I begin with a heavy huff of my breath, picking up a bag of hair supplies we risked a lot to go and get, "we've got bleach, almost every color of the rainbow, including fashion colors. I think I've figured out what I'm going to do, no cutting involved. But what about you, Blondie? What would Mommy and Daddy say when they see you looking like some ragamuffin with colored hair? They'll blame me for corrupting your innocent soul with all my wicked sexual prowess."

Unable to help myself, I arch my back and grind my ass into his front, immediately seeing the blood bloom on his cheeks and elsewhere, too.

He bends down and whispers in my ear, "I'll die ten times over again to be your ragamuffin, Thumbelina."

He presses against me this time, forcing me to brace my hands on the cold sink. A soft gasp escapes me. His words were sensual, seductive, and I can't help but feel the heat spark within me. I clear my throat and my dirty thoughts.

"Let's bleach me first," I say, completely trying to ignore Ardelle's massive hard-on so we don't get completely distracted. "Then, while that's doing its thing, we'll dye you. Your hair is light enough it'll soak up pretty much any color, but if you want a bright color, I suggest we lighten you up a bit with bleach. It depends on what you want."

"I know what I want." His voice is confident, but as he says it, he looks directly into my eyes through the mirror, laying his hands on both my shoulders as softly as a butterfly. His broad frame takes up almost the entire width of the bathroom, one shoulder brushing the side of the shower stall with the other only inches from the door.

Awkwardly giggling, I step away from his body and dig into our products. My eyes widen as I see the color Ardelle chooses, but he smiles back at me, as confident as ever.

The two of us laugh and joke while helping each other with our hair-dying processes. Hours go by, and it takes us forever to finish.

"I'm going to rinse this off back at my place. I need a shower after you absolutely murdered me with his hair color," Ardelle says, streaks of dye cascading all over his neck, ears, and arms. The latter is from my hair, the long strands finding their way onto his forearms despite the gloves.

I nod, agreeing. "I should take one, too. Come back when you're done."

We part, and when I finish my shower, I'm standing in front of the mirror once more, this time alone but feeling conflicted as I stare at my reflection.

The look I chose doesn't exactly scream "blending in," but that's not the point. The point was not to appear like me. So, I've accomplished that, at least.

The majority of my hair remains black, like my father's, except the front pieces—what Pacey calls "the money piece"—shine in Moonbeam White. The ends, teal dye removed and refreshed with a round of bleach, are now baby pink. I feel so different, so unlike myself. I'll likely dye it back once the tryouts are over. It looks good—it's just not me.

I dry and style it quickly. I also manage to have time to put some makeup on, and when I finish dolling up, I feel like a bit of life has sparked into me.

When I exit the bathroom, the apartment is empty. I change into my usual clothes, ripped jeans, a lace bralette, and a sweater that's too big for me and hangs off one shoulder.

I look down at my forearm, at the dandelion tattoo I haven't looked at in months. The guilt I feel for getting rid of Gav's teal in my hair is more overwhelming than I expected it to be, and it's like I picked up that baggage all over again. That moment of peace sure didn't last long, did it? Am I ever going to be happy? Or am I simply destined to suffer one hardship, one disaster, after another? If someone truly knew how much I was hurting, would they still judge me for my actions?

The apartment door clicks open, and I almost fall straight off the couch due to the smoking hot piece of man that comes waltzing in.

Ardelle walks in casually, shirtless, scrubbing his wet hair with a towel. He's wearing dark sweatpants that show off his chiseled abs, and I bite my lip so hard at the sight of him.

Holy fucking stars . . .

His hair is long gone from mousy blond and has been transformed into a deep, dark blue in the shade of Midnight Sky. It's practically black, so much so that the blue will probably only be visible in the sun, and we dyed his eyebrows so he wouldn't look like a browless weirdo or be mistaken for an extra. But damn, had I known making him dark-haired would have turned him from tattooed hottie to drop-dead gorgeous—becoming shadow and darkness and danger incarnate—I'd have never let him go through with it.

I'm in so much trouble.

Ardelle laughs as he throws his towel in my face, but I let it flop into my lap. "You've got some drool on your chin, Thumbelina."

Come lick it off me, then . . .

Stars.

"It's a good choice," I say, words jumbled and heat rising to my cheeks.

He comes and sits down next to me, smelling of fresh sage and cinnamon—him. "You look beautiful, too."

That makes me smile.

"Why'd you pick your blue?" I ask, knowing it's a radical choice for him.

"For Pace. It was the first color she dyed her hair once we left home. It was a big *f-you* to our parents and their rules. I want to show solidarity with her, hopeful that, if she is allowed to watch the games, she'll know that I'm doing this for her. That I haven't forgotten about her. That I'm coming."

Grabbing a hold of Ardelle's hand, we lace our fingers together. "For Pacey," I say, squeezing tightly.

He squeezes back, firm and strong and sure. "For Pacey."

CHAPTER II

We're back at the Titan Games arena to ensure we make it through the tryouts, but I can't breathe. We walk up the small set of stairs that leads up to the entrance, a majestic piece of alien architecture. It's a minimum of seven stories tall and double that in width. The building is dark and sleek and highly technical-looking, all angles and hard edges, nothing round about it despite the fact it's technically shaped like a giant bowl. On the east end of it are a bunch of scaffoldings and other materials used for repairing buildings. The catastrophe I nearly prevented at the last game's finale still caused a ton of damage to the arena itself, and being here brings it all back into focus. Geonni's death, finding out about Gav, the truth being revealed, and the fight with Malakyte.

My footsteps falter as we crest the stairs, and I can practically smell the burning of things in the air from that night. The stench of blood and of magic and of death.

This is where the Titan Games tryouts are being held. Today. Right now.

And I am not ready for them.

Standing in the shadows of a pillar, Deimos glares at us on our approach, leaning against the concrete with his arms crossed. "Wow, you two really know the meaning of blending in, don't you? These disguises do absolutely nothing. They're just superficial. Couldn't you have at least used some prosthetics or something to hide who you are from people?"

I try not to scowl at Deimos, imagining picking his eyes out with my pointy nails. "You're literally a green alien, dude. You stick out more than anyone." We glare at each other in earnest before Ardelle comes between us.

"We're not starting out like this," he says firmly, and I sneer over at the extra but don't say another word.

Jance—who will forever be called "Jance" and not "Dad" or, stars forbid, those sappy epithets like "Father" or "Daddy"— intercepts in the situation. "The kids know what they have to do. It's up to you to follow through on your end. Get them through the tryouts unnoticed."

"Just be sure to follow my lead, kiddos." Deimos walks toward the entrance without us, wearing another one of those full-bodied, skintight body suits made of leather.

Sylo makes a disbelieving sound in his throat and shakes his head dismissively. "This is a bad idea, guys. If Malakyte finds out, he could punish Pacey as retribution. Her life is in our hands. By doing this, we're putting her in danger. What if they notice it is you guys and push this surgery date up sooner because they suspect you're coming for her? I don't think it's a goo—"

"She's already in danger," I interrupt. "She's up there, a prisoner of war, because we didn't act when they took her. We spent months sitting around twiddling our thumbs, doing it your way. Your daddy didn't help us. SSPARROWs don't help anyone but Arianyte. Any minute, they can perform that operation on her, and she's dead. We have no way of knowing. We act now."

That comes out a lot harsher than I intended it to, and by how Sylo's cheeks redden and eyes avert down to his faded shoes missing half their decorative metal accents, I can see it hit harshly.

"What Kara means to say, Sylo," Jance begins, placing one of his massive hands on each of our shoulders, "is that, sometimes, in situations where there're no right answers, we have to take risks. This is one of those times. I'm hesitant as well. But we need to give these two our confidence and have faith that everything will work out."

Shaking off Jance's hand, Sylo angrily shakes his head.

"Hey!" Deimos yells over from the door's entrance, waving us down. "Enough hugs and kisses. Let's go."

I blink in surprise as Jance's huge body fully envelops me, blocking out the sun. "Be careful. If you're recognized, leave. Nothing is worth them getting their hands on you, understand?" His voice is sure, strong, and confident as he holds me.

This is either going to work, or we're about to add a few more Starseeds to Malakyte's collection.

CHAPTER 12

Somehow, we must both compete well enough to be chosen as Titans but also stay completely under the radar. Easy.

The three of us stand in a crowd of roughly a hundred people. Mostly Terran, but far more extras than I expected. Races like the stray Reptilian and Grays. Others like Lyrans, the cat-like people, whose planet was apparently destroyed in a war long ago. Terran-appearing extras such as the Pleiadians, who are really only identified as such by their abnormally tall height and so on.

"Attention, maggots." A hefty extra claps once, looking more like a walking, talking pig with tusks that swallowed a man and ended up turning into this monstrosity.

"His snout is glistening," I whisper to Ardelle, and he bumps my shoulder and shakes his head, but he cracks a smile anyway.

The crowd silently looks up at the hog man, who's dressed in a one-shouldered black toga with the Arianyte "A" on the breast. Roughly two dozen others mulling around of all shapes and sizes, races, and sexes wear the same uniform. Those must be the judges.

"We're testing each of you maggots in four areas of strength: agility, upper body, lower body, and intelligence. Each one will be tested in its own individual heat. In order to even be considered for the Titan Games, each maggot must be in the top sixty out of three of the four heats. If you don't place, you don't compete. Got it?"

"There are dudes here double my size," Ardelle says as we spread out and await the first heat. "I don't know if you're going to be able to outperform them in overall strength, Thumbelina."

Deimos snorts, his own variation of agreement with Blondie over here—well—Bluey? No. Doesn't work. Blondie, it will stay.

Biting my lip, I eye the competition. Blondie isn't wrong. "I'll figure it out."

Worry clouds Ardelle's eyes as we're told to line up shoulder-to-shoulder on the far end of the pristinely rebuilt arena interior.

There aren't many women, maybe a dozen, and I'm, by far, the smallest of them all. I've already been getting the looks of indignation from insecure alpha males who believe a woman's place is in the kitchen instead of here.

Well, I've always been underestimated. This is no different.

A pull deep in my stomach causes my thoughts to shift as I notice Deimos's crystal beginning to swell in power. Ardelle senses it, too.

"We've been spotted," Deimos snarls as we line up, each of them on either side of me. "By that Terran on the far right side, next to the two Gray judges."

I look and see the vacant, eerie green glow of Deimos's Elendril crystal in the eyes of the middle-aged man at the judging table. Here we go. Let's hope Deimos is good enough to do this. If we need to help him through the qualifiers, then we will.

My heart begins to race.

"Maggots!" the ugly hog man shouts as he stands beside the judge's panel. "The first heat is agility. Race to the end of the arena. First sixty will place."

Many arrogant snickers clank down the line of would-be Titans, like this is far too simple of a challenge for most of them, and they've already got it in the bag. I look straight ahead, palms wet with sweat and a nervous flutter in my chest.

"At the sound of the horn!" shouts the hog man.

Here we go.

I brace my body down low, pinning my right leg behind me so I can push off from the jump.

"Be careful, Thumbelina," Ardelle whispers.

The horn blasts through the air a split second later, and I fly like the wind.

CHAPTER 13

ARIANYTE WILL DEPLOY DRONES AND ROBOTIC SURVEILLANCE UNITS TO PATROL TERRAN ZONES, COMMUNITIES, AND NEIGHBORHOODS. ANY SUSPICIOUS BEHAVIOR OR UNAUTHORIZED GATHERINGS WILL BE SWIFTLY SUPPRESSED.

Ardelle manages to keep me from being trampled as a hundred of us take off at once, sardined too close together not to have several casualties get flattened right from the start.

From there, he takes off ahead of me, the gap in our distances widening quickly. I'm fast, but my legs are short, and my stride is even shorter.

Shit.

I thought I was fast, but sprinting is a highly different skill than having good reflexes in battle, I realize. I fall behind quickly but manage to stay ahead of the slowest quarter of competitors, which isn't saying much. At this rate, I won't make it into the top sixty, not by a landslide.

Then the earth-shaking thunder of cannon firing erupts.

Straight ahead of us, emerging out of the opposite wall of the stadium from dark square openings in the concrete face are two dozen high-tech cannons. They're the size of a basketball and glowing—practically sizzling—a white-hot blue in the shade Icicles. The cannons are aimed directly at us.

And they go *boom*.

The front runners get the brunt of the hits, too slow or too stupid to get out of the way. Somewhere up there, I feel Ardelle's crystal spiking. He must've had to use his to prevent himself from getting clobbered.

I can't worry about him right now; I've got to push myself and get ahead of these people.

Straining my muscles, I fly past the bodies of those who hesitate, making it halfway across the arena floor before the cannons begin to fire again. The sounds are roaring, their echoes reverberating along the stadium's walls, pounding against the barrier of my skull like a battering hammer.

I shriek just in time to see the blue ionized sphere shooting right for me, and I have no option other than to dive to the turf belly-first to prevent myself from wearing a hole inside my chest. The heat that passes over my head is insane, and I can feel it sizzling my scalp before hitting some idiot who was trailing too close behind me to see the cannonball coming.

His screams are left behind as I heave myself back up and continue to run. If I can hurry, perhaps I can get to the end before the next ball fires.

When I look ahead, the square openings are closed. There's no way to align myself up with a gap in the firing mechanism; I can't see them.

Many people have made it to the end by now, and my nerves begin to crawl up my neck like an incessant, panicked spider, its legs tapping and tapping and tapping. Go, go, go, *go!*

I listen, pushing myself and ignoring all the pain as it screams at me to stop. People litter the turf floor, along with their dismembered body parts. Arms, legs, and I think I see a head, but I avert my gaze so fast I'm not sure if that's what I saw. I won't glance back to find out. This is sick.

The added adrenaline allows me to run faster, and ahead of me, I see the openings of the cannons begin to open back up. I'm close to the end but not close enough, and there are too many people already at the finish line for me to count. What if it's too late? I need to win this heat, or I likely won't make it through the other three.

I hop over a big guy, who's holding his hand and writhing on the floor, and he actually tries to grab my ankle as I do. My foot slips out of his grasp but barely. Asshole! And he costs me because the boom of the cannon comes mere milliseconds later, and panic explodes within me just as quickly. My crystal involuntarily reacts, burning my chest, as my eyes try to find a cannonball. I don't see one in my direct path, and I breathe a sigh of relief. Then I hear Ardelle's voice booming out like it is cannon fire all its own.

"Thumbelina!" I hear Ardelle cry, and I'm face-to-face with a barreling cannonball coming straight for me.

Another cannon fires unexpectedly right after the last one. I'm too close. There's no time. No time to duck or steer out of the way.

There's only time to die.

CHAPTER 14

Regret floods my body faster than the cannonball barreling toward me at full speed. I think of Jance—of my father—and how he'll never know who I am.

He'll never know . . .

The heat hits me first, burning my cheeks and lashes in a whoosh of Hell's inferno, blowing my braids back. All I can do is brace my arms over my face in hopes it keeps me from somehow getting my head blown off, but that's unlikely. I'm about to be one of the people dismembered and dead on the turf floor.

What did we get ourselves into?

The cannonball hits.

But I'm not dead.

Parts of the ball explode and shatter in all directions, its bits raining down around me . . . but somehow, my body is intact.

Stunned, I blink, dumbfounded, the world seeming to slow. The cannonball did hit me. It's sitting in tiny pieces at my feet, but . . .

My crystal.

It sizzles alight on my chest through my clothes, the three of us agreeing to keep them hidden today. An antimatter shield glowing before me gradually fades into nothing but soft bits of sparks around my body.

"Thumbelina, keep running!" I hear Ardelle shout. He's right. I should run.

I should also be dead.

Go! I hear a voice inside my head shout. *Go*!

I go.

There's not a whole lot of room on the sides of the cannons, so as I pass the finish line, I'm only stopped by running straight into Ardelle. His body bounces against the concrete wall of the stadium as I slam into him, his arms and scent both enveloping me. An emotional wave of relief hits me all at once.

My pride alone keeps my cheeks dry, but it doesn't stop Ardelle from feeling me tremble in his arms. He bends down and says in my ear, "You're okay, you did good. I think you're one of the sixty."

"This is insane, Ardelle," I say, voice muffled in his shirt. "If this is merely the tryouts for the games, what are the actual games going to be like? People are literally dead and dismembered out there."

I was almost one of them. If my crystal hadn't instinctively saved me . . . I can't even think of the consequences of what would've happened. Worse is that I shudder at the thought of what could've happened to Ardelle. What did I get him into? Why did I ever allow him to come and do this with me? Deimos, he's fine, I suppose. The guy tried to kill me, so he isn't exactly at the top of my favorite people list. However, I don't want to see him hurt or captured, either.

"People noticed your little stunt, kiddo," Deimos barks as he walks up to the two of us. There's hardly any room between two of the cannon blasters, so I stand with my back against Ardelle's chest as Deimos stands beside us. "Is it hard for you or something? Do you have some attention-seeking coping mechanism we all don't know about that draws conflict and eyeballs to you? I'm managing to keep it quiet for now, but one more stunt, and it's game over, kiddo. Keep it on the down-low, or we're all *screwed*."

He hisses at us and walks off, the final stragglers trickling in across the bloodied, body-strewn field. Well, so much for me not wanting to see Deimos hurt.

"Ignore him," says Ardelle, his eyes scanning the remaining competition. "You've got bigger things to worry about right now."

CHAPTER 15

The following two heats aren't nearly as deadly or intense, which I sigh a measurable breath of relief for. I nail the heat for intelligence, actually finishing in the top twenty even before Ardelle and Deimos, and I walk around with a smile plastered on my face.

For a whole five minutes between heats.

The current heat is a test of upper body strength, where we're meant to hang on bars until we can no longer hold on. It's a gamble because I can either do really well or really bad. Ardelle, Deimos, and I all positioned ourselves strategically so we can all three see each other in case someone needs help. The flaring of Ardelle's crystal shoots through me. Which is smart. He's using his gravity magic to keep himself up. When I begin slipping, feeling the burning and pulling in my muscles and bones, I glimpse over at him for assistance, but then I see Deimos. He's struggling badly. Ardelle and I lock eyes, and I see worry there. He looks between Deimos and me. Shit, he's probably telling me he can only help one of us. Deimos's eyes are closed in concentration. My hands are sweaty, my shoulders on fire. I peek over at Deimos again, then back to Ardelle. If I lose this round, then I have to win the last one. Otherwise, I won't make it to the actual games. But I need Deimos there, too, and he's doing extra work. It's likely he'll lose a second heat rather than me. I nod my head towards Deimos, indicating to Ardelle to assist him instead of me. It's the best overall choice.

I drop several minutes later.

Deimos makes it through, landing somewhere in the top ten, thanks to Ardelle's gravity magic. Ardelle, on the other hand, is the last little peacock to finish, and he struts around like one, garnering glares from the men—and the women.

"Thanks for the assist," Deimos says afterwards.

"It was a team effort, but I expect you to be nice to me since I took a dive for you," I tell Deimos. I slap Ardelle playfully on the back when I turn to him and say, "The old Blondie would've been far too pretentious to cheat like that. I'm proud of how much I've corrupted you."

"The old Blondie has had a makeover."

Why that makes the spot between my thighs tingle, I have no idea, but stars, it's hot as hell.

"Not too bad, maggots," the hog man says to the remaining eighty or so of us that haven't quit or been too injured to continue. "You pitiful idiots made it to the last heat. Shocking."

The hog man is standing next to an odd-looking device that's almost as tall as he is. "This next heat calculates lower body strength, and what better way to analyze said strength than with a classic kick." The crowd muffles a bit, interested. "This machine here registers the newtons of your kick per square inch. The tech in this machine will analyze each of you maggots individually before the kick is measured. Each candidate's height, weight, speed of kick, et cetera, will be measured by the target area you see here."

He points to the big blue circular pad that's protruding outwards.

Nerves begin to itch at my skin. I look over to Ardelle, and his face says it all. There's no way I'm passing this heat. Not with all the men here. Only a handful of women are left, but even still, just by mere mass alone, I'm not going to be able to generate enough force to outscore the remaining grown men with my size and stature.

Man after man walks up. The machine analyzes their body and then they kick. We don't see their scores, which is somehow even more anxiety inducing.

What the hell do I do here? My mind tinkers with ideas, plan after plan falling apart with each person that goes up against the machine, until there's only a few people left to kick.

"Any bright ideas, Thumbelina?"

I bounce on my toes nervously beside him, getting looks and laughs from the people who've already kicked. I lean into Ardelle and whisper, "Can you use your crystal to put enough force behind my kick to get me through? Like before?"

"I should be able, yeah. That's probably our best shot to get you through this round."

There's some relief that calms my anxiety, but it doesn't do much for it.

Deimos manages to kick a few people ahead of us, his head down and shoulders hunched.

Ardelle is second to last to kick, and I feel naked and exposed without his body beside mine. I'm alone out here, being watched by a pack of hyenas. The men don't bother me when Ardelle is near, but the moment he steps away and I'm on my own, they pounce. So sexist of them. However, they're soon forced to stare at Ardelle when his kick manages to scoot the entire machine backwards an inch.

That's right, assholes. Gape at my hot, powerful boyfriend. You're nothing compared to him. You're weak little twerps.

I smile despite myself.

Wait, did I just call Ardelle my boyfriend? Is he my boyfriend?

Focus, dammit.

"Next."

The hog man impatiently ushers me forward, the blatant whispers of the astonished onlookers distracting as Ardelle takes his place back amongst them.

I walk to stand in front of the machine, and as it begins to scan me, it lowers the target surface to better enable my kick, and it takes a while to get there. Which garners a ton of mocking laughter from the crowd beside me.

"Watch out, boys. We've got a threat on our hands," says this big Terran, a dark-eyed man, his top half looking disproportionately top heavy with his bulgy veins and muscles about to pop out of his skin. Did someone say steroids?

"Man, I'm shaking in my ballerina slippers," another mocks.

"We got us a ninety-pound fighting machine. I think I might drop out."

"Where's my mommy when I need her?"

Ardelle's voice cuts through the mockery with a sharp hiss. "The next person stupid enough to speak will regret opening their mouth, I promise you that."

It shuts them up real quick.

Even though I'm grateful for Ardelle defending me, it doesn't prevent the damage they each intended on inflicting. I ball my fists, anger shooting through my veins, as my cheeks redden with pure pissed-off embarrassment. I could dust them all in two seconds flat, and I'd likely kick their asses in hand-to-hand, too. Those sexist jerks don't know who they're dealing with, what I could do to them. Despite myself, my crystal tingles and speaks its sweet song to me.

Blast them, it purrs to me. *Show them all who you are. What you're truly capable of. You're a goddess, you're a queen, an empress.*

I shake its voice from my mind. *No.* No, I can't use my crystal. It'll kill them. I don't want to do that.

Then an idea tickles the corner of my mind. I can't use my crystal on *them*.

They think my grin is because Ardelle came to my defense, but that isn't why I'm beaming. Oh, no, it's not why at all. Because I don't want to be defended. I want to be *feared*.

I turn to Ardelle, trying to tell him with my eyes that I won't be needing his assistance, after all.

The machine beeps, indicating that it's ready for me to kick.

I get into place, getting my footing just right. Thankfully, the blood pounding in my ears drowns out the testosterone-fueled snickering to my left. Something else takes over my anxiety, and damn, it feels so good.

My eyes catch Ardelle's, and he shakes his head subtly; he knows what I'm about to do. He feels the monster within me surging to life.

But he can't stop me, and I don't dare look at Deimos. He probably sensed what I'm about to do sooner than Ardelle had.

I'm practically delirious and crazy with pleasure.

These men, these assholes think I'm merely some fragile little girl who's absolutely no threat to them on the sole presumption that, because I'm a woman, I'm weak.

Well, screw them.

Screw that outdated sexist assumption. I am not weak or helpless, and I no longer allow *men* to hurt me. Men have always harmed me again and again, and what I hate most is that I let them do it. What's the purpose of having my strength if I do not use it to teach men like them a lesson?

I swing my leg lightning fast in a powerful roundhouse kick, my body gliding through the air like I'm a trained dancer of many years. The moment my back foot leaves the ground, I channel my crystal's antimatter energy down through my core and into that leg. My magic hits my foot as it collides with the machine, and in a boom of pure annihilation, the contraption explodes and goes flying across the arena floor. Ten, thirty, fifty feet, it flies. Until finally it slams into the wall of the stadium, crushed into a million pieces.

My heart is absolutely soaring.

Even more so by the absolutely stunned stupid silence of all these assholes standing beside me.

The look I give them as I return is sheer unadulterated "fuck you," and I wouldn't have it any other way.

Fuck. You. All.

Only then do I fully show them all my teeth.

Their eyes are about to bug out of their heads, and as my crystal coils back into its sleeping position, it winks at me and whispers one last time.

Good girl.

Show them all exactly who you are.

CHAPTER 16

THE ARIANYTE EMPIRE DECREE #19

ARIANYTE CLAIMS OWNERSHIP OF ALL NATURAL RESOURCES, INCLUDING WATER SOURCES AND FERTILE LAND. TERRANS MUST PAY FEES TO ACCESS THESE RESOURCES FOR FURTHER PRODUCTION.

MALAKYTE ARDEEN

She did not.

No . . .

No!

Karalevine . . . what are you doing, you reckless girl?

I can hardly believe what I'm seeing. The Dezlar in my hand is on the verge of cracking from the sheer force of my grip. All the chosen Titans and their pictures stare back at me through the screen. The name and hair are different, but it's those eyes, that soul that I'll never forget. It's unmistakably Karalevine.

This is the last thing I need right now. Aside from my current responsibilities running the Aurora System, I have a commitment to assuring what happened at the last Titan Games never occurs again. Certainly, with the tension between Terrans and Arianyte at such an emotional fever pitch since those games, Karalevine entering these new ones will only cause that hostility to rise—to boil over. She could lead this planet to war.

This throws a wrench into everything I've been planning.

And with Selenyte here as well, stars above . . . I can't even concentrate on what's in front of me, let alone be observant enough to glean the information I need.

I stand within the central hub of the prison, each of the square cells encircling the hub like a snowflake, more cells expanding further beyond the central command. Hours earlier, Naresteé walked out onto the platform and entered the prison of my VIP prisoner, where I watch her continue her work. It's deep within the Azurite, where the windows are few and the vermin are many. The smell is dank this low into the bowels of my ship, and it's a bit staggering how many prisoners I have down here. I must find better uses for them at some point.

Each cell is made of transparent temper-nano glass and is organized side by side. There isn't much to these cells. They're not meant to be comfortable. It's more about what she doesn't have that's important to me. Elements. Natural elements are hard to come by in space, which is why we're on the Azurite in the first place. The elements she is allowed to encounter are strictly monitored, yet even so, she's escaped thrice already. Even with the collar.

Pacey Dawson is far stronger than she appears. Like it or not, I do have to admit my admiration for the girl; she has more fire than I initially expected. Looks can be deceiving. But wouldn't I kill to have that crystal of hers.

Listening in on Naresteé slowly and methodically breaking down her defenses has been informative, but not enough information has been retrieved. Now, with this ludicrous stunt by Karalevine, I am having trouble focusing on their conversation.

All I can think of is *her*. Why would she do this? She must know that, the moment she enters, I'm going to take her. Or perhaps she's counting on that?

I begin to pace in circles within the space, hoping that moving my body will ease some of the grief this wretched girl has been causing me as of late. Does she even know the danger she's putting herself in? Not only the stupidity of this move because I now have her right where I want her but with the dangers of the games, period.

My mind tinkers away as to why she would do this. Surely not for money or fame, so what's her motive? How do I deal with this, and how does it change the plans I've already put into motion?

I come to the conclusion rather simply. Karalevine is entering the Titan Games for the same reason I'm floating in space on this ship.

Pacey Dawson.

That is why she's been savagely attacking my Nests, from what the reports have told me. Someone must have leaked the information that Miss Dawson was here, within the Azurite.

The only place my Starseeds cannot reach . . . unless one wins the Titan Games.

Bold. Stupid. Comical, even.

Karalevine truly believes I'll simply let her get away with this? That I will allow such a farce to take place directly under my nose? Permit her to mock me publicly after all she's already perpetrated against me? After what she did to my face . . .

My fists ball, and the control over my Elendril slips yet again. The feel of it fires against my chest, and it's an unfamiliar sensation, one I haven't felt since first fusing with the Elendril all those years ago. Back when Zariya still lived and breathed and loved me . . .

The sound of the main door opening to the central hub rips my thoughts from Karalevine, and when I see the person standing in the entrance, I wish for the Terran girl and all the problems she brings if it means I could exchange them for this.

"Big brother," Selenyte coos, her outfit silver and glittering, loose against her body. "You've been spending quite a lot of time down here in these gutters. It made me curious as to who could possibly be more important than your sweet baby sister, whom you haven't seen for many star rotations. And my goodness, the smell.

No wonder you've been showering so much lately. I thought it was because you've been trying to wash all the shame and guilt from you, but I must've been mistaken."

I won't even deign that with a response.

Her dark eyes pass my shoulder and land on Naresteé, her back to us. Selenyte finds the Dawson girl immediately thereafter, studying her intently.

"Surely, sister, there are better uses of your time than to dirty your shoes with the likes of these criminal halls."

In the bright lights of the hub and surrounding opaque cells, my sister looks practically colorless—besides those eyes, of course. They're searching, lurking, waiting to pounce.

She makes a humming sound in her throat when her eyes focus back to mine. "I thought you were done with those Elendril crystals, Mal. Father and Mother would be quite dismayed to hear you're dabbling in those artifacts again. Aren't those the relics that got you into so much trouble last time around? When you had to be punished so severely . . . I thought you'd have learned your lesson from that unfortunate experience you had. I would be very unsettled to see you fall from grace twice, especially since Father and Mother are questioning whether to abnegate the throne to you again. I doubt they'll consider it a third time."

My eyes narrow at her, teeth grinding down with increasing amounts of pressure. No other additional outward indications that she's affected me manifests. Internally, however, the roaring in my ears is only dampened by the pounding intensifying within the back of my skull. Only Selenyte can get me this worked up.

Turning my back to her, I allow my mask to falter for only a moment. It's all the reprieve she's going to allow me.

"Oh, Mal." Her voice is sweet, calm, and calculated. "I really hope you're not involved with that one girl again, the one who caused all that damage to Arianyte and was the sole reason for your marooning. What was her name again? Zarmee? Zara? Zarzar?" Her tone scraps with disrespect. "I think if you're committed to your little crystal folk, then, fine. I personally don't care. You know

I think Father and Mother are awfully pretentious and severely behind the times. There's no reason they have to know a thing, as long as you abstain from the throne. Keep your little playthings all you want. The fact you have one held up here is proof enough that you're committed to them again. Allow yourself to have what you so clearly desire. I won't judge you for it. I certainly won't maroon you on a subpar world for a few decades for it, either."

Behind me, I can see my sister's reflection in the glass panel, her frame like a ghost cursed to haunt every moment of my existence. At the very least, I know the arrows she's aiming, but what I didn't expect was for her to fire them so soon.

"My dear sister," I finally say, voice barely on the brink of being contained. Not since Karalevine marred my face have I been this seething. "Let me make one thing perfectly clear to you. The only thing I desire more than my Elendril crystals is my throne. And if we're playing games, little sister, be prepared to play dirty, salaciously, and ruthlessly. I never lose twice."

CHAPTER 17

All revolutions begin with a spark. Something that lights the match of freedom or war, depending on which side you're on. Tonight, I plan to set this revolution ablaze.

All of us haven't gone out in public together in months because it's risky. Yet, given what we suspect about the tryouts, we're out here to celebrate and rally support, get the public on our side before Malakyte can tarnish or arrest us. Let's hope he hasn't gotten wind of all this yet. The well-known rebel nightclub named The Steam Maker has music that booms around all seven of us Starseeds and Ringers as we pass through the door. It is not a night for battle but for celebration, so we don't carry our Elendril weapons with us. I'm dressed simply in a tight black dress, hair down in loose curls, and a dagger strapped to my thigh. But, according to Trinity, the entire world is about to know my name and face, so I'd better look hot tonight. As we enter the bar, we're given special bracelets at the door that indicate we're VIPs.

"Looks like your girl, Trinity, is hooking us up," Sylo says to me, feeling happier now because my plan seemed to have worked.

Although a few other members of my select team aren't so happy with me.

"I can't believe you people dragged me out here." Deimos's grumbles are hardly audible over the booming pounding of the music, but my ears detect his animosity.

The club is set up where the dance floor overlooks a massive stage, a mega screen behind it forecasting the new Titans coming soon. We're ushered into the VIP section, where Trinity and about three dozen top Resistance members linger. I find myself subconsciously searching for Geonni sitting at the center, but he's not here. He will never be here again.

"Kara!" Trinity calls as she waves us over to a corner booth that overlooks the dancing area full of bodies having the time of their lives. She kicks out the four people who are sitting with her, all besides Terryn and Shante.

Once our private waitress takes our orders, Trinity leans over the table with a wicked grin. "I've got good news from my contact within Arianyte," she claims, looking between Ardelle, Deimos, and myself. "You three are in. And you, our little badass, made quite an impression on those judges. You're a savage. I can't believe you destroyed that machine like that. The recording Arianyte made was leaked, and trust me, as soon as you're announced, that shit is going all over the Network feeds."

"She's reckless. She almost blew the entire operation," Deimos says instead, but I can still see the glint of pride in his eyes, regardless.

I elbow him in the ribs playfully.

Trinity's eyes are on fire with excitement. "You're already trending on the Network. It's been too hard to keep you under wraps. The rebels have an army out there ready to make you their mission. They may not be willing to do battle or directly oppose Arianyte, but they're willing to push the rebel's agenda. You represent our freedoms and autonomy, and you're entering the Titan Games to prove the point that Arianyte needs to go. You worked for them, and now, you're standing up against them. Nobody on this planet has had the balls, girl, to do what you're about to do."

"And it can get her killed." The vileness in Jance's voice practically slaps the smile right off Trinity's face.

Trinity's eyes narrow at Jance. She hates him. I can see that—I've noticed it ever since we came back into the city after the heat on us from the last games cooled off. Jance is the one who's supposed to be in a grave, not her father, and Trinity hasn't forgotten it.

"You agreed this was worth the risk to bring Arianyte down. I'm doing this so you can get that other girl back, the hacker." Trinity's gaze never breaks away from Jance's.

"Her name is Pacey, and her life is just as valuable as every other kid here. You're all kids, and you've got to be careful with who you're taunting and how you're taunting them. Throwing Kara in Malakyte's face will only aggravate him further."

Before this gets out of control, I interrupt. "He's going to be pissed, no matter what we do." My eyes soften when I look at Jance because I know I'm practically taking Trinity's side.

Trinity continues to talk about all the things the rebels will be doing to push our agenda and keep me as focused on the public eye as possible. The more visible I am, the safer I'll be from Malakyte doing anything bold. The risk of that is, he'll likely try something far sneakier. I begin to zone out as I watch the people dancing below us. How carefree they seem, drunk and completely oblivious to the weight of what we're trying to do.

It takes me a minute to notice that, behind the bar, along the mirrored backdrop lined with liquor bottles, is my star symbol.

It must be created with some sort of vinyl because the edges are straight and lines are perfect. How crazy is this? As my eyes continue to watch the crowd, a cloaked figure draws my attention. Sitting at the corner barstool, the person is wearing a solid black hood and cloak that covers most of their face, a glass of dark liquor in their hands. I can tell by the stature that this person is male, long legs casually crossed and laid across the brass bar footstool. The stance feels oddly familiar. That couldn't be him, could it? No . . . Malakyte wouldn't dare.

"I'll be right back," I tell the table as I stand, their faces concerned. "I just need to use the bathroom."

As I make my way down the stairs that lead to the dance floor, I keep my eyes on the hooded figure. They haven't moved an inch, an unnatural stillness that's only found in extras. Could this be the shadowy person who's been stalking me? The one from the alleyway and the graveyard? I wasn't sure there was someone there while Jance and I were walking, but it was oddly suspicious. Perhaps they're here now? Because no way in Hell would the prince be stupid enough to come behind enemy lines without his little birdy squad here to back him up.

As I make it to the dance floor, I zigzag my way through the bodies and towards the dark figure. A few people stop me, congratulate me, and call me "the Star," which only delays me. Anxiously, I politely get past them with fake smiles and waves when I finally arrive at the bar.

The hooded figure has gone. What in star's name . . .

My eyes bounce between the bartender and the empty seat, the drink still full. I swear he was here.

I'm being ridiculous. There's nobody stalking me. There's nobody here. I need to get back upstairs before Jance burns the place down looking for me.

I turn and begin making my way through the bodies again, but then my skin gets an icy jolt along it as a figure passes right by me. A waft of ice-cold air . . .

I'm immediately clutched by strong, frigid hands. There's no time, no way to stop the speed and strength of the figure that's got hold of me. I'm shoved into a dark alcove under the stairs, away from the people or any chance of help.

Malakyte Ardeen has me pinned beneath him.

Malakyte's tall cloaked figure stands, leaning over me, both his arms on either side of my body, hands braced on the wall. The staircase is to my left, the allies on the dance floor so close yet so far; I don't think anyone can save me now.

I can only see his strong chin under the hood and the shadow it casts, but I know that coldness and his scent anywhere. I cannot see the scar on his face.

"Malakyte . . ." I breathe, voice shocked and breathless over the booming music around us.

He leans in and whispers in my ears, "What a fine evening it is, my dear *Star.*" He says the nickname with pizzazz, his tone playful and veritably aware of how much power he's got right now. Although my body trembles with fear, it also sings with . . . something else, too.

"What are you doing here?" I managed to say. "Are your soldiers coming to try and take us in? I won't go anywhere without a fight." I have a dagger strapped to my thigh. I can use it to cut that crystal right out of him and make sure he stays dead forever so that it'll never revive him again.

He chuckles like I'm a silly child. "Dear Karalevine, you think so very little of me. It's disappointing. Especially when I know that, one day soon, you'll be pleading for me to whisk you away."

My chest heats. "I'll never want to be with you after what you've done, Malakyte."

The prince leans in closer, his coldness enveloping me. I'm caged in by his arms. I cannot get away. I do not inch back. My hand creeps to my dress's hem, fingers lifting it higher and higher . . .

"Must you say my name like that? Especially when all I want to do is punish you for being such a bad, bad girl." His voice is a low, deep growl in my ear.

Fucking hell.

"Why are you here?" I ask again, trying to keep my mind from the gutters. How'd he even slither in here with all these rebels?

My fingers finally curl around my dagger's hilt.

His face is so close to mine I can feel his lips graze on my cheek. My body is covered in goose bumps. I can't help it. I can't help feeling an icy fire building within me at his closeness. At the immutable danger and beauty of him contrasting in a fucking oxymoron I cannot get out of my head. Why? Why does he do this to me?

Kill him, I say to myself. *Kill him now. End it all, now.*

"I had to see for myself if you were truly entering my games. I came to stop you." He brings one of his hands down and wraps it around my throat. It's so cold. I tense under him, both our bodies shifting beneath the other's, both sensing the danger and threat of death.

I free the dagger from its holster at my thigh. All I've got to do is stab him center mass, and it'll all end. Still trapped beneath him, I slip my blade between us and stick the pointed tip directly over the center of his chest where his black alien heart beats wildly. All he has to do is squeeze my neck, and it'll be over.

Yet, he doesn't begin choking me.

And I don't stab him.

My eyes investigate the dark void where his face should be as the tension cloaking us hits its crescendo, so damn torn between wanting to kill him and wanting to kiss him. I hate myself for it. I'm sure he hates himself just as much, if not more.

"Aren't you going to kill me, Karalevine?" he whispers directly into my ear, and a jolt of something that feels way too much like pleasure goes through me as his icy lips touch the pointed tip of my ear. My breath hitches, but I don't inch back. "Be the rebel's hero, save all the people from the wicked tyrant. Do it. Prove how good you are by slaying me. Behind this whole hero façade, you seethe with explosive fury, and it obliterates everything in its wake. We're both aware you are darkness, Karalevine. With me dead or alive, you'll forever be darkness."

I push the blade harder, likely drawing blood.

He squeezes harder, cutting off air.

"*Do it*," he hisses, voice much sharper than before. Pierce his heart, rip out his crystal, and end all of this.

Fucking stars, just do it!

His grip on my throat tightens, even as his thumb caresses my jawline tenderly.

"You do it," I echo, calling his bluff just as he calls my own. We're both screwing with each other, both as turned on and fucked up as the other. I hate him. I hate what he does to me.

"I should," he tells me. "Just as you should. But that's the mystifying phenomenon between us, Karalevine. One I have yet to decipher. If only I knew why you destroy all my sense of reason."

Those lips of ice kiss my cheek and then he's gone like he was never there—taking his coldness with him. Quickly, my body is replaced by heat I don't know how to simmer. Stunned, I stand there, dumbfounded by what just happened. Are SSPARROWs going to come? Or is Malakyte alone? Should I tell someone he's here? Warn everyone so they can get out before something terrible happens? I had the chance to kill him, so why didn't I do it? Dammit, why didn't I do it?

"Girl, what the hell are you doing hiding under the stairs?" Trinity barks, standing before me with her arms crossed, her makeup heavy and hair pinned up elegantly.

I look up at her, eyes wide and shocked. She looks instantly confused.

"He's here," I yell over the music. "Malakyte, he's here, in the club."

Trinity looks alarmed but only leans in. "There's no way. I had every single person checked upon entry to the club. He's not here. You're seeing things, girl."

"No, Trinity, I'm not. He is here. We've got to go."

"He was here? Then, why didn't you blast him halfway to hell? We could have taken him hostage and ripped that crystal from his chest. I know you wouldn't have left him alive if you truly thought you saw him. Meaning, you either saw him and let him go, or you simply thought you saw him, but it was just a Terran who looks like him. Come on, girl." She actually starts laughing at me. "You think a rebel owned bar is going to let the biggest squid in the entire Aurora System in for a drink? Seriously. You're just freaked out. I don't blame you."

"But, Trinity—"

Suddenly, the music stops, and I look around, fearful of what that could mean. A man steps out onto the stage and shouts into his floating microphone, "The Titans are about to be announced! Let's bring our leader and new competitors down to the stage!"

Trinity grabs my arm and gently tugs me from under the stairway. "It's fine, Kara. I promise you, he's not here. Now, let's go take down this motherfucker."

I have no other choice but to go and start a revolution.

The roaring of blood in my ears is all I can hear as I stand on the stage. The lights blast my eyes, and the cheers sound like I'm under water.

Ardelle, Deimos, and I are positioned side by side as Trinity makes an impassioned speech to the crowd. The fake names of all three of us Starseeds appear on screen, along with the photos they took of us. Malakyte likely hasn't left, and I scan the people for his hooded figure. Movement to my immediate left draws my eye, a shadow deeper than the shade Nightvale. Malakyte is watching me from the crowd, and I have no doubt those onyx eyes are pinned directly on me. I glare him down, unafraid.

Trinity's voice pulls me back in as she speaks in a way I've never seen before.

"We are done kissing the ring of the hand that doesn't feed us," she seethes, her hands talking in conjunction with her words. "No more cowering and hiding in fear of those filthy squids and their sky-rats. This is our time to fight for the people of Earth!"

The crowd cheers along with their approval, shouting out racial insults for the extraterrestrials, causing Deimos to shift uncomfortably to my other side.

"Let's stop pandering to their tyranny, to their injustice, to their so-called protection and order. What they do is control and plunder and take. How many raids have they done this month alone? How many of those raids have been on people of color, the poor or unhoused, or other vulnerable communities? There's a new decree coming out every other day. They're desperately trying to regain control, bit by bit, because it's slipping away. This city has had enough of their public whippings, with no trials in most cases. They allow their SSPARROWs to get away with murder, and the only person doing a thing about it has been *her*!"

Trinity turns and points to me, and I didn't realize that my Nest-hunting would come to so much applause and approval. If only the people in my actual life felt the same way. I wonder how *he* feels about it.

"Speech!" someone shouts.

"Show us who you are!"

"Fuck Arianyte!"

"Screw the squids! Screw the squids!"

Trinity's eyes sparkle, and she's more alive than she's ever been before. "When my father was murdered before my eyes last winter . . ." She hesitates, her face falling, as she remembers the disruptor shot that ended Geonni's life. I remember it, too. The crowd begins booing. "When I saw my father die, when I looked into the eyes of the monster who did it and saw no remorse, I knew I'd take him down some day. He took my mother away under the bullshit guise of a Tribute, and he took my father through cold-blooded murder! As most of you know, the Rebel's Song was created by my father as our anthem, along with his *A Rebel's*

Guidebook to Mischief, both of which I hold dear to and live by. So, if we ever were to lose our way, we had a beacon of light to guide us back home."

Trinity holds up a ratty old journal. It was her father's.

The crowd immediately starts reciting a part of the official passage of Geonni's Rebel's Song; even though in the end, he ended up losing his way, never to find it again.

"So, let our footsteps echo with thunderous might,

A symphony of defiance, resounding through the night.

We are the vanguards, the guardians of Earth's might,

Together, we rise, embodying freedom's eternal light.

In this human rebellion, we paint destiny's art,

With love as our weapon, compassion in every heart.

For justice, for freedom, our spirits shall soar,

As we reclaim our world, like never before.

Unite, oh warriors, let your spirit ignite,

For in our hands lies the power to set all things right.

In this battle for truth, we shall never be undone,

For we are the Terran rebellion, and our
victory has begun."

The building almost comes down from the roaring that follows the passage. Trinity holds up her fist into the air, and the room instantly quiets.

For justice, for freedom, our spirits shall soar, as we reclaim our world, like never before, I repeat to myself, the line a special one to me more so now than ever.

"The prince of Arianyte is a parasite, leeching off this planet and its people. Me and Karalevine, "the Star," know this all too well. She worked with him closely—undercover for the rebels—and she is the one who scarred that piece of shit's face in retribution for my father's life!"

The crowd erupts with shouts.

That's not exactly how that happened, but I don't dare contradict her. I bet Malakyte is fuming down there. The thought makes me smile.

Trinity doesn't stop. "The Star is our beacon of hope now. As an official competitor in the Titan Games, she will bring the occupation to its knees! She is one of us, and she will fight for us!"

"Speech!"

"Give us the Star!"

"The Star! The Star! The Star!" the crowd begins to chant, and I look over to Ardelle for help. There's nothing but a proud smile on his face as he looks back at me, his eyes slanted down to meet my own.

"Go get 'em, Thumbelina," he says, slapping my ass as he shoves me towards the front of the stage. I take my place beside Trinity, the lights brighter and hotter up here.

I swallow, one of the bar workers tossing a floating microphone over to us. Its spherical shape bobs at eye level, moving in tandem with me. Trinity's face is encouraging, expectant.

Hurry up and say something, girl, she tells me with her eyes. *Now!*

But Malakyte is right there . . . He's watching. We're tipping our hand here, directly in front of him. I really wish Trinity wasn't so amped up. She's not listening to me. Well, fine. I'll just control the narrative to keep as much of our plan from this speech as possible. It's all I can do. Let him watch. I'll be talking directly to him, staring him down, and forcing him to hear every single word of why I hate him. And I do hate him; I was simply being stupid under the stairs.

When trying to remember why I began to hate Arianyte so much in the beginning, that twelve-year-old boy's face pops into my memory. What's left of him that I can recall, anyway. My eyes glance down at my dandelion tattoo, the only piece of him I have left. Like always, he gives me courage when I'd otherwise have none. He always did that; he's always been my true north star— the *real* star. Always guiding me home. *I'll dye my hair back to teal as soon as I can*, I silently promise him. For now, I'll try to keep his memory alive. His, Pacey's, and all the Hijacked like them. I'll do it all for them.

"Let me tell you all about the night the Arianyte Empire came for two little kids and what happened next."

CHAPTER 18

"I really didn't think Trinity was going to be able to get this much attention on us," I say as Jance and I sit on the couch, the dog between us and lights turned off. We watch the television coverage together in the dark undersewer apartment. It's strange to see my face on the screen. Ardelle's and Deimos's are there, too. We've created an uproar.

"Reports close to the Arianyte prince say he's given little thought to his old Starseeds taking part in this year's upcoming games," a blond news anchorman says, and I roll my eyes. Bullshit. I know that after our encounter under the stairs and the way I glared him down while on that stage, he's giving it tons of thought. I hope he's squirming. "The prince was asked by reporters if he's going to ban the wanted fugitives from participating."

The frame switches to Malakyte. Stars, that scar on his face . . . I couldn't see it the other night, but there's no hiding it here.

"Are you going to ban your fellow squad members from this year's Titan Games?" a reporter asks.

Another chimes in. "What about their current fugitive status? Can a wanted fugitive even compete in the Titan Games?"

Malakyte answers before more questions can be thrown his way, and I lean forward to listen, despite myself.

"The three fugitives will be allowed to participate in the games this year," Malakyte says calmly, and Jance and I both look at each other with mouths hanging wide open. "I've listened to recent protests regarding this matter and would like to personally guarantee their safety during the games. As of this morning, their official status as fugitives has been dismantled. I believe my former teammates have chosen to participate in these games due to a convoluted belief that Arianyte is unjust to the citizens of the Aurora System, which is ghastly untrue. As a token of good faith, I hope they'll see my promise of freedom during these games as an olive branch to continue our work together in keeping this beautiful planet safe from those who wish to destroy it with threats of war."

The rebels.

Me.

He continues to speak over reporters, but those eyes are throwing daggers straight into the camera, as if that menacing gaze is boring right into me exactly like the other night; our roles reversed. *What are you trying to tell me, Malakyte?*

"I believe that all things come in time, and they *will* come. I have nothing but patience in that regard. Given that and due to rebel activity, we in Arianyte have decided to dismantle the Titan Games parade this year. This decision was already in the works before the contestants were chosen. The public has been given access to each of the sixty Titans and their profiles, available on the Network for anyone to access at their leisure. The masquerade ball at the Glass Crystal Castle will continue as usual for the Titans the night before the games."

"Will there be any other changes to the schedule?"

"Yes." Malakyte grins devilishly. My chest heats. He might as well be right in our living room with the way he's pinning me down with those eyes. "Due to safety concerns, the games will take place at three separate, undisclosed locations around Zarmenia. The main arena is still under construction from last year's games, and as such, there will be no live audience. Arianyte takes the safety of our citizens extremely seriously, and we do not feel it safe enough, even with tightened security, to allow a live audience for any of the three games. Each game will be streamed live to Earth with high-tech recording technology, designed specifically by Arianyte engineers for these games. In addition, the games will take place within three days, one game per day, in attempts to lessen the risk of a volatile attack."

"One game a day?" I say, fear striking me. "By the time one of us makes it to the end, we'll be exhausted and useless when it's time to get up there and find Pacey."

"He's likely done that on purpose," Jance growls, and I huff in annoyance.

That asshole.

I hear the keycard unlocking the door, and Ardelle slides in. "You watching this?" he barks as the door closes behind him. My heart still does a little pitter-patter at the sight of him.

"Yeah, and Scarface just said they're doing one game per day, so three in a row."

Ardelle squeezes onto the couch, causing the dog to jump off.

"I'm shocked he's taken our fugitive status away. Why would he do that? It makes no sense." Ardelle plays with my hair—the money piece and ends dyed back to teal—as he contemplates Malakyte's motives. "Does he think that's going to make up for what he's done? For what he continues to do? Because it won't."

No, it won't.

Malakyte can't be redeemed . . . right? I mean, he didn't kill me the other night at the bar . . . That counts for something, doesn't it? I shake the thought from my mind. He's a bad guy, despite what lingering feelings may exist regarding him.

I shove thoughts of him away. "Is he going to be at the masquerade ball? Isn't it in two weeks? I need a dress. And so do you." I nudge Ardelle.

He laughs. "Yes, I absolutely need a dress, Thumbelina. A bright pink one."

I glare playfully.

Jance answers my question. "Given Malakyte's unnatural obsession with you, he'll be at that ball. I'd expect him there, both of you, and anticipate anything from him."

I swallow dryly. I'll have to face him again. My chest blooms with an unnatural flutter, and I press it down faster than it can emerge.

I know for a fact I'm going to have to get a gorgeous dress and look drop-dead stunning in it. The Titan Games may be a tournament of battles, strength, and will, but I've learned that there's more to winning a game than brute strength. I've got assets, and I plan on using every single one of them to win. So, I've got to look marvelous. And with Ardelle on my arm, I'll do my best to make Malakyte Ardeen jealous as fuck.

CHAPTER 19

REBEL ACTIVITY OF ANY KIND, DIRECT OR INDIRECT, WILL BE
SEEN AS AN ACT OF WAR AGAINST ARIANYTE.

Walking up to the Glass Crystal Castle for the ball sure wasn't how I expected it to be.

The paparazzi flank both Ardelle and I as we're escorted from the Arianyte-issued hover we were forced to commute in. Ardelle's arm is wrapped around my waist as we ignore shouts, catcalls, and questions that are thrown at us like bullets from a disruptor. My ankles are weak from the attention, and I hold on to him tightly to keep from accidentally tripping as we climb the massive set of stairs leading up to the castle.

A woman shouts, "Karalevine, who are you wearing tonight? That gown is gorgeous!"

She isn't wrong.

Stopping Ardelle, I turn back to the flashing lights and cameras, addressing them. "I'm wearing one of Annie Drannaka's pieces," I say with as much confidence as I can muster, holding my chin high as gasps ring out amongst the paparazzi. I swear, even the flashes from the cameras stop for a split second.

"Annie Drannaka's clothing is banned by the occupation," the same woman says, utter shock pouring from her overly lined pink lips. "She's been convicted of crimes against Arianyte and a convicted rebel. Where did you find this piece? Do you know where the fugitive is? What gives you the right to defy the empire so blatantly?"

Wherever Trinity is watching coverage of tonight's events, I know she's grinning like a cat. It was her idea, actually, to wear Drannaka's clothing. Beyond its immaculate, artistic, and flattering style, it'll piss Malakyte off, and I've been doing that like it's my job lately.

I turn and continue up the stairs, ignoring the barrage of ongoing questions, not even trying to hide the smile upon my dark painted lips. I can tell Ardelle doesn't approve. The others thought using this designer was too much of a slap in Arianyte's face, but I disagreed and obviously got what I wanted. If we're counting on the feral attention from the public to keep Ardelle and I safe, then we must make big moves, ones that tremble the earth beneath our feet and cause the skies to burn asunder.

The gown is heavy on my frame. Somehow, the organza fabric is infused with tens and thousands of glittering jewels that resemble stars. The dress fades from a deep plum in the shade Depthless Nightshade to Violet Flower Bomb, then ending in Orchid Lavender—the color of Gavrielle's eyes. The top portion crisscrosses around my chest, leaving my back and shoulders bare. Along my shoulders is an intricate metal and jeweled piece, dangling down my back and matching my earrings and hair jewelry as it holds my locks up in a loose bun. We chose the color purple to match my crystal's color to show defiance to this entire charade. Ardelle is wearing red to match his Elendril.

Though all thoughts of resistance seep away when we see the shining rock on a hill before us, and it is mesmerizing.

The surrounding night brings the crystal castle alive in a way only the moon and stars and darkness can. The twinkling along the glass-like surface is brighter than I ever could have thought possible. The contrast of the night and the glowing castle reminds me of my tattoos, how I create shadows to brighten up a section I want to stand out. This is exactly like that. To truly appreciate the light, you must first be swallowed up by the dark.

"Is the whole thing made entirely of crystal?" I ask Ardelle as we continue climbing the steps, the press not allowed any further than the base of the stairs.

It's made up of the colors Yogurt Pink, Baby Boy Blue, and Lemon Custard, all a desaturated blend mixed into the silver glass-like crystal that holds the structure together. The cuts and edges and angles all make it glitter like some grand engagement ring, the marital tradition from the Old World still managing to survive the alien takeover.

Ardelle ponders my question with a sound deep in his throat, the structure a bright reflection in his eyes as we inch closer.

"The aliens built it as a peace offering after the Devouring Accords were signed, so I don't think so. There's likely not enough quartz crystal on Earth to make something so grand. It's alien technology for sure."

"Well, regardless," I say, "it's beautiful."

He suddenly looks over at me, but I continue to gawk at the castle when he says, "Yes. It's the most beautiful thing I've ever seen."

His voice is low, hardly a whisper on the night wind, and his words touch a distant, deeper part of myself I hadn't allowed to be seen in a long, long time. I look over at him; he's not talking about the castle anymore.

And it's not an act. It is not for show. It's a true and genuine smile. I'm really happy that I gave him a second chance because I've waited a long time to be looked at like this.

He squeezes me tightly as we continue up.

People meander outside the twenty-foot-high doors in their fancy outfits and masks. I scan through my own mask for Malakyte but, thankfully, don't see him. We both know he will be here tonight; he's going to try and play his manipulative hand on us. There are no weapons here, but neither of us are under any delusion that we're not playing war games tonight.

The battle has already started.

And it is on.

Leaving behind the ornate shrubs and over-the-top landscaping for the inside of the castle, we both take tentative breaths.

As soon as we enter, it's like we step back in time.

It looks like a castle from thousands of years ago except made from that iridescent crystal glass. All the decor and furniture are from the historical period of the eleventh century, along with the candlelight lighting that casts deep shadows onto the museum worthy paintings of medieval times.

"Don't you two look like a pair," says a flamboyantly dressed servant, his outfit a bright Tangerine Orange with hair and eyebrows to match. His face is covered in heavy makeup, including his lips and eyes. His bow to us is deep and gracious. "The main soiree room is straight ahead in the main ballroom. Dance your beautiful, tattooed bodies away—I'd love to watch you, my dear." He wiggles his eyebrows at Ardelle, who merely smiles awkwardly back. "Dinner will be served within the hour. You'll find your names on the place settings. You two have been invited to sit at the main table with none other than the prince of Arianyte himself. How lucky are you?"

Lovely.

"After the feast, guests and Titans are invited to partake in the finest of liquors and dance in the Starlight ballroom, where the festivities will end at midnight. We can't have our Titans staying up all night before the big games tomorrow, now, can we?"

Both Ardelle and I stare at each other as the man ushers us forward, greeting the next group of people arriving behind us.

Below my heels is a white, glittering marble that shines so brightly I can see our reflection in it as we walk down the long hallway. It's as if we've been transported inside of a diamond. Humongous archways loom over our heads as the clanking of my heels echoes out into the massive space. The ceilings are grand vaulted concave domes, curving up and down in gorgeous, angled architecture, matching crystal chandeliers every fifteen feet or so.

Pillars of smooth, icy blue and velvety curtains follow us towards the sounds of music playing and people mingling.

"Are you ready to see him?" Ardelle whispers to me, his voice unsure. His Adam's apple bobs as I look up at him. I'm a bit higher up on his shoulders, thanks to the heels. Ardelle looks at me through his black-and-red feathered mask. "He's going to search you out the moment we walk through those doors down there. He likely already knows we're here."

My mouth instantly goes dry. Ardelle doesn't know we've already seen each other recently, but I'm still extremely nervous.

"I'm surprised we haven't been attacked yet," I say in a snarky tone, peering around marble pillars and statues for assassins ready to pounce. No one is there.

My heart races as we enter the main ballroom, my grip on Ardelle's hand becoming sweaty as I prepare for the assault about to barrel down on us. To see the man who's taken so much from me, who's lied and schemed and hunted me. Played me like a fool, tricking me into thinking I had feelings for him . . .

The man whose face I permanently scarred.

Malakyte.

There will be no hesitation this time. If I get the chance to strike—in any fashion—I'm going to.

The moment we pass the threshold of the ballroom, the air smells sweet as plums and sugar. Dozens of people stop as their stares fall upon us. After the show I put on at the auditions, it's not entirely surprising. Looks like my mask isn't going to hide me, unfortunately. However, despite all the sets of glares currently being thrown our way, there's one pair of eyes I feel more intently than all the others.

Our eyes lock immediately from across the room.

Heat rushes into me, Malakyte's tall body exactly as I remember. Muscular but lean. The slight blue tint to his skin shows through his one-piece suit as it dips down to expose his bare chest in a deep V. I see his Elendril symbol, but I force myself not to look directly at it, fearing another vision would take me over. The outfit he wears is matte Midnight Blue, paired with a silk belt that wraps several times around his waist, tall black boots and a sparkling navy half mask finishing the outfit off. His long black hair is combed into a sleek waterfall down his back, combed away to show every sharp angle of his face. He looks dashing and intimidating and so fucking good . . . I swallow hard, mouth dry and breaths shallow.

"Hey." Ardelle pulls on me and steals my attention away from Malakyte. "Ignore him. He isn't going to risk a scene here. Play it cool. Let's get a drink."

Together, Ardelle and I walk to where drinks are being served in orb-shaped glasses. The entire ballroom is quite dim, the domed ceiling giving way to the night sky above us, the lighting bouncing off silvers, creams, and variations of icy blues as they cascade over the ornate architecture. Crescent moons and stars of all shapes and sizes mix with the soft tunes of the live band and voices of Titan participants.

I chug the contents of the glass in one gulp, feeling the alcohol hit my stomach like I swallowed a boulder. "Damn, that's some strong stuff," I choke out, my chest and cheeks already getting hot from the alcohol. There's no time to drink, so the sensation is foreign. My head begins to fuzz almost immediately. The regret of not pacing myself comes shortly after. And perhaps it's hitting me a little harder than I anticipated when a dark shadow catches my eye. I think I'm seeing things that aren't real for a moment because standing along the wall all by himself is a giant man that can only be described as a huge looming shadow. Oh yeah, he's definitely there. He's so out of place I don't know how I hadn't spotted him earlier. I instantly recognize him. Now, even in the glowing candlelight of the ballroom, I can see more of his details. He's an enormous extra, with dark-gray skin and long black hair. He's not watching me, from what I can tell, but it's hard to judge given the mask over his face. This person looks a lot like the figure from the alleyway and fits the shadow I may have seen while walking to the graveyard. A woman dressed in purple approaches him, a wide smile on her face. The horns tip me off. *Narestéé.* They're talking so casually, both relaxed with drinks in their hands. This is worrisome and one hundred percent something I'm going to file away for later. I don't like the two of them together . . .

I turn back to Ardelle to see him sipping on his orb pretentiously like a good little rich boy, when he takes my glass and places both on the tray of a passing servant. "Dance with me."

I'm not given much of a choice.

Together, Ardelle glides me onto the glass dance floor, our bodies reflecting as if it were a mirror. He takes my hands in his, sensing how awkward and stiff I am. There was no time for dancing in the Resistance.

Smiling, he guides us to the left slowly, then to the right and back again. I snort as I step on his foot, but he continues to smile at me. Eventually, I start to gain a sense of the music's tempo, and together, we glide across the dance floor as if we've been doing it for years.

As if we've been together for years.

As if our souls understood how to move these bodies of flesh and bone to make them one, knew how to arouse and entice and engage, like they've done it again and again for over a thousand years. Continuously learning and forgetting, finding, then losing until the end of time . . .

The heat of the alcohol is nothing compared to the rush that infiltrates my chest at the intensity of his gaze. I genuinely smile at how good it feels to be in his arms, their muscles strong and safe. He looks so handsome tonight, and although it's taken me a minute to get used to the Midnight Blue hair, it's growing on me more and more.

Only his mouth is exposed under his mask, and I can't help but continue to look at it. My eyes fill with desire as his tempting lips grazes over the tip of my ear.

"Did I tell you how beautiful you look tonight?" His voice is hardly audible, dripping with his own lust.

But suddenly, there's a deep pang of regret somewhere in my heart . . . that I'm not dancing with Gavrielle. The thought makes me feel so unbelievably guilty that I instantly push it away. I don't want to suffer guilt tonight.

And you deserve to be happy, a voice reminds me, even if I have a hard time believing it.

"I couldn't tell by how hard it's been for you to keep your eyes off me."

Oh, this alcohol is making me bold tonight.

Ardelle spins me. The lavender bottom of my dress twirls around my ankles, the sparkles glittering in the low light like a meteor shower. The smile on Ardelle's face as he chuckles makes me laugh, too.

"You caught me, Thumbelina. Looks like I'm busted. Tell me, what are you going to do about it?"

His challenge blooms in me like a firework, and I have the overwhelming urge to ravage him. Even though the entire room is watching us, I don't care. Leaning in closer to him, I'm tall enough in my heels to reach his neck with my lips, and I softly press a kiss there, fighting back the urge to bite him playfully like a vampire would. Although, my lips must suffice because I feel his skin prickle against me.

"Thumbelina . . ." His voice is a low growl, the grip on my hands rougher. "We're not alone here."

We both know what he means, who is watching us. I don't care. Let Malakyte see. *Let him fume.*

Pulling back, I look deep into Ardelle's eyes. "I want us to be together, Ardelle. I want to wake up and know you're going to be there and that I'm safe with you. I want to trust you and forgive you and let go of anything keeping us apart."

There, I said it. It's terrifying.

But his silence is even worse. Giving him the ability to reject me—to shatter my heart again—is more frightening than jumping off a cliff with no parachute.

Ardelle looks as if I've given him the entire world, and I don't expect it.

"Thumbelina, I want all of that, too, and more. I know I messed up and destroyed your trust with all that went down with Deimos. I'm still so sorry. Everything I do is my attempt to win back the trust I shattered between us. But I don't want to rush you or force you into anything. I—"

Stopping him the only way I know how, I abruptly drive my mouth onto his, the both of us ceasing our dance to melt into each other. It's soft, slow, and tender. The first time I've felt his lips since all those months ago . . . and I've missed them more than I realized. Missed his taste, his scent, the way his hand curls into my nape as he glides his tongue over mine.

The only thing ruining this moment is the spike in power I feel coming from Malakyte, our public display of affection causing his crystal to momentarily slip its leash. I don't care.

Breaking the kiss, Ardelle's hands cup both sides of my face as his eyes barrel into mine through his mask. "My life is yours in these games, Thumbelina. I'll give it up to keep you safe," he declares, knowing how much danger we're about to be in. How does he not hate me for putting him in this type of situation? I don't understand how he can be okay with doing that *for me*.

"And I'll get Pacey back to you." I make my own promise, my own declaration of love, without saying the actual word. That's what this is, I realize. Our promises are the two of us sharing how we truly feel. We can't say the words yet, but we can sure tiptoe around them for now.

I lean my head sideways against his chest, hearing his heart beating wildly under his immaculate suit jacket. He holds me without saying a word, slowly beginning to sway to the music once again.

Scraping at the edges of my mind are Malakyte's words from the bar. Is he right? Am I simply darkness and, sooner or later, Ardelle and Jance and everyone is going to see it?

CHAPTER 20

Song after song plays as the other Titans and their guests frolic around us with peeping eyes, none daring to get too close to the "Arianyte Renegades," or so they've been calling the three of us. Deimos, we noticed pointedly, is not here. Our detractors are not straight-up labeling us rebels, but it'll come sooner or later.

"Let's get some air. I can't take his glaring any longer," Ardelle suggests, and I let him take me out onto the sprawling balconies that open right off the ballroom floor. The night air feels perfectly cool as the two of us walk out, leaving the intensities of the glances and heat of the bodies behind. The music can be heard playing softly from out here as I lean my back against the balcony's ledge.

Ardelle's hands make their way up to my mask, softly pulling on the satin bow at the back. I let it fall as he removes his own, and there's that painfully handsome face staring at me.

"Miss Ruzz." A cold voice breaks the connection like the two of us had just been thrown into an ice bath, and I gasp at the boldness of Malakyte as he stands behind Ardelle, eyes pinned on me.

I didn't even hear him approach.

Immediately, Ardelle whirls, forcing me to remain behind him with a protective arm. "You've got a lot of balls." Ardelle's voice is on the edge of violence.

Malakyte remains calm and passive. "Let me speak with my Star, Mr. Dawson."

"No way in Hell."

The tension between them is lightning building to strike. We can all feel it in the air, and at any moment, it will explode into fire and smoke.

"I'm not here to make a scene," Malakyte says, his body language open and calm. It's so hard to know what his game is. "However, if my hand is forced, I will make things very unpleasant for you, Mr. Dawson."

The threat is clear. *Pacey.*

"You bastard," Ardelle growls, hands balled into fists, his crystal spiking. This is the boy who didn't curse once in the entire time I've known him before the Titan Games last year and hasn't since. "Leave her out of this. Better yet, let her go if you know what's good for you."

"You'll be pleased to know, Mr. Dawson, that I have the full cooperation of your parents. I also don't take too kindly to threats. That being said, understand this. I do not lose twice, and I always get what I want."

Under Ardelle's thick black jacket and red undershirt, his crystal mark lights up. Because we all know what Malakyte means, and it's infuriating Ardelle—it's infuriating me. And although I want to scar the other side of this man's face, we can't allow this to blow up into something that jeopardizes our mission. Stepping away from Ardelle, I place my body between the two men currently fighting over me.

A girl's dream, right?

"Stop it, both of you." I look at Ardelle, begging him with my eyes not to lose his cool. Something I never thought I'd have to do. Not with him. I continue firmly, "You have five minutes, Malakyte, and then we're done. Ardelle, go get us a drink. I'll be right back."

The suggestion causes his eyes to go wide, as if I'm telling him to jump off the balcony and fly away from here on his nonexistent wings.

"No" is his only response.

"Then, I'll extract you myself," Malakyte threatens. It's sharp and unambiguous.

Stepping closer, Ardelle's eyes are like fire incarnate. "I'd like to see you try."

Both men's crystals are lighting right the fuck up. Red and yellow clash. Primary colors rarely look good together, but that's neither here nor there. These two men will never be agreeable again, and it has nothing to do with their Elendril crystal or their colors.

"Ardelle." I grab onto his arm, feeling the tension there. "Look at me." The snarl on his lips doesn't move as his eyes focus on mine. "Five minutes. I'll be fine. I can handle him. He won't do anything here. He's not stupid."

He's trembling with anger, and I can see his indecision spilling over just as much as his rage.

Trust me, I beg him through our crystal's connection. *Trust me.*

As if he could hear me somehow through a bond connecting both of our souls, I can feel Ardelle's body soften slightly, his posture a tiny bit less threatening.

Trust me.

I trust you.

Chafing the space between us, he walks up to the prince and stops directly in front of his face. The two are almost the same height, but Ardelle's broad shoulders and mass have Malakyte beat, even though the alien has an inch or two over him.

"Touch her, and I will kill you."

Malakyte's smirk is dangerously contemptuous at Ardelle's words, seemingly unaffected by the threat.

With one look back to me, Ardelle nods and crashes his shoulder into Malakyte's as he leaves the balcony and heads into the ballroom.

I can finally release my breath.

Why was that so damn attractive?

Stars . . .

Once he's gone, my eyes meet Malakyte's. For the first time in person, I see a portion of the scar I gave him peeking out from under his mask; a part of me elates in it, and the other feels absolutely terrible for it.

"I'm surprised you're not wearing black," I tell him, trying my best to defuse the tension.

He closes the space between us effectively, and that ice-cold waft envelops me quickly. "Perhaps I've turned over a new leaf? Transformed into your Prince Charming."

I snort. "I highly doubt that. What do you want, Malakyte? We already spoke a few weeks ago."

"Dance with me?" He holds out his hand, gloved and welcoming, completely ignoring my comment about the rebel bar.

Fuck me . . .

What I hate more is I still—*still*—feel that inexplicable pull toward him. I loathe him for all the hurt he's caused. I hate him for being the genesis of so much of my pain, yet he's the only one who sets me on fire like this—who sees all of me and doesn't shun away.

Even though all of me hates that I take that hand, I allow him to walk me back to the ballroom and into the crowd of people, all masked and drunk with no idea what a pair of monsters lurk so close to all their finery.

He leads the dance—of course he would—and we don't speak as the music sweeps us up in its melody, allowing us to pretend for a small moment that we aren't enemies.

That he isn't my villain.

 136

Pretend that we didn't almost kill each other a couple of weeks ago.

"Where did you go just now?" he asks, causing me to blink away my thoughts and focus back on him. Despite myself, I blush. How can he see the subtle shifts in me, even now?

He's so close. The clean, citrus smell of him—the strength and the power he commands—drives me mad. Another addition to his arsenal. Malakyte wields every weapon he possesses very strategically, and even indirect nuances, like the way he lays his hand on my lower back, draws me in closer. It's subtle yet enticing. We're basically back underneath that stairwell all over again.

Shove those feelings down, I order myself. *They don't mean anything.*

"What's so important that you had to ruin another one of my evenings, Malakyte?"

He sighs as if he wished I'd just let it all go.

"To tell you what a mistake you're making by entering these games. Relinquish your position before it's too late. I won't be able to protect you in those arenas, Karalevine."

My eyes roll condescendingly. "You think I'm going to do a damned thing you say? After what you've done, you still want to try and control me? You don't get a say in how I live my life. You're going to have to arrest me to stop me."

Instant regret. He could do it; he could do it right now, and I'd be whisked away and never seen again. Why he didn't do it at the bar, I'm still wondering.

Malakyte chuckles slightly. "The increase in your heart rate suggests you think I may do just that. Perhaps I should arrest you. It'll surely save me an immense amount of grief, I'll tell you that much. Although, the thought of forcing you to my will is a travesty. I can't even imagine you being confined. Like caging a phoenix. It's why I relinquished my bounty on you, even after you've been savagely tearing apart my Nests. I was fascinated by your valiant, rallying cry with all those rebels at the bar. It's a shame we're on opposite sides now. Unfortunately, this cat and mouse game must end. The real games are being played now, Miss Ruzz, and I don't want to see you lose. Stop this childish behavior now before it's too late for you."

"A threat, wow. Creative."

"It is not a threat," he coos, lips turned up, eyes slanted down at me. "You think so little of me, yet have I not ensured your protection? Have I not kept my word thus far and allowed your freedom? The freedom of all the people you care about. Your father?"

Jance.

"Don't talk about him."

"Miss Ruzz—"

"Stop calling me that," I interject angrily. "And what do you expect, me to grovel at your feet for not jailing me and my family after what you did during the finale? After you shot and killed Geonni in front of me, making me choose between him and my own father? You're the reason I have nightmares."

Malakyte looks wholly offended. "I chose to end the life of the leader of the Terran Resistance instead of allowing your father to perish. If I had shot Jance, like you chose, your father would be dead right now. I knew that would devastate you. I had your best interests in mind. Don't you see that I did that for you?"

There's no way to slam my face into my palm, since Malakyte is holding both hands, so I simply roll my eyes instead. "Sure, Malakyte. Yes. You forced me to choose whose life to save, between the two father figures in my life, and did me a favor by not shooting and killing my biological father. Thank you so much for that."

There's a long pause.

"You sound displeased with me."

"No shit."

"I apologize," he says softly. I'm so taken aback by an apology I actually flinch a little. "I knew the rebel leader had abandoned you, and it infuriated me—for you. I thought you hated him for what he did and was sure you'd choose your Ringer instead. What I did was terroristic. I can confess that I was wrong. I'm sorry, Karalevine, for all of it. I've regretted my choices every dawn since then. It's why I had to speak with you tonight, in case . . ." he hesitates, faltering. "In case you don't survive the games. I couldn't live with myself if I didn't confess my truth to you. I couldn't talk with you that night at the bar, not like this. I understand if you hate me still. Just know I do not hate you for what you did that day."

I know what he means. It's literally staring at me right in the face underneath that mask.

But I do not apologize for it because I am not sorry. And he has not earned such a proclamation from my lips.

What I am, however, is confused. I doubt this so-called apology is even real, but a part of me wants it to be. I practically crave for him to transform back into the man he was in the beginning. I want him to be the good Malakyte, the one I had manufactured in my head and maybe sort of fell for . . . but he's not that person, is he? No matter how much my heart wishes he were.

"You do that to me, too, Karalevine." As if he's read my mind, he continues. "You're the only person who can. I know I make you feel that enigmatic sizzling between us. You don't have to hate it so deeply, you know. I feel every heart pounding inch of it, too. I haven't been able to stop thinking about our recent time together."

He feels it, too? He can't stop thinking about under the stairs, too? Malakyte senses that heat between us, despite his body being encased in ice? The ghost of his lips on my ear tickles in my memory—

No, stop it.

I step back a bit as we continue to dance, not realizing how close we've drifted. Surely, Ardelle isn't torturing himself by watching this.

I don't answer him regarding our time under the stairs. I'm not going to let him play with me, flirt with me. Regardless of his reasons why, Geonni and Gav are still dead. And I'm proud of myself because I'm strong enough to spot the games he's playing this time.

When we've danced halfway across the ballroom floor in silence, I say, "Malakyte, what you've done, it's terrible. To me and to this world . . . and I can't forgive you for that. It isn't just what you've done. It's that you're not good for me. I don't want to embrace the darkness, okay? Maybe consider that perhaps I'm not good for you, either."

He's quiet, holding onto me like I could become smoke and vanish from his grasp at any moment. I hate that when I see the sadness flash across his face. "You're the air I breathe, Karalevine. Even if what you are is a toxic gas, I'll still breathe you in until I'm choking for breath and my lungs give out. And likely far after that, too, knowing me. Perhaps consider the darkness is simply a part of you, and with me, you don't have to pretend like you do with *him*."

"My emotions and the way I feel them does not make me evil like you, Malakyte," I tell him very sternly.

He contemplates my answer. "Are you trying to convince me or yourself, Karalevine?"

When I don't answer, the dark-haired alien leans in close as he continues to lead us in song and dance. "You contemplate that. Be aware that it's just a matter of time before you're begging to be with me. I don't have to lift a finger; you'll see it soon enough. You'll realize that they don't see you like I do. They don't accept you or understand the way you need to ravage the world to cinders so you can assuage your violent, dark nature. Your family will never accept you, not like I will. Remember, you cannot escape who you truly are, no matter how much of a hero you pretend to be."

I am a hero . . . I am *good*.

Although . . . a vindictive hero isn't a hero. They're a villain.

"Is this all you wanted to tell me?" I ask, pushing away those darker thoughts.

Malakyte's jaw clenches. "There's more happening behind the scenes of the games that puts you in grave danger. You will be at the mercy of what lurks in there. As much as you believe me a monster, I do not wish you to die, Karalevine."

He's doing his best to manipulate me into getting him off the hook for the political pressure. I'm not stupid or naïve this time around. I won't fall for his tricks.

"You know what will get us to drop out."

Pacey. Give us Pacey.

His sigh is all the confirmation I need to hear. At least I tried.

"There's nothing else for us to discuss, Malakyte."

I let go of his hands, stopping our dance. As we stand there, face-to-face, I remember the man I met in the beginning, the level-headed prince who laughed at my sarcasm and thought my boldness was a breath of fresh air. I miss him.

"You know," I begin, taking a deep breath in through my nose as I look him dead in the eyes through the mask and into the man in there, "had you just been the person you were when we met and not done a one-eighty into psycho territory, I likely would have fallen in love with you."

Shakily, I let out the breath I held nearly the entire time I spoke those truthfully betraying words. He stares at me, wearing a completely different sort of mask than the one on his face.

"I'm not worried, Karalevine," he says smoothly, voice cocky as he grins down at me. He leans in and encompasses me completely in an icy hug. My arms automatically move to wrap around him but then I stop myself—dropping them to my sides. He whispers in my ear, "You'll choose me in the end. You can kiss him all you want because it'll be my lips on yours at the end of the day."

I pull away at those words, not liking the serpentine edge to them . . . the haunting promise. We're done here. But before I turn from him and begin walking towards the balcony, I swear I see his eyes mist and show a man full of pain and regret and grief, having just lost the woman he wants more than anything.

That's a dangerous man if I've ever seen one. As my heels clank against the ballroom floor, I scan the room for Ardelle.

However, another figure catches my eye instead.

It isn't the dark shadowy man from earlier. This one is the complete opposite. He's in all cream, his tux adorned with clips and hanging bits that give it a disheveled yet chic look. His mask is cream as well, layered with feathers and jewels, but none of that is what strikes me cold in my heels. He's glaring right at me.

Standing in between the archways that lead out onto the balcony, he takes a step towards me but abruptly stops himself. The man's sheer mass is dominant and overpowering, and it instantly reminds me of the figure that's been stalking me. Is this him? The way he's glowering directly at me is causing my warning bells to ring. He doesn't look like a shadow, but the body type is the same and so is the long hair. It's silver, practically white, and is tied tightly to the nape of his neck. It cascades down his back in a mix of silky strands and braids.

My heart beats wildly as we stare each other down from across the room. He's too far away for me to see any more details. Who is he? And why is he glaring at me? Is it possible there are *two* people stalking me through town?

Could Malakyte be right? Could these games be more dangerous than I previously believed? Is there more happening that I simply cannot see? No. They're just stupid games, that's all. I can make it through them easily. Because, no matter what he says, I am a hero, and I am going to save my friend. Save Earth and all her people, too.

At least, that's what I'm hoping for.

Otherwise, I'll just be fulfilling Malakyte promise and Jance's fears, leading everyone I love into nothing but a highly sophisticated mouse trap.

CHAPTER 21

Sleeping after the masquerade ball is nearly impossible. Partially because of the ball, partially due to what's coming next.

I stayed up all night, pondering both.

I think I dozed off around dawn. It's hard to say when we're underground, but I awake with a dull headache and Ardelle nuzzling my neck.

"No," I mumble, as he pulls in closer to my back. "I don't wanna get up."

He kisses my cheek. "You need to get up and save the world, Thumbelina."

"I'm too short to save the world."

Ardelle's laugh is low and deep, and I feel it vibrate through me as he spoons me tighter. "That'll make it even more interesting. Surprising the masses seems exactly the type of thing you'd fully enjoy."

I mumble in reluctant agreement.

A knock disrupts our giggling, and I lift my head up to see Jance in the doorway.

"Arianyte will be picking you both up in an hour. Trinity will be here in half. Get up. I'll make you breakfast."

That hour passed quickly.

Sylo and the remaining Ringers enter our apartment with Trinity, and we go over our strategy for the games.

"I scoured the city for the best stealth tech for you guys." Trinity hands Ardelle and me two small cases each, in the color Army Man. We open them, seeing an earpiece in one and a single contact lens in the other. "I gave Deimos his already. That earpiece will connect back to us at home base, where everything is set up, and the rest of you will come and monitor. The earpiece isn't all that hi-tech, other than it should be undetectable by Arianyte's systems or scans. Remember, any outside assistance like this tech is strictly against their rules, so don't get caught with them, or they could use that as a reason to kick you out, even arrest you. What's cool is the eye lens. It can transfer text from us directly to you, visible right over your field of vision. Those on the outside looking at you can't see the text. Only you can. It'll stay there until the next message comes in, like a Dez message. Both Kara and Ardelle and Deimos will have different feeds, so you won't be able to see the other's messages, but you will be able to hear each other on comms."

"We should wear these in," Ardelle suggests. "In case they throw us directly into the games from the start."

I nod in agreement.

Ahren looks at his watch. "It's time. We need to meet the Arianyte hover over by the hotel they believe we're staying at."

We pop in our spyware, collect the dog, and leave the undersewers. Jance walks extremely close to me, his stride rigid and responses short. He's worried about me, I know, and I wish I could ease his anxiety. As a sick-in-the-head foster kid, I can't shut down how his concern makes me feel good. But as a daughter, it causes me to feel terrible. I can't help it—I want to be wanted, to be cared for, and I don't know if that'll ever change. But I must remember what he said to me in the graveyard—keep a level head. Not be angry or vindictive or out of control with emotions.

We arrive at the address where the Arianyte hover is already waiting.

We say our goodbyes, and I save Jance for last. He pulls me up in a warm hug, enveloping me in his safe, strong arms.

"I'll be there watching and communicating with you the entire time," he says, kissing the top of my head. "And we'll see each other before the first game starts, when they allow family to visit. Keep your wits. Stay sharp. Remember what I've told you. And be sure to listen to me, alright? You got your sword, and Ardelle will watch your back. Don't trust Deimos either, got it?"

Still hugging him, I nod. It's hard to let go, but we have to. I consider bringing up that he's my father, but the timing is wrong. The car is waiting, and the others are all right here. So, I leave Jance without giving him the knowledge that he needs to know. Maybe I'll have the opportunity when he comes later, like he said.

Together, Ardelle and I slide into the Arianyte hover, and we watch as our loved ones slowly disappear and become specs on the distant streets of Zarmenia.

"Looks like we're still within the city," Ardelle says as the self-driving hover glides us into the parking garage of a giant building, somewhat on the outskirts of Zarmenia but still close enough that we aren't out in the boonies.

Bags in hand, we go into the lobby of the building, where the other Titans are waiting. To say we were met with a plethora of dirty glares would be an understatement.

"You just had to destroy that kicking machine, didn't you, Thumbelina?" Ardelle whispers to me as we stand awkwardly off towards the side of the group, waiting for someone to tell us what to do.

I laugh lightly. "You thought it was hot."

"It was. Only because I got to watch all those other guys gawk over what's mine."

"Who says I'm yours?"

"You don't want to be mine?" He looks down at me with a sarcastic and playful tone, but I can see his eyes flicker with worry.

Fear that I might say no.

"Do you want me to be yours?" I ask simply. "Actually," I interrupt before he can answer, "why don't you just take the initiative and show me how you want me to be?"

Mischief flashes in those blue eyes. And then, without hesitation, he grabs the back of my neck, and kisses me full on the mouth. In front of every single one of those glaring eyes.

"Is that initiative enough for you, Thumbelina?" he breathes as he breaks our kiss, that damned cocky smirk sending a blast of heat to my core.

I glide my tongue across my lips, relishing in the taste of him. "I guess it does. I'm officially yours, then."

"And you're mine," he echoes.

The rush I get from those words is enormous.

"Welcome, Titans!" A cheery voice breaks our not-so-private moment, and both our heads snap to the front of the lobby. The man is a human-looking enough extra, if not for his gangly and exaggerated features, like his long spindly arms, legs, and fingers.

The building itself is fancy. It resembles a ritzy hotel. Although, I'd bet credits to donuts Titans are the only people staying here. There's elegant furniture staged near a fireplace, plants and intricate lighting fixtures, marble flooring, and patterned ceilings. Silent staff members, both Terran and extra, pitter-patter around us, carrying all things from linens to platters of food to what looks like matching clothing.

"For those of you who remain in competition, this will be your lodging for the length of the games. For reference, we're calling it the mansion. At the mansion, your every need will be attended to. Eat and drink to your heart's desire, take a swim in our spa and sauna, and of course, hit that gym. Each Titan has their own individual suites, and fraternization is strictly prohibited. All remaining rules and amenities will be listed in your rooms, and we suggest you go over them first thing. On the table to your right, you will find your names and attached key cards. To receive your room keys, each contestant must temporarily relinquish their Dezlar devices for the duration. Get settled, have some fun, and be back in the lobby at 1 p.m. sharp."

"That's it?" I ask.

"That's it, kiddo." I turn to find none other than Deimos sporting his typical grumpy glare.

I cross my arms. "Nice to see you show up. We missed you last night at the masquerade ball."

Deimos huffs and looks to the side. "I'll dress up in a suit and mask once the cold-blooded bastard is dead."

Fair enough.

"I'd use this time wisely," he suggests. "Stretch, meditate, fuck each other silly—I don't care. Just be ready in a couple of hours to kick some ass because, by the looks of these people, they're going to be coming for the both of you."

And with that, he skulks off.

"Well," Ardelle ponders, "he really knows how to motivate, doesn't he?"

"Should we fu—"

"Thumbelina." Ardelle cuts me off, and I try—I really try to keep the smirk off my face, but I can't help it. That glint in his eyes doesn't go away, either.

He totally wants me.

Our rooms are nice, huge, and on opposite sides of the mansion from each other. I have a funny feeling it was done purposely to keep Ardelle and me apart. It's not like it's all women on this floor or anything. There isn't enough to fill the floor, anyway. From what I saw, there's maybe ten of us here, and the rest are men.

The three of us agreed to drop our stuff off in the pristine rooms and head back down to the lobby to brainstorm and check out the competitors with a keener eye now that we've got the time.

Once we meet back up, we talk for a few hours, strategize what each game could possibly be based on years prior. We look at the competitors who we think will likely be the biggest threats to Ardelle and me, picking out their possible weaknesses and strengths and how to exploit both. Once Deimos shows up, our conversation changes to how we want to play, either as a team and a unit or entirely separately. Each option can better our odds or weaken them. Everyone knows how I'd rather play, but I don't know if going at it alone keeps them safer or not. If it means I can be there to protect Ardelle and even Deimos, I'd rather we do this together. I got them into this. I need to make sure I protect them with everything that I have.

We return to our rooms a second time to change. The first game is about to begin.

Sitting upon my bed is a uniform, which I assume are all matching. It's mostly a solid black one-piece with flattering design accents that flow off the curves of my body in Bloodred and Moon Phase White. The thick leather fabric zips up in the center of my stomach and chest and ends by my neck. It fits nicely, skintight, protective, and high-quality. If it didn't have the stupid Arianyte logo on the back and front, I'd almost like it.

"You look hot." Trinity's voice bounces in my ear as I stare at myself in the bathroom mirror now that I'm clothed.

All I do is shake my head in response.

I grab my sword, then leave the room, shaking out the anxiety from my sweating palms as I walk downstairs.

I find Ardelle and Deimos quickly, and we're all corralled again before the same alien man from earlier.

"Follow me, Titans."

We're taken down a server's tunnel, entirely made of concrete and harsh lighting, looking nothing like the rest of the building. All sixty of us are smooshed into the narrow hallway as it leads to wherever our destination is.

I do my best not to act like the other Titans intimidate me.

Hold your chin up high. You're strong. Your blood is strength and battle tested, and you have magic. You can do this; you're going to rescue Pacey.

A flash of sunlight draws my attention, but I'm too short to see.

"What's out there?" I ask Ardelle, staggering on my tiptoes as I try to see past the others.

Eyes searching, Ardelle shakes his head. "Can't tell yet, still too far back."

Please don't let Malakyte be out there.

After our conversation last night, I worry I've said too much. I shouldn't have shut him down so blatantly. What if he retaliates against me for it? Or goes after Ardelle or Deimos or even Jance when he comes to see me before the game starts? What if all the things he said about me being full of uncontrollable darkness turns out to be true?

Once we finally squeeze our way through the single door, I look around at the giant outdoor space we fill out into. It's not a room because there aren't any walls, but there is a roof. We're standing in a hangar of some kind. Guessing from all the hovers, it's a sky-hover hangar. So, does that mean our arena is far away if we're flying there?

"I don't see Malakyte's bitch-ass," Deimos says, and I snicker. Despite our history—the fact he tried to kill me—he's growing on me. Plus, I'm glad to see Malakyte hasn't made an appearance.

"Attention, Titans!" Our escort claps his hands, a plethora of SSPARROW lining up on either side of him. "This is how the logistics of the games will proceed. If you are not aware, the Titan Games will be played today, tomorrow, and the following day. Each game, players will be eliminated until the Titan is crowned on the final day of competition. The winner will receive five million Cato credits, an immediate trip up to the Azurite fleet for a congratulatory award dinner with royalty of Arianyte, and the offer to travel freely throughout the Milky Way Galaxy."

"Where are we competing?" one of the competitors yells.

When one idiot coos, others follow. "Yeah! Where's our arena? Why can't there be an audience like always?"

The alien announcer waits a beat or two before answering. "I was just getting to the logistics of the gameplay. The Titan Games has been outfitted with three individualized arenas for each game. These arenas are floating above the city on our exclusive Arianyte technology Sky Daises."

"So, the games will be taking place in the sky?" a person asks, one of the few women here. She's broad and muscular, of old-world Asian descent, like Saris, but looks more formidable, if that were even possible.

"Correct," the alien announcer confirms.

Ardelle leans over and says to me, "That explains that strange platform we saw in the sky when we tried rescuing Pace."

That's right. I had forgotten all about that thing.

"After press interviews and family meetings, which will take place directly before the day's game, Arianyte will fly contestants up to the Dais. Winners will be transferred back down separately from the disqualified. Now, the press is eager to see Arianyte's Titans."

I sigh heavily. We're in for one hell of a ride.

CHAPTER 22

THE ARIANYTE EMPIRE DECREE #74

THE SYMBOL KNOWN AS "THE STAR" IS NOW
PROHIBITED FROM USE.

MALAKYTE ARDEEN

The Titan Games are scheduled to commence within the hour. Soon, I'll no longer have my own eyes on my Star, but many are watching her. Hell, the eyes of the entire planet are on her. My Karalevine is becoming quite a legend. It appears, at least, with all this attention on her, she's safe in one regard. Although, I do not like sharing what's mine.

Selenyte cannot use her manipulation to try and harm me by going after Karalevine. She knows any public embarrassments will make their way to Father, I'd ensure it. Although, it's apparent Karalevine inadvertently put yet another target on her back by entering these games. Rash, heedless girl.

My office door blasts open, robbing me from my current thoughts. Standing in the doorway is my incessant sister.

Selenyte blasting in is jarring to say the least. She's dressed in full royal glam, a deep blue gown hugging her thin figure. Stars, does she look like our mother.

"Brother," she says as a way of greeting. "Your goons alerted me that you wish to speak before your silly little games begin." Selenyte sits on the chair opposite my desk and leans far back into it, disregarding her royal etiquette the moment the door shuts behind her. The chair is black leather, and its hinges squeak with her weight. We convene at Arianyte Tower within my main office space, but soon, we'll leave the tower and enter the western arena to watch the show in a more inconspicuous fashion. My impatience is evident as I obsessively and meticulously adjust the objects on my desk. The label of my cup is crooked. There. No, now the label is too far to the right. There, that's adequate. Now I see the keyboard isn't straight, either. It's also uneven.

"Stop fixating," Selenyte huffs in my direction. I straighten out the tape dispenser before pinning my glare on her white hair as afternoon light peeks in from the window behind me and onto her ornate crown. The golden chains and sparkling jewels bounce rainbow light back into my eyes. "Don't give me that look. You know how you get when you begin to do your rituals obsessively. You spiral. And I'm only looking out for you. I know you're all worked up over that rebel girl or whatever her name is. She is such a little pest, isn't she? I found out through the Azurite grape vine that she's the one who gave you that hideous scar across your face. I don't understand, Malakyte. Why did you let this trashy Terran get away with that? More importantly, if you're so worried about her in this ridiculous game of yours, why don't you just snatch her out of the tournament entirely and end this all now? It's not like you don't have the resources and power to do it. Why is she of so much importance to you that you allow her to get away with murder? You wouldn't even let me get away with some of the crap she's doing. You're so rigid, like Father, never wanting to have any fun. Unless it benefits you, that is."

"You get away with plenty, Selenyte," I tell her. "Karalevine is nothing but a rebel out of control. I keep her in the games because that's where I want her to be. I want to make an example out of her. Show the Terrans exactly what happens when they defy me.

What better way to show my power than to have it streamed to a worldwide audience that's eager to watch her fall?"

It's partially true, Karalevine is nothing but a piece on the board. I don't need to yank her from these games to make her mine. She'll come to me naturally, beg to be with me again. And if she doesn't . . . well, I've got a plan for that, too.

"You're more twisted than I am, brother. Where has this version of you been these past decades?" She giggles, placing the tip of her nail between her lips and looking at me suspiciously. Does she buy my ploy? Does she believe Karalevine is nothing to me?

"You haven't been here to see it," I say.

She shrugs. "I suppose. But I have my little birdies. They do like to chirp in my ear about things. About little girls who bite off much more than they can chew."

Is she talking about Karalevine? What can she already know? "You're not talking about yourself now, are you? I figured you're far too self-absorbed to unveil yourself in such a vulnerable way."

Selenyte spins the chair, and she circles several laps before coming to a stop and facing me. My irritation spikes slightly when I notice the pens sitting in their dispenser. There are too many red ones. I've told my assistants an unholy amount of times that there must be an even number of colored pens.

"Perhaps you haven't been around to see how much I've changed, either."

I snap my eyes back to hers. Did she just parrot me?

I change the subject. "Why was Marett coming and going off the Azurite these last few weeks? His diet of blood isn't satisfied with what you provide him? I do not like him feeding on my Terrans. Each one of them is a potential worker or body for the Silent Breath and other experiments, not midnight snacks. My Terrans are a fuel source for us. Production of the serum has slowed on this planet due to the political pressure I've been under. Each body is an asset for war, for expansion, or for the Silent Breath, which is what funds all those extravagant gowns you like to tout around in.

It's why I don't simply blast this planet into orbit and be done with this farce. I still need them. Keep your hound off my property."

The contrast of her cold façade and the playfulness of her spinning in the chair unnerves me. "Marett likes the hunt."

"And why were you two at the Titan Masquerade ball last night? You weren't invited."

She huffs, annoyed with me. "I just wanted to have some fun, Mal. The way you keep me cooped up on that spaceship is driving me crazy. I needed fresh air! I wanted to dance, have some fun. What's the big deal? I didn't cause any trouble. Nobody even knew who I was. We look nothing alike. And Marett was my bodyguard, if my safety is your big concern."

Her safety isn't my concern. Karalevine's is. Did Selenyte see me dancing with her? What could she glean from that single interaction alone? That's why she's here, so I can fish out what she saw. Had I known my sister was there, I wouldn't have been so foolish.

"The Terrans are suckers for royalty. I had a plan to roll you out today, publicly. Now, because you're reckless and wanted to play—as you claim—you've ruined that. You can dance with Marett on the ship, Selenyte. This is my planet. You signed it away to me decades ago. Just because you used to own it doesn't mean you get to waltz down her and cause amok because you're feeling some ship fever. The humans will use any excuse to persecute me. I don't need you adding to their list of grievances."

Selenyte abruptly stands, plucks one of my pens, and begins twirling it as she leans against my desk. "And whose fault is that?" she asks, chewing on the end of the pen before she drops it back into the holder upside down. My nails scrape against my thighs in annoyance.

Frustrated, I take the pen and put it back the correct way.

"Your anxiety is beginning to pester me, brother."

"I do not experience *anxiety*," I snap. "That's a ludicrous human emotion. I am nothing like them."

She sighs heavily, scooting herself onto my desk enough to sit on it. All the items get bumped. "Then, do something before your obsessions begin to show in public. Nobody cares how your pens are organized, Mal. You're going to embarrass the family if you keep going on like this."

A small growl escapes my lips, but she only laughs at me.

"I know mother said it wasn't your fault you have your odd compulsions, but they're so strange. Why do you care if you have an odd number of pens?" She flicks the container over, and they spill across the desk. "You've been glaring at them for the last five minutes. You're as controlling over your desk as you are over me. I'm not a child anymore. You don't need to control every little thing I do. I'm more than capable of taking care of myself."

That's exactly what I'm perturbed about. "While you're here in this system, you will abide by my rules, or you will leave. Period."

A pen rolls onto the floor, and it takes everything in me not to pick it up.

My sister's playful taunting stops abruptly. She doesn't like being told no.

"Stop trying to be like Father, Mal. It doesn't suit you well."

"Stop trying to scheme like Father, *Selly*. It doesn't suit you well, either."

The tension can be cut with a knife.

She scoffs. "I am not scheming, brother. If anyone is, it's you. Living amongst these savages all these years has made you paranoid. Perhaps messing with those Elendril crystals again has made you go mad? Are you trying to hide them from Father and Mother so they won't find out? You know if I tell them, they'll never give you the throne. Not after what happened last time. After what that Zariya girl did to our reputation and our profits. You know, ever since you've been gone, Father and I have worked tirelessly to replenish the stock of Silent Breath that your *mate* systematically sabotaged. The Races and the Counsil were furious with us after her announcement to the galaxy went out. The planets rebelled. Squashing that alone took decades, which you wouldn't know because you didn't have to clean up your mess. We've only now been able to harvest the Silent Breath on a consistent basis again. If Zariya has returned, she must be put down."

"Zariya cannot return, Selenyte. She is dead."

Her eyes slit at me. "So you say."

"Be prepared to watch the first games. We're leaving shortly," I tell her, dodging this topic altogether.

She stands, knocking more items askew. "No," she states aggressively. "Those games are stupid and ridiculous. It's just you peacocking around. I won't be part of them in any way."

"The Arianyte Council has flown in to watch the games. You're coming whether you like it or not."

So I can keep my eyes on you.

Her eyes narrow at me as she scoffs, making her way out of my office. Before she leaves, she says, "You may think me wicked, big brother, but did it ever even occur to you that I came here because I missed you? Or are you that self-involved that you think all I'm trying to do is steal your crown and hurt you?"

Selenyte slams the door as she leaves, not letting me reply. I still see that's her favorite way of telling me to fuck off. I need to keep her close now that my plan is coming into play. It'll be a delicate balance, juggling all these moving pieces. Nevertheless, I need to stealthily watch for flying daggers lest one stabs me right in the back, knocking my crown right off my head in the process. Could she be here because she misses me? Perhaps . . . We'll have to see how she behaves to deduct if that's the truth.

I spend the rest of my time meticulously reorganizing my desk, noting that the pen Selenyte played with has bite marks all over it.

CHAPTER 23

People from all around the world are gathering their popcorn. Their chicken wings, their chips, and dip are all being sprawled out next to decadent charcuterie boards and cups of fancy alcohol of all intensities and flavors. The games are an entire festivity for everyone to watch, to bet on, to forget about their lives and sink their teeth into something primal and uncensored. And today is the day: game one of the Titan Games. The action will begin soon. But behind some players, there are whispers. Webs of networks that have been spun, secrets that have been shared, codes that have been given under the cover of mundanity. Behind soccer moms and waitresses and tattoo artists, there's an entire operation going on right under the occupation's nose. There's a twinge in the air. A buzzing that only those who listen can hear, and it speaks to those willing to come together and fight. Battle for themselves, their children, their freedoms. They are the rebels, and they are waiting to strike.

Before we're all flown up and suspended on the Sky Dais, the competitors are subjected to the paparazzi's questions. There's also a short time for the competitor's family to wish them luck and say their goodbyes. Jance is somewhere within the crowd that waits, which we'll see after the press gets their own licks in on us. I'm still so torn about whether to tell him the truth or not. If I don't mention it, then I'm lying to him by omission. If I do say something to him, then he could lose me in these games and be crushed. He could also reject me, and that's a factor I can't shake, either. Having these fears and keeping secrets doesn't make me a good daughter to him. It isn't fair. And I don't know if I can compete without saying something to him. I couldn't do it earlier today because of the timing, and if I don't do it now, I may never get another opportunity.

The SSPARROW organizers shove the Titans before the paparazzi. So many questions are flying at us I'm not sure where to look.

"Karalevine!" Several people shout my name in earnest, lights flashing so fast my eyes are having trouble pinning the details of their faces.

"How do you feel about being only one of six women competing this year?" some woman shouts. I look around for Ardelle or even Deimos, but both have been pulled away by their own gluttonous paparazzi.

Eyes blinking rapidly, I say, "Well, I think it's pretty sexist."

"Are you a pioneer for young women, or are you secretly a rebel looking to destabilize peace between Terrans and Arianyte? Why join the games if you're hell-bent on destroying the fragile balance of peace between our species? Terran leaders have called for your disqualification."

My eyes roll before I have the forethought to remember there are about fifty cameras recording me, and they're going to have dozens of shots of me with my eyes going into the back of my head. Trinity will slap some ridiculous slogan over the images and throw me on the Network, no doubt.

It's time to do what I came here to do, and in the meantime, I'll make my old tattoo mentor and fellow rebel proud. *For justice, for freedom, our spirits shall soar . . . as we reclaim our world, like never before.*

"Arianyte has proven time and time again that they've abused the power we've given them, Devouring Accords or not." My voice is strong because that anger never truly leaves me, and this part is no act. "The Hijacked—the same people you said didn't exist— were found and rescued. I did that. When I privately worked for Malakyte Ardeen, I saw things that I knew in my heart were not okay, and that is why I am here. I cannot fight the occupation directly, but I can fight in these games. Fight for a voice that will carry far beyond what I can do as one single person. I could have easily been one of those Hijacked children, as I grew up parentless and alone in the broken foster care system of this city."

Step one is complete. Grab their attention, tell them what I stand for.

Now, step two. Bring in sympathy.

"I saw the way Arianyte treated their orphans. I lived it every single day. I struggled and lived in fear of becoming one of the lost Hijacked. Who would come for me? Who would save me? Nobody, that's who. I bet the Tributes and every single adult on this planet feels that exact same way, waiting to be taken. It's wrong to force *children* to live in such fear!"

Make them relate to you.

"Don't you wish it could be different?" I ask before they throw more questions my way, voice booming out over the other paparazzi. "Don't you want to wake up and not feel fear? What would life be like knowing that we don't have to worry about our fathers and mothers, brothers, sisters, and friends being chosen as a Tribute? None of us, except the Terran leaders—they and their families exempt from Tribute drafts, the ones demanding my expulsion from these games—have lived without that bone-chilling fear for years. I don't want anyone to know the terror I've experienced, the terror of watching Arianyte take away someone I love. Because that's what they do. They take. And to that end, what else is Arianyte pilfering behind our backs? We all know that the Terran government knows way more than they're letting on. You should be asking them some harder questions instead of me. Let's demand they stop using Arianyte for their own political and financial benefit and start doing something for their own people."

So many voices erupt my way. Questions, remarks, threats, and accusations—so much that it's overwhelming. Perhaps I got a little overzealous there.

A familiar voice comes over the comms piece hidden in my ear.

"Damn, girl, now that's a speech. I taught you well," Trinity says. "I'm with you. Make them pay for it."

Malakyte is likely watching the live coverage of this because a dozen SSPARROW come barreling in, separating the press people from the Titans. I'm relieved they do. That was a lot.

Strong hands squeeze my shoulders, and I jump but then relax with a heavy sigh when I see Ardelle standing behind me. "Stars, don't scare me like that," I tell him, voice on edge.

"That speech was epic, Thumbelina." He beams, face glinting with pride. "I hope wherever Pacey is, they're letting her watch, and she sees this."

"Me too, Ardelle."

He grips me by my waist and brings me flush to his front. Cranking my neck skyward, I ask, "Are you as terrified as I am for this wild ride?"

Ardelle shakes his head. "No. I'm excited. This is going to work. We're one step closer to getting Pacey home."

Deimos interrupts, "Don't think it'll be that easy, pretty boy. Malakyte surely has something up his sleeve for us. Watch for it. He's being way too generous for my liking. It's suspicious. Especially letting you"—Deimos nudges towards me—"get away with all the shit you're spewing about him and Arianyte. I can't believe he's allowing it."

"Chill out. You're giving me anxiety." I already know what I'm doing is risky for everyone, not just me. There's nothing I can do except protect those I love, and hope that's enough.

"There they are," Ardelle says, pointing towards the crowd of families and waving them over.

We squeeze past tons of people to find a quieter spot towards the back corner. Only Jance and Sylo came, due to the risk they shouldn't have come at all, but Jance insisted he be here. There he goes again, being far better to me than I am to him.

Our talks are grim, if I'm being generous. I know Jance only wants to prepare me and Ardelle for what we may face up there on that platform, but oddly enough, I'm way more nervous about telling him the truth than I am about competing in the first game. In my uniform pocket are the DNA results. I know he'll need proof to accept this. Because what if he thinks this is some sick act to replace his dead daughter and he gets offended? What if this changes everything between us? He's here for me now, cares for me *now*, but he walked out on me recently. He could do it a second time. It makes me nauseous, but I'm just going to have to risk him abandoning me. If I don't do it now, I won't be able to focus on this damned game at all.

It's time.

Time to finally tell Jance he's my father.

My chest begins fluttering.

"Five-minute warning."

That's not a whole lot of time.

The others have been talking strategy while I've been mulling this over in my head, not hearing a word of it. Only one thing matters to me, and I've got five minutes to spill my guts and say it.

"Jance," I say, clearing my throat awkwardly as I interrupt the conversation. My eyes avert downwards, staring at the stiff Arianyte boots. "Can I talk to you alone?" My eyes fall on Ardelle's, and it takes him barely a second for understanding to flash on his face, and he guides Sylo and Deimos away.

We're alone.

When I'm silent for far too long, Jance closes the foot or two of space that separated us and embraces me in the safety of his arms. Leaning into him, I want to cry. All my emotions regarding this decision have haunted me, the fear of our relationship being irrevocably changed, keeping me frozen with indecision. He'll have so many questions—as I do—but there's no time for that now.

My timing sucks.

"You'll be alright, kid. If anyone can do this and win, it's you. I'll be right there with you on comms. I'm going straight back to the rebel headquarters, and I'll be watching your every move. You won't be alone out there. I have complete faith in you and your ability to do this."

His voice is sure, assuring, and comforting. I feel his hand brushing the back of my head. Because the touch is so much more than what it seems: it's all I've ever wanted. So, then, why is it so damned difficult to accept it? Why can't I trust him? What's wrong with me?

"What is it, kid?" he asks, eyes penetrating me in that piercing way where it's hard for me to hold his stare. "There's not much time left."

"I . . ." I try, but my words fall flat. How am I supposed to say this? I should have rehearsed or something. "I want to tell you something. It's important, and I think you should know now before I go up there. In case—"

"You're coming back." He allows zero room for negotiation there.

Nodding, I look away from him, seeing as the SSPARROWs are guiding the sky-hovers over to the hanger's opening. I dig the paternity test out of my pocket, the cheap plastic flimsy in my clenched hands. I hold it close to my chest so he can't see what it says.

He tries smiling to assure me that I can tell him anything, those white teeth straight and perfect, a little like mine, a little not. He

is my father, right? This test isn't wrong, is it? *Stars—stop posturing. Just tell him. Say it, dammit.*

"Back at the last games, Malakyte and I were alone for a while. And during that time, he told me things . . ."

"Okay." Jance's voice turns from intrigued to confused.

My mouth opens, but nothing comes out. He's not going to believe me. He's going to hate me for saying this and will think I'm making it up. Everything will be ruined, and I'll lose him. My heart increases rapidly, and I feel heat bloom in my cheeks, throat, and chest. My mark peeks its eyes open, the sleeping dragon curious as to what threats lay ahead. Little does it know that losing Jance is the biggest danger of all.

"Kid . . ."

"Time is up!" A SSPARROW shouts. "Wrap it up and head to the sky-hovers. Now!"

I can see Ardelle looking our way, concern in his eyes. He can tell I haven't told him and can see my hesitation even from there.

"Umm . . . I . . ." I stutter, watching as more and more people begin to clear out. Against my will, my eyes fill up with tears.

"Kara." Jance takes my hand, not even going for the plastic there. "Whatever it is, you don't have to tell me. You're coming back to me. It can wait. Bundle it up, put it back in your pocket, and let it be. You need to focus and stay sharp. It's okay. I'll be here when this is all done. I promise."

I pull my hands back, grabbing onto his ring necklace without thinking about it.

"I can't promise you that, though." My voice is a breathy whisper, desperate and weak, the core of who I am. "Please don't think I'm making this up because I would never do something like that after everything you've been through. I wouldn't."

"Titans!" The impatience in the SSPARROW's call is evident.

I shift uncomfortably, and without thinking about it for one more second, I shove the test into Jance's hands.

"Malakyte told me that I was your daughter." My words come out fast, jumbled, and practically incoherent. "I didn't believe him at first, but I couldn't shake this feeling that he was right, so I tested our DNA. And he was right. I've got to go. I'm sorry."

I release his hands and run off, passing by Ardelle and Deimos as they wait by the hover entrance for me. Jance doesn't call for me, doesn't say anything as I push my way through the other competitors in line for the sky-hovers and disappear behind them.

I am a damned coward.

At least I told him. I did what I believed was right. All I can hope is that this doesn't change everything between us. I've lived without my father my entire life. It's not that big of a deal . . . but I need my Ringer now more than ever.

Like my life depends on it.

Because it does.

CHAPTER 24

id I make the right choice so I can focus on the games? I can't get the vision out of my head. Jance looking down at the flimsy plastic in his hands, his hair blowing in the wind as the sky-hovers lifted into the air and blasted off into the sky. His face expressionless, brows furrowed, eyes never looking up. That's the last I saw of him before I'm being flown through the sky.

"Girl, seriously?" Trinity's voice comes over the comms. Dammit, I forgot she was listening. Shit . . . "That's how you inform that dude he's your father? How long have you known? Your Saris woman is absolutely losing her mind over here. They all heard it. Was that your intention or . . ."

Jupiter's rings . . . I completely forgot about the damned earpieces.

"Thumbelina?" Ardelle places his hand gently on my shoulder, keeping his voice low as the dozens of other competitors are sardined into this sky-hover along with us.

I look at him, mortified. "You heard?"

Awkwardly brushing his hand through his deep Midnight Blue hair, he ultimately relents. "It was too late to tell you once you already started. I figured you knew."

Deimos shoves a few meathead-looking Terrans out of the way as he comes to stand beside the two of us. "We don't have time for your daddy issues, kiddo. We've got a competition to win."

He's right. I can't worry about Jance anymore. I've got to focus and make sure I keep Ardelle and Deimos safe. I did what I had to do. Now, it's time to compartmentalize it so I can compete.

From what everyone's been saying, these games are different. I peek out the hover window in awe as we approach the Sky Dais, which is the first thing that's new. I'm mesmerized by its sheer size alone. It's gigantic. The top half where the Titans will be is flat, green and lush with trees and grass. The bottom is like a rock, brown and jagged, with pointy bits hanging down like icicles. It's high up in the sky, higher than it appears from the ground. If anyone were to fall, they'd be dead for certain.

As the others gawk at it in amazement, too, I ask, "How is it floating like that with nothing holding it up?"

"Their ostentatious tech, that's how. Showoffs," Deimos mumbles, ever the Arianyte hater.

"Has anyone been able to figure out what the first game is going to be?" I ask, but both of them shake their heads no.

"I heard it's going to be a team game." An interesting dialect answers from behind me, so extremely close I can feel their breath on my neck, yet not even my ears detected their approach. Jumping and turning around, I bump into Ardelle, who then smashes into a few others, and they mumble insults at us.

It's one of the two men from the masquerade ball, the one dressed in cream. The one who was watching me. Tall doesn't begin to cover it. He's wearing the same uniform as me and the other Titans, but it's a little too tight in all the perfect places. However, it's not his massive chest and arms that make him stand out, not by a space mile. It's everything else. Pointed ears. White hair—parts of which are in small braids. Violet eyes. Elongated canine teeth. What the actual fuck? He looks exactly like Gav. *Exactly*. But wait . . . Gav's supposed to be dead.

My eyes immediately go toward his hands, but they're covered in black leather gloves, the kinds that have the fingertips cut out. I stand there, dumbfounded, but as I stare at him, he looks back at me with absolutely zero regard. No recollection flashes in that burning purple gaze of his. Although, I do see something flickering in those eyes: dangerous cunning. He says nothing else and simply saunters off like he didn't just interrupt our conversation out of the blue. The other competitors part for him, even at the cost of crushing several others.

"That guy looks just like Gav!" I hiss, mind reeling. "I have to go talk to him again."

Ardelle catches my arm before I can make it a single step. "Let's hold on. You said the reason you lost it on Malakyte at the last games was because you found out he was killed. That can't be him. He's just one of those Sky-Fae extras."

Sky-Fae. Extras that looked like faeries or elves, beautiful and hauntingly skilled in battle, like old folklore creatures. Which is how they secured the nickname, short for faeries from the skies.

I turn on Deimos and point my finger at him in accusation. "Did you lie to me about him being dead? I swear to the stars, if you're messing with me about him, I will kill you."

Deimos puffs his chest at me, his own canines bared. "You think I would have attacked Malakyte the way I did if I was making up the fact he killed my Ringer? Think again, kiddo."

"There's nothing I wouldn't put past you. You're a snake."

"You're seeing shit. I had the information Geonni gave me, and it said the kid was dead. Whoever that person is, it ain't your Gav, and it ain't my Ringer. I would feel something if it were him . . ."

Deimos looks back over at the Sky-Fae, and I swear something flashes on his face for the briefest of moments. Although, as quick as lightning, Deimos shakes his head, and in a flash, the cool steel returns to his eyes.

Before I can answer, three other extras aggressively squeeze their way through the wall of bodies, stopping our bickering dead in our tracks. Another lurking figure as big as the last comes to cast a literal shadow over me. He's dressed all in black, his hair Hell-Pit Charcoal, down past his ass and mortifyingly greasy. Skin is Soot Gray, with a nose that's more animalistic than human. His fists are massive, and his nails are claws. A beast on two legs. He was the one standing with Naresteé at the masquerade ball. I figured I'd meet both men from the ball at some point during the games, but not back-to-back in this fashion. How they each approached me, it sends off warning bells. The Gavrielle look-a-like has a completely different vibe than this dark one, however. The extra in front of me is straight-up fucking terrifying. Out of the two, my instincts tell me he's the one who's been following me. The way he feels and stands and controls the shadows is identical to my prowler. Now add the knowledge that he's involved with Naresteé in some way, and that makes it all the more insidious. And he came to talk to us? Why?

"We thought we'd come see what all the commotion was all about," the only female of the trio says. She's a black-haired, blue-skinned extra of average height and build. The third man looks relatively normal—compared to Terrans, anyway. Auburn hair, scruffy bearded chin, but it's his Bumblebee Yellow eyes glowing like a wolf's that tells me he's not from around here. The slight diamond shape of his pupils makes me squirm uncomfortably. "Nice weapons." Her beady dark-gray eyes in the shade Haunted House bounce between each of our Elendril weapons, each Titan being allowed one. "They certainly broke the mold when they made you three, didn't they?"

Her comment causes all three of us to glance at each other in suspicious confusion.

"Sure," I say, voice slow and unsure. "Same goes for you three."

The dark one, he hasn't stopped glaring at me—like I'm a meal to him.

Startling me, the sky-hover jolts as it docks on the platform. We must be all the way up on the Sky Dais already, and the timing couldn't be better.

Taking Ardelle's hand, I move us away from the three creepozoids and towards the door. When I look back, they're gone, but in their place a pair of violet eyes are watching me with the intensity of all three.

CHAPTER 25

Shit. Shit. *Shit!*

How the hell did this happen?

Moments ago, we landed on the Sky Dais inside another hangar, but this one had no line of sight to the outside. We'll be going in completely blind.

Here is where we were told what type of game we'd be playing in round one.

"Now, listen up!" A SSPARROW stood upon a small stage before us. "Each arena will be outfitted with Arianyte stealth tracking cameras to catch all the action. In addition, stationary cameras are placed strategically throughout. Now, game one is located on the western Sky Dais and is simply put—a game of Capture the Flag."

The room went silent.

"Take heed. This is no child's contest. Teams will be randomly selected by each of you drawing a card from this dispenser." The SSPARROW pointed to a silver cube, seamless, aside from a slit at the top. "Teams Gold and Silver will be separated at opposite ends of the Sky Dais. Each team will have a designated location known as home base, where they'll hide and defend their flag. The opposite team will cross enemy lines and attempt to steal your flag. A team can only win this round when they successfully bring the opposite team's flag back to their home base. Sixty of you will enter. Only thirty will continue on. Those on the losing team will be eliminated. Any competitors from the winning team that are deemed too injured or are permanently eliminated will be disqualified. Now, line up."

I shouldn't even be surprised by what happened after that.

"Do you think Malakyte designed it to be this way?" I ask Deimos as he and I stand across the room from Ardelle. Ardelle is on the Gold Team. Deimos and I are on the Silver Team. This means, no matter what, one or more of us is going home tonight. On the first damned round. The person I trust most is now playing against me, and what am I supposed to do, ask him not to try and win? His sister is the one being held captive, for stars' sake . . .

I can't ask him not to fight for her.

And he can't ask me not to fight, either. He knows this isn't only for Pacey. It's about so, so much more.

But worst of all, Ardelle won't be there to protect me . . . and I won't be there to protect him.

Deimos shakes his head. "Sounds like something he'd do, but there's no way of knowing."

Ardelle and I stare at each other from across the room, and I'm sure I look just as devastated as he does. How is this going to play out? How are we expected to fight against each other for the win, and how dirty will that conflict become? We've decided to trust each other again, but can we truly do that in this situation?

Jance's stable voice finally comes through on the comms. He's seen what happened, what we have to do. "We all knew this was inevitable at some point," he says, calm and steady, like I hadn't dropped a literal bomb on him thirty minutes ago. Why is he acting like nothing happened? Is he simply going to ignore this and pretend I never said anything, or is he merely trying to keep me focused? "Only one of you kids was going to win. Do your best, but we continue the plan no matter what happens. Just don't get so caught up in this you ruin something far more important to the both of you than a game."

I know that one is meant specifically for me.

But it's not just a game. It's Pacey at stake. Her life.

It's destroying and bringing down the empire.

It's freeing all of Earth.

Taking a deep breath through my nose, I exhale through my mouth, nodding my head in agreement. He's right, I got to keep my emotions under control. I can accept losing if I know Ardelle will win, I suppose . . . Or maybe, I can't. I don't know.

However, I'm not going down without a fight. Ardelle will have to work very, very hard for his win.

Ardelle must see the resolve that fortifies my spine because he sends a smirk across the hanger at me as the doors begin to open behind him, the stark wind blowing in cold air and sunlight. My cheeks burn at the radiance in his eyes as the sun's glow sets them ablaze. Both his hair and eyes glimmer in the cloudless light of the sky coming into view behind him. The gaze he flings me is one of both hesitation and determination. Adoration and anticipation. Hope and fear. I try to give it all back to him in earnest. I've got to trust him now, and I also need to trust myself. I'm not sure which is more difficult, having faith in him or in me.

"Don't you hold back, Thumbelina," he says through comms. "I'm expecting a fight from you, and I don't want to be let down. I want to see some of that little-dog energy again. Just remember how much you adored me this morning."

His tone is playful, confident, and cocky—*so Ardelle*— and it makes me grin in response. I do enjoy a challenge, but I also hate to lose.

CHAPTER 26

"Our little white-haired friend is on our team, at least." Deimos tries to cheer me up as we're shuttled to the opposite side of the Sky Dais as Ardelle, but it doesn't work. Why he cares anyway is beyond me. He said that guy isn't his Ringer. But can I trust him to tell me the truth? Deimos is a wild card.

"Well"—I clear my throat—"I swear he looks exactly like Gav. And the fact his hands are covered is even more suspicious. You really don't feel a pull towards him?"

Deimos's eyes narrow. Wind skates in from the hover windows as it lands on our side of the platform, rustling his paper-thin Winter White hair around his enormous ears. His delay is an answer in and of itself. "I don't know," he admits. "Something about the kid is off. I can't explain it or what it is, but I don't trust it. You shouldn't, either. Remember, he came up to you specifically. Why?"

"He's also been watching me ever since the masquerade ball you never attended," I comment, not answering his question solely because I have no answer to give.

The hover jolts, then relaxes. We're on our side of the platform, and now the games begin.

The thirty of us on our team funnel out of the hovers, and we finally get a good look at the terrain up here.

"Insane," a player says, voice in awe.

The faces of the other competitors mirror his astonishment, and I'm pretty sure a bird will fly into my open mouth at any moment.

We're standing in a fairytale world.

The basic landscape is wooded, pines, giant redwoods, maples, blue spruce, and tons of other types of vegetation all cover the platform in lush amounts. A few of the trees don't even exist on planet Earth. Their size and shapes are either so massive or odd to be native to the planet. There're also mushrooms everywhere, a few taller than me, in several different colors and shapes. I can also hear the soft trickling of a stream nearby, and I have no idea how they got running water all the way up here. Although, that's the last item on my list of questions about this place.

"Are we supposed to get up there?" a scrawny man asks, and the group of us looks up at the platform's most astonishing feature. Floating above the Sky Dais are miniature islands. They're of all sizes, big and small. Some are connected by roped ladders, others hovering independently of the others. The islands have moss covered at the tops, and the bigger ones have tiny little structures on them. How are they getting them to hang in midair like that? Hell, how is any of this even possible? The science Arianyte has at its disposal terrifies me.

A woman, who's taller than most of the men and has short sandy blonde hair, points towards the largest building directly in front of us. "Our hideout is a castle?"

"This building is where the Silver Team's flag will be stationed. You will need to obtain Gold's flag and place it within this building to win. There's tech within the flags that'll alert us when this happens," a SSPARROW confirms. With that, we're given our silver flag, a spike to tie it to, and all the remaining SSPARROW soldiers take back off in the sky-hovers. Rather hurriedly, I might add.

Buzzing around us all like bees are spherical cameras the size of baseballs. One cruises close to Deimos and me, and he swats the thing away like it's an annoying gnat.

"We need a strategy," I say to the group, ready to get in gear.

That gains me a few chuckles from the group, and I firmly plant my hands on my hips.

Don't let them intimidate you. You've got this.

A big guy, tanned-skinned and bald, looks down at me like I'm a toddler. "Okay, little girl. First, I want to make sure all your makeup is in place. We don't want you to break a nail, either. Or have that pretty hairstyle of yours come undone."

Their laughter and my clenching fists remind me of the last time they got a kick out of it at my expense. In fact, this guy seems to be the same dude that started the sexist comment to me during the tryouts.

I march up to him, showing no fear. "I seem to remember you saying something very similar during the tryouts, right before I kicked that machine halfway across the stadium. I can do the same to you. Maybe we'll all get lucky, and you'll roll right off the edge."

The same people laughing at me mere seconds ago adjust their mocking chuckles towards the meathead who started this ridiculous farce.

The man bares his teeth at me. "We all know that was some sort of trick. You taped explosives to your legs or something. Ninety-pound little girls don't scare anyone. You're not in charge here, I am. You all hear that? We do this my way."

Nobody speaks up against him.

A voice comes to my defense, and my head snaps over to the source of it. "I, for one, agree with her. We need a plan."

 174

He's the tallest one here as he takes a few steps towards the meathead and me. His white hair sways softly against the dual blades at his back. We're only allowed one weapon, so how'd he sneak in two, I wonder? "What's your name?" he asks the meathead.

"Emmers," he says, with far more respect than he ever granted me. Sexist pig.

"I'm Damon," he says, and it hurts to hear him say that. Not Gavrielle . . . it was never going to be Gavrielle. He's *dead*. "And I think we can all agree a plan is a great place to start, so let's begin."

Trinity's voice comes over the comms. "I'm sorry, girl. I know you wanted it to be him. From Pop's files on Gav, it does look like he is deceased. It says so right here. I'm looking at it now. He died when he was still a kid."

So, all this time, over all these years, he's been dead? I swore I felt him out there, waiting for me to find him . . .

"Offense and defense are smart. We should split into two teams," I say to the group before anyone can interject. "I think it would be best to split those two teams into quads. For the defense, two should be out in the woods surrounding the castle as the first line of defense. The remaining defend the flag. For offense, four teams should advance together into enemy lines and break off once we're within range. This will give their forces a much more difficult time stopping us. Whoever can maneuver within and retrieve the flag does so, and the remaining quads escort them back to home base. Any questions or comments?"

Damon's Lavender Petal eyes twinkle at me—impressed. His smile is all sharp canines and everything Gav was. He's the same rare species of extra—that, I know for sure. "That's an excellent strategy. I'm in agreement."

My body reacts to his gaze as if he's physically touched me. Yet, there's nothing behind those beautiful eyes that leads me to believe he recognizes me. Which makes sense. He's not Gavrielle.

Stars, stop, I scold myself. *It isn't him. You can't obsess over a damned ghost anymore. Pacey could be strapped down to that surgical table at any moment, and you have to rescue her. You couldn't save Gav. It sucks, but that's the truth. Save Pacey by focusing.*

Emmers, surprisingly, doesn't object. Neither does anyone else.

Deimos chooses to stay on offense while I take defense. I need to have faith he'll keep the flag protected. When he walks into the castle, he snatches the flag from some poor guy who looks terrified of him.

Damon takes the lead on splitting up the remaining Titans into our main and sub teams.

Shocked to find out, he put me with that asshole Emmers and who else? Himself. Odd. The three of us are also paired with a young Terran man slightly older than me. His body type is like Ardelle's but not as tall or broad, and his hair is like the Treebark Brown shade.

"I'm Sam," he says, holding his hand out to me. "It's nice to see a girl participating in the games . . ." He places his hand behind his head, his boyish looks compounded by the blush growing on his cheeks.

"Are we going to braid each other's hair, or are we going to get a move on?" Damon asks, words posh.

I squint at him as the four of us begin walking away from home base and out toward the opposite side of the floating platform.

"You literally have braids in your hair. It's a sign of the warriors on your home world, a sign of great respect. Only those who've bled in battle or are kin to those that have are permitted to braid their hair."

Gav told me that.

As Emmers and Sam continue to walk ahead through the trees, Damon stops so abruptly I practically run into him. I catch a whiff of his smell, and it immediately brings me back to the orphanage. That scent . . .

"How would you know any of that, Earth girl?" he demands.

I study his face, his eyes, his soul. Forget it, I can't hold back. "Is Damon your real name?" I ask boldly, and he flinches but only for a moment. My heart swells with hope. *Say no, dammit.*

 176

Say no. "Because you look like someone I used to know. A long time ago . . ."

"We've never met," he claims. "I'd definitely remember if I had."

He turns towards the other two and keeps walking, but he looks back at me for a split second, as if he's also trying to pick up a forgotten memory he misplaced.

A shadow from within the trees flashes past me in my peripheral, drawing away all thoughts of my old friend. My neck snaps towards it, but when I look, it's gone. This is exactly like when I was walking to the graveyard with Jance. That's perplexing because it looked massive. Perhaps this ghost of Gav isn't the only thing I'm seeing that isn't actually there? Or . . .

"Come along, little girl!" Emmers yells from far up ahead. "Or we're going to leave you behind."

I hate this jerk.

"Damn, it's cold up here," Sam complains as he rubs his arms. The chilly air pulls at my braids, pieces already coming loose without Pacey's skilled hand to tie them down tightly. I remember the night she taught me how to do her crazy braids. I could barely do a basic one. She'd probably see this hair style and laugh at the absurdity of it in comparison to hers. She's so talented, so good at everything she puts her mind to. She doesn't deserve what's happening to her. "I wonder how far away the edge is? You think they'd really let us simply fall to our deaths?"

"If death or murder wasn't a thing here, they'd have made it clear, and they haven't. I'd watch your back. The last thing you need to worry about is falling off the side of this platform."

The guy doesn't reply. If anything, he grows a little paler by my words. Maybe I shouldn't have been so harsh with him, but what's done is done.

Sam's gasp draws my attention to him instead. "What in Hell's gate is that?" He points straight ahead, where I do a double take.

The four of us sprint ahead towards the unholy sight set up before us, and it's the sounds that disturb me the most. I long for the eerie silence and occasional bird chirping to this because . . . this is haunting.

Snarling and gasping, unnatural crying and screaming. Shouts of things unseen, begs for things unfelt. My body shakes as I long for my father's warmth and comfort, but what I have instead is the frigid blanket of death wrapping itself around my shoulders, freezing my spine in place.

Before us are three small cages set roughly ten feet apart from each other. Those pop-up jail cells are made poorly because I can see their flimsy metal frames beginning to sway against the weight of what's inside—against the fury of the monsters trying to escape . . .

"What are they?" Sam gasps in horror.

I glance over at Damon, and he doesn't seem surprised. Worried, potentially, but his face is cold as stone. He's the most composed out of all of us. Even Emmers appears like he's about to lose his lunch.

Within these cages are what appear to be people . . . but they're not human anymore.

"You seem to know what these poor souls are," I say to Damon, and he tears his gaze away from what's inside the cages to look over at me.

His hand glides over his smooth chin as he looks contemplatively between me and the monstrosities before us. "These are Tributes."

The three of us gape, and I look at them closer this time. Their eyes are tinged red in the whites and around their irises. Darkened veins bulge along their pale bodies, which are covered in filthy rags barely distinguishable from their paper-thin skin. Given their gray coloring and inhuman, wild, and ravenous eyes, they appear like diseased animals. I'd assume they'd be frail and feeble with sickness, but they're just the opposite. Their bulging muscles pop their veins out under their skin like black snakes. Their nails are brittle and coated in dried blood, and their hair is wispy corn silk barely holding on to their scalps.

"What do you mean they're Tributes?" I demand.

"I don't know," he admits, voice sounding frustrated. "I've heard rumors of Arianyte experimenting on the Tributes turning them into Jupiter knows what. Stars knows what they've done to them up there over the years." He looks up, up to where Pacey is being held, up to the Azurite. Are they experimenting on her like this? Is this procedure just another experiment? Will she become one of these . . . these *things*? Damon continues with "It's simply my guess. Whatever or whoever they are, we need to get out of here before they get loose. Those confinements will not hold them much longer. Soon, they're going to be chasing all of us down."

"Are they contagious?" I ask, thinking of what would happen if they managed to bite one of us.

"Oh, stars . . ." Sam clasps both his hands around his head, panic boiling up inside him like a hot pot of tea about to scream.

Damon doesn't seem to consider this question for long before he says, "I doubt it. That would create too much of an issue for the occupation, especially with two more games to go. They're likely here as a scare tactic. Let's keep moving and pick up the pace."

"It's too late for that," Emmers says, and we all look in horror as the cells furthest from us begins to come apart under the weight of the bodies pushing from within.

I draw my sword. There's no time left to run.

As if sensing their freedom, these monster Tributes begin thrashing their bodies wildly. One of them pulls his head through the loose gap in their cheaply made prison. Then its shoulders pop free, and his entire upper body is hanging there between two bars as it screams this unnatural sound at us. Reaching, reaching, reaching . . .

The Tribute is almost free, the cage hanging on by a thread.

Damon unsheathes his dual blades from his back.

I swallow nervously.

The Tribute finally escapes. So does another and another, then several more behind that one until the cage is demolished under their ravenous, frenzied weight. Seeing their friends gain their freedom so quickly, the Tributes in the two other cages scream with rage. They want out, too. But if they find their way out as easily as their comrades, I don't know if we'll be able to stop them.

I grip my sword's hilt hard, my hand warming the cold rose gold metal.

"Stay together," Damon calls, each of us back-to-back and forming a circle. "We'll slowly make our way toward Team Gold and hope those other bars hold until then."

"We've still gotta come back," I remind him, but we've got to focus on the here and now.

The wild Tributes run up on us fast, and I'm surprised by not only their speed but their size.

Emmers swings his hatchet at one of them ten feet away and immediately breaks our ranks to go and retrieve it from the neck of the woman he slaughtered. He's already barreling towards another one coming in hot. So much for staying together. Asshole.

My back shifts and presses against Damon's, but my shoulders barely reach his mid-back. His scent hits me like a bat to the skull a second time, some memory resurfacing, but it's quickly replaced by the rotting smell of the Tributes as they close in on us.

"Fuck, they stink. They smell like death and rotting ass," I barely manage to gag out.

One beast launches for me, and I keep my sword high until it's in range. Its teeth are browning, decay taking root within their entire mouth. How long have they been like this? What has Arianyte done to these poor people?

I strike the Tribute down with one efficient slash across their jugular, and they scream out into the haunting woods. Quick, clean, concise. I'm a warrior. I can fight them. Their wail ping-pongs within the walls of my mind, inducing genuine terror. But despite the fear, I cannot let myself falter. My eyes widen in surprise. That attack was a kill shot. However, the man that used to be this now-monstrosity is still standing, a waterfall of near black liquid pouring onto its pale body as it stands there before me—bare chested and simply lurking.

Sam shoots his stunner rifle at several Tributes, and even though I can't see what's happening at his end, I can tell the shots aren't doing enough damage. Damon steps away from me to slash three Tributes at once, two men and one woman. Him leaving makes me feel way too exposed when two others come my way. They shove their injured comrade aside to get to me, and I dive to my knees. My sword slices the legs of one on my way down, and it howls in a painful rage. Yet, the other is on me before I can reach it.

It knocks me square in the chest—brutally.

The back of my head whacks the ground hard, and my vision is replaced with black stars. Perhaps that part is a bit of a lucky break because the screaming face bent over me is terrifyingly scary, and I don't want to see it.

"Get up, Kara, get up!" I hear Jance roaring in my ear, and in my slight delirium, I think he's here to save me. Then I realize, no, he isn't here . . . I'm thousands of feet up on a hellish platform competing in the Titan Games about to get eaten alive by what looks to be a damned zombie-person. Jance isn't here . . . my father isn't here. He's never been here. "Kid! Now! Get up now!"

Filthy hands wrap around my throat and squeeze. They shake me violently, as if I'm a child's toy being jostled so aggressively my head might pop right off.

I can't breathe . . .

"Kara! Use your crystal. Come on, kid."

Even though his voice is directly in my ear, Jance sounds so far away. I'm getting hit harder than I initially realized, the back of my head splitting as the Tribute continuously wallops my skull against the ground below, squeezing and thrashing me violently. No . . . I refuse to let this ugly fucker take me out. I've got too many people to fight for and protect. I'm not going down this early.

As if done waiting to strike, the viper that is my Elendril crystal awakens with delightful savagery.

The Tribute monster with its hands around my throat is the first to die, my antimatter taking the form of a giant blade and sticking itself directly through the chest cavity of the once-human being.

It then rips the poor creature to ribbons. Pouring out of my chest is a torrent of antimatter, loads of branches spindling off in every direction. One blasts into the skull of an older woman whose body is barely clothed. Another spike disintegrates a pair of Tributes that have Damon on his knees. I soak the forest floor until it rains with their black blood, and I soar higher than the islands floating before my eyes. All of this happens in the span of an instant as I lie on my back. It feels too good to get up and do much more than watch and enjoy my power destroying these terrible things. Freeing their souls, more like it. I don't feel guilty about it. Why should I? The crystal does all the work for me now; I don't need to tell it how to destroy. It knows how all on its own. It's amazing. Celestial. Addictive. *Powerful.*

Stars, I fucking love it.

"Kid, that's enough," Jance says through comms. He's such a hypocrite. Telling me to use it one minute and not the next. What will make him happiest, I wonder? If I pulled an Ardelle and try to remove the whole thing altogether, would my father accept me? Where is the line for his love? If I become an out-of-control monster like these Tributes, would he walk away from me then, too?

"Kara, stop!"

Snap!

The crystal's power retreats into me, snapping me back to reality—back to *me.* Damn, my head is absolutely throbbing.

I hear rustling next to me, and I'm met with those eyes again— twin to Gavrielle's.

Damon sits me up as I wince, and the moment my hand touches the back of my head, I feel the wetness of blood there.

The Sky-Fae looks at me with concern and fear, his own face covered in dark gore, cuts, and gashes of his own spewing Cherry Red blood across his muscular body. "What in star's name was that?" He rips a piece of his uniform's sleeve off, revealing a forearm of muscle made practically of marble.

I hiss when he presses the fabric to my head. "I . . ." I look down at his hand, tempted in my delirium to rip the damned glove off. I don't bother to explain what just happened. If he wants to know, he can simply look me up on the Network feeds and read all the conspiracy theories of my magic powers and how I got them. Let him decide for himself.

"Where's Sam?" I ask, ignoring Damon's question.

Damon's face turns grim. "They got him before you . . . before you saved us. Emmers took off towards Team Gold's side. Stars know if he's dead or alive. It's just you and me now."

Guilt hits me harder than the pain in my head at the news of Sam. I didn't know him for long, but I thought he seemed like a decent kid. Sadly, I was too late. I saved one, however, and I suppose if I had to choose, I'd choose to save the Gav look-alike.

Stars, I sure hope Ardelle is having better luck than I am.

CHAPTER 27

Somehow, Damon and I make it all the way across the platform to Team Gold's side without another incident. Thank the stars because, if I didn't have the time to recover from that Tribute's attack, I doubt I would have been very effective in any battle.

For whatever reason, Damon stays with me. He walks twice as slow as his long gait would typically take him, all to keep pace with me. The drones don't find us very interesting and eventually putter off to other contestants.

Jance and the others have been giving me various forms of encouragement, mostly through the lens this time. I'm guessing they'll think Damon might be able to hear any comms communication with his pointed ears, with even finer hearing than mine.

The brush is thicker on this side of the Sky Dais, which is both good and bad.

"We're likely going to start running into other contestants," Damon says, and it's exactly what I was thinking, too. "How are you feeling?"

"Better." And it's true. The thudding in my skull is now only a dull ache, and I feel my well of energy replenishing. We draw our swords.

The two of us stalk through the forest on stealthy feet, watching for every twig and fallen leaf. Our goal is to sneak past other players, not engage them. It doesn't seem like the wild Tributes have made it out this far. Makes sense—most of the danger is in crossing the Dais. I fear what else is out there waiting for us.

I see the alien part of Damon in how unnaturally still he can become, a thing I watched in awe when Gav would get caught doing something he wasn't supposed to be—which was often. With his stillness and my ability to hide behind nearly anything, we make it all the way to Team Gold's home base with only needing to engage four enemy members.

Their home base castle looks like ours. The easy part is over. It's getting that flag that's going to be difficult.

"The place is crawling with them," I whisper as the two of us duck behind a tree, practically sitting on top of him to keep the two of us hidden behind the trunk. I really hope Ardelle isn't lurking out in these trees somewhere, watching this. He may get the wrong idea . . . but I can't lie, it's not a bad view.

It seems as if Damon is thinking of something insane because, when he finally looks at me, those violet eyes are a burning flame.

"What?" I demand, feeling like I know this look of mischief. "Whatever it is—hell no."

"I mean this with all the respect, but I'm sure people underestimate you. If you come running out of the woods, looking all disheveled like you do, with an act of 'please save me, I'm a helpless cute young girl'"—his voice travels to a higher pitch than mine as he mimics a female in the most ridiculous way I've ever heard—"then they'll come to your aid. I have no doubt. Not with how you look right now, which is like shit, by the way. I can sneak in during your distraction and come out with that flag. I can take on anyone they've got in there."

"Not everyone."

A silver brow raises. A challenge. I roll my eyes. What's with men and their little pissing contests? Jeez.

"I don't know about this plan . . ." I don't like having to use my sex and/or my sexuality to get what I want. But this is for Pacey, and degrading myself is a price I'll willingly pay.

"Do it." The message comes over my lens. Sighing heavily, I reach my hand out to Damon as a sign of solidarity, but he does something bizarre. Instead of taking it, he slaps it on one side, and on instinct, I smack the other. Before we know it, we're fist-bumping like a pair of old pals. Gasping, I jump off him, almost revealing our location. He also looks at me in confusion, unsure if a glitch just happened, or what.

"An old friend of mine used to do something similar with me when we were kids . . . did you ever live in an orphanage as a kid?"

"Never." His voice is deep and clear in this regard, at least. "Not only did Arianyte kill my parents, but they also enslaved me. I spent the majority of my youth in an assassin's camp run by the occupation. They suspect I'm dead. I hope to win these games and finally get a chance to be within striking distance of the occupation's leader. I want him dead at my feet."

I thought the Silent Breath and the Hijacked were bad, but child assassin camps, seriously? Is there anything Arianyte won't do?

However, his motives pose a problem for me. If someone has gone through what he claims and is after a prize such as his own vengeance, that means he's highly motivated. I know from experience. This is all good and well for me now, while he's on my team. But that's going to change when we go back to playing for single wins again.

I tell him plainly, "Well, you're not the only person in this game who's got a grudge match with the Arianyte prince."

CHAPTER 28

SPPARROW ENFORCEMENT IS AUTHORIZED TO ESTABLISH CHECKPOINTS AND ROADBLOCKS THROUGHOUT ZONE TERRITORIES TO MONITOR AND CONTROL MOVEMENT. ANY ATTEMPTS TO EVADE OR BYPASS THESE CHECKPOINTS WILL BE MET WITH LETHAL FORCE.

"Help me!" I cry, fake hobbling on one leg as I stumble my way directly towards Team Gold's home base. "I've been attacked!"

A few of the guys guarding the front of their home base immediately abandon their posts, just as Damon predicted they would.

Laying it on thick, I fall right before the men reach me, crashing myself into the dry dirt of the Sky Dais.

"Stars, is she okay?" a younger guy asks, a little chubby but muscular, and he sounds genuinely concerned.

A pair of combat boots encompasses my vision. "Hey, what do you mean you were attacked? By one of us? I don't think we're allowed to help you . . ."

"Oh, don't be a dick, dude. She's obviously hurt," the first guy says. He lifts me up, and I feign weakness as he does.

Shaking my head, I look at the man in the combat boots. He looks militaristic, with tightly cropped blond hair. Likely a twenty-something. "It wasn't Team Gold," I inform. "There are crazy people out in the woods. They're mad with fever and attacking people. They got loose. Attacked. You're not safe out here."

Suspicious as my act may be, it begins drawing a crowd of other players. The blond military dude asks, "Why didn't you go back to your own team and warn them?" Whispers of a few others makes my cheeks heat.

A suggestion pops up on my lens. "You were closer to them and ran in the only safe direction." I'll take it. When I say as much to this group of guys, they seem to buy it.

"Well, she looks like she's been attacked. That's enough for me," another Titan says, a young Asian Terran man. "I'm concerned about these infected people you spoke of. You're sure they were diseased?"

This part of the story is, unfortunately, all true. After I describe the Tributes to them, I reach back and find half dried blood matted into my hair, and the others see the sticky red on my hands. "I don't think your team is safe out there."

"She's just trying to get us to bring our guys back in so her team doesn't get their flag stolen," Mr. Combat Boots says, looking down at me incredulously. A few others seem to agree, and I feel anxiety begin to bloom. What's taking Damon so long? He entered their building the moment the two men guarding it ran up to me. He's had ample time to run up there and grab the damned thing. I hope he didn't run into Ardelle. If he's here instead of going after Silver's flag, he'd be posted inside. I don't care how good or motivated Damon may be. He's not better than Ardelle and his Elendril crystal.

"We should tie her up, hold her hostage until the game is over," Mr. Combat Boots says, and my stomach roils at the fact that so many of these jerks seem to agree.

"So much for trying to do you people a favor," I mumble, and the sweet guy who offered to help me throws me a sad smile.

"Guys, come on," he says, trying to reason with them. "If we keep an eye on her, no fowl. She's no good to her team with us anyway."

Mr. Combat Boots doesn't agree. "No, I remember this one from the preliminaries. She's too fierce to be a helpless little girl lost in the woods."

Well, at least for his own sake, he's not a total idiot. Unfortunately, I was betting on men being their typical selves and thinking with their less intelligent heads.

Another man standing behind me throws his own ideas out there, just to see how many of his fellow men bite. "Why not have some fun with her while we're at it? Arianyte says there's no rules. Hell, we can use her up and kill her if we like. People die all the time in these games. Toss her over the edge once we're done, and it'll look like an accident."

This is why I hate men.

I stand, all signs of my physical ailments long gone. The twinkle in Combat Boots's eyes reveals he's fully convinced of my guilt. And that's fine . . .

Because I am guilty.

The very tip of my sword's hilt is slightly pointed, not enough to cut or anything but hell if it doesn't hurt when it hits.

I'm overly impressed with my own speed and grace as I unsheathe my sword from my back, swing it gracefully a time or two, and ram the sword's hilt right into Mr. Combat Boots's sternum. The cracking of his bone comes first, his howls of pain second, him thudding to the dirt is third.

Hushed whispers of awe and impressed howls follow, the chilly wind blowing my hair around my cheeks and the cameras almost as close. They caught all that, it seems.

Jance's voice comes through comms, ever the disappointed father. "Was that truly necessary? If you were going to hit someone, it should have been the one who threatened you."

"He wouldn't stop running his mouth," I say aloud, speaking both to Jance and this group of men. *Come on, Damon.* "And I don't like being questioned when all I was trying to do is warn my fellow Titans of a common enemy. That being said, any sick pervert who even thinks about putting his hands on me, let alone says it out loud like it's some kind of bonus round in a video game, will get their balls cut by my blade."

Trinity comes on comms this time. "You tell 'em, girl. I'm totally taking this sound and uploading it right now."

The men surrounding me look either horrified as they clutch their legs a little too tightly or shocked that I'd have the gall to speak to them like that. I feel them inching in on me, and I grip my sword firmly. Nobody speaks, but nobody needs to. It's inherent in the tension clawing through the air, the narrowing of their eyes and the bracing of their gaits. Some men hold back. Some don't.

My mark tingles in response, sensing danger. I knew this was a bad idea from the start. But if I can go toe-to-toe with an entire Nest of SSPARROWs, I can take on these goons. They're not as trained as the sky-rats, despite their colorful array of weaponry. That's the threat here. Most of these weapons can kill, unlike the Nests, who were strictly ordered not to end my life. I brace for their attack when a horrific roar shatters the tension.

Each head snaps towards the direction of the sound, not sure what made it but confident that it isn't human. The snarls are closing in, and a few of the men look aghast that there was some truth to my story, after all.

As if his timing couldn't be better, Damon comes blasting through a window—broken glass, a shit-eating grin on his face, and the gold flag in hand.

Holy stars, he's as crazy as a moon fox.

"She's been a damned distraction this whole time!" one of them yells, and it sounds like the pervert who suggested he and the others have their way with me.

The animalistic roar echoes in the forest again as I point my finger at the man, allowing my crystal to build. "That's right, dickhead. I was. Sorry you don't get to tie me up and fulfill whatever sick, perverted fantasy was playing out in your head, but I'll make sure you never get the chance ever again."

Before he can reply, I take a reserved shot at him with my crystal, straight in between his legs.

 190

The rapist screams.

Then a pack of off-world hellhounds, jet-black fur with Harvest Moon-colored eyes, triple the size of a German Shepherd, come bolting our way, maws open and dripping with blood.

Damon seizes me by the wrist before the men around us can react. Perfect timing because Mr. Rapist is writhing on the ground with just enough blood coming out of him to draw the hellhounds to him instead of us.

"Did you just send that electric magic of yours into that man's balls?" Damon asks, half horrified, half impressed.

I shrug as we dash away, echoes of screams from their home base erupting behind us. "Well, he did suggest he and his buddies rape and murder me, so, yeah, I did."

"Damn," he says, voice slightly breathless and face bloodied up from his encounter with the window and whoever he ran into on the inside. "Remind me never to piss you off. But otherwise, nice. There is no honor in such disgusting acts."

"None at all."

CHAPTER 29

"Is it too much to ask for these hellhounds not to come after us, too?" I complain as we run like wild animals ourselves, zigzagging through trees and mushrooms, barely managing to keep from tripping on foliage. Even the cameras are having trouble keeping up with us. Surprisingly, Damon doesn't sprint ahead of me. Rather, he stays on par with my pace, as fast as I can go with my stature.

His voice is joking when he responds. "You can always blast them in the balls. That'll get them off our hides."

"Or I can blast you in the balls for continuing this conversation when it's clearly not the time for it."

Damon only snickers back at me.

I dare risk a glance back, and it appears like four of the hellhounds are in pursuit.

I shout over to Damon. "We've got to stop, so we can shake them. There's four. Two and two?"

"Back-to-back?" he suggests, and I remember how we fought with the wild Tributes.

My nod is all the confirmation he needs.

Practically skidding to a stop, the two of us reverse our direction and face the hellhounds.

As they near, I feel a twinge of guilt. I'm an animal person. I don't like hurting them in any circumstances. I'm sure Arianyte has done something to them to force them to act this aggressively, and they're likely not the bloodthirsty beasts they're forced to be.

"Try not to kill them," I suggest to Damon. "If you can, knock them out instead. They're innocent."

He looks at me like I'm insane, then stares down at the beasts as they finally reach us.

The first one chooses me as its target and lunges for my neck, maw open wide and level with my neck. The only action I can take that isn't fatal is throwing my sword up horizontally. With one hand on the hilt, the other on the blade itself, the Hell beast latches onto the sword like it would a dog bone. It propels me backwards past Damon, and I stagger until my back is thrust up against a tree. Soon, I'm forced all the way to my ass just to get some leverage. Its long pointed teeth stop an inch or two from my throat as its mouth clamps down on the dark steel. The force of this animal ravaging on my sword is agonizing. I'm barely strong enough to hold it off, and as I push against it, it shoves back. We both tremble. The beast snarls and growls wild and eager to taste flesh as we each wildly battle for control of the other. My arms burn and feel like they're made of sand.

"You second guessing that no-killing thing yet?" I hear Damon yell over at me as I grit my teeth hard. He's, somehow, keeping the other three at bay.

Using my legs, I wiggle them under the canine's belly and kick, but that does nothing. It isn't fazed. Again and again, I try, but the more I fight, the angrier the animal becomes. Its eyes are all wrong, like its sole purpose in life is to destroy and kill and tear whatever it sees into ribbons.

"Kill them!" I shout back, knowing my mercy is a fallacy under these circumstances. I can't help them. I can't save them. The only kindness I can give them is death.

To my left, a cry of one dying comes swiftly, but I'm still too focused on my own situation to pay much attention to Damon.

The hellhound is exuding so much pressure on my blade it's creating new cracks within its dark-amethyst veneer. No way on this green Earth am I letting this demon take this weapon from me. It's too important. My connection to it—to Zariya—is too strong. Unfortunately, I have no choice but to call forth an even more ruthless monster to fight the one before me, despite my guilt.

The power builds quickly, but it's not quick enough. The canine whips its neck sideways, causing the hand holding the blade to be cut and out of instinct I let go. Once the beast realizes the change in the dynamic, for whatever reason, it begins to run in a random direction. With my Elendril sword still firmly within its jaws. Not willing to sacrifice my sword, I hold on to the hilt as the hellhound drags both me and it across the Dais floor.

We're far from Damon in a blink of an eye, my face and chest racking against all sorts of twigs, rocks, dirt, and stars-know-what else.

What the actual fuck is happening?

Blast it, a voice tells me. The crystal. It speaks yet again.

I don't hesitate this time.

With my free hand, I create a ball of antimatter no bigger than a baseball, but that's enough.

I chuck it blindly in front of me, unable to open my eyes unless I want a cornea full of debris. The yelp of the animal comes first, and it immediately releases the sword and me by extension. It's dead before it skids to the dirt, charred, steaming, and missing body parts.

I lay there on my stomach, arm feeling as if it's been ripped out of its socket.

Since there's so much emphasis on balls all of a sudden, I have to say, this sucks *massive* balls.

"What the fuck, girl? You okay?" I hear Trinity say on comms, her voice as stunned as I feel. "Oh, umm, your dad—he wants to talk with yo—"

"Kara?" Jance's voice is urgent, concerned, worried. "That looked rough. What happened? We couldn't see much through the lens."

Thankfully, I had the lens in the one eye that was closest to the ground. It probably saved my eye. My other one, however, burns with irritation as I continue to lie there, body weak and feeling as if it's been through a stampede.

It takes me awhile to respond, but Jance waits for me. "The animal had hold of the sword. I wasn't willing to let it go. It dragged me through the forest. It's dead now."

My voice sounds weak, even to me.

"Is there anyone else around you?" he asks, and I forcefully take a peek at my surroundings.

"Doesn't look like it."

"Good," His voice is stronger now. "Rest. Your comrade had the flag. Hopefully, he'll get it back in time and this'll all be over with."

My laugh is cynical at best. "Sure. Until I've got to do this two more times. This is insanity."

The pause on the other line is agony for me.

"Kara . . ." Something in his voice has shifted, and it doesn't sound right. "There's a person hiding in the trees directly in front of you, and he's huge."

CHAPTER 30

A twig snaps somewhere to my right, and I straighten.

Looking into the trees, I scan every mushroom and bush and rock for any signs of the other team, but nobody is here. What did Jance see? There aren't any cameras or drones puttering around, so I must be off the beaten path or on the edge of the arena. It's also unlikely Damon will find me, either. I should locate him—and quickly. It's too risky being so far out here alone.

Yet, that spindly gut feeling continues to creep through my body, creeping up my spine like a demon with wicked claws.

Someone is watching me.

Creeping. Waiting. Anticipating.

I hear a deep growl and a sharp intake of breath from directly behind me. A giant shadow blocks out the sun.

A flash of fangs catches my eyes as I turn just in time to see the gray-skinned alien from earlier flying right for me, but I'm too late to do a damned thing. He's too close. My body goes all tingly as the extra completely encases me in a vise of his giant arms. Then he buries his teeth into the soft tissue between my neck and shoulders.

I scream.

My chest explodes.

The shadowy alien only gets a short drink of my blood because I rip his fangs from my flesh while my crystal fries him simultaneously, zapping him straight off me as if I were an electric fence. I watch as his body is thrown across the forest floor, rolling several times before he hits a large mushroom and rips it right from the earth. He lies there, smoking and motionless.

I guess he was my stalker, after all.

Fuck.

Did he just actually bite my neck like a damned vampire? If I hadn't turned around when I had, he would have ripped my jugular completely out of my throat, no problem. What in the actual fu—

I'm hit from behind, my head ringing like a bell so hard I see stars. My vision tilts sideways before it blurs.

Immediately, I bring my crystal's power back to my fingertips, but I'm too late this time. The feel of cold metal wraps around my neck and panic instantly replaces the feeling of my magic's surge.

No . . . Stars, no, not the collar again.

Malakyte finally comes to remove me from this game. He's put a collar around my neck to block my magic and has come to wrench me away. Fear clasps me like a vise and paralyzes me; I can't move, can't even fight back.

I hear snickering laughter from behind me as I'm kicked in the back, face slamming into the dirt.

"I thought you'd be a lot taller for how much of a threat you're supposed to be," a feminine voice chimes wickedly from above me, filled with cold indifference and that woman-on-woman condescension. Given the dark extra that attacked me moments ago, I'm guessing the female voice is the blue extra that was with him earlier. It must be. It's definitely not Malakyte. She walks over to me, a pair of feminine boots stopping before my face, as I'm forced down on my stomach by a much heavier body. This third person plops on top of me, ripping my arms around to tie them behind my back. This has to be the alien with the yellow eyes, then. Shit . . .

Getting a bit of my senses back, I struggle with all my might, but I'm too weak to get out of this hold. Who are these people, and why are they doing this?

The male extra on top rips my arms aggressively. "I thought you'd be a hell of a lot tougher to catch, too. Although, you did get a good lick in on our friend. That dumbass should have known better than to try to play with his food."

The female squats down to look at me, my teeth bared at her. Yup, she's one of the three Titan competitors who approached us on our flight up to the Sky Dais. The man who bit me comes to stand beside her. It didn't take him very long to recover from my crystal attack, although he looks like shit because of it, body burned and bloodied, clothing practically scorched off.

They've caught me . . .

"Our Mistress will be so thrilled to know we got the Star," the dark one says, voice so deep it's almost animalistic. A drop of my blood remains on his chin.

Mistress? What the fuck do they mean by Mistress? Who would . . . Oh no. Naresteé . . . She's the one who orchestrated this. It has to be. She hates me enough to do it, to go behind Malakyte's back and have me assassinated. What would Naresteé want from me? Only one of two things . . . and both leave me dead.

I feel rope of some kind being wrapped tightly around my wrists, and no matter how much I struggle and buck my body, I can't get loose.

"Damon!" I cry out, my voice panicked. I barely know the guy, but I hope beyond hope he's still out there somewhere close enough to hear me. Would he even come? In turn, I shout for Ardelle, throwing my panic down the connection that our crystals share. What I hear in turn is the tremble in my voice, the fear bouncing off the walls of my own mind. This isn't good. Whatever is going on here, it has nothing to do with games, and I know they have something far more nefarious intended for me. And without the use of my crystal, I'm just a small girl. I'm helpless. No, fuck that, I'm not helpless. I've trained for this. I can free myself. I can find a way.

"Shut her up," the female says cruelly.

Rougher than necessary, a disgusting tasting rag that smells of diesel or oil is shoved into my mouth and tied around the back of my head, my hair caught in the tie. I don't stop screaming at them through the gag.

"Oh, what do we have here?" The yellow-eyed extra on top of me touches my ear, and like an idiot, my cries and struggles stop on a dime. "I see. You're a little cheater, aren't you? I knew you couldn't have gotten this far without some help. This whole time, we thought you were talking to yourself while you were sitting out here. I knew better."

The man digs out the earpiece from my ear against my protests. Jance's panicked voice goes with it.

"Hello, hello," he says into it as the other two snicker with soft laughter. "Whoever's listening, I hope you enjoy the show. You get to hear her die. Just know that there was nothing you could have done to save her. People die in this tournament all the time, especially vulnerable little flowers such as this one. Enjoy the show."

He tosses the earpiece down by my face. Then his hands gingerly glide their way across my body, and I scream in response.

Get out of this fucking collar! I order myself, knowing I've done it once. I can do it again. *Don't let this happen.*

"We don't have a ton of time," the extra woman says, knocking the man off me. "The Mistress told us these arenas are monitored heavily. We take the crystal and get out of here. Kill her now."

She kicks my ribs for emphasis. So, Naresteé is after my crystal, then . . .

I try to crawl away now that I'm free of his weight, but with my hands tied so tightly around my back, I don't get far.

"Awww, look. She's trying to escape. How adorable," he taunts. If it weren't for the creepy yellow eyes, he'd look human. The extra picks up my sword from where it sits on the ground. "This is some weapon. I wonder how it's going to feel being killed by your own blade?"

"The crystal resides in the Terran heart," the woman instructs. "Stab her there. No, the left side, you idiot."

"Here?" he asks, hovering the tip of the blade over my back, but he knows he's in the right spot. I feel my own sword's tip coming through my clothes and into my skin. I know what it feels like to be stabbed by an Elendril weapon, and there's no Ahren on this Dais to save me this time.

Sparks bounce around my fingertips but barely, and this situation is too chaotic for me to focus. My power builds inside me like volcanic lava, the same as last time. My mind spins as I feel my sword cut my flesh, my muffled sobs breaking through the gag and echoing out into the woods. Yet, all I can think of is Jance . . . and Gav and Ardelle and everyone else. They're listening and watching this go down, likely feeling helpless and as powerless as me.

"Oh, look, she's crying." The man bends down to look at me, a smile on his face and glee in those haunting yellow eyes. I pour my rage and the promise of his death into the glare I give him, feeling so much anger. At them. At myself. I can't believe I allowed this to happen.

"Wait, did the Mistress say we destroy the heart first and then take this crystal, or that's just where we get it once the girl's dead? If we accidentally destroy it, *we'll* be dead." I feel the pressure of my sword ease up slightly.

Sounding annoyed, the female says, "Just slit her throat, then, and let's be done with it before some idiot comes along and we have to kill two pathetic Terrans."

The blue-skinned bitch must be the one leading the three of them. The shadowy one hardly speaks, but his eyes are as cold as I've ever seen as he frowns at me.

The alien holding my sword stands on either side of me. I try to swing my shoulders around enough in an attempt to trip him, but that only results in all three of them laughing at me again.

Remember what Deimos said that night at the games when you broke through the collar last time, I try to remind myself.

But there's simply no time.

 200

The extra is holding my own blade at my throat, above the collar.

I feel its sting before I can register that I'll be dead in less than a minute.

Jance and Ardelle flash across my mind, their faces . . . my father watching me die through my eyes. I close them, sparing him the nightmares of this moment as best that I can. The sounds will be haunting enough . . . Regret plows into me. I just told the man I'm his daughter, and now he's about to watch me die? Who cast such a cruel hex on this man? He doesn't deserve to see this.

And stars, I should've told Ardelle how I truly feel for him. And Pacey . . . I've doomed her, too.

I've doomed them all.

CHAPTER 31

SSPARROW ENFORCEMENT OFFICERS POSSESS THE AUTHORITY TO STOP, QUESTION, AND DETAIN ANY CITIZEN REGARDLESS OF CAUSE. EXCESSIVE FORCE IS PERMITTED AT THE DISCRETION OF THE OFFICER.

My blood drips down the front of my chest. My tears meet the hands of the person about to kill me as he holds my face skywards. The muscles in my neck scream as my Elendril blade betrays me. Will they take it, do fowl things with it? Who will find my body once I'm dead and gone? What will happen to my crystal? Will Jance be okay? Will Pacey and Ardelle?

I try to zone out their wicked laughter. The wind whistles through the branches of the trees like a phantom song, orchestrated by some lost soul who bestows her melody upon me in hopes I wouldn't die alone.

Then I hear a gasping, wet sound, and all at once, the weight of the man at my back collapses on top of me with a loud grunt. The blade at my throat loses all its tension and falls, and I sag in relief. I desperately try to push him off me, but he's too heavy.

"What the hell?" the woman gasps, voice angry and confused. The surprised yelp that comes from her lips next is more gratifying to me than I expect it to be, and I see her body fall to the dirt moments later, blood spraying from the crack in her chest.

Damon or Ardelle must have found me. Elation and hope fill my heart that I might survive this.

The only one left is the gray-skinned extra, and I hear nothing but the pounding of bodies tussling. I can't see either, just their feet. Whoever is fighting the man who took a bite out of me is putting up one hell of a fight against the fanged extra. Grunts and hisses fly, but neither speak to me or each other. Not even sixty seconds pass when a sudden slicing sound is followed by a few hollow thunks, and the brawl stops . . . It sounds a lot like a head rolling . . . but who's head? My savior's or my soon-to-be murderer's?

The weight of the dead man is kicked off my back and then I feel cold hands touching the collar around my neck. I gasp, flinching away from the touch. My face is still facing the ground, drops of my blood pooling under me and mixing with the dry dirt below.

The collar is removed fast, too fast. As the binds at my wrist are cut, I immediately rip the gag from my mouth and flip around. Then I'm eye-to-eye with the last person I expected to see as my rescuer.

"Malakyte," I breathe his name, genuinely shocked and wide eyed. *What the fuck is he doing here?*

He's covered in alien blood. Dark green and violet is splattered all across his face, chest, and immaculate clothing. He leans over me, face cold and impassive, yet his eyes . . . they're full of emotions and fury and . . . relief? But there's more, too. I sense sorrow there.

"What—" I begin, but I don't even know what to ask I'm so dumbfounded by his presence.

Kneeling closer into me, he presses his freezing hand around my throat in a grasp of ice. My instincts are to push him away, wildly striking against him, but he holds me in place. My body is too shocked to fight back.

"My skin will slow the bleeding."

I stop. He's right. As much as I hate to admit it, his hand does feel like soothing ice against my neck. Blood continues to drip down my front and through his fingers as I allow him to continue to try and staunch the bleeding. I need to release my crystal's energy soon, so if he tries anything funny, he'll get another scar on his face.

Keeping eye contact, I lay my hands over his own and press down on it. He responds in turn, squeezing a touch more. Pressure will stop the bleeding, too.

"Twice in a couple of weeks, you've had your hand around my throat, and it hasn't been to kill me. You're not a very good villain, Malakyte. Why are you here?" I ask. I'm scared to look at him in the stark daylight, but I force myself to keep eye contact no matter what. "How did you even know . . ."

Malakyte smirks confidently at me. "I had a personal surveillance drone monitoring you the moment you entered my Titan Games, in case . . ."

In case what? In case I divulge my plans. Told someone what was going to happen after I win these stupid games. I should have known.

"I would have seen it," I say, looking around and seeing only the sky and trees.

Pointing to nothing in the sky, I follow his finger when I spot what looks to be a fly buzzing about seven feet in the air. It's practically invisible it's so small. Taking my one opportunity, I zap the little guy with my crystal, allowing some of that pressure out at the same time. It's overkill, but I make my point.

"Well, that was foolish. Figuring if it wasn't for that drone, you'd be dead by now." Malakyte's voice is as cold as the hand against my throat.

"I'll have to take care of myself from now on," I say, pushing his hand off my neck before he decided to choke me out instead of helping me. Hopefully, it was enough to stop the bleeding because I don't want anyone to touch me after what just happened.

Grabbing my sword before he can try and steal it, I take several steps backwards as the blade slides into the sheath. We stand, facing each other, like enemies should. The scar on his face somehow makes him even more handsome as he glares down at me with as much hatred as I have for him. Why'd he save me? Is Narestée the Mistress? And why does she want my crystal and me dead along with it?

"Leave the games, Karalevine. While you still can. I won't be able to save you a second time."

This again.

"Maybe I don't need to be saved," I posture, but it's total bullshit, and his lips tilt up in a way that shows me he knows it is.

Wiping the blood on my neck with my sleeve, I come back with the only phrase I know that'll convey my point the clearest. "Let Pacey go. What could you really do with her that's worth keeping this up between us? What's worth all this political pressure? Let her go, and I'll stop all of it. The Resistance will ease up, and we can end this war between you and me."

Not really, but I'll say anything to get Pacey back.

Malakyte pauses before replying, and it seems as if he's genuinely considering my offer.

"I can't do that."

My arms cross, sticky with blood, dirt, and sweat.

The tension from both of us wanting to embrace and yet destroy the other crackling off us like lightning, and his words only intensify it. I want to hate him for not letting Pacey go, but he did just save my life. Villains typically don't rescue the lives of their adversaries, so what's his play?

Or can there be some small pinprick of hope, a kernel of redemption that exists within his shredded sliver of a soul? Can Malakyte be saved? Can I salvage his soul, as he saved me? Is he even worth it, after all he's done? Maybe he's changed? What he risked by coming into the arena like this . . . if he were caught, he'd lose all credibility. The Terrans would certainly turn on him. Yet, he jumped in and gambled it all to protect me. He risked so much to assure my life was spared.

He reaches his hand out to me, hands stained with my blood. "Come back with me, Karalevine. I'm not sure what you believe about me, but I have never wished harm to come to you. Be with me and, like you say, end the war between the two of us. Why else do you think I've allowed you to do all this nonsense?"

I stare at his hand with wide eyes.

"Let me give you the world and the life you deserve. Stop suffering. Stop bottling up all that rage within you. End the war within yourself that tells you we can't be together because, if we were, you'd be a bad person. That's why you resist your feelings for me, isn't it? Because I make you look like the villain instead of the hero you pretend to be. But being a hero isn't the real you."

My pulse races, his words a genuine offer.

I certainly don't feel like this great hero, mostly because I don't automatically reject the offer . . .

It just sucks that it has to be so complicated. It'd be easier if I fully hated him, if what he said wasn't spot on.

But he's wrong about one thing, and that is that I'm not pretending to be a hero. I am one, and I'm going to rescue Pacey and save this planet.

"I'm sorry about your face," I say, before I turn in the opposite direction of the prince of Arianyte and run.

"Karalevine," he yells, and for the life of me, I don't know why I stop. "When you're unsure, go fast. As fast as you can."

I take his advice, and I run like my life depends on it.

CHAPTER 32

I'm relieved to see Malakyte isn't following me, and I slow down once I get out of his sight. As I walk, I notice message after message coming in on the lens. I've been too distracted to read them, but I can now. I also realize I left the comms unit back there, so they can't hear me.

Jance is freaking out, as he should be. That was awfully close, but even though I'm bleeding heavily, if the slice at my throat was serious, I'd have been dead already. I throw a bloodied thumbs-up in front of myself, indicating to them I'm alright. I'm not. I can barely keep walking. My legs are jelly, and my blood sugar is so low I could faint at any minute. The adrenaline has finally purged itself due to the last few hours of pure madness, and I'm weak.

This isn't good.

I can't face one more opponent, not one more fight. I don't think I can even call forth my crystal now if I needed to, my energy completely zapped.

I also can't believe all that happened with those extras, and how Malakyte asked me to leave with him . . .

An abrupt sound causes me to jump. I reach for my sword when I see Damon coming into view from within the trees. My body sags in relief at the sight of him, and I can't explain why.

"You look like shit," Damon tells me as he approaches, his jog light and effortless despite the fact his face and uniform are as ripped and bloodied as my own.

"Same goes for you. Looks like you took out the hounds okay by yourself?"

Taking more than a casual glance at me, his face frowns in concern. "You're bleeding severely."

Without another word, he comes to stand behind me as he pulls a gray piece of cloth from his uniform pocket. Gently, he presses it against my throat and begins tying it around the back of my neck. I think it's an odd thing to hold in your uniform, but I'm too tired and too grateful to give it much more thought than that. The other team's flag is also tucked into his pocket, he informs me when I ask him about it.

"I thought I heard someone calling for me. It was you, wasn't it? You were attacked? By whom? This is too clean for a beast attack."

"I took care of them," I answer quickly. "It looks worse than it actually is."

Slowly, we continue forward, our pace slowed only by my weakened state. I tell him several times to go on without me, but he refuses to budge.

"So, should I expect an ambush after whoever gave you that wound comes looking for you?" He's pressing about that again, but I can't let him know anything. It'll only put him in danger.

I shake my head, but it hurts. "No. Like I said, I took care of it."

Why am I protecting Malakyte? Admitting to murder—not very classy. However, it doesn't seem to faze him. *He is a child assassin*, I remind myself. They do see death every single day.

All thoughts snap from my mind when an arrow flies past my face, directly between Damon and me. It strikes the closest tree, reverberating from the sheer force of the impact.

No . . . stars, no.

As excited as I am to see him, I also really don't want to see him.

Damon reacts first by swinging his body around, but he's too late. Ardelle pounces on him like a cat. I'm shoved out of the way by his gravity magic, and I can do nothing but watch as the two go at it. I'm mesmerized by them both.

Blow by blow, they battle each other, both practical gods in their own right. Ardelle moves as if he's been doing this his entire life. Damon is otherworldly and so smooth, long hair and braids flying around him. Ardelle lands the first punch, a terribly painful right hook directly at Damon's chin. Damon doesn't appreciate it and comes back with a roar and a ferocious hit of his own to Ardelle's gut. My hands cover my stomach in sympathy pain as I wince—he got Ardelle good. I can tell by the saliva that forcefully ejected itself from his mouth.

I go to shout for Ardelle, except my voice comes out weak and lacking conviction. The pang in my gut tells me I sort of don't want him to win this fight. Because, if he wins, that means I lose.

And I can't lose.

The boys continue their ferocious brawl, getting more violent by the second. It's way too close for Ardelle to use his arrows, and he'll only use his crystal if he knows he can't win any other way. He's no longer using it on me because I can move freely. Should I join in? Although if I jumped into the fray, I'm not sure I'd know who to fight with.

Why am I being like this? Ardelle is my boyfriend. I'd fight with him, right? Morally, yes. Strategically, stupid. I know we all agreed that, if either Ardelle or I made it to Malakyte, then both were as good as the other. But I really want it to be me who wins.

I gasp as Damon's grip on Ardelle's neck drives him down on his back, and it seems to shake the entire Sky Dais. They're both on the ground now. Even though all the breath is taken from his lungs, Ardelle manages to wrap his legs around Damon and flip him so he's on top and in control. My lip is raw as I bite at the skin there, so nervous I'm tasting copper.

Damon doesn't take to being on the bottom very well, and their scuffle transfers the power over and over again. Each time, one of them gains the upper hand, and the other finds a way to steal it right back. Elbows and knuckles fly like bullets. Knees and feet also make an appearance, and it's getting so bad I wonder if I should step in.

Could I even stop them? I've never seen Ardelle battle so ferociously, so primal. He's typically so calm, so steady, when he fights. But this is much dirtier and scrappier than normal.

Blood is spilling from both, and each blow they give hurts the other. Why is this bothering me so much? I just met Damon. He's nobody . . .

That isn't true, though, is it? I've been seeing him as Gav this entire time, despite not truly knowing if it is him. That's why I can't stand watching this fight, because I can't imagine the two of them going at each other so brutally.

Somehow, as both men balance on their knees, Ardelle gets Damon in a choke hold from behind. I can see Ardelle pulling as hard as he can on his wrist, arm looped around Damon's throat. Damon isn't making it easy for him, not by a long shot. He's thrashing and bucking and elbowing Ardelle in the ribs. Damon hits him again. Then again and again and again. Each one breaks my heart so badly.

I can't watch this anymore.

Not after everything else I've been through today.

I open my mouth to shout at them when I feel it—that familiar pull in my stomach.

Damon is slammed face-first onto the forest floor, unmoving. As if he were dead.

As if he can't move a muscle, the gravity far too intense.

Ardelle's eyes glow red.

This fight is over.

The next thing he does is rummage through Damon's pockets, grabbing his team's gold flag.

I run up to them, both men panting like dogs and covered in blood, sweat, and forest debris. Ardelle's eyes are soft as I approach, one of them already forming a bruise around it. Although, he can still see what I'm eyeballing, and it's clutched in his hands.

"Thumbelina . . ." he warns gently, bringing both his hands up in a nonthreatening posture. "No."

My jaw aches from how hard I'm clenching it, like I may crack it in half completely.

He can't do this. He can't come here and take this win from me. Not after I bled and almost died for it.

"Give it back, Ardelle," I don't ask, I demand.

My voice must be firm.

When Ardelle doesn't respond, his face a little shocked, I explain further. "I went through too much to get that thing."

He knows I mean more than just today.

His shoulders bounce as he continues to catch his breath, and with his new dark hair and glowing red eyes, he looks utterly different from the guy I first met. Although the red embers within his pupils are a bit eerie, I see that he does consider what I'm saying. He'll give it back to me. I know he will. I trust him now.

"I can't, Thumbelina. Not this time."

What?

"Something terrible is happening to Pacey. I can feel it. I haven't been able to shake it. That surgery can happen at any moment. They've likely already done terrible things to her, and I can't let it continue. She's my sister. *I* have to save her."

I can't exactly tell him he shouldn't go save his sister, but this sends such an unfair pain through me. I do not expect it, and I can't accept this.

"So, you just waltz up in here and take it from me, and what? You expect me to let you?"

He can't stop his light chuckle before it comes, and he knows right then he fucked up.

"I can kick your ass just as easily as that guy." I point to Damon, still under Ardelle's gravity control. I'm bluffing big time because, in my state right now, I probably can't beat Ardelle. Not fair and square, anyway. But the anger building up is fueling me with more strength, so maybe after this recent conversation, I might have a shot.

Ardelle tries to placate me.

"I know you're strong, Thumbelina, stronger than anyone else I know. That isn't why I laughed."

"Bull."

In a flash, I snap and reach for the gold flag, and I manage to grasp it in my hands, but Ardelle keeps hold of it.

He circles away from me, holding the damned thing high out of my reach.

"I'm going to end you," I say angrily, even though I'm not serious in the slightest. He even smiles just a little. He knows I don't mean it like that, no matter how angry I am at him.

Jumping, I try for it again, but he's too damned tall. His chuckle at my pathetic display pisses me off even further, and I shove him in the chest—hard.

He stumbles a pace or two, looking back at me slightly wounded. When he comes to stand face-to-face with me, my heart is racing.

"Give it back," I say through gritted teeth. "It was mine first. Finders keepers. You lost, just admit it."

"I'm not the one having difficulties accepting their loss."

Angrily, I push him hard against his chest once more, and this time, there's no ambiguity about the hurt flash in his eyes.

"Come on, then. I'm fighting you for it."

I shove him again, my anger clawing out of my throat like a demon possessed. Malakyte's words echo in my mind. *Remember, you cannot escape who you truly are, no matter how much of a hero you pretend to be.*

"Jupiter's rings! Fight me, dammit! Fight me like you fought him!" I yell as my emotions begin to tumble. "What, am I not big or tough enough for you to fight? Too afraid you'll ruffle my feathers? I don't care. I'm not giving up. Do it!"

When I throw the first punch, his hand stops the hit easily. This pisses me off even more. Looks like my anger isn't giving me the strength I need, after all. But I can't give up. Not yet . . . not this quickly.

I draw my sword, fuming.

"Thumbelina, stop it." His voice is serious now. "Enough."

 212

My body and sword are trembling. "No."

I lunge at him, slicing through nothing but air, but my heart isn't fully in it, and he can tell.

We go at it. Tit for tat. He lets me attack him, and he does nothing but dodge each and every time.

Angrily, he uses his magic to pull the sword from my hand, and it flies twenty feet away. I'm distracted as I watch it go, and I don't see him come up close to me. He grips me firmly by my waist and draws me into him, our hips flush against each other. I squirm, but he doesn't release me. I fight him a little bit longer, but the attacks are weak and lacking conviction. He takes them all until I can't keep them up.

My anger-filled cries quickly turn to saddened sobs, and I go from attacking him to crying in his arms. That's it, then.

I've lost.

I've failed.

He doesn't get it . . . He doesn't understand why I need this.

"I'm sorry, Thumbelina," he says softly, brushing my hair from my face as he looks at me with sad yet firmly resolved eyes. "I know how badly you want this, too. I know what I'm taking away from you, and I hate it. I must get to Pacey. She needs me. It's my fault she's up there, and it's my responsibility to get her back. Please understand. It's not that I don't trust you with this. It's that I have to be the one. She's my sister, my responsibility. It's my duty to rescue her."

What he doesn't get is that I do understand. I do. I just . . . I just . . .

Who am I kidding? I've been a complete jerk, a brat, and a terrible girlfriend. Shame immediately reddens my cheeks, and I'm so embarrassed by my actions I can't even look him in the eye anymore. Is Malakyte right about me? Am I just an awful person pretending to be someone good?

His arms bring me tighter into his body, and he continues, "Go be with your father. He loves you, and I know he'll be relieved to have you back safe. Let me carry the burden this time, please. You don't have to be the one who holds it up every time. Allow me to take the risk instead. Because, as much as I need to get Pace back, I'm also doing this to save *you*, Thumbelina. Go back home and root for me, okay?"

He's a way better person than I am. So much more than I ever deserve.

"But I can't protect you anymore," I say, and it scares me.

"You'll be protecting me by giving me the peace of mind knowing that you're out of harm's way." I wrap my arms around him, tears falling silently at his words.

"It'll be okay." He separates the two of us finally. We both know he has to go.

He looks at me for what could be the very last time. He wipes the half dried tears from my cheeks, eyes lingering far too long at the material tied around my throat.

Then he bends down and kisses me.

I kiss him back.

Fully and passionately and with every bit of my heart and soul.

His tongue glides into my mouth softly at first, the taste of him intoxicating and, altogether, *him*. Then it's as if time and the competition and life and death all stop around us as he kisses me fully and deeply and with everything that he has. I give him all of me in return. Pouring all of me into him as my hands hold his face, and I feel the wetness of a single tear glide down his cheek onto my fingers.

Then he leaves me, the abrupt separation a sensory shock to my system.

"If you blame her, retaliate against her, or hurt her in any way for letting me walk away with this flag, I'll find you, and I'll kill you," Ardelle tells Damon, his tone laced with venom and promise. My brows raise in surprise. Holy shit. "You'll be able to stand again once I'm gone."

Ardelle gives me one last glance goodbye and walks into the woods towards our side of the Dais. He's going for Team Silver's flag, knowing that's the only way to win. I'm not sure if he'll get past Deimos, but he likely will.

There's so much I want to tell him, yet anger sews my lips into silence.

The wind dries away the last of the tears on my cheeks, and the tears he left on my fingers, too.

CHAPTER 33

What am I supposed to do now?

"Well," Damon growls as he finally gets back on his feet. "That's your man? What'd he do to me?"

I can't help but cynically laugh at his appearance, all ruffed, hair a mess, uniform torn and covered in blood. It's that, or I'll start crying again.

"Now, you're the one who looks like shit," I say, flipping it back to him. But I probably should answer his question. "Ardelle can control gravity."

Damon's icy brows raise with admiration, teetering on impressed. Which is weird, because Ardelle just thoroughly kicked his ass. Boys are so confusing.

"So, you two are some supernatural power couple or something?" he asks, skeptical but clearly fishing for answers.

"Something like that."

Closing the distance between us, Damon stops in front of me and clasps his giant hand on my shoulder. "I heard what went down between you two. Sort of hard not to."

I cringe with embarrassment. "Yeah . . . I lost myself for a second there. I'm sorry you went through all that for nothing. We can't win unless we have that flag, so it's over."

"I wouldn't say it was for nothing," Damon says, his mischievous smile making my belly tingle slightly. A butterfly of hope. As if I know what's going on behind that devilish grin of his. "He's not the only one with a trick up his sleeve."

My brows knit together in confusion.

Without saying a word, he reaches for me. Confused, I swat him away, which he responds to by patting me on the top of my head like I'm a toddler. With our size difference, I might as well be. Letting him do his thing, he unties the fabric he put around my neck earlier. Suddenly, the Gold Team's flag is right before my eyes. Not with Ardelle currently making its way to the Silver Team's home base.

"What . . . ?" I say, completely dumbfounded. I point towards the direction Ardelle ran off in. "But he . . ."

Damon is grinning like a sly cat, fangs glinting in the sunlight. "You two aren't the only ones with magic."

"How'd you get the gold flag from Ardelle and swap it with the one around my neck?" I ask, and he chuckles at me.

"The real flag was always around your neck, hiding in plain sight. When he arrived, I made him see a gray fabric tied around your neck and a gold one sticking out of my uniform pocket."

He smiles like he's the smartest guy in the room.

Then it all falls into place.

All of it.

I knew it.

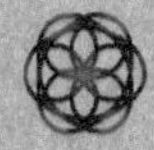

Without saying a word, I grab hold of his right hand, my nails digging into the leather glove. Gav's power was illusion magic. If he so chose, he'd make a room full of kids experience whatever he wanted them to see. He'd create it out of thin air. Snakes, spiders, bats, monsters from his home world. He excelled at creating illusions. His little ass would constantly be pranking everyone from the bullies to the mothers who watched over us. It wasn't his Sky-Fae alien race magic, either. It was Elendril powers. His eyes glowed green when he did it. I'll never forget it.

This is happening *now*.

"What are you do—" he protests, but I rip the Velcro on his glove too fast for him to jerk away. When he ultimately does, the glove is now in my hand.

Damon holds his hand up close to his chest, the look of shock reflected there. But it's too late to hide, I already saw it.

Deimos's Elendril crystal symbol is etched into his hand, where all the Ringer's marks reside, between the pointer finger and thumb. It looks just as I remember it, all those memories flooding back to me. Tears rim my eyes.

It's him. It's Gavrielle.

I knew it. I fucking *knew it*.

After all this time, all these years . . . I can finally—*finally*—allow myself to feel the elation and relief of finding him. It's like this big dam I've constructed within blasts apart, emotions flooding in unchecked. I don't stop them or try to push them away because he's here. An unfurling of a six-year-long ball of tightness and pain finally coming undone to glee, the only good nostalgia of my childhood—all of it bursting within my heart. Nobody understands how he is my true home, my guiding star, my best friend. My everything. Somehow, he came right to me. Gavrielle is alive.

I don't stop myself from jumping into his arms, unable to hold in my sobbing. He smells the same yet a little different. The fresh citrus of him mixed with a warm masculine ginger and ozonic smells, he's like a clean breeze on a foreign alien shore. But there're parts of him that are changed, too, and I can't quite figure out what it is.

But that doesn't matter. It's him. I found him. Right now, I don't really care about the how or why. I'm just elated that he's *alive*.

It takes him a minute, but he finally wraps his arms around me.

"Gavrielle," I whisper, his name sounding so foreign on my lips. "I'm so sorry."

The moment those words escape my mouth, he grasps me firmly by the shoulders and separates us. I look him directly in the eyes, the bright light of the sun blasting into them as they dance like wildfire.

"How do you know that name?" he demands, voice serious but also . . . afraid? "Nobody knows to call me by that name."

I furrow my brows in confusion, a tiny spider made of fear crawling up my spine. "Gav, it's me. It's Kara. How do you not recognize me?"

Fear flashes on his face, but he masks it quickly. "I've never heard that name before."

My mouth falls open. "Kara? Karalevine Ruzz? You've never heard that name in your life before?"

He tries to answer, attempts to search his memory, but I can tell by his expression and confusion in his eyes there is no recollection. "I have not."

It's like being given a diamond ring only to drop it down a sewer grate. What is going on here? There's no way he couldn't remember me. And he's not lying. The horror and uncertainty reflected on his face is absolutely real. It's as if he knows he should remember me—remember my name and my face—but he doesn't.

Gavrielle doesn't remember me.

He doesn't remember what I did.

Who gave him those burns I see all the way down his neck?

"Do you remember living at the orphanage? Outside Zarmenia City limits. You were nine years old when you came there. You were there for a few months before a little girl with black hair came to live there. She was small, alone, always getting into fights with the other kids. She had a strange star mark on her chest, remember?"

I unzip my uniform down far enough to expose my Elendril mark, and his eyes go wide at the sight of my star. He stares as if a memory is trying to smash its way through whatever barriers are preventing it from seeing sunlight.

"I . . . I . . . the orphanage? No. I grew up at the assassin's camp."

My sigh is so loud within the silence between us. What the hell is going on? Where is Gav? Where has he gone? This is nothing short of the sickest torture I could've ever conceived happening. I find out he's alive, and I didn't get my best friend killed but then I realize he doesn't recall me at all. All this time, I've been killing myself mentally and emotionally over what he must've thought of me ditching and blowing him up. What a shit person I must have been—but what was it for? He doesn't recollect any of it. Whose sick idea of a joke is this? Why does it feel like someone just stabbed my sword right through my heart?

"You look very upset," he says, appearing abhorrently confused.

I can't help but laugh bitterly, although it's full of fury building within my blood.

"Is your name Gavrielle Abraxas?" I ask blatantly, needing to confirm and set a baseline.

He glares at me, conflict written plainly across his face. After hesitating way longer than I thought acceptable, he finally answers me.

"Yes."

I inhale sharply. That simple word causes my entire vision to blur and turn sideways. It is Gav . . . he's here, he's just lost.

He's lost, and I'm going to find him. I'll never leave him behind again.

"And you truly do not remember me?" I press once more. "This isn't one of your stupid jokes or pranks? You seriously have no idea who I am?"

Genuine sadness replaces his typically strong Sky-Fae features. "I do not remember you, Kara."

As if being struck by some unseen force, he flinches away from me.

"What is it?" I ask as I notice him blinking rapidly as if he's seeing something only he can visualize.

It takes him almost an entire minute to respond. "When I said your name just now, I . . . I felt something. However, I can't grasp it, it's fleeting. The moment I give chase, it slips away."

I try something that might help him. "Do you remember the bouquet of dandelions you gave me the last night we saw each other?" How special he made me feel that late afternoon before everything changed. "You went to the field out back and picked them in secret. You didn't have anything but your shoelace to tie them together with, and after the two of us got into trouble, you took me upstairs and gave them to me. You used your magic to change them into the most beautiful flowers from your home world. They were black and tapered into a bright teal at the tip of the petals. They were your mother's favorite. You did that for me, and I did this for you."

Pulling up the uniform's sleeve, I show Gav the single dandelion inked into my skin. Forever a reminder of him to never give up until we are together again. No matter what.

His face is one etched in pain and sadness. A part of him knows, even if he can't fully recall. His soul remembers.

After a moment of silence, Gav is drawn to my hair, the teal ends coming out of the braid I didn't secure tight enough again. He stares down at it, and I refrain from saying anything as I watch emotion after emotion flash behind his eyes. As if he's alone in the wilderness, never knowing what sort of wild beast or dangerous path will thrust him into peril next.

I feel so helpless.

So angry.

This is Arianyte's doing.

When they took him, they must've Reconditioned him. There's no other explanation for his amnesia. Yet another crime Malakyte has committed. He's not allowed to try and seek redemption; he doesn't deserve it. I hate him. I *hate* him! My crystal surges, my control slipping for the first time in months.

"I can feel you," he says quietly, eyes still drawn to the ends of my hair—the colors that remind him of his mother's favorite flower. "Your magic is strong."

"They're called Elendril crystals. I have one. You don't, but you're connected to a person who does. It's complicated, but I'm what's called a Starseed, and you're a Ringer. Each Starseed has a Ringer. They're like a divine pair."

"I see. But we are not a pair? I'm not your Ringer?"

My eyes look at him with devastating sadness. "I'm not your pair or your Starseed, Gav, but I'm your friend. I promise."

"And you knew me when you and I were children? Not at the assassin's camp?"

"Gav," I breathe, "you were never at the assassin's camp. At least, not before they took you. Arianyte kidnapped you when you were twelve from the orphanage. I know because I was there. They came for me, too."

Pain creases in his near-flawless face. The features I had let time dissolve from my memory. I do not allow this moment to pass without permanently etching every line, every shape, and angle into my mind.

"And they did not take you?"

Can I tell him the truth? Can I admit fully to what I did that night? Shame blasts into me like a sky-rail train. Seeing Gav is dredging up a lot of old shit. I don't know if I can handle all this right now.

"I got away," I say quickly, regretting it immediately but unable to utter the truth. Not when I just halfway got him back. I can tell him later, when we've both acclimated a little bit.

"You're sure it was Arianyte?" he asks.

"I'm one thousand percent sure it was them. Malakyte Ardeen, the prince himself, ordered it. He sent his number two, that bitch with the horns, to come for us. They took you, and I escaped. Arianyte has the ability to alter memories. It's called Reconditioning. They've clearly done it to you, swapped your old memories with new ones so there's not this gaping black hole in your past where your old life should be. Why they did it, I don't know. But we'll figure it out together, okay? I promise. All that matters is that we found each other again. I've been searching for you ever since that night. I never forgot about you, Gav. Not one day went by that I didn't think about you. You don't know all that I've done in the name of finding you . . ."

His hand reaches for my cheek, and I do not flinch away. He searches all of me, penetrating my eyes to my very essence and beyond. I get hot from it, my body tingling. Why is this so unreal? He's here . . . he's alive. It's like a dream, but it's not a fantasy or make-believe this time. I see that little boy within this grown man's face. I find all the mischief and playfulness and strength and bravery that's always been at the core of who Gav is. His memories may be gone, but Gavrielle Abraxas is in there.

But why are you here with me *now?*

It's too suspicious to be a mere coincidence. It can't be.

Finding Gavrielle creates way more questions than answers, and I'm pretty sure, once we get to the bottom of it, the two of us will wish we never opened Pandora's Box.

CHAPTER 34

The Silver Team won.

Gavrielle is alive.

I'm one step closer to liberating Pacey and ripping down the Arianyte Empire.

All great things.

So, why do I feel so shitty?

After our conversation, Gav and I had nothing more to say or do, and we knew we were already on stolen time. Given all that, we walked our way back across the Sky Dais, taking the long way closer to the edges and away from the freaky Tributes, whose deranged eyes still haunt me whenever I close my own.

Once we returned to our side of the Dais, our team welcomed us with enthusiastic applause when they saw we had Gold Team's flag. Ardelle had somehow managed to wrangle our flag from Deimos by sneaking in through a window and pinning him down with his gravity, which thoroughly pissed Deimos off. Ardelle was on his way back when we arrived. It's likely we returned in the nick of time.

No longer am I seen as some layup who somehow lucked out at the tryouts. Hell no. I'm the one to beat.

It's all a blur after that.

The celebration of my team members swept me up in their shouts with pats on the back and congratulations, but the win feels hollow to me. I was even picked up, thrown about, and tossed upon shoulders so many times I began getting dizzy. It wasn't until Gav finally swooped me up and onto his own shoulders that the other players left me alone.

It isn't that I'm unhappy with the win—because I am. It's just . . . I feel different now that it's all over. Nearly being killed so violently, the shit Malakyte said, all the stuff with Gav. Today has been a lot, and I'm numb, drained, and exhausted. I also really wish Jance was here.

I close my eyes, the memories of everything that happened today flooding back in so fast I can't keep it straight, the flashes coming in like rain pellets I cannot stop. They seem endless. I've only been in my room at the mansion for less than twenty minutes, the silence tormenting. My adrenaline hasn't come down yet. But it can't, not when I don't know where he is.

Ardelle.

They flew Gold Team off on a separate sky-hover, so I haven't got to see him since we parted ways. Perhaps I'm paranoid, but I'm afraid Malakyte will capture Ardelle and we're going to have to rescue both siblings.

We knew this was a risk going in, and it was one we were willing to take. Now, however, the worried flutter in my chest is telling me an entirely different story.

Does he think I played him? I had no clue the actual flag was around my neck until Gav pulled it off me, but will Ardelle believe that? I'm sure if he gets out of here a free person, he'll see what truly happened on the news feeds. I turn the television on for some background noise, and it's all over every station covering the games. Our passionate kiss along with the brawl we had moments prior plastered for the world to see. I had no idea it was being recorded. I've watched our interaction play several times as the minutes tick by. I sit, dazed, on my king-sized bed, not knowing what to do with myself. The room feels way too large for only me. It reminds me more of a hotel suite than anything, every towel and lavish piece of furniture in its perfect place.

I should probably shower. I'm covered in dirt, blood, mud, and stars-know-what else . . . I'm just so tire—

An urgent knock thrusts me out of my thoughts, and my neck snaps in that direction, still on edge. My eyes immediately search for my sword, and I rush for it on the small table by the dresser. Who's at my door now of all times?

The knock comes again, more persistent this time. Could it be Gav? There's certainly a myriad of questions to ask regarding our past. Perhaps he's as haunted by our conversation as I am?

Or is it Malakyte? Coming to retrieve me, scorned because I didn't take his hand and run away with him.

There's no peephole, but I keep the safety chain on as I crack it open.

My body sags in relief at who's staring back at me.

I slam the door shut, remove the safety chain, and swing it wide open.

I'm in Ardelle's arms before the door closes behind him, and I can't keep my sobs under control.

"How?" I ask through my sniffs, my snot getting all over his uniform.

Before he can even answer me, I spill up everything that happened with Gav and the flag. "I had no clue you didn't have the actual flag. I thought you walked away with it. It was Gav. He's alive. That guy named Damon is actually Gav."

"*Your* Gav? I thought he was dead?"

I shake my head in disbelief. "So did I. Apparently, Malakyte believes him dead, and he's assumed a fake identity because he says he doesn't even go by that name anymore. His Ringer powers were *illusion magic.*"

Realization flashes on Ardelle's face. "That would make a lot of sense. I swear I saw a gold cloth around your neck when I was approaching you both from behind, but when we were talking, I noticed it was gray. So, I figured I must've seen incorrectly. How did you not notice his eyes glowing?"

"He put the damned thing around my neck while he was behind me, the slippery little shit. He's smart like that. Even as a child, he knew how to avoid getting caught when playing his stupid little games. It's completely something he would do."

Ardelle stops me before I can rant further at being played. Softly, he unravels the makeshift bandage tied around my neck, and his eyes go absolutely dark. It doesn't take him long to notice the blood and bite marks through my uniform, either. His face tells me he would kill whoever did it. Too bad they're already dead.

"Who did this to you?" he demands, fury boiling in every word.

I explain everything to him, about the three extras and their so-called Mistress, and my theory of it possibly being Naresteé, how she was at the ball. I tell him what Malakyte had done . . . but not what he had said or asked of me. Ardelle looks as horrified as I feel once he's been filled in.

"So, someone else is after your crystal this time around," he concludes, and I nod in agreement.

"Never thought I'd find myself wishing for Deimos as an enemy again . . ." My attempt at humor in this dark situation. At least he cracks a tiny smile. He simply looks at me, so much sadness in his eyes it's unbearable. I now wish he had won because, after finding out about Gav, I don't know if I'm emotionally stable enough to keep this up. I'm afraid the promise I made to my father will inevitably shatter.

"Ardelle," I whisper, voice vulnerable and raw.

"Yeah, babe?"

"I'm really scared," I admit. "I don't think I can do this."

Wrapping me in his arms again, I'm enveloped by his warmth and scent. "You're the strongest person I know, Thumbelina. If anyone can do this, it's you. I believe in you. We all do."

I snort but say nothing. Ardelle sets his bow and arrows to the ground, picks me up, and leads me to the bathroom.

I don't fight him an inch.

I suggest to Ardelle we take our lenses out, and he agrees.

"I lost my earpiece," I tell him as I pluck out the contact lens and place it in its container. He does the same.

"So did I. Otherwise, I'd give you mine," he informs, and I'm bummed; it'd be good to have.

Although exhaustion is beginning to settle in, I bring myself flush to him, feeling the hardness of his body against my own.

"I'm so tired, but I want to spend whatever time I've got left with you. So, what are you going to do in order to keep my mind from wandering off to sleep?" I ask mischievously, a wicked smile playing on my lips.

A twin smile flashes on his own, and I tingle in expectation.

Bending down low, he whispers seductively into my ear, "The only thing you'll have on your mind, Thumbelina, is my name."

CHAPTER 35

Ardelle's right.

He's the only thing on my mind.

Even though we bathe separately, I anxiously rush back to him. I wait impatiently on the bed for him to finish his shower, still wrapped in my pristine white towel as my body sits naked beneath it.

"Looks like the people are disappointed we're not competing together any longer." Ardelle's voice surprises me as I see him standing in the doorway, his own towel wrapped around his waist far lower than I've ever seen before. I swallow dryly, and what comes out of my mouth is some gibberish agreement.

He laughs at me.

I blush.

How can I not?

The V and indents of his hip bones are striking against his abs and tattoos, that body of his honed to absolute perfection. The water beads dripping along his neck and chest are enough to drive me wild. I beckon him over as I lie down sideways with my head on the pillows. He slides onto the bed behind me, and I shimmy closer.

"You're not trembling like you were earlier," he says, brushing my half dried hair over my ear as he lies behind me.

"That's because you're here, silly." But then I'm instantly reminded I'm going back into this hell game alone tomorrow.

Without him. "I don't want to talk about the game. We've got such a short time here. Let's not waste it."

He squeezes me closer to him as he nudges his head towards the screen mounted above the dresser. "Did you know the cameras were watching us when that whole thing happened?"

Our scuffle is being played on one half of the television as reactions of popular Network influencers and celebrities are shown on the other. The caption at the bottom of the screen in bright red letters reads, *Star-crossed lovers separated in Titan Games love-match.*

"I had no idea." I bet Malakyte is absolutely fuming over it. Good. Let him be jealous.

"I think they're more disappointed we won't be rage-kissing anymore," I say.

"That can still be arranged. Minus the rage part."

"What if I want a little rage? Keep it spicy, you know?"

"Spicy? I'm not sure you can handle spicy, Thumbelina," he murmurs, and I flush. "That'll cause way too much trouble."

Grinning, I say, "What if I want trouble?"

Ardelle's chuckle vibrates through my ear as he drags his fingertips softly across the skin exposed above my towel. It gives me goose bumps, but it also begins to stir something in me. The longing and desire that's beginning to spark, to set fire and burn away this entire day. I need him to take every bit of pain and fear and make me forget everything that happened today. He leans down and nibbles on my ear. "Maybe trouble isn't such a bad thing, after all? You've successfully corrupted me, you wicked thing, you."

I gasp as if he's actually hurt me, rolling away with a fake cry.

Chasing me, his entire body pushes up against my back, and I'm suddenly reminded there's only two fluffy towels separating our naked bodies.

"Don't cry, Thumbelina. I'll kiss it and make it all better."

And he does. His lips touch the back of my neck, my shoulder, moving down my spine until there's no more skin to be found.

I turn my face towards his, meeting his Sapphire Sunday-colored eyes. "Kiss me, Ardelle," I tell him, but it comes out as

a bit of a plea. I need to get lost in him, all of him. I don't care if it's an unhealthy coping mechanism for what happened today—I need him tonight.

Ardelle kisses me slowly, tenderly, softly building up the tension between our lips in the perfect rhythm. I taste him tentatively, taking my time with him. I wrap my free hand into his wet hair as he gently holds onto my neck, so careful of the slash there.

The heat between my legs builds quickly, turning into a maddening hunger I don't know how to satisfy. Ardelle scooches me so he's spooning me again. His free hand moves lower, touching me in places he never has before. I let him, eager for his hands to explore all of me. I'm ready for that. It makes my heart thrash wildly. *Why doesn't he just rip the damned towel off me already?*

I grind my ass against his front, feeling the full hardness there for the very first time. A part of it scares me a little but then I remember this is Ardelle. I am safe. If I say stop, I know he will stop. And I am not afraid. Because anything that happens here is my choice, and that's all it ever should be.

Our kisses go deeper, tongues meeting each other eagerly. He grabs my thigh but doesn't go higher; the desire in me is overwhelming. Stars, I need him to touch more. I take the hand on my thigh and glide it up under my towel.

Stopping our kiss immediately, Ardelle asks, "Are you sure?"

The sincerity in his eyes is everything I need to see.

"Yes," I breathe. I am sure. He goes to explore my body, just as I want him to.

"You sure you want me to touch you here?" He slaps my ass through the fluffy fabric, all the playfulness back in his tone.

"Yes."

A deep growl emits from his throat as he cups my ass in his hands, skin-to-skin.

"Stars, you know how long I've wanted to squeeze this perfect ass of yours?" he barely manages to say before kissing me again. The pressure between my legs soars as he holds all of my bottom in both his hands.

He sits up and rolls me to my stomach, opening my towel to reveal all of my backside to him. I can't help but blush into the fluffy pillows. I feel the tips of his fingers trace my tattoos, the touch soft yet agonizingly taunting. Trouble it is, then.

"Thumbelina," he breathes, voice low, "do you trust me?"

Difficult question, one I've been grappling with for a while now, but the answer comes to my lips immediately. "Yes."

Ardelle checks that his towel is still firmly tied onto his waist, but as he does, I peek over my shoulder to catch a glimpse of ink I've never seen before. It's so low on his flat stomach, and I can only see a small bit of it, but I'm intrigued. Ordering me to turn back around, he opens my legs wide. He places both his hands on my hips, pressing himself against my ass so I can feel just how excited he is.

And stars, do I feel *all* of it.

"Move with me," he instructs, taking control of the rhythm as he drives his hips into me from behind.

I press myself against the mattress, feeling wetness from my own excitement. It feels so good as we move together, the friction drawing his towel down farther and farther. I feel him pull it back up again. If only I could just rip it off him . . . see that concealed tattoo there, to see everything, nothing hidden.

The pressure builds and builds and builds. Stars. Do I want this to go further? I think of what that would mean, how good I know it would feel to have all of him buried inside me.

"Ardelle." His name is a plea for more. Stars, please, give me more. Grant me all of it so I don't have to think about anything other than him and me and this moment. He grips my ass with both hands—hard, and my back arches, shoulders pinching together. He then dances across my skin, greedily feeling every inch, every tattoo, every scar, and devouring all of me. He is so fucking hot. His arms, his chest, the way he touches my body like I'm his god.

His rhythm increases, and I feel his towel slipping. Yes, stars. Come off. I moan his name once again. Stopping suddenly, he leans over me, most of his weight on my back. "Say that last bit one more time."

Asshole.

I can't help but love it, though.

His hands glide along my bare back, slowly making his way to my hips where he dives to my ribs then to the sides of my breasts. I feel him shimmy back a little, sliding his fingers along my thighs as he opens them a little bit.

Slowly, to the point it's almost pure torture. He reaches between my legs, touching the wettest part of me first. I practically whimper with pleasure when he finally touches the apex of me. He uses the wetness there and glides his finger along my clit, the touch sending shivers through me.

Torturously slowly, Ardelle glides his finger inside me, and a small cry escapes into the pillows. He's gentle, safe, and I melt into the feel of his delicate strokes.

"Ardelle," I gasp his name, pleasure taking over all my senses. I'm mad, crazy with it.

"Do what you did before," he instructs as he begins finding that perfect tempo again. "Move with me."

As before, the two of us move together, but this time, I feel his finger inside me as I'm pressed up against the mattress, moaning his name. My hands grip the blankets, my body trembling. The pressure is too much. I've never felt anything so good. My heart is a wild thing, thudding and thudding so hard I can hear pounding in my head.

It happens then. Ardelle's towel finally breaks free, and he stops to catch it.

"Don't," I gasp, arching up and looking back at him. His face is flushed, eyes primal and dark with need, the towel firmly back in place. "Let me turn over."

Without a word, he slowly slips his fingers out from me, and my eyes widen when I see him dip the entirety of his finger into his mouth, tasting me; the heat in me doubles. *Fucking hot.*

I turn over onto my back, my body completely naked before him, and his eyes absolutely devour me whole. Slowly making their way down around every curve, every peak and valley. He's like a parched man seeing water for the first time in days. My body is his oasis, and Ardelle eagerly traces my curves with a heady gaze darkening his eyes. I love the way he licks his lips, tilts his head, and looks at me like I'm everything.

All it takes is a flick of my foot to undo his towel, and it finally falls to the bed. He doesn't catch it this time. He's on his knees, that perfectly sculpted body standing up in all its glory before me. I bite my lip at what I see there, his cock hard and ready for me. I need it. I need him. I can't wait. Not when death could come tomorrow. Not when neither of us are guaranteed another day of life. I notice the solid black raven silhouette tattooed far below his hip bone, done in brush strokes with wings wide open. I'm happy, knowing I get to see this hidden part of him. *All* parts of him.

"I want this, Ardelle," I breathe, voice trembling with need. "I want you."

That's when Ardelle's self-control finally snaps. He crawls onto me, and the two of us slam into each other, kissing in a wild frenzy of lips, tongue, and teeth. My bare skin against his feels like everything I've been missing, his tattoos melding with my tattoos. Our desire coming loose in a way that leaves no room for what must come next.

Breaking our kiss, his lips find my neck, then my collar bone, down my chest, and when his lips flick the crest of my nipple, I cry with pleasure. I throw my head back into the pillows, enjoying his mouth, his hands, not wanting to forget a second of this moment.

As he makes his way back up to me, he kisses the pointed tip of my ear. I bring his face into my hands and force him to look at me, the expression tender and terrified all at once. My heart leaps and soars at the adoration and care I see there. He asks one last time, wordlessly confirming my choice to cross this line.

"I'm ready for all the trouble, Ardelle. I'm sure."

 234

We kiss each other softly now, delicately, the roaring wildfire simmering down just long enough for this moment to flourish between us as sweet and memorable. But we're both ravenous, starving, and we cannot wait any longer. We need each other. It's primal, unsatiated hunger.

I bring my hands to that V at his hips where the raven tattoo sits, sensually drawing my fingertips up and down the sensitive skin there, teasing him. But I am greedy, and I want the whole thing. Softly, I take the length of him in my hand and begin stroking him up and down, the skin velvety soft. He's thicker than I thought, bigger than anything I've ever had before, but I'm eager for all of him. He moans in my ear, bending down to lick my nipple in tandem.

Wrapping my legs around his waist, I guide him to the wettest part of me; I'm ready for him. I release my hand once he's positioned in the perfect spot between my legs, and I release all my control over to Ardelle. My heart is thrashing as he laces both his hands through mine, the mark on my chest a steady burn. The pressure within my core maddening. Ardelle is slow and so gentle as he guides himself into me, deliberately filling me inch by precious inch. It hurts some, the thickest part of him, and it takes me a minute to adjust to the absolute fullness of him inside me and how he feels. My legs tremble along his waist as he buries himself completely into me, the two of us lost in the other. I'm high off this feeling—this ecstasy.

The growl in his throat intensifies as he begins to move, assured that I've adjusted to the feel of him deep within me.

We move together, my nails digging into his back as moans of pleasure break past all sense of modesty.

"Stars, the sounds you make, Thumbelina," he barely manages to say, increasing his tempo as he thrusts his hips into mine. Over and over and over. He releases my hands and sits tall, that body an absolute specimen before my eyes as he drives himself into me. Harder. Faster. His chest, his shoulders and arms are tattooed, sculpted perfection.

His hand comes down to cup my cheek, thumb tracing the edges of my lips. The heat and intensity build, and I ride that wave all the way to the end.

My body begins to tremble, the tension in my core climbing and soaring to heights I've never known. My chest swells, and I'm going to tip over the edge. Any second . . .

Then I explode in the best way possible.

I cannot hold in my cries of pleasure as my body is racked with it. Like waves of pure ecstasy hit me, sending me tumbling a thousand times over again. My entire body shakes with it. Ardelle pounds faster into me as he drives me over the edge. I cry out his name, my crystal shooting to life as it lights up the room. It's never ending, the wave upon wave of satisfaction that overtakes me.

Ardelle is so turned on by my climax that I begin to feel him teetering on the edge as well, and I squeeze my muscles around him as he drives himself even deeper inside me. He holds me close to him as he comes undone before me, my body reducing him to nothing but growls and moans of pleasure. His crystal, too, lights up, and for what feels like endless seconds, the two of us float several inches above the bed, his gravity magic taking over. It is astonishing to witness our hair, the blankets, and pillows all floating around us. It's more thrilling to experience the high it gives. He's both stunned and amazed by it, too, slowly bringing us back to the bed once he's finished, never letting me fall.

Once back on the mattress, our breaths echo in the air, chests heaving and bodies covered in a thin, albeit sexy, sheen of sweat. Both our crystals have returned to normal, and we're lucky I didn't blow up half the room with how fucking good he made me feel. We simply stare at each other for minutes, for hours, who knows. But we can't separate or leave this moment or dare peek outside the safe walls we've constructed together.

Once he leaves my body, he crawls back to me and finds my cheek, kissing it.

"Feel good?" he asks, way too much pride in his voice.

My ridiculous giggle is my response.

 236

"Good. The way you called my name makes up for how you attacked me earlier today."

"I'll probably cry your name again if you fuck me like that a second time," I say honestly, a chuckle in my tone. He looks at me all smug.

"What's the raven tattoo mean?" I ask, unable to help myself.

Ardelle shrugs casually, but I can tell it's personal for him. "I just . . . wanted something only for me, you know? A symbol that I can fly and soar and be myself. You helped me see that, too, Thumbelina. I'm glad you saw it—besides the person who tattooed it, nobody else knows it's there."

I do nothing but smile up at him. "Thank you for sharing it with me."

He smiles and taps me softly on the tip of my nose. Did he just *boop* me?

"You've got to be starving. I know I am. Want to order food?" he asks, changing the topic. I nod as he stands from the bed and walks towards the small table, my brow rising at the immaculate view of his perfect ass. He looks back at me, that damned cocky smile on his face. I chuckle and throw a pillow at his head for good measure. This time with him will certainly be on my mind as I fight for my life in that arena tomorrow. Because he's who I'm fighting for.

Him and all the others.

He returns to me once the food is ordered, and it feels so nice to have him back in my arms even after that tiny amount of separation. Taking my hand, he interlocks his fingers into mine, and we hold on to each other for dear life.

CHAPTER 36

ARIANYTE WILL NOW ENFORCE A STRICT NETWORK SURVEILLANCE SYSTEM, MONITORING KEYWORDS AND PHRASES TO IDENTIFY POTENTIAL REBELS, DISSENTERS, REFERENCES TO THE STAR, AND REVOLUTION. ANY PERSON FOUND TO BE SUPPORTING REBEL ACTIVITY WILL HAVE THEIR USE OF THE NETWORK REVOKED. ANY ENCRYPTION OR PRIVACY TOOLS, VIRTUAL PRIVATE NETWORKS, OR CIRCUMVENTION OF ARTIFICIAL INTELLIGENCE TO SUBVERT ARIANYTE WILL BE DETAINED AND QUESTIONED FOR REBEL ACTIVITY.

Waking up in Ardelle's arms is both beautiful and tragic. Beautiful in the sense I feel safer and more seen than I've ever been, so glad I gave him a second chance.

And tragic because, now, we must leave each other. It's made even harder by the time we have in the shower together, where Ardelle gives me all his flesh once more, and I let him take me over the steaming water until my legs are too weak to stand. Anything to forget what's waiting for me at the start of game two later today.

"I'll sneak out of here with Jance and the others," he tells me once we clean and finished getting ready. I put the lens back into my eye before we walk out the door. "Hopefully, Malakyte or his goons will see right past me and let me leave."

"Your bow and arrows are hidden in the bag?" I ask, making sure he doesn't get spotted over something as stupid as that.

When he confirms they are, I get an inkling and ask, "Can you leave me an arrow, actually? Never know when one could come in handy. I can shove it in my sword sheath."

"You're a crazy girl, you know that, Thumbelina?"

I shove him with my shoulder playfully, and he responds by coming down to kiss my lips. The fresh cinnamon of his toothpaste blooms under my nose, and I blush slightly at the memory of last night and this morning. How I moaned his name over and over again.

I bite my lip playfully.

As Ardelle and I make our way down to the hangar from yesterday, I remember something I meant to tell him last night.

"So, you know how I told you my old friend Gavrielle is actually alive, right?"

He nods, keeping the two of us to the shadows as best we can. Ardelle isn't supposed to even be here. We can't get caught.

"Well," I begin as we sneak past a couple of maids, "there's something wrong with him."

I explain to him Gav's memory loss and how it's like he was given an entirely different life and remembers that one rather than the life he actually lived. We hurriedly sneak down a set of servant's stairs and through the kitchens. Once there, we find a heavy metal door that leads out to the hangar from yesterday. Many of the remaining Titans are already crowded around and waiting for their interviews and meetings with their family members.

"Go," Ardelle tells me, pointing towards the group. "I'll meander into the crowd of families. I'll get out of here just fine, Thumbelina. I—" He stops short, eyes a bit conflicted. "I know you're going to kill it today. I believe in you, babe. I'll be rooting for you, and I'll always be with you."

He kisses me goodbye, his lips soft and warm against mine. It's over too soon as we part, both of us walking in opposite directions.

It doesn't take me long to find Deimos. He sticks out like a sore thumb. Plus, the crowd is a lot slimmer today. The hangar's ceiling is really high, and warm air blows through the big open door.

"We need to talk," I say as a hello. He only mumbles in annoyance.

Head on a swivel, I look around for Gavrielle; he isn't here yet.

"That Sky-Fae dude is Gav," I hiss in his giant ear. "Your Ringer is alive."

"What?" His voice is irate but hushed. We don't want to draw unnecessary attention.

"You're the one who said he was dead," I remind him.

Deimos slams his palm into his face. "You're sure?"

"Well, he's got your Elendril mark right on his hand, so, yes. That being said, we've got a problem."

I explain Gav's amnesia just like I had with Ardelle. Deimos merely scratches his giant ear, contemplative.

"Also, you smell different . . ." he says, eyeing me suspiciously. "Like pretty boy." My eyes go wide, and I feel my cheeks heat. Oh, my stars, can he smell that Ardelle and I had sex? Why did nobody tell me extras could do this?

"I don't . . . I—just, mind your own business. Stars. What about Gavrielle?" I quickly change the subject.

"There's nothing to talk about for now. I need to focus on this game." Deimos crosses his arms and walks off.

"But—"

A big fat meathead approaches, and I stop talking immediately.

"Emmers." My hello is less than enthusiastic.

Slapping me on the back way harder than necessary, he patronizes me right off the bat. "Surprised to see you here and not your little boyfriend. Seems like Damon got you there and back, eh?"

It's so hard not to deck this guy in the face.

"Actually, it was her who did most of the work." Gav's voice breaks in before I can reply with some smart-ass remark.

Laughing awkwardly, Emmers tries to backtrack. "You know I'm just messing with the little girl. Come on, look at her. *So cute*."

"Screw you, dude," I finally say with a roll of my eyes and a disgusted scoff. "I know what you're trying to do, and it won't work."

"Oh, yeah? What am I trying to do?"

I step up closer, barely coming up to the guy's breastbone. "You're threatened by me, and your little psych-out isn't going to work. I've faced a lot scarier dudes than you, my man. And I promise, you won't even make it on the list of people I'm worried about today."

Emmers's laugh is deep and cynical. "Oh, sweetheart, you're adorable. Nobody is threatened by you."

"I am," Gav says before I can respond. "And if I were you, I would be, too."

I raise my chin in triumph. What I just won, I don't know. It doesn't matter because Emmers putters off with a grunt and some sexist bullshit, muttering under his breath.

"Thanks," I say, seeing "Damon" in an entirely new light this morning. "That guy has had a stick up his ass for me since day one. I have no idea why, but whatever. How are you after yesterday? Did any memories resurface?"

Gav shakes his head, and he looks a bit sad. Until he suddenly squints his eyes at me, sniffing the air as if he's caught a whiff of something in the air. Then that look of sadness transforms into another wholly unexpected emotion. *Jealousy*. Stars, how mortifying. Does everyone know Ardelle and I had sex? Jupiter's rings. But there's no more time to discuss or analyze it before the SSPARROWs let in the paparazzi. Which I'm incredibly grateful for because I am not discussing my sex life with my childhood friend I just reunited with yesterday.

The shouts of questions come down on us all like pelleted rain.

"Karalevine, are you disappointed your lover is no longer competing with you?"

"Are you defying the empire, Kara?"

"Any news on the man whose genitalia you set on fire and his condition? Will he be seeking legal damages against you?"

"Is it true you're working with the rebels? Are you a Renegade, Karalevine?"

A female reporter points at Gav and me. "Who is this new mystery man? Should your lover be worried? Sources say he's beside himself at the fact this icy-haired Sky-Fae is gunning for your heart."

I look at Gav, my cheeks blushing. He smiles back at me and tilts himself over to say in my ear, "You caused all this. Deal with it."

It goes on and on for the next thirty minutes. So much so, half the Titans simply walk off, knowing the press isn't remotely interested in them. I can't believe all the attention I'm getting.

"The Silent Breath is no hoax. We all saw the children as they were liberated from Arianyte's clutches. They testified to being bled dry, many to the point of death. Arianyte claims those children were sick with illness, that they were curing them, but we all know the leader of the empire lies."

Questions erupt.

"Is Malakyte Ardeen a liar, Kara?"

"Was the Silent Breath why you stopped working for him?"

"What should be the consequences of breaking the Devouring Accords?"

Before I can even think of an answer, dozens of SSPARROW soldiers emerge from nowhere and aggressively remove both me and the paparazzi.

I'm seized and dragged back towards the building by three SSPARROW, Gav hot on our heels. I'm thrown against the concrete wall and flung so hard all the air is forced from my lungs.

"Hey!" Gavrielle yells, shoving his massive body between the soldiers and me.

The distorted voice of the person inside the metal uniform berates both Gav and me. "You talk to the press about the Silent Breath one more time, and there will be consequences that your new celebrity will not protect you from. He is finished watching you disrespect him and this empire. He made that exceptionally clear."

We all know who *he* is.

"Shut your mouth, or else. We will not warn you again."

The soldier speaking to me rises, turns, and shoulder-checks Gavrielle before him and his other two assholes-in-arms walk back towards the rest of the Titans.

"Stars . . . are you alright?" Gav asks.

I crack my neck once or twice as I rub the slash at my throat. The gauze that's covering it seems to have loosened some.

"I'm fine," I say, the SSPARROWs announcing that families and friends are coming in now. "Don't worry about it. There are people I need to go see."

Crossing the hangar with Gav in tow, I meet the crowd of our closest supporters, the other Titans doing the same.

"Kid!" I hear Jance's deep voice calling, and his height allows me to see him through the crowd.

We both run towards each other. The way I left things yesterday was so childish and stupid, and I just hope he still . . . still *what*?

Malakyte's words slam into my mind, amplifying my insecurities. Spiking the fear within me that who I am at my core is far too dark and unlovable for these people. Good people don't love bad people . . . It doesn't work that way. Can Jance accept me, even though I don't necessarily have his morals or principles? I have both morals and principles. They're just different from his.

I meet Jance's eyes hesitantly, a bomb of anxiety waiting to blow within my chest. He hugs me just as tightly—just as warmly as ever, but I watch for any minute changes.

I'm relieved to see Ardelle made it to them, and we hug tightly.

Ahren has come as well, likely worried about his Starseed's return home.

"Everyone, this is Gavrielle." I introduce Gav as he stands behind me.

"The same Gavrielle you told us about? He's alive?" Ahren asks pointedly.

I turn, cranking my neck to look Gavrielle in the eyes. "I thought you were dead. Arianyte has you listed as dead in their system." I turn to the others. "He's got some amnesia. He doesn't remember me."

The two Ringers eye each other skeptically, which shoots a pang of fear straight into my gut like a spear.

"Gav, this is Jance, he's my—" I stop short, unsure what to call him.

Jance steps forward without hesitation and holds his hand out to Gav. "I'm Kara's father."

I'm unable to help myself as my entire body tingles at his words.

Although this seems to confuse Gav, the uncertainty disappears from his face quickly.

"Gav, you met Ardelle already," I pan to Ardelle.

Gav smiles cocky and cool and wholly unbothered. "The one with the magic tricks. I remember."

"I'm not the only one with tricks," Ardelle answers just as slyly.

The two simply grin at each other.

After the introductions are over, Ahren forces me to show him the slash on my throat. We separate ourselves from the crowd and the others, Jance following like a shadow.

After pulling the makeshift dressing from my neck, Ahren looks at it intently as he throws on a pair of gloves he stashed in his pocket. I also inform him of the bite marks.

"Kid." Jance finally breaks the silence. "Who attacked you yesterday?"

I rake my tongue along my teeth before I answer. "The Mistress."

I explain everything to them.

"We have to assume if they came for you once, they're going to come for you again." Jance's black coffee eyes show worry, fear, and concern. He isn't wrong.

Ahren speaks before I can.

"A centimeter deeper, and this wound would have ended your life. I must heal this if you wish to keep your windpipe."

"Lovely," I breathe. "Thank the stars Malakyte—*my knight and shining armor*—came to rescue me. What the hell is going on? It's like everything is ass backwards in this tournament. Is Malakyte setting up for a redemption arc, or what?"

"I wouldn't count on that," Jance answers dully.

"Whatever it is"—Ahren removes his gloves—"you better traverse these next two games with extreme caution."

I meet Ahren's gaze as he drenches his hands in sanitizer, the smell of alcohol so strong it's a practical slap in the face. The red glow lights up his pupils, and I instantly feel his magic enter my body as the two of us link up through eye contact. Jance's hands squeeze my shoulders as he stands like a comforting statue behind me.

I hiss, teeth gritting hard as Ahren's magic seeps into the gash in my throat. His bare hand cups along the slash, the other above the puncture wounds of the bite, and I close my eyes and try to be anywhere else but here. Ahren's power sears its way through my flesh at lightning speed. Burning and pulling and ripping and reforming. Until I am made new again.

Hurried footsteps approach us from the crowd's side.

Ardelle runs up to us shortly after, taking my hand in his; Gav stands by, watching, too.

"As good as new," Ahren says, releasing our connection as his magic ceases. My neck burns as if it's on fire, but it feels like smooth baby skin. I thank Ahren just as the five-minute warning is blared, and Jance not so subtly pulls me aside. The others walk away, giving us privacy.

"I'm sorry about yesterday," I blurt out, knowing we don't have a lot of time. "I just . . . I don't want this to change anything. I promise I'm not making it up. And—"

Jance forces me to turn and face him, but I can't meet his eyes, and my cheeks flush with heat and fear.

"Kara, look at me," he says, bending down to my eye level. But I don't, I can't. I can't see him tell me what so many other so-called father figures have said before. It's too hard to bear him leaving me like Geonni left me; he promised a lot of things, too.

It's too unbearable, all of it is. And I'm simply too weak to handle it. And heroes aren't cowards, either, are they?

His face keeps following mine until I can't crank my neck any further to avoid him. With a frustrated huff of my breath, I finally look at him.

He smiles softly. "I knew something was odd the moment I first saw you at the confinement center the night we brought you home. I suspected as much because you looked so much like Astoria. I couldn't deny it. The sight of you practically brought me to my knees. It was like seeing a ghost. There are questions that I have, but I've known you were my daughter from day one. I didn't tell you because I wanted you to find your own way to me. You didn't want to be with us initially, and I knew there was a lot on your plate, so I waited. It's why I told you what I did that night you came to my room distressed, 'You're mine, kid.' You've always been mine, and nothing you could ever do will cause me to abandon this relationship. I failed you, not knowing you were out there. I should have known. I should have known whoever killed your mother wasn't after her . . . Darling, I think they were after *you*."

My whole world tilts.

They were after *me*? Whoever killed my mother wasn't targeting her at all, no . . . that wouldn't make sense, would it? If I was taken—which I was because I'm alive—it's only logical to surmise that I was abducted for a purpose. And there's only one reason that could be.

This damned Elendril crystal.

"All that happened to you in those years you could've been with me . . . it's all my fault. Your scars are from my ignorance. Your trauma is the fault of my disregard of the truth. I should have demanded to see proof of both bodies but identifying your mother broke me. I couldn't handle seeing . . . I was a weak man, and it cost you your childhood. It's likely that, if Malakyte knew of our relationship, he's involved in your mother's death somehow. How deeply involved, we'll have to discover on our own. Get your mother justice, if we can. I'll spend the rest of my life making it up to you, Kara. Can you ever forgive me?"

The flash of what my life could have been like with Jance there from day one comes on heavily . . . the what-ifs of who I could have been had I not grown up in a world of chaos and trauma and abuse—but in one of love, support, and stability . . . the cruel irony is crushing. I should have been with him. I should have been a happy, healthy, normal child. Instead—well . . . I'm just *this*. Maybe this darkness wouldn't exist within me if so many people hadn't tarnished my soul.

"Of course I can," I choke out, voice trembling with emotion. I don't blame him for my life. It wasn't his fault. The pain in his eyes tells me how deeply he blames himself. "There's nothing to forgive, Jance."

He embraces me, and I never want him to let me go. Yet, that orphaned girl in me sinisterly whispers, *But he knew all this and still walked out on you. He left and said he couldn't deal with you anymore.*

No. I'm ignoring that voice. It's wrong.

"Had I known you were alive, I never would have stopped looking. Never. And I would have found you and brought you home to me."

Tears fall to my cheeks.

"I know."

I never thought I'd be reunited with either of my parents, let alone have one who was this wonderful.

Ardelle comes back over to us, and instead of breaking our embrace, he joins in. Wrapping his arms around us both, I'm smashed between the two giants.

"Group hug!" he hollers, Ahren joining in—because why not?

"Gav!" I yell, voice muffled as I'm practically drowned in bodies. "Deimos! Get your grumpy ass over here."

Gav jumps in like he's been with us for years, and when Deimos reluctantly sulks over, Ardelle snatches him as if he's a prisoner of war.

I realize something all of a sudden. There are so many people behind me, those who have my back. I was trying to do this all alone, convinced that I had to conquer this impossible challenge by myself because that's all I've ever known. I wasn't aware of how else to solve a problem other than to suit up and get that shit done alone. There was nobody to count on.

That isn't true anymore. I do have people to lean on, those who love me and care and want me to succeed as badly as I do. I'm surrounded by them, and I need to stop being stupid and sabotaging these relationships. Protect them, keep them safe. That's what I've got to do.

Eventually we break off as we're told it's time to leave.

Ardelle gives me one final hug, and we kiss each other hurriedly and passionately, as if it could be the very last kiss we ever share. It won't be. I know it won't be.

"Be careful, kid. We'll be with you the entire time." Jance's words are comforting as I watch them go.

Text begins funneling in on my lens, and it says, *Aw, that was sweet. Good luck, girl. I'm watching your ass. Don't die.*

I won't die, I say, as if to Trinity herself. In actuality, I'm saying it to myself. There's no fucking way I'm going to die. I've got a teammate to save and a prince to kill.

CHAPTER 37

HIT THE ECONOMIC NERVE:

FOLLOW THE CATO TRAIL, REBELS. TARGET THEIR ECONOMIC CENTERS, DISRUPT THEIR FINANCIAL OPERATIONS, AND LEAVE THEM BROKE LIKE A GAMBLER IN OLD TOWN. CATO CREDITS TALK, BUT WE'LL MAKE IT SCREAM FOR OUR CAUSE.

The others aren't gone for more than two minutes when all the SSPARROWs line up before us.

"We've got a special gift for everyone before we fly you up to the eastern Sky Dais," one of them explains, and not more than ten seconds pass when an expensive ground-hover drives up to the hangar's entrance.

My blood pressure instantly drops.

That's Malakyte in there, he's come here. I just know it.

My panicked eyes flash to Deimos, knowing we got too lucky with Ardelle being able to just walk out of here.

He looks concerned, but he's composed.

"It's fine, stay behind me," he says, and even though he's the last person I want to take comfort from, we have agreed to be allies in this tournament of death and trust has to go both ways.

"What's wrong?" Gav asks, clearly confused.

Before I can answer him or explain, the doors to the ground-hover open skywards, and my mouth falls straight to the floor.

"What the fuck?" Deimos says before I can, and I'm so thrown off guard I almost fall over.

This cannot be.

Emerging from the hover are two pristinely dressed Terrans, a couple with platinum blond hair done up so not a hair is out of place. Their clothing is immaculately made, tailored, and styled to say they've got both money and power. The man's suit has gold cufflinks, and the woman's jewelry is as expensive and sparkling as her fake smile. I'm familiar with these two, but their faces are older versions of the two people I know well.

Mr. and Mrs. Devil Incarnate, as I like to call them—Emily and Richard Dawson.

That's not the surprising part. It's the person they brought with them that shocks me halfway to Saturn.

She's dressed in a hideous pink-and-gray two-piece skirt and jacket combo. It's made of a thick and itchy material and its plaid pattern screams *stuck-up bitch*. The white turtleneck under the jacket completely covers her crystal mark. It's accented with a pearl necklace and earrings to match. Her hair is no longer colored blue but instead mirrors the flawless butter blond of her parents, styled and cut into a bob that looks more pompous than chic. But that's not even the worst part.

It's the look on her face—the expression in her eyes.

Rage replaces the shock that first formed at the sight of her—of this girl I thought I knew that wears the face of someone I do not recognize.

Pacey.

What did they do to you? Wait . . . oh no. Have they done it? Have they successfully removed your crystal?

Fists hardening into rage-filled balls as my nails cut into my skin, teeth threatening to crack as I hiss, "Deimos, what the hell is happening?"

"I don't even know," he admits, eyes wide with shock. "Do you think she's playing along to appease them?"

"I've got a better question. Her turtleneck is covering the mark, so there's no way to tell, but could they have already taken her crystal out? Do you think they knew we were coming and they went ahead with the surgery early?"

Deimos doesn't answer.

Standing before a floating microphone, Richard Dawson smiles at the group, but it's fake as shit and cold as ice.

I bet you're regretting not killing these douchebags when you had the chance, huh? Trinity's words appear on my lens, and though I can't tell if she means it sincerely or sarcastically, the sentiment is the same. Regret fills me up to the brim.

"Remaining Titans," Richard says, his voice a deeper and more sophisticated vibrato than his son's. "As sponsors and leaders of Zone Seventy-Seven, the home of Zarmenia City, we share our admiration and pride as you valiantly battle your way through to become the Titan Champion."

It takes everything in me not to scoff in disgust.

"For today's game, many other Terran government officials have been invited to participate in the day's events."

"That doesn't sound good . . ." Deimos mumbles under his breath, and I completely agree.

Figuring Pacey can't see my short ass in the crowd, I slowly make my way forward. If Malakyte were here, he'd have shown his face by now, so I feel confident that he isn't.

Mr. Devil Incarnate continues his speech. "With a generous donation to Arianyte, each Terran official has the opportunity to throw a sabotage onto the field. It can be dedicated towards any player."

"So, you're paying to sabotage us?" a player asks, not sounding particularly thrilled.

I'm halfway up to the front, but the closer I get, the more worried I become. Something about Pacey isn't right. Her face is off, her *eyes.*

Her father answers the question coldly. "That is how the game was designed. The Titan Games are supposed to be challenging, are they not? But don't fret. Only two sabotages are permitted per contestant, so no Titan is unfairly targeted. It can also skew the betting pools."

Pitting us against the rich and powerful elite surely isn't the way to keep the public happy, Malakyte, I think to myself as I finally get to the front of the crowd. There's no way she won't be able to see me now.

I discreetly wave to get her attention, but she ignores me.

While her father goes on and on about sportsmanship and whatever bullshit he's using to justify betraying his own kind for money and power, I do my best to try and get Pacey's attention.

I cough three times, hiss at her, stare her down like a crazy person, but nothing works. She's got to be purposely ignoring me at this point because nearly everyone here can see I'm trying to get her attention.

"Can I help you with something, young lady?"

It takes me a second too long to figure out the question is directed towards me, and I look up to see Ardelle's father staring me down with eyes that are the same Cerulean Sea Blue as his son's. It's bizarre, because even though they're the identical color, all of Ardelle's life and goodness are stripped away, leaving nothing but an icy veneer instead.

"Richard," Emily hisses, trying to get her husband's attention on the down-low. "That's the girl."

Likely, nobody other than those of us up front could hear her, and thankfully for them, all the families and press have gone, because whatever fire is lit up under Richard's ass is a big one. Recognition floods his gaze, matching his wife's contentment for me from the moment her cold large eyes came upon me.

"Ah, yes. *Her.*" His voice takes on a certain edge to it, one I've heard in Ardelle's once or twice when we first met. I see where he got it from.

Finally, Pacey looks me in the eyes, and my heart soars.

Only for it to plummet once more.

 252

There's nothing behind those giant, once life-filled eyes. Almost exactly like Gavrielle. When she looks upon me, there's absolutely zero recognition there. As if she's never seen me before. I'm nothing but a homeless person on the street, dirty and gross and foreign. Completely irrelevant.

"What did you do to her?" I demand. "She's your daughter, for star's sake. Can't you just let her be who she is? Can you not simply love her without ordering her to be 'fixed' of some nothing-affliction you worry will make you look bad? Must you brandish her as your porcelain doll while scooping out her soul in the process? Stars, look at her! That is not Pacey."

The smug look on both their faces in response makes my blood boil.

"We have no idea what you speak of. We love our children dearly." Emily's voice is sweet in tone, and to the outside world, she almost pulls off the loving mother act, but I see right through it.

"Your children hate you both. It's why your son was in my bed last night and not anywhere near you."

The Titans around us respond to that, some snickering and others cursing impressed words under their breath.

Pacey finally speaks, and I'm not prepared.

"We'll see about that. My brother will see through your pathetic, low-class act soon enough. Whatever you're doing to manipulate him, he'll come to see you for what you truly are. It's disgusting to take advantage of his pain. You're lucky your fifteen minutes of fame is protecting you in this game because, if all these cameras weren't on you, I'd beat your little ass myself."

"Pacey, darling, we do not threaten low lives," Emily tells her daughter pointedly.

"Pacey, what the hell?" I breathe, so confused as to what's happening here. "Snap out of it. They're messing with your head."

He did it. Malakyte Reconditioned her. It's the only explanation. We're already too late, aren't we? Whether her crystal still beats within her chest or not is also a mystery. But I doubt it's gone. She'd be dead if it were. Did Malakyte figure out our plan to enter the Titan Games was a rescue mission, and instead of trying to risk the surgery quicker than planned, they opted to Recondition her first? Is this all because of me? Even if we somehow manage to get her back with us physically, the Pacey we know and love so dearly—is gone.

She's *gone.*

I almost throw up right here, the nausea hitting me like a baseball bat to the skull.

"Pacey, please. It's me. It's Kara."

She scoffs at me like I'm the dirt on her perfectly scuff-free white pumps. Looking down her nose at me, she says, "I know exactly who you are, Karalevine Ruzz. And I know trash when I see it. You may have manipulated and tricked my brother in the first game, but I promise you, in the second one, you won't have the opportunity to use whatever poison you carry within you to weasel your way into another win. We'll make certain of that. And we'll make certain Ardelle comes home to us, too. Just you watch."

I do not know this girl.

I feel a presence walk up behind me, and I'm surprised to see Deimos there.

"That's enough, kiddo. Time to go."

He grabs onto my shoulders, his pointed nails digging into my skin.

I resist him. "No. Pacey, wake up! You're a Starseed. You're one of *us.*"

I can't help but let my anger overflow in the form of tears as I search her eyes for any recognition of the girl I once knew. This isn't real. Not after all we've been through to get this far. This can't be happening. This cannot be all my fault—the guilt will destroy me.

Deimos is now pulling on me, and I'm pushing against him—hard.

"We're done here," Richard Dawson says to the lot of us, but I am not done. Not by a space mile.

"No!" I scream as the three of them turn back to their hover like I'm nothing at all. "Pacey! Stars, Pace! Snap out of it!"

I'm losing it in front of all these people, those who are supposed to be my competitors. No doubt, this was a trap set specifically to trigger me. And damn, has it worked.

Gav arrives at my other side, the three Dawsons entering their hover and slamming the doors shut, my cries completely closed off to them.

"They're gone, Kara, let them go." Gav lifts me up in his giant arms and carries me back through the crowd. I don't care that the other players all stare at me; I don't give a fuck what they think. The only reason I'm even here is because of that girl.

A SSPARROW signals to the group to enter the sky-hovers immediately after the Dawson's hover takes off, and I don't know how I'm supposed to go up there and battle these people after this. What the hell is the point?

"Hey!" Deimos shakes me roughly, and I have no choice but to look him in his Black Lagoon eyes, even though mine are full of angry tears. "Get a hold of yourself, kiddo. This isn't the time to lose your shit. I get it, what you just saw was messed up, and I don't even know where to begin, but the best thing you can do for her is to stick to the plan. Got it?"

"What plan?" Gav asks, and Deimos shoots him with a distrusting glare before looking back at me.

The arch in one of his fluffy white brows is enough to tell me to keep my mouth shut about said plan. He doesn't need to say another word. I understand.

Deimos is right. I need to get my shit together because there's no time and no mercy from these competitors. I've got to win this game and get onto that spaceship. But that reminds me, if Pacey's now mind-fucked and potentially working for the enemy, which is likely, then this throws a major wrench into our plans. The panic in my eyes finally causes Deimos to think a bit further into the future. He figures it out pretty quickly. If she's on their side now, how are we supposed to hack their systems and disrupt the digital flow of communications the moment war breaks out? That was our one chance to hit the occupation hard and swift so we can end this war before it ever began—with as few casualties as possible. We can't do any of that without Pacey.

"Just get through the games," he tells me with a frustrated growl. "And keep your damned head on straight."

It's all I can do to keep my head on at all as we pile into the sky-hover and zoom into the air towards the next Dais and the next game. Whatever is in store for us up there, it's not going to be easy.

I check my lens, and there's no comment about what just conspired. Jance and the others likely aren't back to base yet, so I know they didn't see the encounter with Pacey. I try waving my hands in front of my face to signal Trinity, but she doesn't say anything. Perhaps she's as stunned as I am and trying to come up with some alternative plan.

I don't care. I don't care how hard it is. Pacey wouldn't give up on any of us. She'd fight and think and figure out a way to get us back. There must be a way to undo what's been done to her. I must find it. When Ardelle sees this, he'll be crushed. I don't want his heart to shatter, see the pain he's going to experience. I love him too much to see his world fracture apart before his very eyes. And it will; he'll break. I know it. If I save her, I can prevent his suffering. Prevent all of them from feeling what I'm experiencing now. The last thing I want is for them to be blindsided like this. It's beyond cruel and twisted.

Malakyte will not get away with this. I'm even more determined than I was, and if this is a low blow attempt to throw me off balance before this game, it isn't going to work. I do my best when I'm mad, and I am thirty-paces-to-the-moon enraged and ready to kick some fucking ass. He poked the bear, and now he's getting the monster. He loves darkness. He wants darkness—I'll give him darkness.

He better prepare because this game just got dirty, and I'm here to fucking play.

CHAPTER 38

You have got to be kidding me.

We've just learned what game two is going to be.

Today is colder than yesterday, and my teeth chatter as the other Titans and I stand huddled together in the hangar on top of the eastern Sky Dais.

"The race will be one solid lap around the Sky Dais along the designated path," says the SSPARROW. "Anyone who tries to get smart and divert from the path will be disqualified. There are twenty-seven of you remaining from yesterday. Only the first fifteen Titans who successfully cross the finish line will continue to the finale. Everyone else will be disqualified."

Richard Dawson's little speech about sabotage is making a lot more sense now.

Stars . . .

"Line up to select your vehicle. These will consist of old-world internal combustion engines—petroleum based. Others will be ground-hovers, electric engines. It all depends on which one you get. Players will approach this device screen at random, and once your vehicle has been selected, the machine will spit out a miniature version which you will take down to the race pit, where you'll be suited, strapped in, and lined up to race. Get moving."

We all collectively look at each other, a bit stunned and not having expected a race. I don't think Arianyte has ever done one in the Titan Games before.

Doing as we're told, we line up in a single file behind what looks like an arcade game mixed with a vending machine, the only difference being its rounded edges and sleek metal design.

What happens next depends completely on which type of car or hover a person gets. Either shouts of joy or whines of disappointment come from the people in front. As Gav and Deimos stand behind me, discussing which would be better, I really don't care about the type of car I'm going to be getting. All I can think of is Pacey, what they did to her. How I let this happen and how it's all my fault.

"Get it together," I hear Deimos growl from behind me. "I can feel your emotions slipping, and it's going to make you sloppy. You have to be here and take part in this race if you have any hope of getting your friend's mind back. Lock it up in a box for now and focus."

"I can't!" I hiss back, blinking away the tears that come.

Deimos leans down to my ear and whispers quite cruelly, "You don't have a choice."

He's right. I don't.

Finally, it's my turn. I approach the machine and follow the prompts, inputting my player ID and letting it generate the car I'm supposed to get. They claim it's random, but I doubt it. I'm probably going to get a junky piece of shit.

A pleasant jingle chimes as a picture of a spicy looking car comes into view on the screen. It's got wheels, so it's not a hover. Knowing absolutely nothing about cars, I press the accept button—like I've got any other choice—and a miniature version of my car pops out. It fits in the palm of my hands, and my brows are high with intrigue as I walk away and wait for the other players to get their own ride.

Once everyone has their miniature vehicles, we enter an underground half-dome area that opens into the racetrack's starting line. The overhead is massive, at least three hundred feet tall and one hundred wide. The track itself is much less wide, likely around sixty feet or so. Lined up in rows are all our vehicles, spanning seven cars in each of the four rows. I'm taken to one of the pit crew people for a quick orientation.

The person before me is an average Terran, a young man with short brown hair and brown eyes. He wears a one-piece suit as he nervously rummages through his portable locker.

"Please put this on." The boy hands me a helmet, and I take it from him. It's all black except the Arianyte A logo on the back in Scarlet Rouge. The helmet is tight on my face, slightly pressing my cheeks together as it sits snugly over my head.

"You have your visor here," he says to me, the visor rising over my eyes with a push of a button on the side. "Give me your car model, please."

The young man holds out his hand, and I toss him the mini version of my car. His brows rise slightly, but he says nothing as he turns and begins walking away.

"I will take you to it now."

I scan the vehicles before following the kid through the starting pit, zigzagging by other players and the colorful array of machines. I see slick ground-hovers, high powered, sleek, and monstrous old-world cars with wheels as big as me in. A few are the typical Malakyte black, while others shine with colors I can only dream of tattooing with. One is Bumblebee Yellow with black lightning bolts. Another appears almost as sloshes of thick, wet paint collided into each other on this ground-hover as Butternut Squash Orange and Ocean Breeze Blue melt together. I ogle at another one that's got spiky edges protruding out from all angles, including its tires. Each one is different. There's even one that's a juiced-up mountain vehicle of some kind; stars, I don't even know what that is. Those types and the few motorcycles look like the most difficult ones to drive.

It's only when I finally set eyes on my car that I completely forget about all the others because damn.

"She's got a variable-compression two-liter, four-cylinder engine but packs quite a punch for being more eco-friendly, with some other alien tech in there I doubt you care much about. And it's a V12, too." For the first time, this young man comes to life as he talks about the car before me. "Even though it's technically a combustion engine—an old-world engine—she's fast. Just look at those curves! You see, the aerodynamics of this car are sick. She's sleek, fire on turns, and did I mention she's *fast*? If I'm being real, you've probably got the best car here. Lucky you, being a girl and all."

My brow rises at him. "A girl and all?"

"I meant no offense. It's just . . . girls typically don't care about cars. That's all I meant by it . . ."

The car, however, is stunning. Its base color is white, but it has iridescent sheens of purples, pinks, and blues. It looks as if it's already blasting at the speed of light, despite it sitting completely still. The way it was designed makes it appear like it's shooting through the stars. The headlights are narrow and point down towards the grill—which, alone, has intricate shapes and colors of purple accents. The wheels are average size, but the rims have some glowing violet light emitting from within them. The windshield is angled more flat than other cars. The open canopy does leave me exposed, though.

"We've been calling it the Warrior Angel," the boy says, all smiles.

I chuckle a bit at the name, only because it's quite fitting. "Does it have wings or something?"

Eyes sparkling, he walks up and presses a button on the side. "Practically."

Before my eyes, both doors simultaneously open in sync with each other, opening out skywards—like a pair of angel wings.

Pacey would absolutely adore this car. It's totally her, in every way. It has all the bells and whistles she loves. It has all the extra stuff to make it special . . .

My fists ball up in anger, that overwhelming panic settling into my chest again. How did they turn her? What did they do to her to create such a fracture in her psyche? The dark images of all that must've happened come scorching into my thoughts, and I absentmindedly brush my nails along my star mark under my uniform. I want to burn this entire place down for all they've done to her. Make every person involved pay one hundredfold for each moment of her suffering.

"You okay?"

I blink, the boy looking at me as if I might pass out.

"Yeah," I lie, "I'm fine."

He doesn't look like he believes me, but he nods anyway and leans into the car. Bringing me along with him, he points down to the vast- and complicated-looking dash.

Stars, how am I supposed to drive this thing? It looks like a spaceship in there.

"Things to remember," he begins. "It's an automatic transmission, which is good. It shifts gears for you. That means all you gotta do is press on that pedal. That's the gas, and she'll purr for you. Try to keep your RPMs below four, five max. Go over that, and you can blow the engine. These babies are fast and powerful but finicky. That's the trade-off, I'm afraid. If you're in a pinch and need a little boost in speed, press this button there."

He points to a Lime Green triangle-shaped button in the very center of the dash.

"But be careful with that," he warns, looking me dead in the eyes. "The likelihood of you gaining that extra speed and not being able to control the vehicle is extremely high. You're just as likely to zip yourself right off this platform as you are to pass your competitors. It's a big gamble. I'll leave that to you. It's more of a break-glass-in-case-of-emergency type deal. Just know most of us pros can't even control it, so it's your call. I'm required to tell you about it and its risks."

"Comforting."

"If it were me, I wouldn't use it. Although, I'm not the one in this competition, am I?" He laughs awkwardly and looks down at his shoes, which are covered in grease stains. "I umm . . . watched you battle yesterday and just wanted to say I thought you were amazing. The way you fight with that sword is incredible. I wish more girls were like you, the way you say whatever you feel like with no fear about the consequences. The truth is, I don't even like the occupation. I just do this for the credits—so my family and I can survive. Man, it feels so good to say that out loud. It's too bad you won't really have much use for that sword in this round, huh?"

A part of me is both happy I am inspiring him but also a tad surprised by his reaction to me. Although, aren't I doing this for people exactly like him? Those relentlessly trapped under Malakyte's thumb, either for financial reasons or perhaps pure survival. Regardless of why a person is being forced to kiss the ring of our dear leader, the mission is still the same—change their opinion of the occupation. If we turn the people, we turn the tide.

"What's your name?" I ask, and he lights up like the engines roaring to life all around us.

"Mickey," he says. "My dad is an old grease monkey, and I was supposed to inherit the family business before Arianyte came and its technology and the decrees put us out of business. We weren't able to acclimate to hover vehicles quick enough to keep business open. That said, we had to close and take jobs through the occupation so we could get training to even understand their technology. It's why seeing old-world cars being used here is so exciting to me. They've all but disappeared."

That's right. They polluted the air too much, and Arianyte banned them from use.

"Well, Mickey, I'm here to end this occupation," I say boldly, giving zero fucks about whoever can hear me. The only person who can do anything about it already knows I'm coming for him and his throne. "Perhaps, if I win these games, I can make some real changes."

I hold out my hand to him, and he looks at it like it's something completely and utterly foreign. Eventually, though, he takes it.

"I'll be putting all my bets on you."

CHAPTER 39

As I sit in the driver's seat of this juiced-up, old-world car, I familiarize myself with its properties. The wheel, obviously, is manual steering. There's no artificial computer interface that can assist. This is all me. It isn't round but instead has two handles on either side of it that don't connect to the top or bottom. The Arianyte A sits in the middle, encased by a black circle and glowing in the color Bloody Tear Crimson. The seats are all white leather, stitched with a thick Neon Green thread.

I focus on my lens, expecting some sly comment from Ardelle about my feet not reaching the pedals, but there's nothing. Not anything about Pacey, either. That's odd. There's just a generic "Good luck."

Well, whatever, I guess. They're probably just nervous for me.

The young mechanic, Mickey, finally returns and approaches me with the car key in his hand. "Time to get this baby turned on."

The key is a flat triangle-shaped card. He presses it against a section on the dash, and the roar that comes to life beneath me is nothing less than a beast awakening.

"Man, doesn't she purr like a kitten?" he fawns, but I'm still stunned at the vibration on my ass to say much of anything, so I nod in agreement.

The power of this machine is incredible. I feel it. And she's all mine.

I grin inside my helmet, unable to help myself. Whether this vehicle was given to me randomly or if Malakyte handpicked it, it's straight-up the best gift I've gotten this entire competition.

The dash lights up in the colors Pop Pink, Green Inferno, and Blue Snowflake. There are a lot of buttons and bobs, numbers, and symbols I don't understand.

Mickey sees my discomfort and clarifies a few things for me. "Don't worry about all that stuff. Here's what you need to focus on the most. See this screen above the steering wheel? These are your RPMs I told you about. They're on the left. It also records your speed in miles per hour in increments of ten on your right. It can go up to one hundred and eighty miles per hour, but like I warned you before, that speed is incredibly difficult to handle. And it's only reachable if you push the green triangle. The screen in the center higher on the dash analyzes the route twenty feet ahead and places the image inside this screen for you. Watch out because it can be distracting. Also, twenty feet in this car is a blink of an eye, so keep that in mind. You're also being recorded, see here." He points to a mounted camera sitting on the flat part of the dash below the windshield. "Say hi to the people of Earth." He waves to the camera. I do nothing. That isn't creepy or anything. I bet Malakyte has my car's camera set to his personal viewing screen right this moment. The urge to cuss him out for what he's done to Pacey is overwhelming.

"One last thing," he says, pointing to an arbitrary number double zero on the dash, "this will show your place in the race.

Once you start and get out beyond the starting pit, it'll begin tracking your place."

After finishing up my short orientation, I'm given some leather gloves as a goodbye present from Mickey, and he leaves me at the two-minute mark.

My adrenaline is starting to build up within my blood with each passing second. Since my car is roofless, I stand up high and look around for Deimos and Gav. I'm settled roughly in the middle of all the vehicles, if not slightly towards the back. With all the revving of engines, I can't hear my own heart hammering in my ears, but I can certainly feel it. A lot of the men here are showing off their engine's power. Some are even inching forward and stopping suddenly, unable to contain their excitement. They're roaring to go—pun intended. No sign of Gav or Deimos, and I have no clue what cars they're in. Instead of worrying about Pacey back when we got our miniature versions, I should have looked at their rides, so I knew who was in which one. Stupid. I'm being reckless. As difficult and painful as it is, I've got to put Pacey out of my mind for now. If I don't, it's going to get me killed.

Sliding back into my seat, I double-check all my mirrors, my pedals, then strap myself into the crisscross seatbelt.

Helmet visor down.

Middle finger up.

I'm ready.

A loud blaring sound accommodated by red flashing lights surround the semicircular dome, coming to life along with a ten second countdown.

Holy stars, this is happening.

I spare a glance at the words on my lens, and there's nothing new there. I feel alone and a bit hurt by their lack of support, but maybe they simply don't want to distract me. But I'm not alone. I remember they're here with me. My father, my boyfriend, and even Gav—are with me. Plus, my sword is my ride or die companion sitting in the passenger seat. It followed me across the stars, I realize, and it will continue to bring me strength during this round.

Ardelle's arrow tucked away inside the sword's sheath. A piece of him is with me, too.

I switch gears to drive.

Five.

I take a deep breath.

Four.

I squeeze both sides of the wheel.

Three.

I look forward.

Two.

I focus on one thing.

One.

Winning.

The sound blares once again as my bones tremble in their wake, red lights switching to green.

I slam on the gas pedal.

The car roars to life.

CHAPTER 40

UNCONVENTIONAL WARFARE:

THINK OUTSIDE THE BOX, REBELS. EMBRACE UNCONVENTIONAL WARFARE. USE THE ENVIRONMENT, NATURAL DISASTERS, AND UNCONVENTIONAL WEAPONS. SURPRISE THEM, SHOCK THEM, AND GIVE THEM A TASTE OF REBEL UNPREDICTABILITY.

It's a clusterfuck.

We're all too close together right out of the gate, and I barely go anywhere because there's no space to do so.

"Move your asses! Go!" I yell out, finally discovering what road rage feels like.

The smaller vehicles, motorcycles, and cycle-hovers slither between the cars, easily making their way to the front of the line as they zip forward and pass us all.

I grit my teeth with impatient annoyance, eyes bouncing all over the place, looking for a way through.

There!

I punch it.

Zooming past a dozen cars easily, I zigzag my way closer to the front of the line. A gasp escapes my lips as a car to my left explodes into flames, and I don't even know how. This is crazy. As long as I make it out of this cluster, I'll be good.

The car is a bit squirrelly. Each inch I move the steering wheel, the machine veers double or triple what I intend. The pedal is also super touchy, and it clearly wants to go as fast as it can. I'm here to oblige.

It seems like forever, but finally, I separate from the heard, and it's a straightaway. However, this Sky Dais looks a lot different from the last one. This platform is desert-themed, and far out into the distance is a city, for all intents and purposes, that looks like an apocalyptic wasteland. Above me in the sky are the same floating islands that were on the last Sky Dais, and I don't get what their purpose is.

The first turn comes, and I slow down a bit. Three cars clustered around me do the same. I see the track is leading us towards the ruined city. On the back end of the turn, I press the pedal down and speed up, successfully passing all three other vehicles. Catching movement out of the corner of my eye, I see my rank in the race has changed. I'm in sixth place. Hell yeah.

Okay, Kara. Just keep this up. Stay steady, and you'll be fine. This isn't too bad.

The wind blasts my braid as the ends of it sticks out of the helmet like a horse's tail, but being all the way up here, driving this fast, it feels freeing. I can do this! I am not afraid.

I risk taking a glance at the lens when I finally see a new message pop up. It reads, *You got this, girl. Kick ass. We're all rooting for you.*

That's nice. They are still here. It's what I need.

A gold car creeps up to my right and is awfully close. Where'd this asshole come from, I wonder? I turn to look over and see if I can possibly catch a glimpse of who it could be.

A sausage middle finger waves in my direction—*Emmers.*

He swerves his car so close to mine I panic and jerk away, but I'm going so fast that I immediately lose control of the car. I swing way too hard to the left, veering completely off the asphalt track and into the sandy terrain. The sand blasts onto the car and into the cabin—getting everywhere.

Am I going to crash? Am I on the verge of ruining everything this soon after takeoff?

No, the voice of my crystal says vehemently, *no you will not.*

It's right. Fuck that. I'm not letting Emmers of all people knock me out of this game.

I grip the wheel tightly, letting my foot off the gas. I jerk from the immediate downgrade in the gears. The car revs, as if complaining it's not allowed to go as fast as it wants to. *Well, don't worry*, I promise the car, *we'll be hauling ass soon enough.*

Rolling over some bump under the sand and a grunt of frustration later, I'm back on the track but currently in ninth place.

Emmers is going to pay for that.

It takes the car no time to get back to top speed, the city's dark silhouette getting closer and closer, the details of its corroded buildings becoming clearer by the second. The car revs wildly, its engine purring as it automatically switches gears to allow it to hit higher and higher speeds. The power I feel with this sublime machine directly under my fingertips can only be akin to true elation.

Suddenly, my entire windshield lights up with a red light flashing all the way around its edges, and the word *Warning!* shows up for a split second. What's going on? Is there something wrong with the car? More words pop up in my field of vision across the entire windshield, completely distracting. *You've been sabotaged.*

"Oh, fuck me," I curse aloud. Who sabotaged me, and how is this going to be implemented? The stupid Dawsons are responsible for this. I just know it. Are they watching me through the cameras right now? Will anyone else be affected, or is it specifically me? At least we can only get two sabotages, from what Richard Dawson had said. If I survive this one and my second, I'll be fine.

From above, I see movement or a flash of light or something. Whatever it is, it draws my eyes upwards past the decrepit cityscape and onto the floating islands above the Sky Dais. I flip my visor up and squint, checking the road before I do. It's clear.

Looking up, I see what appears to be little black shapes moving around up there. What would be . . . *Oh, I get it.* Those aren't simply aesthetic islands; those are the damned spectator seats. How had I not spotted them yesterday? No way the public are the ones chilling up there. Which means only one thing, access to those islands comes strictly and directly through Arianyte. And let's just take a gander as to who else is sitting pretty up there while we're down here risking our lives for their entertainment? Terran government leaders, that's who. The Dawsons are definitely up there. Whether Pacey, Malakyte, and even Naresteé are, too, is a mystery I won't be able to solve right now.

Those sons of bitches.

But I have no time to be upset about it because, out of nowhere in the middle of the track, thick concrete slabs spring from the asphalt. Like giant spiky slices of monolithic bread springing up from a toaster. The spikes on them aren't merely for effect, either, and I see the car nearest to me smash directly into one, exploding on impact.

I scream in fright as one pops directly upwards in front of me with hardly any room to avoid it, and I veer to the right just in time to miss it. However, the paint job on this thing has a new spike-sized scratch all along the side of it.

The car swerves for a minute, but I'm able to gain control of it better than I was the last time. My heart's beginning to race again. These things can pop up anywhere.

There aren't many cars around me, but the two behind me slow down as their shapes get smaller in my mirrors. Great. I'm the guinea pig, then, huh?

It seems my sabotage affects the remaining players, then. Which means, other players' sabotages will affect me, too. If this is how this crazy race is going to play out, there could be booby traps anywhere at any time. Whoever invented these games is a madman.

Slowing down, I creep along the track cautiously, jumping at any movement or sign one of those slabs is going to pop out. I hear an engine revving up from behind me, and I look in my rearview mirror and see an Opal Red hover coming in hot.

Fine by me, buddy. Go for it.

I scoot to the edge of the track as the red car zooms past me in a flash of Cherry Bomb. For their sake, I hope they've got fast reflexes.

They don't.

About five seconds after they pass me, a slab shoots up from the ground. They try to dodge it, but they don't. Instead, their car hits a spike exactly as the slab explodes up from the asphalt, and it knocks the car into the sky a few feet. Upon landing, it flips once and lands right on the hood.

I slowly pass the car, checking to see if the person inside is okay. They seem to be alive, and they're neither Gav or Deimos, so I keep moving. But I do notice something curious.

As I pass the slab, I see it sink back down into the track itself from whence it came. Once it disappears, the spikes retreat as well, leaving a rectangular outline of it. That's it. That's how I see them before they fly out.

I got you now, you jerks. I'm coming for you up there on your perch. Try and sabotage me—my ass.

I punch it.

Using the car's camera and my keen eyesight, I search for the rectangular outlines in the track. There's one! On the right.

Dodging it, I skid past it as it pops up directly.

I grin devilishly.

There's nothing I hate more than someone trying to come for me but nothing I love more than watching them fail at it.

I do this several more times before reaching the entrance into the city, where, no doubt, there're far worse traps waiting for me. A green light illuminates the windshield in the same manner as the red warning did, giving me a cheery "Congratulations! You're not dead" notification. They really need to shove this sabotage crap right up their asses.

The buildings cast a shadow on the road as I slow the car, the roar of the engine slowing to a soft purr as I glide down the small slope and enter the lion's den.

My eyes scan everywhere. The track itself is clear, at least free of those pop-up slabs. The buildings look like the city below. However, their windows are broken or blown out completely. The paint is faded and worn, the doors hanging off hinges or simply gone. They even have names for businesses that never existed, their signs and slogans dull or half peeled away. It reminds me of the story my pitman, Mickey, told me about his family's business. Is this how it looks to them? Is this what Arianyte has truly done to Earth? Is it just a different outward manifestation of our true world? Ironic that the aliens are the ones that put this faux city here. Perhaps deep inside, they know how guilty they are.

Red lights up my windshield again.

Without the wind blowing in my ears and the other cars blasting around me, I hear a creepy yet cheery female voice when it says, "You've been sabotaged."

I grip the wheel hard and flip down my visor. My last sabotage. Well, that was fast.

Glancing down at my place in the race, I'm in sixth again. A bit further behind than I'd like, but hopefully, I can make up for time in the city.

It isn't a good sign when the sounds of crashing, booming, and bloodcurdling screams echo from up ahead.

CHAPTER 41

I don't want to go forward. I don't want to willingly drive into a shitshow where the likelihood of death or injury is significantly high.

But Pacey needs me. Ardelle needs me. The world and everyone in it needs me. I must go forward—and, as a bonus, prove to Malakyte that he's wrong, that I am good. You don't fight this hard for those you love if you're evil. I won't let him skew my self-perception.

I press the car forward, going at a cautious pace but not too slowly in case I need to bolt out of here quickly.

Then I see it coming out of the corner of my eye.

Huge. Silent. It blocks out all the remaining light and swallows me in its darkness.

My eyes go wide as I slam on the gas pedal. But why does it seem like the car isn't moving? Is it stuck in quicksand? Or is every mile long thrash of my heartbeat an indication that time has slowed to the smallest of increments? Slowing to a snail's crawl so it can deliver me to death himself. At least that's how it seems, as the colossal wrecking ball comes barreling down alongside the buildings and straight towards me. It's so big that I can't see anything else.

My senses seem to snap back into place, and just like that, as if I'm zapped out of the slow time loop, my car moves like normal.

By a hair, my car zips out of range of the gigantic wrecking ball as it swoops down behind me. It's so close I feel the wind tickle the back of my neck, blowing my braid forward.

I fly down this road like a bat out of Hell.

My eyes shift left and right, not knowing when or where another ball will come barreling down. Movement from behind me catches my eye when I see several vehicles coming in from the desert. They caught up quick.

Not understanding the danger, a Lemon-Lime Green monster truck comes up next to me, trying his best to pass. I'm torn. Do I let him drive on, risking another place in line? Or do I let him go ahead, taking the literal brunt of my sabotage?

I let him pass me.

I let two more pass me.

Does this make me a bad person? Does this make me like Malakyte?

I'm back in ninth place, and that's when all hell breaks loose.

Not just one ball falls from the right, but another comes directly behind it from the left. Then a third, coming straight for me.

I veer left, and I speed up again, but I'm wrong. Speeding up is the worst thing I could do. I need to break instead. I'm not going to make it . . . I'm not going to make it.

Oh, my stars . . .

I shriek before I'm hit, but it's hardly a microsecond apart.

Death is raining down on us all.

CHAPTER 42

I'm spinning. Not rolling or tumbling, which means my wheels are still on the ground. That's a good sign.

My car makes a one hundred and eighty-degree turn before I come to a stop. I'm sitting sideways on the track, another car smashed into one of the buildings in front of me, the stench of gasoline thick in my nose. My entire body is trembling, my hands glued to the steering wheel for dear life.

Words come into my lens. *Are you okay?*

How do I answer that?

Another car passes me, but I'm in too much of a daze to pay attention to it or my place in the race.

Are the spectators yukking it up with each other high upon that floating island at my near death? Did they get what they paid for with their sabotage?

I practically have to peel each finger off the wheel as if they were threaded into its leather binding, but eventually, I let go. I give a weak thumbs-up to the others watching me on the lens.

I've got to get moving.

After straightening my car back out, I move along, hearing what sounds like echoes of mocking laughter from somewhere high above.

I've got to go.

Fast!

I speed up quickly. The turns are sharper, more frequent. The cityscape around me is closing in tighter and tighter.

A flash of black snags my attention in my rearview mirror. A motorcycle. And it's coming in hot.

My butt lifts off my seat as I hit a ramp that takes me up onto a second parallel track, the car gaining some air for a couple of seconds as it leaps to the new path. A motorcycle with big fat wheels in the shade Nightmare Nightshade remains on the main track but disappears as my elevated position takes me high above them.

My number in line changes as the motorcyclist passes me from below. I'm in thirteenth place now.

Fuck.

There's only one thing I know that I can do: *go faster.*

I'm already pushing one hundred miles per hour, and my control is squirrelly at best. I can't push the green triangle here. On this secondary track, it's far narrower, and I'd likely fly right off it and down into Zarmenia City. Plus, this new pathway will likely end soon.

Just as I assumed, I see a dip in this spare line up ahead, and it's a risky move, but it may be my only chance to get ahead of the motorcycle.

I punch it even faster without giving myself time to think it over. I know it's dangerous, but I don't have a choice. One hundred and ten miles, one hundred and twenty . . .

My stomach flies into my throat as all four wheels leave the ground, and I'm free-falling back down onto the main track— completely bypassing the decline ramp and flying directly over the black motorcycle.

I'm banged around like a rag doll upon landing, the tires and engine squealing at me as I try to regain some semblance of control. Thankfully, my movements are too erratic for the person on the bike to pass me, and my spot moves up to twelfth place. Although, I worry when I feel a pull from the machine, somewhere deep within its core. One of the dials on my dash, the one next to my speedometer, is bouncing like crazy.

Then my favorite sound chimes in.

"You've been sabotaged."

Wait . . . *what?* We're only supposed to get two. Why am I getting a third?

Hopefully, I can outspeed whatever is coming for me.

If only I were that lucky.

It comes faster than the others had, and I now wish I wasn't traveling so fast because holy fucking Jupiter's rings with a cherry on top. I stop my car as fast as I can, and the screeching whine from my tires and the engine is ear-piercing.

As the entire Dais trembles, there is no doubt that the mocking laughter I hear is coming from up above on the floating island. This is funny to them, isn't it? The sure suffering that lies before me brings them so much joy . . .

Apparently, it does.

And I'm going to make them pay for it.

But first . . . I must survive what's in front of me.

Before me lies a demon incarnate.

As tall as a five-story building, it's a mix between a scorpion with a hard shell on its back and a monster straight from the depths of some hellish world. How did they even get it up here, let alone transported to this planet?

Stars above . . .

As if sensing me, its glowing red eyes—ominous vows of death—focus down directly onto me. If it wasn't for my helmet, my mouth would be hanging open in pure shock, and I have to physically keep my body from pissing itself. I'm feral for my father's strength at this moment . . . but he isn't here. There's nobody here to save me from this. My hands tremble so hard the only way to stop them is to clutch the steering wheel in a death grip. I try to look at the incoming messages on the lens, but the fear has blurred my vision, and I can't even read them. How am I supposed to get past *this*? This literal behemoth of a monster.

My chest begins to sear white hot and thank the stars for it because it's the only thing to bring me back from the brink of the unyielding vise of pure terror this monster has me locked in right now. My vision focuses, and I'm able to read the two words that keep repeating themselves over and over again.

Your crystal!

Your crystal!

Your crystal!

The gigantic monster crouches down, its tail coming up from behind it high and curved just like a scorpion's.

Oh, fuck me.

Without thinking, I grab for my sword. If this Hail Mary is going to work, I'll need it. But as I go to draw it out, it isn't coming out of its case. What the hell?

I gasp.

No . . . no!

Ardelle's arrow is lodged in. I can't get the sword free from it.

The car rattles as the track below me begins to break apart from the sheer weight of this creature. I can hear other vehicles arriving from behind me, but this time, they see the danger before them and are smart enough to stop.

How dare Malakyte allow such a heinous monstrosity to be released up here? What if it crashed down to the city below? What is he thinking? I thought those zombie Tributes were bad, but this . . . this is something else entirely.

Doing my best, I pull and pull, trying to get my blade free of its scabbard. The monster begins barreling towards us, stocky yet more agile than a creature like that should ever be. I start to panic as I see the light from my star begin to glow underneath my uniform. Maybe that's all I need to kill this monster?

"*No!*" my crystal's voice retorts, "*you need the sword!*"

Shit, shit, shit!

I nearly squeal in pure delight as I finally feel the blade giving way.

There's no time to celebrate.

I sit my ass back into my seat and unbuckle myself from my safety belt.

I wish I knew sign language right now, if only so I could tell the people watching that I love them. That I'm sorry. That I tried so fucking hard. I really did.

There's no time to question my plan. I've got to shove down that fear and go for it, survive this.

And that's exactly what I do.

CHAPTER 43

STRATEGIC RETREATS:

LIVE TO FIGHT ANOTHER DAY, REBELS. STRATEGIC RETREATS ARE PART OF THE GAME. FALL BACK, REGROUP, AND COME BACK STRONGER. WE AREN'T QUITTERS, BUT WE KNOW WHEN TO FOLD AND SAVE OUR REBEL CARDS FOR THE PERFECT HAND.

My power builds the faster my car flies straight towards the beast.

The roar of the engine is the roar of my magic, the two screaming in tandem with each other. Bound entirely by fate, by power, by design.

To destroy something like this, I must shift gears within my mind, fall into the darkness I try so desperately to push away.

The thing before me isn't the only monster in this battle.

What it doesn't realize is that *I* exist. That I am death and destruction and annihilation.

I am the Killer of Worlds.

The beast knocks debris and building materials everywhere, its body so enormous it can't help but level everything within its vicinity. Dust plumes into the air, blocking out the sun and engulfing me in an eerie, apocalyptic war zone.

As I drive up closer, I notice that it doesn't seem to see me anymore. Could it be my positioning? Flipping my visor up, I'm so close I can practically see the pupils of this bizarre creature's eyes as I fly into its shadow. Then that's when I spot it, and I realize why it can't see me. It isn't blind at all. It's being controlled.

Its eyes are blazing green from within, and my laugh is half crazed and half elation.

Deimos, you crazy bastard!

I turn around, seeing half a dozen vehicles and the black motorcycle behind me. The person on the bike I passed earlier raises a hand to salute me. It was Deimos this entire time. And he's holding the monster back for me to get by. I see another figure sitting outside his window next to Deimos, waving at me. *Gavrielle.*

Adrenaline pumping so fast, I drive in as close as I possibly can to the monster.

I'm not leaving the others to face this thing. They'll be killed. Gav will be killed. Even though Deimos is giving me a straight path out of here, I will not take the coward's way out. Not with a power like mine, the only thing that can stop this beast.

Heart pumping blood and magic into my veins, I let it all go.

My rage, my hate, my fury at the Dawsons, at Malakyte, at my own depravity, and at everyone who holds up this corrupt, piece-of-shit empire. I hurl it all into my blade. Until my sword is lit up like a beacon of purple flame in the ultimate darkness. Till it symbolizes not just me and what I'm doing up here. It symbolizes *the Star.* It represents every Tribute, every Hijacked, every orphan and person who's been hurt and terrorized by Arianyte. For the rebels and Geonni and all the people of Earth. *This* is the sword that will bring Arianyte down. This is the symbol that'll undo it all.

They better fucking count on it.

And choke on it.

Because, once I'm done with this beast, I'm coming after the real monsters.

I steer the car right up next to the heaping monstrosity. With my sword in hand and my magic pouring its light and ecstasy into my soul, I cleave my weapon into the monster's ankles as deep as the weapon can go. The antimatter in the blade does the rest, my magic blasting its way into the flesh like it's made of butter, cutting all the way to the bone and beyond.

With my ass back in the seat, I hang a sharp right, using my hands to blast the other front leg as best I can before completely coming up under its belly.

All light is cast away as I'm enveloped in purple radiance, the roar of the engine echoing.

Looking up, I blast into its soft stomach and hope monster guts don't rain down on me.

No time seems to pass until I'm up for my second hit, and I line the car back up for my final deadly strike.

Again, I find the sweet spot and slice my blade into its ankles, and that's when it finally lets out a deafening cry. Deimos has lost his hold at last; I just felt his crystal's magic break away like a snapped twig.

The monster tussles and squirms, feeling its life seeping from its body by the second. Yet, still, it fights, and with each step it takes, I'm one second closer to being squashed or worse.

Throwing my bloodied sword into the passenger seat, I slam on the petal as guts and blood and stars-know-what else comes sloshing down on me in a torrential rain of viscous green goop. I almost vomit from the smell alone.

So much for me not getting covered in demon guts.

Me and the car make it out from under the belly of the beast, and I feel elation as I'm home free, seeing a corner in the track where I can easily whisk myself away.

Until the stinger end of its tail slams down directly in front of me, sliding right into the asphalt track like it's the butter this time.

Faster than I can think, I let my crystal surge once more, pulling at the deepest wells of my power. Even at this level, when there's hardly any left to use, it feels fucking fantastic. And I, tiny little old Kara, am bringing down a literal monster.

I blast that stinger straight off the damned Dais. I do so with a shit-eating grin on my face, my middle finger high up in the air and a colossal sense of pride in myself. As I zip away from the beast and round the next corner, I know that, if I can defeat this monster, I can confront the other ones that are awaiting me.

That laughing from the floating island above has finally gone silent and ceased for good.

CHAPTER 44

I don't get very far before I stop the car, put it in park, remove my helmet, and puke my guts up straight onto this cursed hellscape of a racetrack. Whether it's from the disgusting smell of monster insides or my body's blood pressure, adrenaline, and sugar levels dropping, I can't hold in my lunch as I lurch repeatedly. After several gags that have my body racking and ribs aching, I finally slam the door closed and lean on it, window down in case I need to hurl again.

That was insanity.

Doing these Titan Games one after the other like this has drained me, both physically, mentally, and emotionally. Not to mention my crystal's powers, too. I had to draw on more power than I have in a while just now. And I still have a whole other game to go . . . assuming I get through this one alive. My reservoir is dwindling, and that scares me. What if I'm completely maxed out by the end of all this? When I meet Malakyte face-to-face again, I won't have my greatest weapon to use against him. Perhaps, that's his intended goal all along? It's not a bad strategy on Malakyte's part. Gassing me out works extremely favorably for him, especially when he knows I'm coming for him.

Conserving my crystal's power is top priority now.

"You've been sabotaged."

My mouth falls open as I glare at the windshield. Anger roils in me now. This is no coincidence. The extra sabotages, that monster back there . . . they don't fall in line with the rules.

Then it hits me all at once.

The Mistress.

She's somehow causing this; I just know it. I thought perhaps it was the Dawsons, but it would make much for sense if it were the Mistress—Naresteé—because she would have all the power and access to pull something like this off. Especially without Malakyte figuring it out. Naresteé must be up there on that island, watching and spinning her plots. She thinks she's so smart that I don't know what she's doing.

Bitch.

And to make things worse, I hear the revving of engines from behind me. The other players found a way around that monster's corpse, it seems. I was hopeful it would have blocked their cars from getting through and I didn't need to worry about them for the rest of the race. Can't catch even one break. Thanks, Universe.

It's not the Universe. It's those damned jerks up above me. Whether it's the Mistress alone, just the Dawsons, more of the Terran officials, or a combination of all three, I've got to take the threat for what it is and prepare for it. I won't be caught off guard again. My hunch is they're all in on this together—at least in terms of this specific round, where they have the power to knock me out of the game. I am a danger to what little authority they have, and they don't want me destroying it. Their lives are far too lavish and comfortable to ever allow me to win these games.

As anger replaces the twirling in my gut, I grip my helmet and chuck it up into the sky with a frustrated howl. Screw these people. Stars . . . I'm so sick of them. How much further are they going to push me before I snap?

I can't afford to waste any more time contemplating my mental state, and I strap back in and put the car in gear. Whatever bullshit they've got coming for me, I'm ready for it. The Mistress and those affluent assholes aren't going to break me. In fact, I'm the one who's going to do the breaking. As soon as I can, I'll break Pacey from the spell they cast on her. Then I'll break her parents. After that, I'll break the Mistress. And finally, I'll break Malakyte.

Ending all of this.

My hair whips in the wind as I zoom off, feeling better after puking and my short break, even if I do have another sabotage coming. The finish line must be soon. I've just got to hold on to my place, and I'll be fine.

There's not much on the lens, just another, *Are you okay?* and *Get it all out.* Vague, but fine, I guess.

Movement from behind catches my eye, and it's a brigade. At least six or seven of them, and they're coming in hot.

They catch up to me fast, and I currently regret chucking my helmet because, even with the windshield there, the faster I go, the less I can see. It's reckless. My anger is making me stupid.

Deimos is amongst the garrison of players on my ass. I can't see where Gav is.

While I'm looking behind me in the rearview, I don't realize another alternate track steering me—and everyone else—onto a completely different path that leads sharply to the right. My wheels bump the edges of the barrier, and that's what brings my attention back to what's in front of me. We're being forced to take this new route, the old one blocked off now when it wasn't before.

I'm first, but the others are right behind me. The road thins and thins to the point where only one vehicle can fit at a time, but Deimos manages to squeeze all the way up until he gets behind me. He doesn't try to pass, but I'll be ready for him if he does.

Don't look in his eyes, I remind myself. There's too much at stake to trust him fully right now. But that makes me feel a little gross inside at the thought.

The track widens up, and the other players are now neck and neck with me and Deimos. He comes up to my left, keeping pace with me. I can tell he is looking over at me, but I don't look his way. Instead, I keep my eyes solely focused on what's ahead, jumping at any movement that could be the upcoming sabotage. Where is it? It's got to be coming soon.

My place drops to fourteenth. Then to fifteenth.

Shit!

The faster I go, the more the wind irritates the lens on my eye to the point I can barely keep it open or see through the tears welling up in it. I can't fucking see.

As cars begin to pass me, I hear my place dropping.

And dropping.

Deimos—surprisingly—remains by my side in a very uncharacteristic move. He needs to go, or else he's going to lose, too.

I scoot down in my seat as low as I can go while still being able to see what's in front of me.

It'll be fine. I can use the car's camera to see . . .

I peek up over the dash a bit more, and that's when I see it.

The sabotage.

Deimos keeps looking over at me until I point straight ahead, and it draws his attention forward. He knows he can't remain at this speed. Neither of us can.

He zooms ahead, likely hoping he's not too late as well.

It's either I stop here and lose this race, or I risk going into this with a slim chance of survival.

Then I remember something, something Malakyte said yesterday. I thought it was random, but now I think I know what he meant. What did he say? *When in doubt, go fast. Go as fast as you can.*

I choose the latter option and press my foot straight to the floor.

My body is pressed tight against the seat as the car vrooms and vrooms. I remain ducked down as far as I can, at least for now. I can sit up higher once I get closer.

I've caught up to Deimos now, the two of us gaining on the others. They haven't reached it yet. Not yet . . .

Anything could be beyond this threshold, anything—or nothing at all. Both are terrifying prospects. Both I must face or risk losing this once in a lifetime chance of bringing Arianyte to its knees.

The rest of the pack makes it there twenty feet before we do, and I finally sit up high and brace myself for this. *Faster. Got to go faster!*

I bare my teeth and grind down hard to keep from screaming as both Deimos and I approach a near vertical ramp that goes up into absolutely nothing but air. We reach the ramp at the same time, side by side, and there's a slight bump as the car begins its ascent up, up, up . . .

Then I'm weightless.

The car—me—am sailing through the air. My hair billows around me, the bits that came free of my braid wisping near my face like they did last night with Ardelle. The radiance from the sun peeks from behind the clouds and flashes brightly in my eyes. My hands are white-knuckling the steering wheel so there's no blocking out the light or the spectacular view as I coast across the sky—as if this car were an actual angel soaring through an actual heaven.

I'm unable to hold in my shout of both pure elation and trepidation as I fly across nothing but air. There's nothing but thousands and thousands of feet and the earth under us. Another reason why this platform was placed so far outside the actual city limits—they couldn't have vehicles falling on people's heads.

But the stunning view is short-lived as panic instantly sets in when I realize how far away the connecting ramp is. The others, including Gav, seemed to have made it across. Not one of them missed or fell from what I could tell; they're already driving away.

Deimos's motorcycle is smaller and lighter than my car, so he's flying ahead of me, and I fear I'm not going to reach the connecting ramp.

I'm in midair. I can't boost myself to go further or faster.

I don't have Ardelle's magic.

It's going to be close, and I squeeze my eyes shut, not wanting to see my demise.

I'm racked—hard.

So hard I feel like I may be thrown from the car despite the seat belt but then I feel hardness below me again, and I immediately pop my eyes open to see the track before me.

The way down this ramp is nearly as vertical as the way up, and I slam on the car's brakes to gain some resemblance of control.

I feel the car veering sideways as I try to steer it in the opposite direction.

If I flip and begin to roll, I'm dead. Especially at this speed, with no helmet or canopy above me to protect my head.

Gravity isn't on my side.

I lean in the opposite direction, like that'll make a difference.

The tires on the other side are lifting. I can feel them slipping . . .

Fear strikes me cold, and my star is burning again. A striking contrast, one that both shuts me down yet wakes me up all at once.

Think, think, think!

I hold my hand out and blast a wave of antimatter, hoping the force will balance me back out.

It helps but not enough.

The car is still tipping, farther and farther.

I'm going to roll. It's going to kill me.

Then I remember Geonni taking me on a hover ride late one night in the city. He was forced to use something that wasn't the main break. It was . . . an emergency break!

Without wasting one more precious second, I rip my hand away from the wheel and crank on the lever next to my thigh.

The car whines in protest, the RPM meter squealing in anger as I force the car to slow the fuck down. The brakes are screeching and sparking around me. My leg presses with all my strength on the brake pedal, my arm wrenching the emergency brake.

Come on!

The wheels meet the pavement again, and I begin to straighten out the more I slow down until finally—*finally*—I'm in control and out of the danger zone.

Deimos waits at the bottom of the ramp for me, his visor up.

"Nice save, kiddo. Surely, I thought you were a goner."

I sit there, stunned, my breathing ragged, and my mind astonished that I'm not splattered all over the racetrack.

"What are you doing?" I say, ignoring him. "We need to go. We've got to catch up."

I'm shocked when he shakes his head. "No, you go ahead."

"What? Are you insane? No. I need you."

I hate admitting it, but it's true. We can't pull off this plan without him.

"Only one of us was ever going to win, kiddo. If he let your boy go, he'll let me go, too. Maybe. I'm going to bail out now, see if I can cause some mayhem of my own from the outside."

My mouth hangs open in astonishment. This is the guy who chased Malakyte all the way across the galaxy in search of avenging his dead daughter, and *now* he's going to decide to call it a day?

"But—"

"Go. I can't go back onto the Azurite, not after . . . after all that happened with Zariya. I'll have to help you from the ground. So, get out of here." He points towards the direction the others drove off in, but they're already out of sight. "You're running out of time."

I go to protest, but I stop myself. I don't have time to argue with him. And though I hate it, I give him one last nod and drive off as fast as I can go.

Deimos, it seems, has abandoned the cause.

He's abandoned me, too, and as I watch his black form getting smaller and smaller within my rearview mirror, I'm surprised by how much it hurts.

CHAPTER 45

THE ARIANYTE EMPIRE DECREE #37

ARIANYTE MAINTAINS THE AUTHORITY TO MONITOR AND CONTROL ALL FORMS OF COMMUNICATION, CENSORING AND INTERCEPTING MESSAGES, ENSURING THAT INFORMATION ALIGNS WITH THE INTERESTS OF THE OCCUPATION.

I'm in seventeenth place.

Not good at all.

Chances that I'm losing this race after everything I've gone through to get here are extremely high. Gauging by the position of the sun and the floating islands, we're at the other side of the Sky Dais by now. The finish line must be near.

I'm driving as fast as I can, despite the watering and pain in my eyes. My hair has come undone completely, and it flows behind me like a deep ocean tsunami about to crest. A bit like me, about to explode out in a wave of massive destruction—unstoppable and lethal. My anger the driving force.

I feel slight elation as I turn a corner and see the other Titans up ahead. Perhaps there is hope I can still make it. I'm only two places behind the qualifying spot, merely two spots away from being able to get to the next round, which leads directly to Pacey's freedom and Malakyte's demise. The Mistress, too, because she's really starting to piss me off.

Then most of that hope is snuffed out before catching fire. Way ahead, super far in the distance, is the finish line. I can tell by the large black banner sitting high above the track. Many players have already made it. That's why they're all collected there. A few still haven't.

The track is a straight shot there. No turns, no obstacles, no sabotages. Just a singular passageway that seems a bit too simple for all that's waiting for me at the end of the finish line.

There's no other choice. I've saved it for a moment just like this, and no matter how risky, I must make this move.

I press the green triangle.

Instant regret hits my blood.

I'm slammed into the seat, feeling like Ardelle's gravity is holding me down to it. The engine whines and screams, building and building up like a crescendo.

I veer left, then try to correct, but I go way too far to the right. This keeps happening, over and over again, until I'm sure my next adjustment will be the one that causes me to flip into a barrel roll.

Every small move that I make is exaggerated. It's like I'm driving inside a fun house, where, no matter what I do, everything comes out distorted and not the way I want it to be.

Figure it out, I order myself. This is my last and final shot.

Finally, after what feels like a ridiculous and embarrassing amount of time do I get this car straightened out.

The car speeds up, and it manages to close the gap between me and the last two players—until it doesn't.

They, too, must have some special boost of speed because they zoom far away from me the moment I get close enough to attempt a pass.

That's it, then.

Fine. That's just fine . . .

No, it really isn't. Not when Pacey's soul is at stake. Not when her current condition is all my fault. I can't fail her. I can't fail

Ardelle or my father. I can't disappoint everyone else or feel the shame of it.

I can't fail. As if to pour salt in my wounds, I swear I can hear that mocking, insulting laughter from the Terran leaders above me. They also know I'm not going to win this round, that my time in these games is done, and they're the reason why. They took down the rebel girl that threatens their lavish lifestyle. They did that. To *me.*

Laughing and mocking and ruining everything.

Don't they see what I'm trying to do by being here? Can they not look five feet beyond their own self-interests to understand that my struggle to free the people of Earth from the rule of a sadistic tyrant is for them, too? Are they so oblivious to the suffering of the people they claim to rule that they cannot recognize we've reached our breaking point? Are they so heartless they do not care? *How dare they?*

It's like water that's been simmering inside me all day is finally beginning to boil over. I want to keep my promise to Jance—I really do—but it's over anyway, so it doesn't matter anymore.

I can't let them ruin everything we've all worked so hard for, sacrificed for . . . they've already taken Pacey, already twisted her pure, innocent heart into their cruel, cold one. And now they're about to plunder my one chance to get her back and keep Ardelle's heart together. Take Malakyte down. Bring Earth's day of liberation with Arianyte on its knees. These Terran officials and whoever is working with them are going to steal all that hope away, and they're cheering for it. Cheering for their own demise. I can see them up there on the island, arms raised in triumph, high-fiving each other.

They're the antithesis of everything I stand against and every wrong I wish to write.

Perhaps, there's another way I can make some waves. A different path I can take to cause destruction. Albeit a lot less organized and graceful than the initial plan.

Fuck it.

I only crave justice.

And if I can't have it by making it through the next round, I'm going to bring them down with me.

Literally.

Because *I'm pissed*. And I'm not letting them get away with it anymore. They've hurt too many of us. Stolen too much.

I lean over into the passenger seat and grab Ardelle's arrow. I had no idea why I even asked him for it. Perhaps to feel closer to him, maybe as a small way of still having a piece of him here with me. I hold on to it as my hair flaps around it, questioning if I should do this.

Or if I've gone absolutely mad.

My anger says, *Who cares?*

Ardelle may be upset with what I'm about to do. Blood is thicker than water, after all. I just hope to the stars Pacey isn't up there.

This arrow will likely burn up before it even makes it to the island. Besides, it's more symbolic. It won't do much damage. If anything, it'll scare the shit out of them. And they'll have regretted trying to kill me repeatedly today. They'll regret trying to sabotage their one and only chance of freeing the Terrans after all these years, so they can live like kings and queens and keep their youth and wealth. But most importantly, these people will rue the day they laughed at me.

Before I change my mind, I stand up, brace for impact, and take aim.

CHAPTER 46

They want to call me a rebel. They want to mock and break me down. They want me to feel less than my true worth. It makes me *so angry*. I told myself before that I would stop fearing and hating the parts of myself that aren't so pretty. My darker nature. Revenge, destruction, spitefulness, and likely more. The monster in me is the monster in everyone who judges me for my actions. Now, I must embrace it to survive it. Endure the outside world—but also my inside world as well. This is who I am, and this part of me isn't going out without one hell of a bang.

I'm sorry, Jance, I say to myself—to him. *I want to make you proud, but Malakyte is right . . . He's always been right. I'm the antithesis of a hero, the opposite of light. A hero would never consider the destruction that I'm about to cause, and that's the point Malakyte's been so eloquently trying to make.*

I take my sword scabbard and jam it into the steering wheel to keep it driving straight.

It works.

I stand, heart a wild, hammering thing. Ardelle's arrow clutched tight to my chest. I topple a few times, the car and my knees both wobbly.

Looking into the camera, I'm speaking to the people of Earth and them alone.

"Citizens of Earth, my name is Karalevine Ruzz Gallivan, and like you, I'm a victim of the Arianyte Empire. I joined this death game so I can rescue my friend from their clutches—free all of us. My teammate is not alone in her suffering. We're all victims. I know you're used to it. I know resisting is hard and terrifying and the fear for you and your family is real. I know. I've seen the murders and the arrests and the raids. But living in fear is how they control us. They want our bodies. They require our labor and our minds, and they need our children! The Silent Breath is real, the Hijacked are *real*, and Malakyte wasn't lying when he admitted to kidnapping and farming them to breed his immortal serum. Just months ago, he tried to blow up this entire city. If not for me, he would have succeeded. And our fellow Terran leaders—the people who should have our backs the most—were set to be his victims that day, as well. Yet, they sit up here on this Dais, no doubt with their champagne and fancy things, laughing and gorging on our suffering down below.

"I likely won't be continuing in these games, so I want to give our Terran leaders a message before I go. When you decide that corruption and greed serve you better than doing right by your fellow humans, you will feel the brunt of those people you left behind. Not only because I am one of them but because everyone below my feet is, too, and they're sick and tired of you selling them out for your own benefit."

I hold the arrow up in the air, barely able to keep myself from toppling over backwards. Puttering towards the island are several sky-hovers. They're smart enough to know what I'm about to do. Which is fine. I don't want them dead—just scared. I'll wait a second to ensure their escape. Especially since Pacey could be up there. I don't want to risk her health or safety.

The barrage of messages that pop into the lens are nothing but a bunch of blurry words. My friends and family cannot stop me.

The hovers have landed, and no doubt they're all panicking, kicking each other in the backs while they crawl over each other to get free. I don't intend to kill any of them, but it is funny watching them think that I'm going to.

Since I'm not continuing, I have no qualms about using the tiny last bit of my crystal's power that I've got left. With the arrow in hand, I get my body into position. My right arm cranks backwards as I mark my target and take aim.

I wrap my antimatter magic along the shaft of the arrow, swirling around it like a coil.

Some of the sky-hovers are already taking off. It's now or never.

With a war cry, I chuck the arrow skywards. I use my magic to propel it upwards, and it soars faster than I thought possible.

The arrow holds up far better than I expected it to, likely because it's an Elendril weapon.

It flies. Upward and onward and straight on target.

Towards corruption, towards greed, towards inequality.

The arrow blasts through all the tyranny, hoping to destroy each of them with just as much finesse.

But that's when instant regret breaks loose inside me.

CHAPTER 47

The islands are hollow?

Well, shit. That changes things.

I didn't anticipate that.

And it's far too late to stop it now.

Before my eyes, the entire floating island begins to crumble and fall apart.

It happens so fast.

I hit it relatively center mass, thinking hitting the bulk of it would do the least amount of damage, but with it being hollow, it blasted an opening through it instantly. That hole is now the new bottom of the island, all the materials from below the arrow's mark now falling directly to the Dais.

The rest of the island isn't far behind.

The debris strikes the track dead on, since the island is floating directly above it. Except that isn't the only thing it hits.

The two players, the ones that were about to finish the race in fourteenth and fifteenth place, are bombarded by rubble and metal.

Looking up, I see intricate metal pieces inside the island. That must be the technology that keeps it floating in midair. It doesn't look like it's going to be staying up very much longer, either. If that entire thing comes down, it's going to fall right on top of me.

I've got to move.

Now!

I slam my ass down into my seat again and take the wheel. The car had slowed significantly since I stood up and didn't have my foot on the petal, so it roars to life once I punch on the gas.

Wood, metal, trees, and tech, even chairs are coming down on me as if I were a god and had created my own storm. I had. I absolutely had.

The Dawson's got one last sabotage, after all. They should be happy because this is probably one of the most dangerous of them all.

Any one of these things can whack me on the noggin, squish me like a bug, or simply take my head off; the ways to die are infinite.

My car veers sharp to the right as a gigantic piece of debris crashes in front of me. I shriek in surprise as another chunk lands directly in my back seat, a small bit ricocheting and slashing my cheek. It doesn't hurt. My adrenaline is going far too insane to feel anything other than pure urgency and terror.

Move, move, move!

I pass one of the cars that was ahead of me. My place jumps to sixteenth. Perhaps I can still make it to the finale.

My heart batters my rib cage.

A massive boom racks the Sky Dais, and I swear I hear screams off in the distance. A sudden jolt of pure fear hits me when I wonder if blowing up that mini island could somehow bring the entire platform down? No . . . no, there's absolutely no way. Right?

I'm stupid. I'm reckless, and emotionally reactive. What the fuck was I thinking? I was just so angry . . . but irritation at myself gets the backseat to my survival; I'm well-versed in lashing myself with guilt, so it's fine. I'll get to that later.

The finish line is close, but it's also in the crosshairs.

Finally, I come up to the final car I need to pass. He hasn't crossed the finish line yet, and hope sparks in me even though my soul is soaked and in no way flammable enough to catch fire.

Their car has been hit by something big on the front end. I can tell by the giant dent in the hood of their sleek, matte-orange hover. I've come this far, done so much to get here. I've got to cross this finish line before them. I don't care what I have to do. I'm winning this race.

The person in the car sees me inch up to him, and he tries spooking me by jerking towards me just enough to allow me to think he'll crash us both rather than let me pass him. It's an aggressive move, one I don't fall for.

They aren't going to beat me with cheap little tricks like that.

Not caring about what happens, I try and push the green triangle again, not really anticipating much. Like me, it's probably already tapped out.

But it's not.

Blasting ahead like an entirely new second wind, I come up alongside the orange hover. We're neck and neck.

Twenty feet left till the finish line.

Several people have stayed behind there, perhaps waiting to see who finishes first.

Me or them.

The onslaught from above still hasn't ceased—if anything, it's worsening.

My foot is all the way to the floor of the gas petal. I physically cannot make it go any faster.

They inch forward.

I'm ahead—but then they steal the lead once again.

Ten more feet.

Neither of us slows, and the people still waiting at the finish line break apart and get the hell out of our way.

Come on!

My place in the race changes to fifteenth, then reversing to sixteenth. Back and forth, like torture.

 300

I've got to do this. It's for everyone, for this entire planet—for Pacey! This person driving next to me does not have this much to gain and to lose, I guarantee it.

So, I don't feel bad when I use the same tactic they tried on me.

I jerk my car to the right as if I'm about to bump into them and cause them to crash. But it's a fake-out, exactly like the one they used only moments before.

Five feet. The track is right there.

And they're so nervous or incredibly tense that they fall for my ruse, and they instantly go spiraling out.

It's my only shot.

Go now!

I don't let up, and I try pushing down the pedal even more, but it doesn't budge.

The car behind me disappears into the falling debris, twirling and spinning out.

I cross the finish line with only a few seconds to spare, moving up from sixteenth to fifteenth place.

CHAPTER 48

It takes me way too long to stop.

The brakes can only do so much when you're flying at close to two hundred miles per hour.

I immediately see SSPARROW hovers following me down the track. They're likely coming to arrest me.

The island is still crumbling from the bottom, and over half of its entire structure is gone.

Finally, after hundreds of feet from the finish line, the car stops.

I blink the dirt and dust from my eyes, feeling a deep sense of incredulity. As if I'm floating through time and space.

SSPARROWs surround me, and I'm ripped from my car and thrown into one of their sky-hovers. My body feels like sludge, and I don't fight them. Even if I wanted to, there's no strength or energy left.

I simply let them take me.

Thankfully, I have enough sense to grab my sword and sheath before they do. They don't take it from me as I hold on to it for dear life.

We're flying off the Dais promptly.

It's impossible not to watch as the floating island completely collapses the moment we take flight. The antigravity tech or whatever was holding it up falls to the platform with an intimidating thud, shaking the Sky Dais so severely I feel it in my bones all the way up here.

Then we're flying back down to the Earth, where my punishment awaits me.

Am I still in the competition?

Did I kill anyone?

What's Malakyte going to do to me?

I chuckle to myself, mostly out of delirium, at the image conjuring in my mind of how upset he likely is right now. At least I have that to keep me warm and fuzzy for whatever punishment he's cooked up for me.

Yet, that small bit of joy plummets when I finally look at the messages on my lens. They're hard to read, as the lens is full of debris, but I can still see the words clearly enough.

What have you done?

CHAPTER 49

PEOPLE POWER BLITZ:

UNLEASH THE ROAR OF THE MASSES, REBELS. UNITE THE PEOPLE, SPARK A REVOLUTION. MARCH, PROTEST, AND CREATE A RUCKUS THEY CAN'T IGNORE. THE POWER OF THE PEOPLE IS A FORCE THAT EVEN SQUIDS FEAR. LET'S ROCK THIS REBELLION, MY FRIENDS.

I'm taken back to the mansion, to my surprise. The only thing that's different is that I'm escorted up to my room by soldiers and thrown inside.

When I open the door a few minutes later, four armed SSPARROWs are planted outside.

I pace the room for what feels like an hour, and nothing happens.

There's no way for me to really communicate with the others on the lens, but they're dead quiet. I know they're probably upset with me, but as I'm watching the news coverage of the event, it doesn't look like anyone was killed. Which is a huge relief. So, how mad at me can they truly be? I was going to lose . . . I-I wasn't thinking. I was just so outraged, my anger at believing I had lost everything completely got the better of me. I couldn't stand the fact that these

Terrans were about to ruin all we've sacrificed and risked our lives for. And the mocking laughter at me, too . . . I snapped . . .

I need to explain, but how do I do that when they can't hear me?

Finally, I decide to take a shower and clean the layers of dirt and monster guts off me.

Before going in, I look in the mirror. I see a person who looks more defeated than someone who managed to sneak out the win today.

But I don't look at myself. I look at them. All of them, pouring my apology into my eyes as best that I know how.

My makeup bag sits on the double vanity sink, and it gives me an idea.

Digging into it, I find a lipstick and write onto the mirror two simple words.

I'm sorry.

Standing there, fidgeting and bouncing on my feet, I wait for a reply. Any reply.

None come.

After waiting nearly another half hour with no response, I remove the lens and hop in the shower.

I stay in the shower way longer than needed, the memories of Ardelle and I together in here this morning a stark contrast. I'm huddled in a ball on the floor as the scorching water fails to wash off the shame built up all over me. The exhaustion and emptiness don't rinse away, either. No matter how long I linger or how hot I make the water, I can't erase what happened. They probably thought I was getting better . . . that I wasn't going to act like this anymore. I thought I was, too. Maybe I'm unfixable? A person doesn't become an angel just because their life improves, not when they had to be a devil to survive. That devil will always be in me, I realize, and that's what's scarier than anything. That I can't trust myself. I can't trust my emotions or my judgment, and that means nobody else can, either. Malakyte is right. It's why he's obsessed with me; he knows I'm as fucked up as he is.

And I'm so, so upset with myself that, when I finally leave the shower, I can't even look at my own reflection.

By the time I dry my hair and change, it's late, and I'm starving. I order food and intensely watch the news coverage of the race. Most of it is about me—again. The video of me blowing up the island and my speech right before is being played on nearly every single news station—and likely all the Network feeds as well. Trinity, out of everyone, should be elated. This is exactly what she wanted—to make noise. To raise an army of Terrans Arianyte cannot defy. Or is there something going on that's upsetting them that I'm unaware of? Perhaps something on the outside that I'm not privy to? Is that why nobody has replied on the lens?

Then there's the matter of my fate in this game. My fate, period. The protests on the streets, on the Network, the boycotting of all things Arianyte, it goes on and on. It's incredible. Clearly, the people of Earth suspect Arianyte will disqualify me. Many Network influencers and news anchors are going over the Titan Games rules to see if what I did was technically against the rules or not. However, the Terrans are making it quite obvious that, if I'm kicked out of the games, they will revolt. Night has fallen, and from my window, I can see the glowing of fires that've broken out on the streets from the riots. I never expected it to go this far.

Ardelle's parents and Pacey are likely just fine. If they weren't, the news feeds would be reporting on it by now. They'd use any excuse to vilify me, so the fact they haven't yet is a good sign.

The news shows me amongst the players who made it to the next round, and I'm elated to see that Gavrielle finished in ninth place. Emmers, that asshole, came in sixth. They're currently showing me as an active contestant, in fifteenth. I guess that's another good sign.

A knock comes to my door. Great, my food is finally here and faster than I expected.

I jump off the bed and throw the door open, only to be gobsmacked by the person who's standing before me.

"Move." Her sweet, high-pitched voice hisses at me.

Fuck . . .

Naresteé doesn't wait for me to let her in. Her tall body barrels over mine as she shoves her way inside. The door slams shut, and she glares at me, Burnt Ruby eyes ablaze. Has the Mistress come to finally finish me off herself?

"What are you doi—" I begin, but she cuts me off immediately.

"Excuse me?" she seethes. "Did I give you permission to speak? No. No, I didn't. So, keep that mouth of yours shut until I tell you otherwise."

Even though I want to say something snarky in response, I don't, and I remain quiet.

"Good." She points to the table and chairs. "Now, sit down and let me give you a good talking to about what's expected of you, if you wish to continue playing out your little fantasy in this tournament."

Too tired and hungry to fight her, I do as she says, but I keep my guard up for any sign of attack.

She remains standing. Her outfit is immaculate. It's a two-piece, hand-beaded mix between a suit and a cloak. Both are of the same pattern and color. The top coat piece is long-sleeved, with an attached cape cascading down to her feet. The pants hug her legs tightly, most of the beading towards her ankles.

Naresteé's eyes search me, swirling with indignation and repulsion. I get I blew her up—twice—but I don't understand her hatred towards me. Why she'd send people to try and kill me.

"What do you want?" I demand, leaving zero sweetness in my tone. I cross my arms and legs as I look away from her, unable to stand looking into those eerie red eyes.

Her lips twitch before finally speaking again. "Your little stunt today almost killed both Arianyte and Terran officials. We should have you executed in the streets. Not to mention your so-called rallying speech. Nobody cares, Kara, they truly don't."

"They seem to care." I point to the television where my supporters are picketing and protesting and rallying on my behalf. Half the planet is in an uproar over me.

The people of Earth are sick of being oppressed.

Naresteé willfully ignores that fact. No shocker there.

"The only reason you're not in a cell is because he's infatuated with you, but I promise, you'll have wished he ordered you to death. It's no less than you deserve."

My eyes narrow at her. "Is that why you're the Mistress?" I straight-up ask her. Some expression flashes across her beautifully haunting face before she starts laughing at me incredulously. "I am not Malakyte's Mistress, you daft girl. Stars. Besides, I'm with someone new now, and they're a far better fit."

I search her face for some sort of hint of deception, and there's certainly something going on behind those haunting eyes of hers. But what is it? There's only one way I'm getting answers out of her.

I stand from my chair. "Did you try to get me killed yesterday? What the fuck did you do to Pacey? You Reconditioned her, didn't you? What else have you people done? Did you kill my mother, too?" I yell, my anger getting the best of me as all my questions cascade from my lips.

"Sit your ass down," she hisses, exposing her teeth to me in a clear threat. "After what you did to Malakyte, you should be dead. You deserve to be dead, Terran trash."

I shove her chest in challenge. "Fuck you."

"Bitch." Naresteé shoves me backwards, hard. I hit the legs of the chair and fall into it. When I climb back up, she's already there.

"I'm going to say this one time and one time only, you pretentious little brat. Arianyte knows nothing about assassins, mistresses, Reconditioned girls, or the death of your mother. And if you keep up this pathetic endeavor to try and hurt Malakyte politically, I promise you'll have much bigger problems. Keep your mouth shut. This is your last warning. He will remove you if you make one more speech to the press, to the Network influencers, to anyone. *Shut the fuck up.*"

She pulls up, straightens her suit top, and turns her back to me. The spicy, sweet scent she leaves behind makes me want to gag.

The door slams a moment later, making me jump.

Stars . . .

I stand in the middle of the suite, stunned. Am I surprised Malakyte didn't order my execution, let alone kick me out of the Titan Games? Hell yes, I am. It's out of character for him, but the harder I push his buttons, the less reactive he is. If he hadn't messed with Pacey, I might have even started thinking stupid shit like he's changed and was trying to be better in some twisted way to win my heart back. But that isn't the case, is it? Because he did Recondition her. He Reconditioned Gav, too, a long time ago . . . that type of person doesn't deserve redemption.

Maybe neither do I. Because so much of what's happened, to both Pacey and Gav, is all my fault.

The Dawsons have broken their silence and are on a nonstop campaign against me all morning. They want me removed from the games entirely and arrested. Unlucky enough for them, the man in charge of that has a half-century crush on me, so I think I come first.

What sets me on edge is the nonresponse from the others. I assumed their lack of reply after what I did yesterday was because they were upset with me, but it lasted all night. When I put my lens on this morning, there's nothing there. Not a single word. I thought at least Jance would say something, but I did break my promise to him. Perhaps he broke his to me, too. He promised he wouldn't walk out on me again, no matter what. And today of all days . . . I mean, yes, I screwed up. I acted on my emotions—rashly and selfishly, and I put Ardelle's family in incredible danger. But this silent treatment seems way too harsh. It has me on edge, big time. They're probably just waiting to talk to me in person, I'm sure of it. Their lecture is a lot harder to say over tiny texts than it is face-to-face.

I stand, isolated and alone, within the hangar as the Titan finalists and I await the press and families before the third and final game officially begins. What I notice immediately is the extra SSPARROW presence, but nothing else seems out of place.

Today is darkly overcast and pouring rain. It's cold, and I shiver in my uniform as I hop in place in attempts to keep warm.

I hear a male voice call for me, and I can't help but smile when I see Gav running up to me. "Hey!"

We embrace like we're old friends, and I laugh at myself because we are old friends. However, he still doesn't recall who I am as we break our hug and look at each other. The natural way we vibe together gives me the inkling that some part of him does remember, and I cling to that hope that somehow, someway, he'll shatter past the Arianyte Reconditioning and find his way back to me completely.

His hair is pulled back into a low ponytail with a few small braids thrown in here and there. I'm a bit surprised that I missed how truly drop-dead beautiful he has become. His face hardly looks like it's made of flesh at all, given all the angles and his strong square jawline. He's otherworldly—literally. He watches me with eyes of Royal Amethyst, and I see he's trying so hard to remember me. We've both been through so much together since we were separated, but somehow, we finally found our way back to each other.

Patting my head like I'm a toddler, he grins at me mischievously as hell. "Damn, I couldn't believe it when I saw the videos of you blowing up that island." His voice is chipper and booming with pride and laughter. "It was the best thing I've ever seen. You've got balls the size of an Annameir stallion. It was incredible to see it all up close, but the video of your rallying cry truly brought it together. I'm proud of you. I tried looking for you yesterday after the games, but I couldn't find you. I didn't know which room you were in. Otherwise, I would have come to check on you. Are you alright after all that? They didn't hurt you or anything?"

"They had me on lockdown after my stunt," I tell him. "And they yelled at me, of course. But overall, I'm fine."

Lies.

Pursing his lips, he looks up into the sky as if he's contemplating the fact that what I did would have likely gotten me killed for treason against Arianyte. What do I tell him if he asks why I'm not dead or, at minimum, disqualified and arrested?

"You okay? You look off today." His concern is sweet, and I try to smile, but I know it doesn't show as genuine.

I shrug, playing off my anxieties over my family not talking to me as nothing more than a slight annoyance. "It's nothing. I just need to talk to my dad and my friends about everything."

Before he can answer, each of us is called up by the paparazzi, and I force myself to smile in front of the cameras and look much more confident than I feel. However, before Gav and I can even make it over there, several SSPARROWs intercept us.

"You're not speaking with them," one says, grabbing onto my upper arm so tightly it hurts.

I pull on him, but his metal fingers hold me steady. "Fine, whatever. I got it. Now, let me go."

The soldier releases me but stands watch until the press shouts their questions and leaves. They try to yell some over at me, but I keep my mouth shut. My message has been put out there. I've said everything I need to say to the people of Earth. It's up to them to stop living in fear and revolt against Arianyte. I can't do it for them. All I can do is give them the push.

My anxiety grows more and more paralyzing with every moment that passes by. I look over to the group of family and friends waiting for the call they can come in. It's so much smaller than the last few days, and I try to see Jance, but I'm way too far away.

When the paparazzi are finally shewed away, I'm gnawing on my lip in anticipation of what the SSPARROWs will do. Will they remain where they stand, keeping me in a miniature prison?

Or will they simply wander off, their job of maintaining my silence completed.

I practically collapse in relief when they collectively walk off with a warning to keep quiet and the family group is finally let in.

My eyes scan every face as they make their way into the hangar, Gav planted firmly behind me. It's hard for my heart not to beat in anticipation of how I'm going to explain myself, and I'm nervous they're very upset with me. I bounce on my feet in place as person after person walks by Gav and me. It isn't until there is nobody left to stroll by us that I go extremely still.

"Wasn't your father supposed to be here?" Gav asks, sounding concerned. "Or someone else from your group? Are they truly going to stand you up before something like this? You could die today."

My chest rises and falls in a panicked rhythm, my eyes still searching for people who aren't there.

How do I answer him?

All the more so, how did Jance not come? I can see Ardelle or the other Starseeds and Ringers not wanting to risk it because Malakyte could take them, but they could have told me so on the lens.

Wait . . .

What if Malakyte did something to them? What if that was my punishment for yesterday? Fear instantly replaces the deep hurt that bloomed inside my chest at their ghostly disappearance. They could be in grave danger. They could be exactly where Pacey was. How am I supposed to play this final game not knowing if they're safe or not? What the hell am I supposed to do now?

Then I see movement on my lens, my heart soaring at the text that comes across my vision. I grab Jance's ring as it hangs around my neck, as if it's a security blanket.

I scan it too quickly. That can't possibly be what it says. Then I read it again. And again. And again . . .

"Kara? What is it? You look like you've just seen a ghost." Gav places a hand on my back, sensing my demeanor completely shift from fear to complete annihilation.

Everything I feared them doing to me was irrational, and I knew that. My issues with abandonment go way back, not only from believing my parents dumped me the day I was born but from the myriad of foster homes and families that never wanted me in the first place. I developed trust issues from the ones who threw me out again and again. Like trash. It happened so often, I finally began feeling like trash, behaving like trash, because that's what I believed I was. No good. Damaged. Broken. A monster . . . Too messed up to ever be loved by anyone, let alone a group of genuinely good people—a family. So, I would hurt people before they hurt me. I made many mistakes with my Starseed family doing just that. Until they gained my trust. Until I figured out my parents hadn't abandoned me but instead loved me more than I ever thought possible.

Or so I had thought.

But if love from a parent is this conditional, then that was never love in the first place.

I examine the text again, not wholly believing what I'm seeing, but there it is. Sitting directly in my line of sight for me to read and reread, cracking pieces of my heart each and every time.

> *Kara, we can no longer endorse your wild and unhinged behavior. What we're trying to do is too important, and we can't risk your selfish actions ruining it. We've given you chance after chance to prove yourself as a team member, but all you've proven is how selfish you are. We're continuing the plan without you. We need someone we can trust. Trust with our lives, trust to do the right thing, and you simply don't have the moral fiber that aligns with ours. You're too reckless to be a part of a mission so crucial. Once the games are finished, do not come back to the undersewers. The rebels may accept you back, but Trinity isn't sure she can trust you, either. Understandably, Ardelle is furious you almost killed his entire family. He's broken up with you. He's completely done. Jance says he'll deal with you later. He is your father, after all. He can't simply get rid of you. But he*

said he doesn't want to talk to you right now. He also said he wants his ring back. We're sorry.

"*We're sorry . . . ?*"

ARABELLA K. FEDERICO

said he doesn't want to talk to you right now. He also said he wants his ring back. We're sorry.

"*We're sorry . . . ?*"

CHAPTER 50

THE ARIANYTE EMPIRE DECREE #66

ALL TERRAN FEMALES OF REPRODUCTIVE AGE ARE REQUIRED TO SUBMIT TO A PROCREATION EXAMINATION BY ARIANYTE PHYSICIANS. IF APPLICABLE, ARIANYTE WILL ASSIST ALL FEMALES WITH REPRODUCTIVE HEALTHCARE, INCLUDING INSEMINATION, IVF TREATMENTS, FERTILITY BOOSTERS, AND HORMONAL BALANCING TO ENSURE THE LIKELIHOOD OF PREGNANCY.

The ride up to the northern Sky Dais is a blur.

I'm numb.

I'm detached.

I'm astonished.

The words on the lens are like a knife to my heart every time I look at them, and after self-mutilating repeatedly, I finally decide to take the damned thing out. If anyone saw, they didn't say anything. Gav also says nothing. Although, I can tell he's noticing that something is very off with me.

"Hey," he nudges me with his massive shoulder as we continue flying up to the southern Dais. The hover feels so empty, a lot like what's happening within my heart. All the warmth and love I felt filling me up the last few months has suddenly been ripped out of me. Now, I'm vacant inside. They did it. They finally did the one thing I feared they'd do most. I convinced myself that they wouldn't, that my father wouldn't abandon me. Jance walked away from me weeks ago, and he did it again just now. Like the message said, he's stuck with me, so he can't completely desert me but . . . it's enough. And Ardelle, after everything we shared the other night, I'm flabbergasted. I thought we genuinely had something special. I thought . . . he cared about me. I thought that maybe . . . that maybe he loved me. How could he simply discard me so easily? He must have taken what I did as a direct threat to his family . . . and I guess it was. Yet, he should know me better to think I'd do what I did for no good reason. He should've had faith in me . . . the same way I should've trusted in love and in him, I guess. I want to believe in love stories. They just don't believe in me.

That little voice that told me they'd leave me—it was right. I should've listened to it. At the last Titan Games finale, they were about to forsake me then, too, but Malakyte went from zero to psycho so fast they didn't have the time. They saw through his ploy and lies, but that's the only reason why they didn't. That moment should have told me that our relationship was always conditional, that it was only a matter of time before they'd see the real me and run off. I'm so fucking stupid. I'd do anything to just find that thing inside of me that everybody hates so much and rip it out, destroy or bury it so deep it never sees the light of day ever again. I'd do whatever I had to in order to never feel this way again.

"Are you okay? I know your family and friends didn't show up, and I want to make sure your head is in the game. There's not a whole lot of time left until it's go time."

Go time, he says. What does that even mean? Where am I going to go? Why even continue to participate? What's the point? They don't want me to be a part of the plan anymore . . . They don't want me, period. Where am I supposed to go after this game is over, assuming I survive? My mind is spinning.

How could they do this to me?

How could Jance? And Ardelle?

I messed up. I acknowledge it completely, but they're not even giving me a chance to explain or tell them what happened in the race and how I was attacked repeatedly by his psychotic parents.

And after everything Jance said yesterday, he couldn't have meant any of it. This was just a convenient excuse for him to get rid of me now before he was permanently shackled to me for the rest of his life. Because he knows I'm a shit daughter, a shit friend and girlfriend, and a shit person. Nobody wants someone like me as their child. He wants his stupid ring back, then he can have it. I don't want it anymore.

They don't want *me* anymore . . . nobody ever does.

My worst fears come true.

I'm utterly alone again. Gav will ditch me, too, once he remembers what I did to him. I should go, leave now before he figures it out.

"Listen," he says, Gavrielle's violet eyes look down at me with a plethora of sadness as he stands close. "I know my memories are gone, and trust me, I've been trying to recollect the time we spent together at the orphanage, but I cannot unearth them. The only reason I believe you're telling me the truth is by the reaction you had to me initially and the fact you knew about the marking on my hand and its abilities. My true name as well. So, I believe you when you say you used to know me. That means, at some point in time, you were important to me. Seeing you like this pains me more than it should if I'm supposed to have only known you for two days. There's more here between us. I can feel it. Additionally, something more is going on with your friends simply not showing up. What more do you know? I am not naïve. I know there's something going on between you all, and it involves these games. What is it? You can tell me."

Without confessing to cheating and using the lens, I can't explain all that happened. But looking at him now, how genuine he's being, I honestly doubt he'll mention to someone I've been skirting the rules. So, I tell him about the lens, how we've all been communicating together—but not why or the plan to hit

Arianyte—and what they said to me before we got on the sky-hover. There's not enough time to explain anything else, not now.

"That's extremely harsh," he says, voice disgusted. "And this surprises me. You all seemed so close yesterday. Has anything like this happened before? And they said nothing else to you?"

"No," I say dully, that single word answering all his questions consecutively.

As all the Titan finalists walk out from the hover and into the Dais hangar, Gav sticks close to me.

"I know this is a lot, and the timing is horrendous," he begins, looking around the hangar as if someone should be there waiting, but there's nobody but the SSPARROWs and Titans, "but you must forget about all that and concentrate on this final game. If you don't think you can get into the right headspace, drop out now while you still can. Otherwise, you'll be too distracted, and the likelihood you'll be killed is high. The finale is always the bloodiest game of the three. Everyone knows that."

He's right.

Perhaps I should drop out. Why put my life at risk?

Then Pacey's smiling face pops into my mind's eye.

The last words she said to me all those months ago in the basement of the Titan Games arena. *We're seeing each other again, Kara, so don't even start.* That is what she told me . . .

She hasn't abandoned me—well, technically, she has. In her current frame of mind, she hates me. Likely even more so after yesterday . . . but the real Pacey is in there somewhere, and I know she has my back. I'll see that Pacey again, just like we promised each other. I can't let her down. The others may or may not know about what happened to her, that her mind has been Reconditioned and she's forgotten us. I won't leave her to that fate or sacrifice her soul because of the pain I'm feeling inside.

I can't quit.

What I can do, however, is let them go. If this is what they truly want, then I must respect that. They've put up with a lot from me. They really have. It was only a matter of time before this happened. I get it. There's just something etched into me that repels people. I'm meant to be alone, it seems. As heartbroken as I am, I understand why they're doing it. Saving Earth is too important to risk having someone like me who can't keep their emotions in check and who's wildly out of control. Holding onto them for dear life is only going to strangle them, and I've put them through enough. Perhaps it's for the best. If Malakyte believes we no longer care for each other, then he can't use them against me anymore. In the end, it's what'll keep them the most safe.

I'll be okay, eventually. I've done this before.

"You look as if you're going to faint," Gav says, and he's right. The realization—the finality of my choice to let them go—is a crushing weight within my chest so heavy I cannot breathe through it. It's physically battering me.

The right thing has never felt so excruciating.

I can save Pacey and then walk away from all this.

Then never let anybody in ever again.

"Can you compete, or do you need to drop out?" he asks, voice nervous and concerned.

Gav's question brings me back to the present moment, and I think about the answer I've already come to. If I'm going to rescue Pacey, then I've got to shove the others from my mind—with an iron will if I must. Otherwise, I'll be dead from the distraction of it. The finale is the finale for a reason. It's the biggest game of all three. I have to be ready.

"I can do this," I promise, but I don't know if I'm speaking to Gavrielle or to myself.

In order to survive this final game, the familiar weight of all the sadness I carry swiftly transforms into its ever-persistent companion: seething rage. In response, the devilish figure perched upon my shoulder smirks, their laughter echoing through the depths of my being. It wears Malakyte's face.

"The third and final stage of the Titan Games is effectively called 'The Maze.'" The SSPARROW addresses us as we stand before him for the third and final time. "It will be a battle royale style clash of wills. The last man standing wins the games. It's that simple. One weapon per contestant is permitted. Any contestants who are found to have multiple weapons or weapons that are not a part of a preapproved set will be disqualified."

I'm sure that extra clarification of the rules was because of me yesterday. Sneaking that arrow in alone should have gotten me disqualified. *His* arrow.

I know I love him, Jance, too—in my own way. Their opinions of who I am, how they view me, wouldn't be so damaging to my heart if I didn't. And because of the affection I carry for them both, I must bury it deep within me. Submerge it into the pit of darkness, where every good part of me goes to perish. To be ripped apart, destroyed, and incinerated within the tragic flame that never wavers. Darkness is the only thing that's truly never left me. Sometimes, when I can no longer hold it back, the rage within me blasts to life. Similar to how a star burns in the sky, it's a constant battle between serenity and chaos. But that's the problem, isn't it? It never gets to burn all the way down unless it goes supernova, unless it chooses to consume itself and go out in a blazing burst of glory.

The thing inside me has no such light, however. But similarly, there's constantly been that social leash keeping it at bay. Parts of me—the good parts I've tried to build around it—they've done their job to assure I don't destroy everything that's important to me by losing complete control. This has nothing to do with my crystal. It's all me. The pieces of me Malakyte loves so much, apparently. He's likely the only one who ever will. Maybe that's where I should go? To the person who's always wanted me, no matter what I've done or how black my heart may be. The others are too good to love the true me.

If I were to unleash it fully, completely, without any morals or principles stopping it, I fear it would destroy the entire world. My blackness would reach across every nook and cranny until it snuffed everything out entirely. Perhaps then it would finally find itself satisfied and stop eating me alive.

"Each finalist will be set eight hundred meters apart from each other at an opening to the maze," says the SSPARROW, but I'm hardly paying attention to the rules. I'm honing my pain into a deadly blade. "Deadly force isn't advised but isn't strictly prohibited. Although if a single player kills more than three other players, they will be disqualified. Unless said killings are in self-defense. The last person standing wins the Titan Games."

Sounds simple enough.

They want a monster, they're going to get a monster.

CHAPTER 51

REBEL RECRUITS RULE:

OPEN YOUR ARMS TO NEW BLOOD, REBELS. FIND THEM, TRAIN THEM, AND MOLD THEM INTO WARRIORS. TEACH THEM TO FIGHT, TO THINK ON THEIR FEET, AND TO NEVER BACK DOWN, ESPECIALLY WHEN UP AGAINST A SKY-RAT. PASS THE TORCH OF RESISTANCE LIKE A HOT POTATO OF FREEDOM.

Gavrielle hugs me goodbye before we're all split up. I try to familiarize myself with the way he smells, his body, his face. If I survive this, I'll make sure to draw him this time, cement it to my memory forever. Every line, the way his pointed canines peek out when he smiles, the brightness in those beautiful purple eyes of his. In case . . . in case I lose him, too. At least I'll have this small piece of time together. At least I can put that mission to bed knowing I finally did one thing right.

"Get to the end," he tells me, patting my head in that annoying way he's been doing the last few days.

I hope he finds what he's looking for in that maze. I hope I do, too. But at least we found each other here, in this unlikely place.

"Be safe."

Then he's gone, and I'm being led solo to a hover that'll buzz over to my designated starting point within the giant maze.

A thick fog settles around the entire Sky Dais, and all the way up here the rain is a heavy, misty presence all on its own. Except, when I see the maze itself, I see an entirely new competitor I must face, and it's the most intimidating of them all.

Thunder rumbles far in the distance as I exit the hover, my body shivering against the chilly rain. The grass underneath my feet is slippery. It'll make running difficult, and I file that away for later.

An intimidating presence looms its brutal force over me.

It's not a maze. That name is far too *vanilla* for this monstrosity. It's a labyrinth. An entanglement of black marble or straight obsidian sprawling out for what seems like endless miles. I can't see the end of it. I doubt I could even without the fog ebbing and flowing through its infinite paths. The walls are at least ten feet high, and when I walk up the labyrinth entrance and touch the wall, it's freezing cold. I can see my reflection in its pitch-black surface, beads of water trickling down in endless races to the bottom.

The threshold to the labyrinth is a massive, detailed archway looming over the maze itself. It's crafted of actual stone, fifteen feet high, with strange symbols etched into this ornate archway of intimidating beauty.

Stars above . . . I have to walk through *that*?

Choking vines creep along its smooth edges as if they're trying to reclaim the eerie stone back into the earth from whence it came. The labyrinth looks like it's been machine cut so that each corner and corridor is perfection at its finest, every single clean edge held up to the highest standard of Malakyte himself. Perhaps that's why I feel like the eclectic maze has such a presence. It reminds me of him. It's spewing his essence. It breathes of his dark, corrupt soul.

"Get ready," the SSPARROW that drove me here warns me, his distorted voice making me jump. "When you hear the horn, you can go in."

"Will there be monsters in there this time?" I ask boldly, since the last two games had them.

I don't expect the soldier to answer, so when he does, I'm surprised. "The only monsters you'll find in there this time will be yours."

What the fuck is that supposed to mean?

I jump at the sound of a deep, guttural horn blaring somewhere on the platform. I'm reminded just how fragile I truly am if a damned noise can cause my heart to race and palms to sweat. If only I still had the people I considered my family by my side . . . perhaps I wouldn't be so triggered.

But I don't have them anymore.

With only a slight hesitation, I walk past the labyrinth threshold with an uncertain swallow, imagination blooming wild as to what's awaiting me there.

I draw my sword, the sound of it coming free of its sheath bouncing off the eerie black walls.

At least I've got an outlet for all my pain—I'm allowed to pummel some people today. Use the chaos of battle to soothe the ache within, just like I did with the SSPARROW Nests. That's about the only thing holding me together, as sick as that is.

That, and Pacey.

The others can hate me and discard me—fine. But Pacey is innocent, and I won't abandon her like they abandoned me.

So, I walk down the darkened path, sword out in front, to whatever monsters await me.

And I'll be grinning at them in return.

Let the Titan Games finale commence.

CHAPTER 52

I miss the revving roar of my race car right about now. I'd take the sound of it to this utterly eerie quiet any day. There're no swishes or clatters, not a crunch nor a clank. No birds or bugs, no wind or thunder; there's nothing here. It's graveyard quiet except for one single sound.

My heart hammering against my rib cage.

It smells of rain and soaked earth, a musky smell lingering around the edges as well. If I didn't know better, I'd also say it comes with the scent of death, too.

I turn my first corner slowly, not wanting to be caught unaware by another player or some deformed creature sent from the pits of Arianyte's war chest specifically to torture me. There's movement the second I make my way around a tight turn, and I muffle the shriek clawing its way up my throat when I realize that it's my own reflection in the dark obsidian walls.

Stars, I'm too tense.

Hopefully, nobody is close enough to hear my debacle, and I shake my head at myself in anger. Stupid. Ridiculous. Practically jumping at my own shadow.

The floating cameras bobbing around me likely caught it, however, and my cheeks burn with embarrassment.

Are they watching me right now? My so-called family, father, ex-lover?

Get your head in the game, dammit, I scold myself. *Stop it. You made the choice to let them go, so let them go and do this now or concede.*

Right.

Deal with them later.

If I'm out here thinking about how much I hate my father for ditching me, I'm going to get killed.

Anger. Turn it into anger.

Hone it and sharpen it into a weapon that won't let anyone hurt you again.

Let it burn this entire place down.

I can't deny the tiny smirk that flashes on my lips at the thought.

I turn left, right, right again, then left. Stars, where is everyone? Will there be sabotages in this round? Where are the ravaging tributes and wild beasts? It's far too silent.

Above me, the floating islands stand watch like silent gods, judging my every step. I chuckle lightly to myself, only because I doubt there's anybody actually up there watching us rats run around in the maze. I'm sure they're *devastated* by it.

There really isn't a goal in this game other than to take out the other players, so that means there's either one of two strategies. Option one, search them out and take them down. Option two, hide and let everyone else knock each other out, then pounce at the end.

I'm not really in a waiting sort of mood.

Alright, then, my goal is to track down the other players. Easy. I can focus on that and keep my mind busy with them. Try and forget about what my so-called family did to me.

An odd smell snaps my attention back to focus.

What is that? It's slightly chemical with an acidic twang to it, like the burning of bleach or something. It's not a good smell, and my guard instantly flies up.

My footsteps continue to slosh along the wet ground, the misty rain adhering to my cheeks as I skulk around corners vigilantly.

Then I see it.

The source of the smell.

At first, it appears as a thicker fog, slowly creeping along the soggy bottom of the maze. It's whiter and fuller than any haze,

and it billows with fat, puffy swirls—like it's being pumped out from somewhere.

I stagger backwards. Immediately, I run in the opposite direction of this ominous cloud. Every corner I take slows me down even more, and it's hard to get a good pace.

Taking another corner, I slam myself to a stop, hand slapping onto the cold, wet material of the labyrinth.

Stars, no . . .

I either ran myself into a circle, or there's more of this obscure fog coming into the maze. I'm betting it's the latter.

A scream shatters the silence, causing me to jump in surprise. It's close and causes the hairs on my arms to rise, the man's bloodcurdling cry an anthem of horror.

But I have more pressing matters.

This mysterious fog is steadily crawling closer to me, creeping and spindling till it's time to land its strike; and the only thing I can do is run.

So, I run.

More and more sounds of the other players begin to echo out into the maze, as if something within this labyrinth has awakened, and it is coming for us all at once.

Running is futile.

I know this because the air slowly and steadily becomes hazy and cloudy. The smell singes the inside of my nose, causing my eyes to water and my throat to tickle incessantly to the point that not even coughing eases the sensation.

Whatever this artificial mist is, I can't escape. I've breathed it in, and now, we'll see what happens. I'm on guard, senses heightened and prepared for anything.

Stars, I really wish Gav was here with me. I'd even take Deimos right now. I hope he's okay and made it out alright. Maybe I'll go stay with him after this? If he doesn't still want to kill me, that is.

Focus . . .

Right. I'm supposed to be focusing on this game . . . but who cares? Honestly, who gives a shit anymore? Nobody wants me, so it doesn't matter what I do. I'm as free as a bird! I'm actually glad they left me. Fuck 'em! They're so pretentious and stuck-up with their morals and their high ground. Shut up about it already . . . just let me be who I am. Maybe if my stupid, so-called father looked a bit harder for me, I wouldn't be this way. It's his fault! Stupid Jance . . .

I start giggling, and I don't know why, but I can't stop.

I feel . . . funny.

And I don't really care about anything anymore.

Screw it!

I'm done. I'm leaving this maze.

Actually, no . . . I'm going to find *him*.

"Are you watching me, asshole?" I shout into the gray sky, knowing Malakyte is watching me from somewhere. "I'm coming for you!"

I laugh again, but this time, it's much more cynical. Stars know the cameras streaming out to the public are catching this and the people watching are having a heyday.

What's going on with me? I don't feel right . . . I don't feel like myself.

Shit.

That wasn't a mist that was billowing through the halls of this dark maze . . . it was a gas.

A drug.

Now, I'm high as a kite and only getting higher. I'm both light and heavy at the same time, the edges of my vision blurring as my eyes feel like massive weights pulling them down, but my head is in a whole other galaxy. Nothing matters all of a sudden.

Oh my stars, I am high as fuck.

My feet wobble, and the ground tips sideways at a forty-five-degree angle. The once sleek and sharp edges of the onyx maze are now wavy black slabs. I try to blink out the distortions, but they remain warped.

I turn a corner, expecting nothing but another identical passageway, when a figure stands directly in my path, still as a statue.

Gasping—quiet dramatically, I might add—I stagger away from the figure. It's male. A long brown coat cascades in a phantom breeze as the person's face is looking down at something on the ground. I can't see their eyes. They're covered in black sunglasses; his dark skin is ashen and . . .

Oh . . .

Oh.

Geonni lifts his head and stares at me from behind his sunglasses.

My sword slips from my hand.

I slap my cheek—hard.

This isn't happening.

I'm not only flying higher than a sky-hover, but I'm hallucinating, too.

The slap does nothing as he remains in place, standing there like a practical statue that sprang from my nightmares as a living wraith.

"You killed me, Dynamite." The voice is exactly how I remember it. *Geonni's voice.*

I blink my eyes and squint, not sure if I'm seeing blood trickling down the side of his face or not.

"No . . ." I babble, taking steps back but the distance between us never changes. "I chose Jance. I tried to save you. I didn't know he was going to shoot you."

A shot from a disruptor pistol blasts through the air, and I don't know if it's real or all in my imagination, but it freezes me in ice.

It's the exact same sound as the shot from that day. From the day Geonni was killed. I'd know it anywhere. I hear it in my nightmares all the time.

"You killed me, Dynamite," Geonni's ghost repeats. Over and over again. "Admit you killed me."

I drop to my knees and hunch over them, covering my ears, but it doesn't stop. I rock myself as the words permeate into my skull like a battering ram.

"You killed me, Dynamite. You killed me, Dynamite. You killed me, Dynamite."

"Stop it!" I scream, voice guttural and high-pitched. I squeeze my eyes shut as I hear him approach. I can't look at him. I'll lose my shit if I do. I'm already teetering on the edge of completely falling apart.

My mark is on fire as I continue rocking, trying to drown out his words with my own screams. He's right. I did get him killed. Just like I got Gav and Pacey Reconditioned. What will happen to the others when they try to attack Arianyte without me? Will they be less protected or more protected? I honestly don't know.

Suddenly, Geonni's words stop. Then it's boneyard quiet as the air becomes thick with my fear—the foul presence of it. When I open my eyes, I see I'm sitting in a pool of dark-crimson blood. It's all over me. On my legs, my clothes—blood all over my hands. Where it's always been. My original sin.

I shriek again, jumping backwards as Geonni's legs appear directly in front of me. I never heard his footsteps approach.

There's no escaping him as I skirt back and land on my ass, my arms the only thing holding me up. I crawl away, but my back hits the cold, slick surface of the maze wall. There's nowhere to escape to.

Nowhere to run.

He's glaring down at me, hatred in his gaze.

"Please don't say it," I beg, tears brimming over my eyes and falling to my cheeks.

I can see half his head is blown out, his glasses now sitting in the puddle of blood before me. Geonni's milky-white eye glows against the pink scar above and below it. Malakyte gave him that scar. Malakyte blinded him. In return, I did the same to Malakyte. Although Malakyte did manage to save his eyesight, where Geonni had not.

"You killed me, Dynamite. Admit you killed me. Admit it was all your fault."

"You left me!" I shout back, grabbing my sword up from where I dropped it and holding it before me protectively. Like it'll do any good. You can't kill a ghost, just like you can't kill what haunts you.

Geonni smiles wickedly. "That's the truth, isn't it, Dynamite? You wanted revenge on me for leaving you. So, you killed me."

I shake my head vehemently. "No." But it only comes out as a pathetic whimper.

No.

That's not true. Right? Right?

"You killed all those people at the orphanage, Dynamite. You cannot deny it."

He's right. I did kill them.

"Please stop," I beg.

"You killed the people at the Capitol building."

It's not even a question anymore. I did . . .

"You've killed so many people along the way. It's why the others have left you, too," he begins, voice taunting. "They don't want you to kill them, either. Just like you killed them before."

"Zariya killed them before!" I snap back, way too fast not to be defensive.

"You killed them."

This isn't real, I tell myself. *I'm just hallucinating. Geonni is dead. This is my mind, and Arianyte's drug's fucking with me.*

But why does it feel so real?

"And you're going to kill them again. You and Zariya are one soul. You can never escape what she's done, and you can never escape the fate that awaits you. Each reincarnation, you will face what she's done, face the curse of the Killer of Worlds."

Geonni's ghost bends down, and we're face-to-face, eye-to-eye, soul-to-soul.

"Admit it," he says, and I shake my head in confusion. "Admit it."

"Admit what?" I blurt out.

"Admit you killed me, Dynamite. Admit you killed them all. Admit you're a murderer. Admit that you're full of darkness. Say that you're the Killer of Worlds."

My head shakes dramatically. "No, I'm not. I'm not!"

"You are."

"I'm not!"

"You are!"

Am I? Am I a murdering psychopath and simply hadn't realized it? I know I've killed before, but it's been accidental. I didn't mean to. I didn't want to . . . or maybe I did? I wanted to slay Malakyte, even though I chose not to in the end. I still want to kill him. I wanted to exterminate Deimos after he nearly took my life. So, that desire is within me somewhere, waiting like a parasite to take me over completely. And the others . . . in our other life together; I slaughtered them, too. Maybe I just kill and kill and kill?

And that's why they left me? That's why Jance left me . . .

"Fine," I say to Geonni, tears falling as they mix in with the raindrops on my face. "I'm the Killer of Worlds."

I admit it because it's the truth.

Not in the silly way I claimed it yesterday. That was different. That was hyperbolic. A trivial thing that popped into my head because the moment was insane. However, claiming it for real, like a brand or the curse Geonni claims, requires that I must accept the title and all that comes with it.

That I am the Killer of Worlds, and that I'm no better than Zariya was. No better than Malakyte. It means I'm a killer, and that I've lost my most difficult battle, the one with myself.

"I killed you. I killed all of them in our past life. Ultimately, I was going to kill or get the others killed in this life, too. It was only a matter of time. It's why I'm letting them go. To keep them safe *from me*."

A smile crosses Geonni's lips, the gap in his teeth and golden tooth glinting within the silent lightning that bounces off the clouds. Then Geonni begins to dissipate. Becoming incorporeal, he and his blood disappears with the wind, leaving behind only his sunglasses on the slick grassy ground.

The Killer of Worlds sits alone once again . . .

CHAPTER 53

THE ARIANYTE EMPIRE DECREE #81

ALL SSPARROW ENFORCEMENT OFFICERS ARE IMMUNE TO PROSECUTION OR LEGAL CONSEQUENCES FOR ANY ACTIONS TAKEN IN THE LINE OF DUTY. TERRANS ARE REQUIRED TO SHOW OBEDIENCE AND DEFERENCE TO SSPARROW AND NEST ENFORCEMENT, AND FAILURE TO COMPLY WITH DEMANDS CAN RESULT IN IMMEDIATE PUNISHMENT. SSPARROW ENFORCEMENT HAS THE JURISDICTION TO IMPOSE INSTANT CONFINEMENT, PUBLIC HUMILIATION, OR POSSIBLE EXECUTION, WITHOUT THE NEED FOR A FORMAL TRIAL OR LEGAL PROCEEDINGS IF THEY DEEM THE THREAT IMMEDIATE.

I finally see what the SSPARROW meant when he said the only monstrosities to fear were going to be ourselves.

Makes sense now.

There are no worse monsters to face than the ones in the mirror.

My body is stiff as my back rests against the maze wall; I'm still in too much shock to move. Afraid that, at any moment, Geonni's ghost will reappear to taunt me some more.

How long will this hallucination drug last in my system? My body feels lighter, at least, and I'm slightly clearer in the mind, albeit from pure fright, but I'm still experiencing a pretty severe head high.

Will I even be able to fight like this? I grip my sword's handle tightly, as if it's the only real thing in this haunting place.

Across from me is the grassy pathway and another wall of obsidian stone, and I see my reflection in it. I look so small, so fragile. Can a killer be those things? Apparently, they can.

Then another image comes up from within the black stone like an apparition from the depths of Hell. It's only in the reflection of the maze wall next to my reflection, and the dark prince himself appears to me.

I know this isn't real, so when I laugh, it's soft and cynical.

"From where I'm standing, Miss Ruzz, your situation doesn't seem all that comical," Malakyte's hallucination-reflection says to me.

"Well, whose fault is that?"

He smiles at me, eyes soft and warm and pleasant—almost affectionate. Perhaps I can get the version of him that I wish he was rather than the person that he is. If this Malakyte is conjured from my mind, then maybe there's a slim chance this won't be as miserable of a hallucination as the last one.

"The key isn't to fight yourself but to accept yourself." This is definitely the better version, then. Thank fuck.

"Why do you like me so much?" I ask, desperate for something—some version of someone to accept me. To want me—*love me.* I need it like I need the air I breathe, like I need the blood in my veins. Even though he isn't real, I can pretend.

He looks at me like he's sad. "*Like you?* You think I like you, Miss Ruzz?"

Oh, great. This is not the direction I thought this conversation was going to go. Yet, Malakyte continues before I can reply.

"Terrans put such weight on the idiom. It undervalues the true depth of emotions that pool beneath the silly phrase. No, Karalevine, I do not like you. A person does not cross the galaxy in search of the soul they purely *like.* Those who merely like do not forgive that person for permanently disfiguring them. It's insensible to just like a person when the last forty years have been solely about them and the goal of being together again. You may think that your soul is ugly or that you're unwanted and unvalued, but I vehemently disagree. The parts of you that you loathe, the portions everyone tries to change in you, are the very things I like most about you. You don't have to change or hide if you're with me. My wish for you is that you wouldn't have to hide, that you can be free and uninhibited. You can be seen and loved and adored like you deserve to be. Have I ever shunned you? Judged you? Tethered you into some mediocre version of yourself? No, I have not. Because, when it comes down to it, Karalevine, I don't just like you, I love you. I've loved you from the moment you first sneaked into the Sun Revolution Ball on the Azurite. You spent all the credits you had on that gown, and you did it so you could get in and rob me blind. Which you did but only because I let you. Back then, I couldn't say no to you, even to my detriment. Not then and not now. When I learned you had died, that Zariya had died, I simply couldn't accept it. My love spans beyond life and mortal flesh and time and space. After losing you for what felt like an eternity and against all the laws of nature, I somehow found you again. And you wonder, naïvely so, why I like you? Why I pursue you in earnest? It's because I love you, Karalevine. I always have, and I always will."

This time, when the tears fall, they're not of sadness and self-hatred or fear but of something else entirely.

I close my eyes, not knowing if this would be better or worse if it were real and not some figment of my incredibly messed up mind. It must mean a part of me truly desires him—wants him to be redeemed. Because, if Malakyte can find forgiveness and redemption, then, stars, that means I could.

When I look back to the maze wall, he's gone.

Probably for the best.

I can't have my enemy blowing kisses my way, even if they are entirely fake.

There's a tickle on my hand, and when I look down to scratch it, a shriek escapes my lips. A fat black bug sits there, and I fling my hand faster than lightning to get it off. Was it real or a figment of the drug?

A soft buzzing noise splits the silence, and it's close. I check my body for another bug and, thankfully, don't see one, but I hear the buzzing again. It's definitely the whizzing of a bug's wings fluttering, and when a bead of sweat drips down my spine, I squirm.

I cry out again when I feel tiny legs crawling up my thigh, and I flick it off before seeing yet another teeny black shape strolling my way.

Then another.

What are they? Are they—

Oh no.

Stars, no.

No matter how cold outer space is, vermin still finds a way to survive. That is true for the Azurite fleet, as well. Because the ship is basically an arc, it's a mixing pot of dozens upon dozens of species. Each time one of them and their luggage arrives onto that vessel, they're not alone. Pests like bugs and rodent-like critters sneak aboard and multiply fast. One such species made its way from some foreign planet to the Azurite, then to Earth. We call them fliders because they're a mix between a fly and a spider. Or a literal fucking demon. Their bodies are fat, especially their little butts. They've got six legs, but they're long and stick out in front and behind. And then there're the wings. The fliders have flat wings that make a buzzing sound when they fly, their fat legs dangling in the air like hairy ropes. They're horrendous insects and have devastated Earth's natural ecosystem, especially in Zarmenia because Arianyte does so much transporting between here and the mothership.

They eat almost all other insects and leave incredibly nasty bites on humans and animals. As far as we've heard, they're not venomous, but their stings or bites or whatever they are hurt like a bitch. I've been stung before as a child and have never forgotten it.

Am I seeing them because of the gas, or are they actually here?

My eye catches a few more as I pull my legs in closer to my chest.

No. No. Anything but this.

It's not real. It's not real.

One lands right on my cheek, and I hear it buzz before I feel it land. My scream echoes out into the maze, bouncing off the looming black walls to the ears of whomever may be close enough to hear them.

I stand, shaking and wiggling my body violently in case one has clung on. I jump at any itch or tickle against my skin, fearing my long hair will make a good nest for them.

Their buzzing noises increase as my head whips in every direction. My breaths become heavier and shallow with each passing second, my eyes unable to keep up with how many fliders I'm seeing both in the air and on the floor.

Please, stars, let this be a hallucination.

A sharp hiss escapes my lips as there's a painful pinch on the back of my hand. I whip it around, but it's too late to prevent the bite. A big welt is already beginning to form. Dammit. This doesn't feel like a mind trip, if I'm being honest. Geonni and Malakyte both blurred at the edges, and these things are crystal clear. If this were fake, I don't think I'd be able to experience the searing pain of the bite or the liquid seeping out of it.

Shit.

These little bastards are real.

So, why am I still standing here?

Sliding my sword into its case, I make a break for it. My skin crawls as my footsteps squash dozens of them, as if they're miniature squeaker toys. Yet, what's worse is the speed and veracity in which they chase after me. Such a thing shouldn't be possible, yet here I am, running from a hoard of fliders as if it's an angry Nest of SSPARROW sky-rats.

Bugs hold a special place in my heart as being one of the most hated creations of all time. Whether they're native to Earth or come from outer space, all insects are disgusting little demons.

One of these demons catches me and goes in for the jugular. It manages to bite me right in the side of the neck. I feel it squirming and its wings beating for freedom as I wrench it from my throat and chuck it to the ground. This one hurt even worse than the first. Stars.

I've lost count as to how many corners I've whipped around, yet when I turn back to sneak a peek at the bugs, the hoard is tactical in how they chase me. They're a calculated hive mind that I cannot hide from. An intelligent swarm. I realize with sudden terror that their sole goal isn't to take me down one by one but instead to devour me as a whole unit.

Holy stars.

Holy fuck.

I got to get away from them, but how?

There's only one way to destroy a swarm such as this, and typically, that one thing is fire.

But I don't got any fire, do I?

No, I do not.

I got something better.

Another one of these flider bastards somehow crawled within my uniform and bites me in the back. I slap myself until I think I've squashed it, but there's no way to know if I killed it for sure. The thought of one of them under my clothes literally makes me jump out of my skin so high I'm practically halfway to Heaven. Although, this place feels a lot like Hell.

I'm flying past corners so fast that, when I dash around another one, I'm stunned to find my own reflection staring back at me.

I've run myself into a dead-end.

CHAPTER 54

What should I do?
   Where do I go?
   How do I get out of this?
I'm stuck, both physically, in the sense that there's nowhere else to run to, but also within my own body. I'm frozen. Halted in fear and in panic. My biggest weaknesses have been cut wide open in the previous hour, culminating in this moment. I'm unable to move an inch due to it zapping every ounce of strength left within me. I have nothing in me. I can't do it . . . I don't want to fight anymore.

Or suffer anymore.

But do I want to die like this? With thousands of fliders crawling their creepy legs up and down my body, in my ears and mouth, digging themselves into my eyes and burrowing their bodies into my own . . .

Stars.

Fuck no.

Which means I have no other choice than to move.

To act.

To fight.

I turn and face the swarm, so close the fast ones have already made it to me. They buzz around my mouth and eyes, but I do my best to ignore them.

The familiar feeling of numb infinity sparks me back to life a tiny bit as I call forth my Elendril crystal's power.

As one of the few things in life I can count on, I reach down into the pit in which this dark curse lives, only to find nothing there.

For the first time since this power has manifested that day at the orphanage, it doesn't come when called.

Stars, no . . .

Has my magic left me, too? Is it "Abandon Kara Day" or something? What the hell is going on? Where is it?

Digging deeper, I reach for it again, the fliders swarming around me to the point I can no longer ignore them. I swat at them vigorously, panic beginning to make my mind crazed and unfocused.

Call forth your powers! I order myself.

It won't come!

It has left me, just like everyone else has left me.

Horror grips me, an icy and brutal hand against my throat. I can't even scream.

From behind the blackened hoard of fliders, I see a flash of white. It's only for an instant, but it's there long enough for me to know exactly what it is—who it is. Gav. But not Gav as he is now, Gavrielle as he was then. As a child. His twelve-year-old body darts across one of the pathways and around a dark corner, silver hair whipping in some phantom wind. Another thing to add to my torment, it seems.

Fliders begin stinging me everywhere, and I no longer care who hears my screams.

How has my crystal failed me? Is it because I've overused it? Too much magic in too short a time? Am I simply gassed out? I can't die like this, I won't. Anything but this.

It's a fucking nightmare.

But it's real.

If I die in this dream, I die for real.

In pure desperation, I reach for my powers once again, clawing and racking my metaphorical hands against the barren and hollow place within me where it typically slumbers, always licking its lips in anticipatory delight. Now, it's as if the conscious entity that is my magic has simply vanished completely.

I thought the feeling of emptiness was bad an hour ago, but now, I've never felt more alone and broken than I am in this moment.

About to be eaten alive by a swarm of damned fliders.

My boots are completely covered by them now, as are my clothes, hair—they're everywhere.

My screams echo out across the labyrinth walls.

The finality pulls at a place deep inside, one I thought left barren and empty. But like the darkness I find so alluring, it beckons closer to me as my desire for it blooms in full. Not only a craving but a ravenous hunger, a salacity that cannot be satisfied.

My crystal.

I feel it again.

With no time to think or plan or strategize, my screams erupt as a blast of my crystal shoots out of me. The fliders all collectively squeak as they're annihilated into fine bits of dust. My crystal blows a hold right through the maze wall, complete overkill. I exhale in shaky relief, shuddering as I swat the remaining bugs from my body.

I hardly get a second to breathe when large hands haul me roughly by the collar of my uniform, literally yanking me up the smooth side of the maze until I'm sitting on top of the cold, slippery stone. I'm in too much of a panicked fit to see who it is, nor do I fight them. Then I'm being violently dragged along the top part of the maze, sliding all over the place.

"Hey!" I cry out to the man dragging me by my uniform's neckline so forcefully he's ripping it. It isn't Gav—that, I can tell right away. Who is it?

The man stops abruptly, and I shimmy my body around as if I'm on fire, shaking off more reminding bugs, skin cold and clammy and no doubt as white as a ghost. When I finally turn to face them, I gasp in surprise.

"Jance?"

He looks at me coldly, and he appears . . . off. Almost possessed by anger and hatred.

For me.

I back away, boots leaving a soft squeaking sound on the stygian marble labyrinth.

"How did you get up here?" I ask when he doesn't say anything to me, my voice hoarse from all the screaming.

What I want to ask is how dare he show his stupid face when he just left me after he promised he'd never do that again, but I don't. I can't bear his answer. I'm one tap away from a complete shatter.

Yet, something about this is all wrong.

He is all wrong.

One of the broadcasting cameras appears behind him, and it bobs like a buoy in an ocean of gray clouds and misty rain. The sun has practically set, leaving the labyrinth in an unnerving darkness.

After a tense silence, my father finally speaks. "I heard your screams from afar, and I knew it was you. So, I came for you."

My brows knit together in confusion at the response. So much is confusing here. His voice, for one, is off. Two, what he says makes no sense.

I open my mouth to reply once, twice. Then, finally, on the third try, I manage to get words out. "Why are you in the maze at all?"

He takes an ominous step towards me before saying, "There aren't many of us left, perhaps four or five. Maybe even less. The maze proved to be far more dangerous than we expected."

What the fuck?

I blink the rain from my lashes, the droplets heavier now as the world around me darkens and thunder booms in the distance beyond the Sky Dais. He's still there, as solid and corporeal as a real person. He does look worse for wear, however. His clothing is grungy, which is strange for him. It's covered in blood, soaked with rain, and covered in mud, as if he's been on the ground in a real scuffle or two.

"Jance?" I back away further, but he follows.

I should unsheathe my sword, but even after everything he's done, he's still my flesh and blood. I can't strike him down.

Aggressively, he charges me, and it surprises me so much I simply don't react fast enough. I trip over my feet, and I go down, back landing roughly on the jet-black top of the maze. Air jumps from my lungs violently, and I gasp as they scream at me. But when a curved knife materializes from Jance's hands and catapults right for my chest, I act on instinct.

My leg shoots up and kicks him square in the chest. And I hold absolutely nothing back.

Whatever the hell is going on here, I can't go down. I must fight. Regardless of who I'm battling against.

Jance grunts as he lands flat on his back, and I don't wait for him to get up.

I run.

Following the path of the labyrinth, I snake my way along the top, but charging footsteps are right on my ass.

The corners up here are even sharper than the ones below, and as I whip left to follow the path, I slip on the slick, wet surface. When I fall this time, I tumble forward, my legs flying up above me, cracking my lower back like a twig.

Jance is on me in an instant. His weight is like a bull's.

The way his hands grip my wrist so tightly and with how forcefully he pummels his knee into my back, I know for sure this person is not my father. Jance would never, no matter what happened, treat me this roughly. He didn't even do that during training, when he was supposed to be beating the crap out of me. And he knows . . . he knows how much it frightens me when men hover over me in this way.

"Stop it!" I grind out as his free hand shoves the side of my face down into the cold, wet marble of the maze. Is this Jance and he's possessed by something, or is it someone else wearing his face? If I kill him, am I killing Jance? What should I do? Can I get out of this hold to do anything about it in the first place? I'm not so sure I can. My crystal's powers have practically left me. My own father has abandoned me—whether this is him or not—he's still gone. The man I have feelings for hates me . . . and he ditched me too. My family has renounced me. Gav doesn't remember me. What do I have left to fight for? What strength can I draw from to dig deep enough to gain the upper hand in this situation?

Fight for Pacey, the Hijacked, Gav . . . all those people down there who are rooting for you right this very moment. Fight for them. Be their hero. Now, force him off!

Gritting my teeth in a snarl, I manage to wrangle one leg up from his weight and bring it up under me. That's it, that's all I need. Using all my strength, I lift my hips up, lifting us *both* up.

"The fuck?" I hear, and his surprise at my strength gives me even more incentive to keep pushing. My father knows where the source of my might comes from, and it isn't from him. The Syrian blood that flows through my veins allows me to sneak my opposite leg up under me, and I twirl my body beneath this person wearing my father's face, breaking free. I elbow him right in the nose, and he grunts as blood sprays in a splattering texture across the maze.

Quickly, I crawl myself out from under this person and take off running a second time.

I've got to get off the top of this thing. It's way too slippery and narrow. Plus, there's nowhere to hide, and I may need that option.

A turn is coming up, so instead of going left, I dive leg first. Thanks to the slick surface and beaded water on top, I slide right off the edge.

The only sound in the entire labyrinth is my tiny gasp as I fall ten feet back down into the maze. It feels a whole lot higher than that.

I hit the ground hard enough to make my bones quake, but there's no time for a reprieve. As soon as my knees and ankles stabilize, I spring forward, hoping beyond hope that "Jance" isn't behind me.

Turns out, hope is for fools.

"Get back here, you little bitch! You're mine!"

He hastens atop the maze, keeping pace with me easily, still wearing my father's face.

That isn't Jance. That isn't him.

I take off right, bridging the distance between us. The portion of the maze he's standing on doesn't connect as I disappear into the obsidian darkness. This is my one chance to get away.

I take two lefts and an additional right before I hear his footsteps sloshing in the soaked grass behind me. My heart hammers, each beat a threat to my ribs as it slams against them. I'm being chased still, and I never thought I'd miss the fliders until now.

I'm soaring around yet another endless corner when my foot slips in a muddy section, and the fall causes me to stumble once, twice, and that little tumble costs me.

He shoves me forward from behind, causing my momentum to topple me over completely.

Refusing to get caught in the same position as last time, I turn onto my back at the last minute. Right before he pounces.

And I no longer see my father's face but the true person hell-bent on killing me today.

Emmers.

That makes sense. Dammit. I've been hallucinating Jance's face this entire time, and I never even thought to assume that.

Although, I see clearly now, and the hatred in Emmers's eyes shines brighter than a star. They've gone mad. Red around the edges, bugged out, wild and crazed. Whatever hallucination he experienced drove him as insane as it did me.

That isn't good for me.

He's huge, and he overpowers me quickly again by using his weight to pin me down on my back. He mounts me, even though I kick and scream and claw and punch.

Rough hands clasp hard around my throat, so tightly I feel my increasing heartbeat in my neck, and he begins to squeeze.

"She told me if I deliver your body, I'll be richer than if I won these silly Titan Games," he begins, voice distant yet almost relieved. As if his task is about to be completed, and he's moments away from collecting his prize. "My Mistress promised me five million Cato credits for your mangled body. An easy thing to say yes to since you've been pissing me off since the tryouts. Nobody makes a fool out of Emmers, nobody, especially not a stuck-up little cunt like you!" My vision is going spotty, my grip on his wrists weakening. The throbbing in my throat is wild as Emmers cuts off all circulation, and I feel the blood pooling in my face, as if it turns entirely into pins and needles.

He grins down at me, ever so pleased with himself. "What my Mistress wants, she gets."

The fucking Mistress again? Naresteé doesn't know when to quit.

Is she going to get what she wants, after all?

Emmers and his wild expression blur as I gasp for any amount of air left to me, but all I can manage to get are pathetic glimmers of hope that hardly resemble a breath of air. The result is tiny, weakened gasps and squeals as I try my hardest to cling to life. I try in vain to draw upon my crystal's power, but it doesn't come. No fancy outmaneuvers will save me this time. This time, I'll die under him rather than escape.

My vision is going black. Before it completely encompasses everything, however, I see a glimpse of a figure appear behind Emmers.

"Jance . . . ?" I manage to squeak out, the figurine nothing but a pair of broad shoulders painted as a dark silhouette.

Unfortunately, it's nothing but another illusion.

CHAPTER 55

The sounds around are muffled bursts that make little sense, let alone definable. My face still feels hot, the blood not yet where it should be since—

Emmers!

My eyes snap open the moment I remember what was happening. Emmers was quite literally choking me to death, and I must have passed out.

So, why did he stop? Why am I not dead?

My mind is still fuzzy and unclear, and I'm coughing harshly as my lungs desperately gasp for air. My lashes are thickened with tears, and I angrily whip them away. I'm flat on my back, too weak to even sit up.

Although, my ears are working just fine, and I hear scuffling and grunts directly next to me.

Forcefully, I make myself sit up on my elbows, and I finally see why Emmers was forced to stop his assassination of me for his Mistress.

Gavrielle.

This time, I pray he's no illusion. That he's real and solid and here to do one thing: save me.

I don't like to be saved. I'd rather just save myself . . . Except, sometimes, a girl needs to be rescued. Especially when she doesn't feel worthy of it in the first place. If I am the Killer of Worlds, then Gav should have let me die.

When I watched Gav and Ardelle fighting in the first Titan game, I was impressed by his wicked grace in a body so large. Lethal. Dynamic. Precise. That's the pillars of a true assassin, a warrior. Gav is all those things. Except, this time, he's quite the opposite. Now, as he brutally fights hand-to-hand with Emmers—who is no slouch both in battle and in size—he's practically feral.

"Gav!" I try shouting at him, except my throat is swollen and feels completely collapsed. All that comes out is a sad, wheezing sound.

I roll onto my side. I've got to help him.

Gavrielle's fangs are barred as he pounds on Emmers, his white hair staining with the blood of the man. Emmers, to his credit, is still hanging in there despite Gav's clear advantages. Gav hasn't even used the twin swords strapped to his back. Instead, he's content with using his raw and bloodied fists to beat the life out of Emmers.

"I will take her heart!" Emmers hisses as he manages to put a step or two between him and my alien friend. "I will take her heart and bring it to my Mistress."

That isn't the smartest thing to have said, because Gavrielle goes still as death. Sky-Fae still.

"She's mine," Gavrielle whispers as he towers over Emmers, who is bloodied and beaten. "She is mine!"

His roar makes my eyes go wide because it practically shakes the entire Dais and something deep within my heart, too.

"Wait, where'd she go?" Emmers looks in my direction, his face shaking with panicked confusion. But I'm sitting right here. Is he hallucinating still? Then I feel it, the slight pull that I've forgotten about until now, Gavrielle's Ringer magic.

Gav's eyes glow green within the pupils, just like I remembered. He must be hiding me from Emmers, in case he tries to come for me again and Gav can't stop him. The act warms some part of me frozen over from the events of the last few hours and days, perhaps longer.

There's no answer from Gav, and he pounces on Emmers, blades now in hand. There's a slice, choking, and then a heavy hollow thud. It bounces and rolls before coming to a stop. Another louder sound follows shortly after, sloshing and leaden. Emmers is dead.

How many more heads will roll before this tournament of death is over, I wonder?

His death was quick, efficient in a way I don't know how to be. Only a person trained in killing other people could artfully end a life in such a way. Even though I know I'm safe, a massive part of me is so sad to see this. He told me he grew up in an assassin's camp that Arianyte ran, yet it still didn't completely dawn on me exactly what that meant until this very moment. Gavrielle, my Gavrielle, is a trained killer. That once sweet boy who gave me a bouquet of dandelions is gone.

Because of me.

At least if I had been taken away with him, we'd have been in this mess *together*.

But that reality will never be true, will never exist.

Instead, we're both left with the fallout of what Arianyte has shaped us to be.

"Kara." He approaches me, falling to his knees and helping me sit up. The way he says my name, it's different somehow. I look into his eyes. The green glow is gone, and I see someone completely distinctive from the person I've spent these last few days with—yet painfully familiar.

"Gav?" I breathe, voice hoarse but clear enough for him to understand. Not the Gav I've known from the past few days, but my Gav. The old Gav.

He shakes his head yes, eyes glassy. "I remember." His voice is full of sadness, bitterness, pure unadulterated unfairness. "I remember everything. You, the orphanage, that bitch, Amera, and Narestee and—"

"How I left you," I confess before he says it. If he's going to leave me, too, then I need all the breaking done at once. "I blew you up. I gave you these scars." I brush the back of my fingers against the side of his neck, my guilt overwhelming yet somehow freeing to say it out loud to the one person who matters. "I left you, Gavrielle. I'm so sorry. Stars, I'm so sorry."

Gavrielle takes my face in both his hands and forces me to look him directly in the eyes. "You don't know how happy I was to know you had gotten away. It was the only thing that kept me going. Knowing they didn't catch you made everything that happened to me worth it. I remember that now. I remember all of it . . . When the hallucination gas was dispersed, it triggered my memories to return. I'm not sure how, and I don't think Arianyte intended for that to happen, but it did. I remember all of it—so many years, as if the veil had suddenly been lifted from my eyes. It's a miracle, I-I remember everything. Right in the middle of battle, I remembered your face. Remembered *you*. Stars . . . and then I ran for you, immediately knowing I had to get to you and tell you that I remembered. I had to make sure you were safe."

He looks down at the dandelion tattoo and my forearm as he takes my wrist in his hand, a single tear falling onto it. He does remember. "I remember this, the weeds I picked for you that day. I was so afraid how you'd react."

"They were never weeds to me," I whisper. It's the truth. By some grace, Arianyte's attempts at messing with our minds ended up freeing Gavrielle's. There's no better outcome that I could have asked for from this. Unless I'm completely hallucinating this entire thing.

"Are you real? I mean, this isn't still the gas making me see things? Making me see something I desperately wish was real?" I take his hand, needing to hold on to him in case this is an illusion. If it is, then, maybe, just maybe, I can keep him here as long as possible.

"I'm real. It's me. The day we met, you came back to the orphanage and I, like such an idiot, threw myself into the fray for you when that scuffle broke out. The kids weren't kind to you upon your arrival, and I couldn't stand to see them hurt you, even then. Plus, the effects of the gas only last an hour, and that has long since passed."

350

I smile, remembering that day we first met. How, exactly as he described, he came to my rescue. Exactly as he did today. But like an itch in my mind, something about what he just said doesn't quite fit.

"How do you know that?" I ask, pulling his hands away from mine.

His brows crease as he flinches his head back from me just slightly. It's subtle, but I notice it. "Know what?"

"How do you know how long the gas lasts?"

CHAPTER 56

THE ARIANYTE EMPIRE DECREE #70

ARIANYTE STRICTLY MONITORS WOMAN'S REPRODUCTIVE HEALTHCARE. FETAL ABORTIONS WITHOUT STRICT PERMISSION ARE CRIMES PUNISHABLE BY CONFINEMENT, FORCED PREGNANCY, AND/OR PERMANENT SEPARATION OF OFFSPRING.

Gav's body tenses at my question, his eyes averting mine as the air shifts within the silence that passes between us. Something is off. What could it possibly be?

It can only be one thing, after all.

Dread cleaves the connection between us in half.

"They used it on you guys at the assassin's camp, right?" I ask, my eyes practically pleading with him to lie to me.

The pain in his gaze tells me that isn't how he knows about the gas.

"There was never an assassins camp, Kara." His tone is cold and distant. "At least, not in the way I described it, anyway."

His eyes close, as if he can't even stomach looking at me when he says the words. "It is true that I've been trained to kill, as such is my birthright. My family, my race—we're killers. We came to Earth to kill, and that's what we did. That instinct in me was honed as sharp as the blades at my back, and I embraced it. It's also true that I had forgotten my past, forgotten you . . ." He shifts, pulling something from the pocket of his uniform. It's a piece of paper, folded up and crumpled to the point where it could rip and fall apart with the gust of the wind. As if he's held onto it for a long while. When he unfolds it, I gasp. It's one of my old drawings of him. One of the very same sketches that was stolen from my loft months ago.

No. Stars, no.

He recognizes the shock on my face, that I've put two and two together.

"It was you who broke in . . ." My thought trails off as my mind spins for the reason why. It comes a beat too late.

"Yes," he says, barely a whisper. "Malakyte chose to make me one of his invisible guards and workmen. I would work in the shadows, sometimes for recognizance, to intercept assassination attempts, do his personal bidding . . . He sent me to your loft to search for anything I could uncover regarding you. He was convinced you had a connection to the rebels, which I was sent to prove or disprove. I had no recollection of you, us, the orphanage—nothing. I had no idea who you even were. I was there because it was my duty. It was simply another job. Until I found this. The other drawings, too. That's when I began to dig. Began inserting myself deeper into you and the other Starseeds in the background. I had to know what these drawings meant. So, I watched you from afar. He sent me to follow you, watch you, spy on you. Although, I found it harder and harder to report to him what you were doing, especially when I found out you were working with the rebels. I could not inform Malakyte of what I had found, and so I didn't. I had never lied to him before then. That part of me, the part I now understand is the thread that connects us, simply would not let me put you in danger. I could not do it. After last year's Titan Games . . . after the finale, I had to get closer to you. But you disappeared. Not even I knew where you had gone. When you and the others joined the Titan Games, I volunteered myself for the position to enter as a contestant so I could finally gain access to you. I knew that you and I were connected somehow, but this is not what I thought I was going to find. I did not expect this outcome. Malakyte ordered much of this, yes, but I—Kara—I needed an excuse to get into proximity to you. Because of this."

He pushes the drawing towards me again, but I'm frozen solid.

No.

No.

No!

I recoil from him, and I see the immense hurt that flashes across his face.

"Kara, please. I didn't remember you. I couldn't have known. The moment I remembered I came for you. I killed everyone in my path so I could get to you and tell you this. To also tell you—"

"Tell me what?" I yell, voice all sorts of crackly, from the injury and from sheer pain at what's happening.

What the actual *fuck*?

"That, no matter the circumstances, I cannot allow you to win these Titan Games. No matter what, you mustn't win."

CHAPTER 57

I practically laugh, although there's nothing funny about this. Not in the slightest.

I hate him, I realize. I hate him. I hate everyone. I hate myself. For being so foolish. For seeing the sweet, innocent boy I ditched way back then, when what I truly should have seen is the calculated killer before me.

A spy should know another spy when they see one. Geonni is likely rolling in his damned grave right about now.

I hate him, too.

I hate all of them.

"Go away," I tell him in a hushed, cruel whisper, and he flinches, as if I've punched him hard in the face. Who knows, I still might.

This is what will do it. This is what's going to make me snap.

Even though my legs wobble, I force myself to stand and begin walking away from this traitor. If I don't leave now, who knows what I might end up doing.

Thankfully, we're in a maze. It shouldn't be hard to lose him.

"Where are you going?" he demands, but I ignore him. I owe him nothing.

Stars, I'm such an idiot. I should have known Malakyte would pull some sick move like this. I practically gave him the ammunition; he merely played the hand.

Idiot! I'm a fucking dumbass!

"Kara!"

"Fuck off!" I yell back, my strides increasing in pace. "After everything I've sacrificed to bring us back together . . . all so you can go run back to your master. Just go. I'm sure he's incredibly interested in all the intel you've gathered on me."

"That isn't what I was sent here to do," he tells me, and this causes me to pause. My head cranks over my shoulder. He's right there. My Gavrielle, standing right here before me, like I've begged to the stars for years. Turns out, getting what you ask for isn't all it's cracked up to be. My eyes narrow at him, the rage building up inside me palpable. He knows the question I want to ask, and he answers it, knowing that, if I must ask, it'll make things worse for him.

"It's been my sole job to make sure you finish and win the Titan Games. That's my only purpose here."

"Why didn't you help me in the race, then? I barely saw you once."

"I was with you up until the end, up until we all hit the ramp. You just never saw me, Kara." He laughs a bit bitterly. "To be honest, you didn't need me. You had it all under control. So much for me being your knight and shining armor."

"Shut up, Gav."

"You cannot win these games." He switches back to the topic, chuckles gone.

I turn back towards him and ask, "What? Why? That makes no sense."

"Yes, it does."

I go to argue but then realize he's right. That my suspicions were spot on when fearing Malakyte was setting a trap in case I did end up winning. However, what I did not expect was Malakyte *wanting* me to win the games. Why would he want me to win?

"What is he planning for me?"

"I do not know," he answers quickly, and I roll my eyes with a frustrated sound and continue walking away.

He runs right up next to me. "I swear it, Kara. I do not know. What I do know is that it's bad. He wants you. He's obsessed with you."

"Yeah, no shit. That's why I'm going to kill him." And not be scared this time. Killing Malakyte is the one reprieve left to me now. The only way to keep those I care about safe. Destroying Malakyte keeps them safe. Freeing Pacey makes them happy. To end this nightmare, bring freedom to the people unable to fight for it themselves. However I must get this done, I'll do it. Everyone I love is gone. If Malakyte kills me in the process, so fucking be it. I don't care. I've got nothing to live for anymore, anyway. If he's planning to get me, then I can at least prove to those I love that I have changed, that I am better than they perceive me to be.

Gavrielle grabs my arm to stop me. "You cannot."

"You cannot!" I spit back, chest bumping him in challenge, not caring how silly it may appear with our size difference.

His head shakes, and a smirk dances across his lips, which only irritates me more. "What?" I demand, blood boiling.

Rubbing his chin, he sighs heavily. "You haven't changed a bit, Kara."

This surprises me. It also breaks me.

"You're wrong!" I cry, my voice weak and fragile and cracking with emotion—exactly like I am on the inside. "I have changed! Losing you changed me. I spent all these years risking my life in search of you. Year after year, it *destroyed me* knowing you were out there, not knowing what was happening to you under Arianyte's thumb. Because of me! It destroyed me. Running from Arianyte, day after day, knowing they were coming for me—that changed me. Having no family, no parents, nobody who actually cared about me, that changed me. Knowing I let the only person who did care about me get taken away by the occupation tore me apart! I'm not good anymore, Gav. I changed when you left—when they took you. I had to become someone else in your absence, and you don't know me anymore. I've been alone this whole time. Until Malakyte found me a few months ago and introduced me to the other Starseeds and Ringers and then I found out one of them was my father, my real father, and he just left me out here to die in the cold because I must be so disgusting of a person he doesn't want anything to do with me. That is going to change me. So, you don't know me. I'm not the girl you used to know. She's gone. She died the day they took you away. So, go!"

I shove him firmly in the chest this time, as hard as I can. "*Go!*"

He stands there, not having moved an inch because he's a massive fucking tank, doing nothing but looking down at me with those stupid, beautiful eyes. I push him again, and this time, my rage gives me enough strength to propel him off balance, and he staggers backwards. "Leave! I don't care what happens to me when I'm up there. *I don't care!* Let him try to hurt me. There's nothing left of me for him to break apart. He's already done it!"

Tears well up, but I refuse to cry. I'm done crying. I'm done feeling self-pity and sadness, and all I want to do is let this fury burn until it's all-consuming and I go up in flames with it. Take Malakyte down with me for good this time.

"You tell him that I'm coming for him, and I'm ready for whatever he's got."

With that, I turn my back to Gav—my Gav—and walk away. Something I never saw myself doing.

His hand grasps around my wrist, stopping me.

"You may not feel like you have anything to live for, but I know that isn't true. I saw the love those people have for you. The guy with the bow and arrows, the one whom I fought the other day and whose scent is all over you, I felt his conviction with every blow."

"He wasn't fighting for me," I correct him.

Gav doesn't believe me. "He was. I know because I saw him watching for you, making sure you remained safe, even when he should have been focusing on me. It cost him hit after hit. So, I do not believe the look of love I saw on his and your father's faces simply disappears because you blew up an island."

My eyes close, remembering them but also hating them for this pain, too. "Well, they did. Now, let me go. I'm going to take out anyone else who's left up here before I miss my date with the devil. Don't try to stop me. Nothing you say is going to change how I feel."

He skitters around to face me, and I roll my eyes at how blatantly ignorant of my boundaries he is. "There is no one left. It's only us."

"They're not all dead, are they?"

Gavrielle looks confused. "No, of course not. Each of us was given a panic button to press in case of emergency or if we wanted out of the maze. It has a count of how many contestants are left. Didn't the SSPARROW who drove you to your starting point give you one?"

I laugh bitterly as Gav pulls out the circular device, the number two glowing in red lights at the center. That must represent both Gav and me.

"No, no, he didn't."

Another gift from *the Mistress*, I'm assuming.

"Goodbye, Gavrielle."

I move to step beside him, but he blocks me with his body. Taking a deep breath through my nose, I try again, and like before, he prevents me from moving forward.

Fine.

Spinning on my heels, I turn around and take off in the opposite direction, but he's fast as lightning and makes his way in front of me yet again.

"Jupiter's rings, stop this," he seethes at me. "I'm sorry. *I am sorry*. I didn't remember you until less than an hour ago. If I had, I never would have gone through with this. When I was a child, after they took me, Malakyte tried to get me to tell him where you were. Through torture of all kinds, I refused. Even as a twelve-year-old boy, I rejected every ounce of torture and manipulation they pounded into me just to keep you safe. That's when he had me Reconditioned, and you were lost to me then . . . but I never gave you up to him, and I never will. I simply did not remember. Please, believe me."

"It doesn't change the fact you're his hitman—his lapdog. Fuck. I don't even know if what you're telling me now is real. If you even lost your memories at all. I can't trust you. I can't trust anyone. Now, *go*."

The few remaining drops of my self-control are drying up, and if he doesn't get out of my way now, I'm going to lose it on him.

"Kara—"

I pull my sword from its place at my back, the metal sound clanging in the moist air around us. This action causes his eyes to widen in both surprise and pain.

"Stop it," I fume through tightly grounded teeth. "Leave. Push your little button. Go back to your master and let me win. Or I'll make you."

"You truly think I'm going to leave you? After everything? Perhaps you believe your family and your lover are capable of that, but I am not. I'm never leaving you again. Plus, you cannot force me."

My head tilts to the side as I glare at him, pursing my lips to keep myself from whacking him upside the skull. "Are you saying that because you don't think I can take you on or because of our history?"

"Both." It doesn't take him long to answer, not long at all.

He can think what he likes. It still won't change things. "I will fight you if I have to. Don't make me have to."

It dawns on Gavrielle that I'm as serious as a heart attack, and I can see the battle going on within his eyes over whether to draw blades against me.

Gav doesn't break our stare as he reaches behind his shoulders for his twin blades.

He's going to make me have to. *Well played, Gav, well played.*

The wind blows hard, cascading our long hair around in dramatic, contrasting arcs. With the dark sky and labyrinth in the background, it must be one hell of a sight for those watching.

Knowing that Malakyte turned Gav's mind infuriates me, and my energy and resolve is back with full force. Do I blame Gav? No. But can I trust Gav? Also no. If it's only Gavrielle between me and Malakyte, then I'll go through Gav. I'll go through anyone to get to Malakyte at this point. He's taken too much, and I'm done letting him get away with it. I'm not leaving Pacey to her fate, either. There are far too many good reasons not to go forward. I don't care anymore. I'm doing this no matter what.

"I'm trying to protect you," he tells me, the tension between us rising like the electric pulse in the air. Lightning must be close.

I smile sadly at him, but it falters quickly. "And I'm trying to avenge you."

My sword swings hard and fast over his chest, and he blocks it effortlessly. Pushing downward, our blades slide against each other as the sound clangs into the air. The space we're in is small, which benefits me over him because I'm more able to move around within it. Using that to my advantage, I squeeze between him and the maze wall, sneaking my way behind him easily. The sharp end of my blade taps along his shoulder, but I don't sink it in.

"Let me go," I try again, not wanting this.

I don't see his elbow coming back towards me fast and hard, hitting my ribs and knocking me backwards.

"If I must hurt you to keep you alive and safe from him, then that is what I'll do."

I pounce on him, sick of this talk. Gavrielle is a force all his own, and I'm shaken at the power of his hit. Our swords slam together in earth-shattering blows, and my arms swing in arcs as we both dance in a waltz of death and sorrow. Neither of us wants to fight, yet neither will yield to the other. He doesn't understand what's at stake; it isn't simply about me. The entire planet depends on me winning this game. I can't let them down because I'm too much of a coward to face my villain.

His giant body blocks me from going around him this time, but I charge at him anyway. He knows I have nowhere to go, and he braces for me to hit him. Instead, I dive feetfirst between his legs, coming up fast behind him as I kick out his knees. I strike his upper back hard, knocking him down face-first. He must drop his dual swords to catch himself, and I use the maze walls as a floor, walking along it with his body as an anchor. As I fly atop him, I steal his blades and throw them over the ledge into some other part of the labyrinth. Now, he's weaponless. Not that he was truly using them, though. We're both intentionally holding back.

"You're a quick little shit, aren't you?" he complains, standing back up to his feet, yet there's still a playful compliment in his tone.

We both go to punch at the same time, each nailing the other right in the jaw. I don't know if Gavrielle is pulling his punches or not, but that fucking hurt.

Taking a step back to steady myself, I shake my head and the pain along with it. "Not holding anything back, I see."

"Likewise." He rubs his defined and sculpted jawline, almost as if he's impressed it stings as much as it does.

"You're honestly going to beat my ass to prevent me from winning? You want fame and fortune that badly, *Damon*?" I taunt, knowing that doesn't mean shit to him.

"I want to keep you safe and alive that badly, *Karalevine*. It's what a good friend does."

A good friend, huh? Is that what he thinks he's being?

I try to convince him he's wrong. "It's about more than just me, Gav. Listen, there's something way bigger happening here than you realize. It's why me, Ardelle, and Deimos entered the games in the first place. We didn't do it for fun or fame or Cato credits. We did it to save our friend and bring down the empire, and I've got to finish what I started. Malakyte setting a trap was already a part of the risk factor, but I can handle him. I've done it before."

Yet, Gav shakes his head vehemently. "You don't know him like I do. You cannot."

There he goes again with this *I cannot* bullshit. Nobody tells me that I can't do something. Nobody.

"You don't know me anymore, Gav. There's nothing I cannot do."

There it is. The truth at the core of this entire scuffle between us. His lack of faith in me because he's still looking at me as that broken little girl I was back then. He believes that's who I am and that he needs to protect me all over again. Defying his master is proof of that, and I have no doubt it's deeply noble of him, but

I don't want or need his protection. What I need is Malakyte's head on a spike.

Unexpectedly, Gavrielle lifts me up and throws me over his shoulder like a sack of potatoes, then begins hauling me down the path of the maze—like I'm nothing but a doll. I'm accosted by his scent first, but the crisp smell of him doesn't distract from how infuriated I am at the audacity of this guy.

"Gav!" I shout, but he ignores me, walking in the direction I threw his blades. "Gavrielle! Put me down right now!"

I kick, punch his back and shoulders, and pull his hair. His reaction? Absolutely oblivious. Complete zilch. Like I'm nothing but an annoying gnat and my hits are not soft.

"Gav!" My voice is ruthless and dripping with irritation. He can't do this. He can't. "Gav!" I scream directly in his ear, causing him to finally acknowledge me by jerking his head back.

"We are leaving this Dais. I can get you somewhere safe before he comes."

No.

I need to free myself from him somehow, and squirming isn't going to work. Stopping my struggle, I close my eyes and feel for my crystal's power. I'd never use my crystal on him, but I can at least use it to distract him.

There it is, a tiny spark to draw upon. My anger fueling it back to life. Knowing I may lose it once again, I only call forth a fraction of its power. A minuscule pinprick of antimatter energy can do a shit ton of damage, and damage is exactly what I'm looking to cause.

I point my finger at the shadowy labyrinth, and I blast it to bits.

The explosion is instant.

Massive.

A thundering boom seems to rack the entire platform as hefty chunks of obsidian are thrown into the sky and surrounding area. Gav is facing the opposite direction, and the explosion catches him off guard.

He falls to the ground face-first. I slither my legs out from under him too quickly for him to grab them back as slink right out of his grasp.

I'm off.

Then I'm not.

Gav manages to seize hold of my ankle, and now, I'm the one falling face-first to the ground.

A fire has broken out where my crystal blasted, likely hitting the technology or something underneath the grass. Whatever caused the blaze to catch, it illuminates us both as it bounces off the reflective surfaces of the maze's walls, giving it the sense that the flames surround us. The Burnt Orange color reflects in Gavrielle's eyes. With his pointed ears and canines, he looks so utterly foreign to me. I had forgotten how alien he truly is until this very moment.

I'm going to regret this, and it's cruel and a low blow, but I've got to get away from him. Reluctantly, I kick Gav right in that beautifully handsome face with my foot. I try not to hit him too hard. He curses and ultimately releases me, and I'm on my feet in seconds.

As I dash through debris, I stop when I see something odd within the rubble.

The small, circular item is no bigger than the palm of my hand, and it's flat. The number two glows red in the center. Gav said contestants can use this mechanism to exit themselves from the game. This is Gav's, so if I push it, then—

My old friend's body slams into me, and we're immediately on the ground again, the heat of the fire more intense down low.

If I'm going to do this, I have to do it now, while I'm still able.

I'm assuming that center spot is the actual button mechanism, and I go to push it, but as I do, Gavrielle slaps it out of my hand. I hiss at him. He growls back. It lands on the grass, and I snarl, kicking and flailing about like a wild thing.

His strong hands and arms pin me down quickly, but I wrap my legs around his waist and buck my hips upwards. It doesn't work as well as I'd like due to our dramatic weight difference—he's a literal wall of meat—but it does knock him off balance enough for me to wiggle out from under him.

Gav and I scuffle back and forth, each making small gains and losses on the other. He's hard to fight, but I somehow manage to swing myself into a sitting position on top of him, Gav on his back.

"This ends now, Gav," I say, the fire burning in intensity behind us.

I take my sword in my hand and whip it around quickly, barreling it straight down.

CHAPTER 58

Gavrielle's eyes widen in shock as my sword's blade plunges down so close to his face it nearly knicks his sculpted cheek.

I've got to release the pressure at the last moment, so I don't destroy the device that allows players to forfeit the game.

The tip of the sword still breaks through it, however, as the circular device beeps several times consecutively.

All the tension in Gav's body releases instantly as he realizes what I've done. That I wasn't going for his head with my blade—for one, but that I just successfully exited him from this competition.

Still sitting on Gav's lap, I pluck the round device from the tip of my sword. The screen is cracked and shattered, but I can see the glowing red number in the center: one.

I have won the Titan Games.

Holy shit.

I've won.

"Congratulations," Gavrielle says, voice defeated—sad. "I hope you know what you're getting yourself into."

I look down at him, feeling terrible for the bruise already forming on his cheek from where I kicked him. In fact, I feel incredibly awful for having fought him at all.

"I'm genuinely sorry, Gav." And I mean it. "But I have to do this. I must see this through till the end. You don't know what he's done to me. You don't know all the things I need to make him pay for. I hope you can understand and forgive me, especially for clocking you so good in your beautiful face."

The Gav I knew couldn't help but chuckle at that, and he does.

A loud blaring sound shocks the air between us. Fireworks blast through the darkened sky as rain falls in buckets around them. I swear I can hear cheers from all the way down below us in Zarmenia City. Outstanding . . . I really didn't think that many people would be happy to see me win. It seems the animosity for Arianyte goes a hell of a lot deeper than Malakyte expected, and I'm going to exploit that hatred. Sharpen it, hone it, wield it. It will become as deadly as any blade made for the throat of an enemy. My enemy.

Sky-hovers appear in the air above us. The SSPARROWs will be coming soon. They'll take me to him, to whatever trap he's set for me.

Gavrielle springs to his feet, and graciously holds a hand out to help me up. I stare at it for a moment, the old nostalgic sensation overtakes me. Gav . . . my Gavrielle.

As I take his hand, Gav lifts me up, and I plow into him, hugging him so hard he likely feels my body trembling. I need this because I don't know if I'll ever have the chance again. There's so much I want to say, so much to apologize for.

My old friend hugs me in return, his massive body envelops me in the safety only a home can provide. I remember why I fought so hard to find him in the first place; it was all for this. For this incredible sense of security that Gavrielle brings me. It's the closest to peace I've ever felt. And now, I finally have him back, for real. No memories lost or stolen, just the two of us.

There is the elephant in the room of what he's been up to within Arianyte all these years and if I can trust him or not. I wonder, due to all the betrayals in my past, if he's being truthful with me. That, unfortunately, I cannot shake. And I want to trust him, but I'm not sure . . .

I'm surprised as he suddenly grips my chin and gently guides my face to look up at him. He's so tall, and I'm so short. Eyes in the shade Lavender Ice stare at me with only the intensity of someone with a lot of emotions in their heart. I can see it. Gavrielle bends down to me, our faces only an inch or two apart. I feel his breath on my lips, the fervor of his gaze on my body. He leans in to kiss me, and I'm taken aback by it but I don't stop him. My chest explodes with the unexpected heat of a veclear bomb, and I am not afraid of the way it feels. His lips brush mine, a touch lighter than powdered sugar . . . but then I pull back slightly at the thought of Ardelle, such a minuscule movement, but he picks up on it.

Gav smiles sadly, as if he expected me to deny him. I'm brokenhearted over what Ardelle did, but we did just sleep together yesterday morning. I can't be kissing another person right now. Even if the prospect of that kiss seems . . . like something I would have wanted if life hadn't torn us apart. Right now, I'm far too stressed juggling my feelings for two guys, let alone inserting a third. I must keep Gav safe, and the safest thing for him is to stay the fuck away from me. Malakyte already knows we're friends. Adding a romantic relationship will only endanger Gav further.

"I'm sorry," I whisper, and I mean it.

Gav shakes his head. "Don't be. I think that blast of yours must've knocked my head around a bit. I . . . I don't know what I was thinking."

"That I'm irresistible and adorable?" I joke, trying to get rid of the tension. It seems to work because he flashes me that fanged smile that I had all but forgotten about.

When he finally separates us a little bit, I see a half dozen cameras zooming in from around us, some coming in close as others keep their distance. Thank the stars they weren't here two seconds ago. Gav looks down at me, the violet in his eyes smoldering with the glow of the fire around him. Those eyes say a million things, but he focuses on me as if he's trying to tell me something specific.

His hand comes up to my forehead, brushing my rain-slicked hair back in place. Why does he look so sad?

Bringing me in close, he holds the back of my head and gently kisses my forehead. It's such a tender gesture yet so meaningful.

So, when he whispers in my ears, I'm surprised by the rough tone in his voice.

"You won't like who I'm going to have to be after this, but I have to do what I must to stay as close to your side as possible. Play along."

He's right, I already don't like it, but I try to keep my face calm and composed for the cameras.

"Do me one favor," I say as I bury my face in his chest. I feel him nod as he rests his chin on top of my head. "If you can, find me the same gas that Arianyte used in this maze. Someone I care about deeply needs their memories back, and it's the only chance I've got to wake her up."

There's no time for Gav to agree or not because the SSPARROWs arrive and split us apart.

The moment the cameras go off, Gavrielle turns into a completely different person. His face and eyes go icy and detached. It's as if the boy I've known and loved for so long is entirely gone and instantly transformed into a stone-cold killer.

"I'm on assignment," he says to one of the sky-rats, holding out his arm to him.

The soldier scans some implant in his wrist—something I've never seen before—and they all but ignore him from there. Aside from him telling them he's ordered to stay by my side, that is.

He takes hold of my arm and roughly drags me through the maze. We find his blades on the way, and as I'm being escorted out of the Titan Games as the tournament's winner, I've never been more terrified.

Now, the true games begin.

CHAPTER 59

SSPARROW ENFORCEMENT OFFICERS WILL CONDUCT RANDOM AND INVASIVE BODY SEARCHES OF TERRANS IN PUBLIC SPACES TO ASSURE THE SAFETY OF ALL CITIZENS. ANY RESISTANCE OR REFUSAL WILL BE MET WITH IMMEDIATE AND VIOLENT REPRISAL.

The attention of the press and paparazzi was intense as a general competitor, but as a winner, it's outrageous.

"Kara!"

"Karalevine! How does it feel to win the Titan Games?"

"Do you know what you're going to do with the money?"

"Are you worried Arianyte won't validate your win because of your filthy mouth?"

"Kara!"

Gav and I—along with our escort of SSPARROW soldiers—reach the ground in no time. I'm not taken back to the mansion but to the main transportation port. The same place where we first commandeered a spaceship to try and breach the Azurite before this crazy plan was even thought of. Fate has brought me back here once more, but this time, I am alone. I really shouldn't have taken my team and my family for granted.

But now, I'm on a rampage to kill the prince of Arianyte, and they'd just try and stop me.

Gav and I walk through the wildfire that is the paparazzi and Terran fans screaming my name and onto the transport ship that flies us into space, and we arrive at the docking station of the Azurite far more quickly than I would have liked.

I only hope to the stars the others were able to sneak on board somehow, that they're still going to stick with the plan.

Gav, for all his charm, is a significant actor. He hasn't broken character once, and his role as Malakyte's lackey is being played a little too well. So good, in fact, I begin to doubt his allegiances to me.

You're just being paranoid, I tell myself as he takes hold of me once again and leads me out of our spaceship and to the loading platform that connects this ship to the Azurite. It's a massive area, hundreds of feet high and several hundreds of feet long. I'm taken out into this huge space where Gavrielle escorts me up a set of metal stairs that lead to some sort of airlock door.

The thought of facing whatever Malakyte has waiting for me has my palms sweating and mind reeling. However, I'm ready for it. I'm ready to take off his head.

The entrance leading to the Azurite beeps, and I straighten my spine to that of a steel rod. It's clear, but there's lettering that's blocking out the myriad of bodies behind it. Once that door opens, we'll be face-to-face. Malakyte will not see my nerves, nor my fears. He will only see what I want him to see: my cold determination to kill him. I'm on a warpath, and he can't stop me.

The door opens with a whoosh sound and a hiss, smoke swirling around so thick I can't see anything but a solid wall of white for a few seconds.

Gav squeezes my arm affectionately as he holds onto it. With his Sky-Fae ears, I know he hears my heart thrashing against my rib cage, Malakyte likely will, too. I wonder, will Malakyte be able to smell the change in my scent from Ardelle, like the other extras have been able to? That will not go over well . . .

As the smoke begins to clear, I take a long, deep breath through my nose, the exhale shakier than I would like it to be. Time to face my tormentor. Show him that, despite my ravenously beating heart, I am not afraid. That this dark and tenacious thing beats not for him, as he would wish it to, but in spite of him. He doesn't get me, and he never will get my heart.

The figure beyond the mist begins to take shape, the silhouette coming into view. Tall, thin, long hair and a stupid crown atop an even stupider head. He would be wearing a crown, that pretentious asshole.

Except, instead of the dark fabrics I know Malakyte to be fond of, I see white. In fact, I see a lot of white.

White hair, a crystal-white crown, a white-and-gold gown. The only thing the woman standing before me has of Malakyte are his cold onyx eyes, which glare back at me with a burning fury.

"Who the hell are you?" I blurt out, my shock that Malakyte isn't here to greet me causing me to forget myself for a moment. The fact he isn't here is both an immense relief and slightly insulting. I won his stupid Titan Games, dammit. I deserve to see the prince. "Where's the little prince?"

The woman before me chuckles at that last bit, but her face remains as icy cold as her slightly blue-tinted skin is. The hallway beyond the door is long and made of sharply angled black walls. Orange stripes of light illuminate the darkness, and the side wall is a seamless window looking out into outer space. The Earth floats off in the distance, half covered by the rest of the ship.

"Malakyte will be arriving shortly," she says, a sharp voice dancing on the edge of a blade. "In the meantime, I have come to congratulate you on your inconceivable victory."

The tension rises as she continues.

"Those of us within Arianyte's command have been watching the Titan game's top players ever so closely but none closer than you, Karalevine. You put on quite an untenable show these past few days. Got the Terrans in quite an uproar. The Arianyte Council has been scandalized by your performance."

I hold my chin up. *Don't you dare back down. Look this bitch in those freaky eyes and say what you want to say.*

"Arianyte has many things it needs to hear in order for peace to be arranged between our people. The Terrans have spoken. They know what they want."

I don't expect it, but she begins to giggle slightly. Her silver crown dangling over the center of her forehead, the icy blue jewel there glinting in the light. She is a stunning woman. From her features alone, she doesn't look much older than me. Except those eyes, stars, those fucking eyes. They're scarier, darker, and colder than Malakyte's ever were. Who is she to him? They're related, that's clear. But with the Silent Breath, this person could as easily be his mother as his sister. Perhaps none of the above.

"I wasn't aware you were the Terran satisfaction ambassador. In fact, I didn't think we even had a position like that. Which then begs the question, who gave you the authority to speak for the Terran population on this planet? Who elected you to this fabricated position, I wonder?"

"Well, nobody did. I just won the games."

The icy woman purses her lips, painted to appear pink, but I can still see the blue blood pooling underneath the makeup. "I see. So, you take what you want rather than ask for it?"

I smile, doing my best to keep my cool. "Twisting my words isn't going to change the fact Arianyte must answer for its crimes. Last time I heard, you aren't the person to talk to about those sorts of things. Where is he?"

Stars, when did I see myself preferring the company of Malakyte Ardeen to anyone?

This woman's laugh echoes out into the hallway as me, Gav, and all the SSPARROWs remain cramped by the airlock door. Little miss snow angel hasn't let us pass yet.

"Yes, of course. The man everyone wishes to speak with." Her tone switches to one a hell of a lot more pleasant. "Like I stated, he was delayed, but as the princess of Arianyte, I am here to greet our newest Titan. Please, come, the Azurite awaits you."

The princess? Sister, it is, then.

Didn't Malakyte mention her at one point? That they hated each other?

Finally, she steps out of our path, and we leave the airlock and walk fully onto the Azurite. Few Terrans have ever set foot here, and now I am one of them.

Where is Pacey? And where is Malakyte hiding?

"It is customary for the winner of the Titan Games to be given an exclusive congratulatory rendezvous tour of the Azurite with the head of Arianyte upon their entrance to the fleet."

Gav and I give each other a hesitant glance, but he looks back towards the princess before I can gauge what he's thinking about this so-called tour.

"I will wait for her after the two of you tour and converse," Gav says, not asking.

Nodding, she reaches out and takes my hand, bringing me close to her. It's freezing cold.

"Of course, of course. And where are my royal manners? My goodness, how could I have forgotten to introduce myself? Silly me. Must be all the excitement from that last speech you made. I watched it just before your arrival. There's a bit of a delay getting the Network feeds up to the ship, you understand. My name is Selenyte, princess of the Arianyte Empire. Let's talk, Karalevine, just us girls."

CHAPTER 60

PRECISION STRIKES:

PICK YOUR TARGETS LIKE A SKILLED MARKSMAN. TAKE DOWN THEIR INFRASTRUCTURE, DISRUPT THE NETWORK, HIT THEM WHERE IT HURTS. CUT OFF THEIR SUPPLY LINES, FRY THEIR ALIEN TECH, AND WATCH THEIR PLANS CRUMBLE LIKE A STALE COOKIE. AIM TRUE, REBELS!

At first, I'm very unsure about this little impromptu meeting she suggests but then I remember I need Gav to go do something far more important than guard me.

"That'll be just fine," I say, looking from her to Gav.

Use this chance to go get me the hallucination drug, I order him with my eyes. I can only hope he understands and is able to track down what I need him to. If he's loyal to me, he'll figure it out. If not, I'll know I cannot trust him.

Selenyte then leads me away, only the two of us walking down the hallway, which is made of the same black steel that blankets the Azurite from the outside. The hallways feel otherworldly and so very far away from the home that I've always known on Earth.

It feels like I'm incredibly far from my home planet, even though the Azurite is sitting within its orbit.

I follow the alien princess silently, focusing on mapping my route back to Gav. It isn't much of a tour, given she doesn't speak. We don't go far before we enter the chosen destination, and it has one hell of a view.

Within the darkened room, my eyes are immediately drawn to the floor-to-ceiling windows that show a stunning view of planet Earth. I'm glued to it in amazement, its beauty mesmerizing from all the way up here. Also very bright, brighter than I would have thought.

"Stunning, isn't she? Planet Earth," Selenyte says as she watches me with those peculiarly probing eyes. "It's sad that it almost perished. If not for my brother's grace, it would have."

My eyes roll.

"I'd have thought someone like you would find sights such as these boring after all your many years and travels across the cosmos."

She huffs, half insulted by my comment, half impressed. "I suppose I can stretch myself far enough to see where you could come to such a ghastly conclusion as that one. To the contrary, your assumptions of me are quite far off. If I were this conqueress you believe me to be, I wouldn't have brought you to this room, in particular."

This causes my brows to rise and piques my curiosity.

Taking a second peek around the space, I realize it's no ordinary meeting room. The gorgeous view distracted me initially, but I see clearly now.

The room itself is dark, the main source of light is along the walls and ceiling, strips of blue that illuminate rows of what appear to be computers that stretch further than I can see. Perhaps they go on forever? As I follow the hallway that leads deeper into the area, the colors of all the computers lighting my path, I find the center of everything.

The central computer, the artificial intelligence that runs all of Arianyte. From the Network to the Tribute lottery to how the planet itself is fairing, flight schedules, SSPARROW and Nest scheduling and deployments, communications between the Azurite, Earth, and all the subsidiary bases in the Aurora System itself—it controls *everything.* The hub is a giant round station with a long keyboard that only Pacey would understand how to use. Screens and other odds and ends surround the hub with a chair sitting dead center.

I turn to Selenyte with what can only be a shocked look on my face. This is no coincidence.

"Why'd you bring me here?" I demand, needing to know exactly what's going on.

The princess's smile is wickedly cruel.

"For you to do what you came here to do, of course. Bring my brother to his knees."

CHAPTER 61

"**W**hat?" I laugh, wondering if Malakyte is around a computer tower somewhere, waiting to pop out and begin giggling at my gullible nature. Although, it's hard to imagine him giggling. "You've got to be joking."

Selenyte approaches me calmly, the beads on her gown making a slithering sound against the smooth black tile flooring.

"It's quite simple, actually. I know things. I hear things, and I have it on good authority you joined the Titan Games to bring my brother and Arianyte down. Am I wrong about that? I mean, you have been flaunting it all over the world and Network feeds, after all."

There's really no point in denying it now. "Fine, but why bring me here specifically?"

"Because why wouldn't I? This is where I'd go if I wanted to cause mayhem and turmoil within Arianyte. Also, a little bird told me that was your plan. I thought bringing you here would show you how much of a team player I am. Convince you we should be allies."

I eye her suspiciously. "You don't strike me as the type to want to work with a team."

I'd know.

Her smile reveals those double sets of pointed canines on the top row of teeth. I shiver. "I do have to keep up appearances. Otherwise, the soldiers would report back to my brother, and I'd be caught . . . I'd be punished. My brother is sadistically vindictive. So, if you found my initial greeting towards you disrespectful, that is why. What you saw before is my public affect, a side effect of my upbringing, I'm afraid. You see, Karalevine, I have a certain aversion to my big brother. I loathe him because he exists purely to make my life a living hell. He always has. When he loses, I win. When I saw you openly defying him when no others dared to even think of such foolishness . . . I knew I had to do everything in my power to help you get up here and then destroy him. I did what I could to help you in the games. I was beyond impressed."

I completely see why Malakyte dislikes her, yet I let her continue without interruption.

"Don't blow up the Azurite or anything like that, but by all means, do what you came here to do. Take down the tyrant, be Earth's champion. I'm giving you the only opportunity you're going to get. The cameras to this area of the ship have been shut off but only temporarily. For now, he'll never know it was us. I doubt I'll ever get a chance to help you like this again."

My mouth hangs open in surprise, having not expected such an outcome.

I look around, seeing all the terrible havoc I could cause by gumming up this tech. Which was the plan, but there's one integral piece missing in this, and I don't have it.

I don't have *her*.

"There's nothing I can do here, not without someone your brother has been holding captive," I tell Selenyte, and her pristine pale face reveals no amount of surprise at my words.

Yet, she turns from me and heads out of sight around the machines. Although, I can still hear her words when she speaks calmly to me. "I feared you'd say something like that. Which is why I went through the trouble of getting that prisoner back for you. However, she doesn't seem so much like a prisoner any longer."

My heart soars in foolish hope as I hear a metal door opening, the slight rustling of clothing and then what sounds like soft whimpering. Then Selenyte returns from around a corner, looking like a practical goddess in her gown and crown—but she's not alone.

"Pacey!" I run towards her, my friend's arms and legs bound with black rope as the alien princess holds her up by her shirt. She appears to be drugged, her eyes glossy and heavy, and she does not struggle. "What did you do to her?"

Dropping her into my arms, I catch Pacey and begin untying her bounds as her weight drags us both to the smooth floor. She mumbles something about how she's not going to do what Selenyte asked her to, but it's all unclear rambling. Selenyte drops Pacey's Elendril scythe on us, as well, like it's nothing but a foam imitation of the real thing. Rolling off my thighs, it clinks to the ground.

"She was uncooperative when I kindly asked her to hack into the Arianyte systems. When I realized the two of you were friends, I thought you could convince her. I had to get her here somehow, so I was forced to sedate her. I hid her in the janitorial closet over there."

Well, that's just lovely of her.

"You . . ." Pacey mumbles as her eyes finally focus on me. "You . . . you're the one who almost killed us on the island yesterday. I remember. I remember you're the girl who's in love with my big brother. What are you doing here? Unhand me right now. You're a monster!"

I shake my head, looking down at her as I hold her in my lap. "Pacey, no. I mean, yes, I apologize for the incident yesterday. I genuinely wasn't trying to hurt you or your family. I swear it. Listen to me, Pace, Malakyte messed with your mind. You've been Reconditioned. You have to remember the last several months. Remember me. Remember your brother, how much he loves you. How you and he fled from your parents, remember?"

"I remember my brother, you dolt. We left, but eventually, we came to realize what a mistake running away was, and I came back. You're the reason my brother didn't come back with me." She tries struggling out of my grasp, but her movements are slow and ineffective. So, her long-term memories are intact. That's good information to know. Now I need to figure out what portions of her memory have changed and which haven't. She's likely exactly like Gavrielle, remembering scraps of her life that never existed and forgetting others. They rebooted her like one of these computers, installing new hardware and deleting others.

I hold her wrists down and press my face close to hers. "Then, remember what you two were trying to accomplish together. Focus on why the two of you ran from your parents in the first place. Think about that, Pacey. All that Ardelle did to keep you safe. Your parents are not good for you. They *hurt* you. They're never going to stop trying to change you. This isn't who you truly are, and you know it. Those scars on your arms are from *them*."

The look on Pacey's face reminds me exactly of the one Gavrielle gave me, confusion and uncertainty plaguing her every thought. My convincing words triggering something lost, a fragment of a memory far away and well out of reach to her.

"You know what isn't good for me? Being kidnapped," she snaps. "Now, let me go."

"We'll let you go," Selenyte promises as she gracefully bends down so she's eye level with the two of us, "only when you've completed the task of annihilating the Arianyte computer systems. I know how skilled you are with computers, how you can hack into practically anything. Do that, and you'll be safely on your way."

No, she's going to stay and come back with me. I'm not leaving her here. But I don't say that. Instead, I remain quiet and let her believe all she needs to do is hack Arianyte.

"What do you mean by 'annihilate their computer systems'?" she asks.

Selenyte answers before I can. "Destroy communications on all fronts. Tear down all SSPARROW schedules and communications. Disable drone and security footage, rip down the Network feeds, blow up the grids. Is that specific enough for you?"

My spine straightens.

"A lot of that stuff would be detrimental to the Terrans. Just screw with the Arianyte operations, like hitting the SSPARROW communications and deployment mechanisms," I suggest instead, but I don't like the glower Selenyte throws my way as the beeping and humming fans cooling the supercomputers pitter in the background.

"You both are insane," Pacey sneers, and the hatred in her voice, in her eyes—for me—is heartbreaking. "I'd never do anything like that against Arianyte. I owe everything to Malakyte."

I shake my head at her. "That's the thing, Pacey, you already have. Several months back, you and I broke into an Arianyte building and planted a bug in their systems, then you hacked the footage of us coming and going. You can probably go back and find your code in their systems if you just get in there and look for it. This isn't you. Malakyte has done nothing but kidnap and hold you captive on this ship. He's messed with your memories. That's what I'm trying to tell you."

Her large eyes search mine for any amount of falseness as she fights through the haze of whatever drug Selenyte got her with, and I know she finds no deception there.

"When did I do that? Does he know? Do my parents know? They can't know. You can't tell them."

"Nobody knows," I promise her. "Just you and me. Well, and now Selenyte. But she's on our side. We just need your help to do the right thing. You know Arianyte will never be loyal to you. They'll never let you be free. Same goes for your parents. Don't you remember? You want to color your hair, right? You want to wear skimpy, loud, ridiculous clothes. You don't want to hide that mark upon your chest."

I pull down her shirt and breathe a sigh of relief when I see the Elendril symbol is still there. This means we aren't too late to stop the surgery, and Malakyte doesn't have her crystal. By some miracle, it actually worked. Thank the stars. I expose my mark, and her eyes widen, as if she's never seen it before.

Stars, what the fuck did they do to her? This is all my fault.

If I could only get her to Gavrielle. Perhaps he was able to get the drug that caused the hallucinations, and I can use that

on Pacey in an attempt to get her memories back. I don't know what else to try.

"I need to get back to my friend, the extra who came up with me. I need to get back to him right now."

"Is she going to hack the system or not?" Selenyte blurts out, completely ignoring what I just said, and anger roils up my spine.

Practically hissing, I bare my teeth at her. "You need to back off," I demand, voice angry. "Her mind has been discombobulated, shaken about, broken to pieces, then put haphazardly back together, so give me a stars damned second to explain to her what actually happened so she has some sense of reality."

"I can't hack into their systems," Pacey claims before Selenyte can reply to me. "My parents would kill me. I can't. Malakyte would . . ." Her hands begin to tremble.

Selenyte rises to her feet with an annoyed grumble, turning her back to us both in irritation.

"Then, use that crystal artifact in your chest to cause a mass weather event on the planet. A tsunami or something would suffice. You can do that, right? Nobody would ever know it was you."

My brows scrunch as I look up at her. "Have you lost your damned mind? Why would you want to do that? Pacey, don't agree to that."

"Trust me, I'm not going to."

At least whatever they did to her didn't make her stupid. That's one piece of good luck that I've got on my side.

"Selenyte, why would you want to harm the people of Earth like that?" I ask, not understanding why she'd want to cause a mass-casualty event.

"Because it'll hurt my brother and his assets. Why else? Causing an event like that leaves his defenses wide open. I'm sure I could find a way in and destroy them from there. So, if you want out of this room, then use that little Starseed weapon of yours and do what I tell you to do. As your princess, I'm ordering you to use your powers and create an extreme weather event on the planet."

Pacey's head shakes side to side. "No way."

Selenyte's scowl is both annoyed and bitchy, and I begin to question her true motives for bringing me here.

"You're both so useless." She begins pacing. "And since you're no longer of any use to me, there's no point to continue playing this inordinate farce."

Leaving Pacey against a supercomputer tower, I stand, the hairs rising on the back of my neck. I swear, the computers are pushing in closer and closer. The room is becoming hotter and hotter.

Selenyte's hair is so white that all the lighting makes it appear solid blue as she faces away from me. It's only when she turns to face me that her solid black eyes cause me to take a step back. They're like depthless pools of an abyss, nothing but a cold, dark hell deep beneath. Calculating and cruel and cunning—just like the Mistress has been. If I didn't know it was Naresteé who was trying to kill me, I . . .

I stop cold in my tracks, a warning tingle crawling up my spine. No, no, it can't be . . .

"You seriously didn't guess it?" she coos, voice practically thrilled. "Stars, you're so dull. I truly don't get what he sees in you."

So much for all those compliments she gave me a couple of minutes ago.

Selenyte turns towards me finally, and the smile on her lips sends sheer terror through me in a way I haven't known unless I'm staring down the long-toothed maw of some monstrous predator. Shit, what am I saying? She's no different.

"Didn't you wonder how you kept getting so many sabotages during the race? You think my coward of a brother would have ever sent that horrific creature loose, knowing you'd be up there, all vulnerable and what not?" Her voice is taunting. "An unknown woman sending mercenary upon mercenary after your worthless little hide. What I did not anticipate was you getting away from my assassins. One in particular has been with me since I was a child, and when I realized you had killed Marett—well, let's say I couldn't wait until I had the chance to slit your throat personally for that irreverence. Having to see his body charred, his head cut clean off . . . Do not think that won't go unpunished. I was planning on delivering your legendary torment once you served your purpose with these computers. Claiming that you coerced me into this room at sword point, forced me to do your terroristic rebel bidding. I barely made it out with my life, but I managed to slit your throat just in the nick of time. I've got my brother too busy preventing his own catastrophe. He won't be paying the two of us any attention, not for a while now. I've got the time, and I won't let you slither away this time."

"You're definitely related to Malakyte because only your tainted bloodline can gaslight someone with a straight face and still act like you don't have a wild stick up your ass."

Oh, she sneers at that one.

"Am I right, Mistress?" I ask, needing the final piece of confirmation. So much for her being Naresteé. I can't believe I was so far off. Despite wanting to be hard on myself, I didn't know Malakyte's sister was even here. There's no way I could've anticipated it was her.

Selenyte glides her tongue along her lengthened canine, as if preparing for a tasty meal. "Of course, foolish little girl."

"Why?" I demand, blinking tears of pure fucking anger from my eyes. "I've never done a thing to you. I don't even know you."

"You almost brought down this entire empire, you little bitch."

Zariya. She's talking about Zariya.

The Killer of Worlds.

"Plus," she continues, "my brother, for reasons I've never understood, genuinely loves you. Personally, I understood it a lot more with the last body you had. This one is . . . well, lackluster. Dull. Childlike. Zariya was at least a bit more interesting looking. You try to make up for it by dying your hair and scarring yourself with ink, but I see the real you under all that fake trash you cover yourself with. You've got an interesting face, I'll give you that, but you're too small. Too weak to fight men, like my brother. Which is why I have no idea how you managed to kill all four of mine, especially Marett. He was my most loyal servant, and you will die for his death, you Terran scum."

"Zariya is dead," I say definitively, hating how I keep getting compared. But I guess I'll never be free of her original sin now, will I? "And for your information, bitch, I'm half-Terran. And proud of it. My other half, that's the half that's going to kick your ass. You're going to wish I was still Zariya because I'm way more reckless than her. Hell, I'm a lot more spiteful, too."

The scoff that comes from Selenyte's throat is bitter, bitchy, and as cold as the ice in her veins.

I draw my sword, and the black blade reflects all the many lights twinkling in the room. I glance down to make sure Pacey is out of the way, but I find nothing on the floor but her scythe.

Dammit!

"She probably scurried off to call my brother, so it looks like I'm going to have to kill you quickly. Shame. I wanted to relish in your agony like I would a luxurious meal. I'll simply have to be satisfied knowing I put to death the little bitch who killed my best friend. That'll do just fine. And once you're dead, I'll rip that crystal artifact from your chest, and it'll be mine. Having one of my brother's precious Elendril weapons, along with him seeing the sight of your bloodied body, will grant me enough giddy satisfaction to last a decade, at a minimum."

The princess glides her long pale leg through the slit in her gown and removes a cylindrical metal shaft from a holster strapped to her thigh. Grinning wickedly, she flips a switch along the side of the silver mechanism, and what fires out of it astonishes me.

"Is that a stars damned photon sword?" I ask in a shocked tone, having never actually seen one. It glows pink along her pale skin and hair.

Can my sword block something like that?

Her grin is absolutely villainous. "As a matter of fact, it is. And it's going to turn you into ribbons."

Seeing the air around the pink photon blade sizzling with hot life—I have no doubt she's telling the truth.

The princess charges at me, and the only thing I have time to do is hold up my own sword to block it. Stars, she's fast.

I suddenly get a rush of fear that my sword will crumble under hers, but as the two demon blades clash into each other, my own holds firm. We dance like two deadly ballerinas. Both beautiful, both in tandem with the melody of death. The sounds of her photon sword slamming against my Elendril crystal is strange. A zipping twang explodes as the two weapons collide together. I duck to prevent decapitation and Selenyte's illuminating blade hits the computer towers behind me. It hisses and whines, smoke billowing out around us as we fly through it, swapping positions.

"The smoke can't hide you forever," she taunts through the white cloud, but I can see the pink blade easily glowing within it. She's right, I can't hide from her. So, I'll go for her instead.

Taking a deep breath, I charge back into the smoke on quiet feet and straight for pink beacon of light, and she gasps in surprise when my sword swings down for her. I smirk. *Got you, bitch.* My sword slices through her upper arm, and she roars, more out of anger than in pain. But my victory is short-lived when she jabs her photon beam right into my ribs.

The rush of pain is a burning feeling, much different from being stabbed by a typical blade. However, I twirl, spinning around and out of the way, my sword arm coming down just in time to block another one of those insidious jabs. Simultaneously, our blades strike each other's, and we get stuck like there is a battle of wills, it seems. What a wild, insane turn of the tide. I did not expect the situation to dissolve into this, but I practically relish the fight—the pure adrenaline.

"What's that smirk for?" Selenyte sneers. "There's nothing that should be crossing your mind in this moment to make you grin, you foolish girl."

For a princess, she's sure strong, and she uses her height against me, plowing down with all her might. One of my knees gives way, causing me to bend the knee—seemingly in subjugation. I'm weak from the last three days, in more ways than one, and my strength is seeping out of me like a leaky faucet. My muscles are becoming useless, tearing under this weight.

Yet, I cannot yield. Not now, not after everything. And not to her, the woman who's been secretly trying to kill me while she stands in the shadows.

When I smile, I leave no room for anything but giddy satisfaction. "I was just thinking how funny it would be to mark up your face the same way I did your brother's. Give the two of you a matching set of scars."

This fiercely pisses her off, and with both her hands, she presses that photon sword down on me so hard my back is bending in a deep backbend to keep her from toppling over me.

My back will snap before I let her win.

"You know what I think, little girl?" she breathes, sounding batshit crazy. But she's struggling, too. It's in the vibrato of her voice, in the trembling of her arms. "I think someone needs to show you some manners. A lesson in civility. Zariya was classless, too. A dirty lowlife from the gutters of all places. My brother's soft heart always getting him into trouble."

Malakyte has a soft heart? Stars, I cannot imagine what it would be like to have to grow up with *this* as my sister.

The heat of her photon blade bites at my cheeks, burning my lashes and singeing the dried skin at my lips. All my muscles strain to keep her at bay because she has every edge over me. She's got the higher ground, needing only to push down. While I have to exert all of the muscles in my arms, to my back, my core, my thighs—everywhere—just to prevent her from winning. But we both know there's little hope of me pushing her back.

Both our blades shake under the intensity, and one of us is going to break before the other. It's likely going to be me.

I grit my teeth, both out of pain and in defiance of her, of all she stands for. And I can't let someone like her win. Not when she's likely to be after something more than simply revenge against her brother or my crystal. There's something bigger at stake here.

Like the throne of the Arianyte Empire, for starters.

But I'm slipping, inch by precious inch, and she can see it, too. I can see the outline of the pink blade reflecting in her glassy black eyes. It's almost at my chin, the photon sword near blinding me at this close range. Selenyte drives both swords down, angling for my neck.

The kill strike.

My entire body is trembling now, and it's taking everything I have, every ounce of strength left, just to hold her off these precious last few inches.

I hear her cackling as I close my eyes, not wanting to see her face of devilish glee, a haunting portrayal of evil.

She's evil. Full of hatred and cold malice. If this is what Malakyte's family is like, no wonder he's the way that he is. If Malakyte had a loving, kind, warm family, would he be a better person? If I had grown up with Jance, would I be a better person, too? Am I just as much of a victim of my circumstances as Malakyte is? Are we both by-products of our environment, made and bred to be the very darkness we wield so eloquently?

I'm either a victim of life's circumstances and allow it to rule me, or I take all that hurt and suffering and do something positive with it. Make it mean something more than just pain and anger and turmoil. Let it be my anthem, a promise to myself that those past abusers will never again find their way into my world.

"You're slipping, little girl." She licks her lips, anticipating my death. Excited for the heartbreak her brother will face from it, too.

"No," I seethe, pushing all my weight into my heels, thighs, ass, and back; I use all my body to drive off her assault and force her backwards. Surprise flashes on her face, contorting from the mask of delight to one of fear. She tries to hide it, but I see the flash of distress in her eyes. Losing would be the ultimate strike to her ego. She'd loathe it more than anything. I'd know because her brother is the exact same way. And though I hate to admit it, so am I.

"You're not going to shove me down." My legs are straightening, and hers are bending before me. I push with every fucking ounce of strength I have. Take all that sorrow and hurt and fury that I've been running from and use it to keep me going. Because that's what I've been doing, I realize. I've been using battles and sex and anything I could to escape the hurt in my heart, and now, I'm going to use that pain to beat this bitch. Maybe after that, I can finally put it to rest.

"You can't beat me, *princess*. You can't win. Because I've got something you'll never have holding me up."

Her teeth bare at me like an animal's, fangs completely out and viciously ready to bite. "Oh, really? And what would that be, little girl? That silly crystal of yours? It won't be enough. You're all tapped out. My brother assured it so."

The boost in her confidence shows, and I feel her shoving me back down again.

"No," I claim again, the muscles in my arms ripping, screaming, and tearing from the pure force of keeping her weapon at bay. "I've got love behind me. And you have nothing but hate. You're alone."

Selenyte laughs, eyes closed and mouth open wide like it's the funniest thing she's ever heard. "You ridiculous child. You don't have love behind you. You have nobody behind you. All the people you love have abandoned you. They've left you all alone here. All you have is your pitiful self. You have nothing, and you are nothing."

One of my ankles gives way, and Selenyte leans over me. There's no way I can overcome her now. Perhaps she's right. Maybe I am alone . . .

No!

I hear my father's voice, somewhere deep in my heart. And despite everything . . . I feel his love there, too. I sense Ardelle and Gavrielle and the old Pacey and Trinity and Geonni. Perhaps they've left me, and I've let them go, but I still love them. And the warmth I have for them will never disappear, no matter what. It was real for me. It *is* real. That is what separates Selenyte and myself; I still feel the love in my heart, and she cannot.

And love is power. Love is strength.

Like a second wind, my body is boosted with the power to force Selenyte back up, both our blades and arms quivering against each other. I feel as if my wrists may completely snap with how much pain there is, but I don't stop. I don't yield to her—to hate.

"I have more love behind me, Selenyte, than you've had in a hundred years."

And as if proclaiming it aloud was some sort of magical spell, somehow, my crystal surges to life, diving within my sword and blasting Selenyte's photon blade. The beam of particles stands no chance against my Elendril weapon, and the princess goes flying across the room.

I gasp as my entire body collapses to the floor, its cold, smooth texture an oasis on my hot and sweaty skin. I look around, not believing I managed to win that dual. At least, for the moment. I doubt this fight is over.

As if on cue, Selenyte moans from her spot on the ground several computer towers down. My body is so weak and limp I have to crawl as I go to knock the photon sword away from her grasp, assuring she can't pick it up and use it against me.

I sit there, my limbs like useless jelly, wondering how the hell this happened. It went so fast. One minute, we were talking about being allies, and the next, she's trying to kill me. This fucking family is off its rocker, and I shudder at the thought of what their parents must be like.

I should get up, go find Gavrielle. I don't know what else to do. Kill the princess? She'd certainly be more trouble for me if left alive . . .

Selenyte suddenly lifts herself up fast, quicker than I'm ready for. Instinctually, I back myself up as she crawls towards me, but she rips my sword from my hand at the last minute.

"You're dead," Selenyte taunts, the beads of her dress dragging against the flooring as she makes her way to her knees. She's disoriented and struggling to rise. I'm shocked to see my sword in her cold hands. "Terran trash."

I look around for her photon sword, but its pink blade has disappeared, and it's too dark in here for me to see the metallic handle. I can barely stand, let alone fight against it with no weapon at all. My crystal is tapped out again, that last attack emptying me out. She's on her feet now, ready to pounce and make good on her promise to turn me to ribbons.

Forcing myself to stand, I back away as she sluggishly approaches me. My Elendril weapon is heavy in her hands, and I can tell she's not used to wielding something so hefty, but I doubt that'll stop her.

Then my heel taps something, and I hear metal on metal scratching the floor. I don't need to look down for hope to swell in my chest.

Pacey's scythe! She left it here.

Selenyte sees what's at my feet and charges. She's not going to allow me a second to get a hold of it. My own sword comes straight for my neck as she, once again, goes for a head. I duck, sliding around her on the balls of my feet, one of them on top of her beaded gown. She gets stuck under my boot and trips—this is it! My only chance!

I seize the scythe in my hands, the weapon massive and as tall as I am. It's heavy at the top, the handle long and smooth and beautifully crafted. I brace my weight evenly as I bend my knees and swing.

Selenyte's eyes go so wide as the curved blue blade comes straight for her neck.

"That's enough!" a voice booms out into the darkened room, and my heart both flies and sinks all at once. I barely manage to stop the blade an inch from Selenyte's throat.

Malakyte.

The prodigal son has arrived.

CHAPTER 62

alakyte and I lock eyes immediately.

My entire body goes numb.

He's here.

Fuck my stupid heart. It thuds as I see him, that pull . . . that flush of energy that enters me every time we lock eyes. I just . . . *I hate it.*

Do I, though?

Both Selenyte and I are ordered to drop our weapons, and SSPARROWs come and take them away. What happens next is a blur of bodies and lights.

Two hulking SSPARROWs drag me out of the room, while Selenyte is escorted by a few others before me. My cheeks burn, and I stare at the floor just beneath my feet. I barely manage to keep myself upright, even with the support of the two soldiers constricting my arms. I had one opportunity to stifle the occupation and cut it off at the knees, and I lost it. How many times will I fail? In what way am I so stupid that I fell for Selenyte's ruse so easily? Stars, I'm enraged with myself. She offered the bait, and I devoured it like a starving animal. I had my chance; it was right there—and I fucked it up. The shame of it burns so hot and I refuse to look anyone in the eye because of it.

If Geonni's ghost has seen what his little protégé has become, he's one thousand percent disappointed in me.

The halls are made of a black material, smooth and matte and overlaid with many straight angles. The lights on the ceiling are whiter and starker than their orange counterparts along the walls. I stare at their reflection in the pristine reflective surface of the floor as I'm ushered down the halls, already lost. Gavrielle slides into step behind me as we march through hallway after hallway. Neither Malakyte nor the SSPARROWs pay attention to him.

We travel through the spaceship, its familiarity hitting me somewhere deep and subconsciously, one of Zariya's memories, no doubt. Doors leading to other rooms and hallways open automatically as we walk by, soldiers standing at each threshold. Soon, however, I become completely lost. With Malakyte at the helm, all I can see is the back of his head poking out between helmets of his SSPARROWs every now and then. He wears a black cape that billows behind him like looming shadows, keeping everyone else off his heels. All except his sister.

I have to stifle a tiny gasp when something round is shoved into one of my hands. It's Gavrielle. I instantly move whatever it is into my pocket. It's smooth and incredibly light, feeling like an orb or sphere. It's cold like glass and so light it must be hollow. The item is about the size of a baseball, so it pokes out of my pocket awkwardly. Did he succeed in finding the drug that could possibly restore Pacey's memories?

It seems like an endless trek through the massive spaceship by the time we finally arrive at a set of grand double doors. They open automatically upon Malakyte's arrival, disappearing into the walls as we enter what could only be described as a giant throne room.

Fitting for a prince of a cursed empire.

It's large, especially for a craft where space is, no doubt, one of the biggest luxuries and lit by large pillars of pale orange light that cast the area in a warm glow. The throne room also employs bands of cyan to keep a cool tone to the lighting. I'm thrown onto a deep blue floor etched with crisscrossing orange lines. It's cold as my palms barely catch my fall. As I look up, before me sits a throne settled atop a simple Dais, yet the throne itself is far from basic. It's made up of some type of dark blue-gray stone, and the back shoots high into the bright spotlight that shines above it.

Wings, carved directly into the backing, are pulled in tightly so the rest of it stands tall and menacing. Behind this seat of authority is a vast window that cascades into a seamless arch that becomes the ceiling, giving us a view of the stars beyond this horrific place. Shining like a beacon of hope is planet Earth, and I wonder if it knows it's the target of so much hate. The space is brilliant; designed to be as aesthetically pleasing as it is intimidating.

As I gaze around, I find Pacey standing near the right side of the room, but she is with NarestÊ©. The two of them are holding hands as if . . .

Oh, stars, no. Please, no.

They're holding hands as if they're *lovers*.

"Haven't you ever seen two women in love before, Karalevine?" Narest!Â©Â coos, the smirk on her lips devious. "You're not prejudice, are you? I told you, I found someone new. Mr. and Mrs. Dawson weren't thrilled with our arrangement, but they're reconsidering it after we confined them in their home. They'll come around eventually, and so will you."

My eyes shoot to Malakyte as he takes a seat on his throne, sitting down slowly. He wields his power as easily as he does the sword strapped to his waist.

"My dear Miss Ruzz," he finally says. "My apologies for not being there to greet you upon your arrival. A certain situation tore me away." He pauses to look at Selenyte, who stands next to him and his stupid throne. There's no misgivings in his expression—he's pissed at her. She tightly clasps her hands in front of her and looks down at her feet, her long hair shadowing her face. "But I'm here now, and as such, it is my duty and obligation to congratulate you upon your victory, as I do every single competitor who wins my esteemed Titan Games. Congratulations, Miss Ruzz, on a well-earned victory."

His eyes practically sparkle. Gav wasn't lying—Malakyte had wanted me to win, all right. And now, he's got me.

"You see, *Karalevine*," Malakyte continues, "I was late to your arrival because I had just been informed that my dear sister here had been scheming behind my back to the Council of Exstacé, the ruling body of Arianyte behind my family. She's trying to steal back Earth."

My chest starts to feel heavy.

"That wouldn't bode well for the people of Earth, now would it?"

I look between both siblings, Selenyte and Malakyte, two sides of the same cruel coin. Malakyte isn't what I'd call a great leader by any means. He's tyrannical at minimum, and that's just the start. However, Selenyte seems crueler somehow. She's colder, she's brutal, and I think given the choice between the two, one would be worse than the other. Selenyte is an unknown. How she'd rule could be vastly different from how her brother does, and I doubt it would be for the better.

"My dear sister likes to scheme, you see. You played quite a role in this so-called coup, Karalevine, but not in the way you likely think. Thanks to your impassioned speeches and rallying up the Terrans to practical war, you inadvertently riled up the Council of Exstacé to the point where they were convinced a full-scale war was imminent. It wasn't until you threw that arrow that I could no longer defend you as some silly child playing foolish games. That arrow was the pretext dear little Selly needed to shoot down my authority. She got the council to vote, allowing her own soldiers to mobilize and take over Earth so they can squash this little rebellion. Because I did not rip you from the games or punish you in any way, I was excluded from this process until it was all but complete. It seems my position as the next emperor is now in question. So, thank you, Miss Ruzz, for one stellar performance."

My mouth hangs open.

"She's no good for you, big brother." Selenyte's voice is soft and sweet, like a little girl. "I know you see what I've done as an act against you, but that isn't so. I did it to finally get you to see how dangerous she is for you—for all of us. If I take back control of Earth and step in as empress, then she won't have this sway over you or the empire. I wasn't going to let her destroy all this family has built and sacrificed for like Zariya did. I did this for *us*. I wanted Earth back, so you'd stop this mission of yours, so you can finally come home. We all just want you to come home."

For someone who's been abandoned like the two of us, those words are heroin to our soul.

I can see the gears turning in Malakyte's eyes as he peers between me and his sister.

Selenyte drives her manipulative knife even deeper into him. "If I take back Earth, make it into what it was intended, it won't be a failure in father's eyes; he won't be upset with you. Let's get production going together and leave for better ventures. I can take over all the responsibilities of ruling after father steps down. You can just forget her and come home to us, Mal."

I roll my eyes. *Mal.*

He cannot be falling for this bullshit? Can he?

Malakyte sits up tall, and I hate that he looks good on his throne. "You've lied and deceived me the entire time you've been here. You forced a secret vote behind my back from the Council of Exstacé—convincing them to deploy your soldiers to Earth for a hostile takeover of my property. You have plotted and attempted to assassinate my Star on numerous occasions over the last three days, and you are attempting to theft my crown right off my head . . . Sister, how does any of that indicate that you wish for the two of us to be together?"

I look between the two siblings. All the hate they have for one another. What a stark contrast to Ardelle and Pacey. They'd never do this to each other.

"It's what's best to save the empire, Malakyte. She's warped your mind. She almost destroyed us last time. I'm preventing her from doing it a second time. If doing what's best for you causes you hate me, then, so be it."

He chuckles under his breath. "Oh, sister, you misunderstand me. What makes you think you were in any way successful in this grand ploy of yours?"

My lips curl in so I don't smile at his words. He catches the slip, and I see admiration there.

Flustered, Selenyte's words stagger. "I . . . you—you heard what the council said. They've spoken. My troops are coming."

"Perhaps," Malakyte drawls, uninterested.

Selenyte looks disheveled and worried.

"The council, and all their inept wisdom have come to their senses, sister, once I explained to them my reasons for my actions. Had you simply asked instead of riling up their brainless fears of some Terran girl, then I would have laid out my plan in full."

His plan. Gav and I lock eyes. He regrets letting me come here. It's all written right there on his face. It's going to be okay; I'm going to accomplish my objectives. It's not too late, even if Gav believes it is.

A cold sweat breaks out on my skin, regardless.

"Karalevine." Malakyte's voice booms along the throne room's walls, breaking me out of my ever-growing panic. "If not for you, I wouldn't be in this farcical mess."

"I'd say if it weren't for your sister, you wouldn't be here," I say.

He smiles wickedly. "Nevertheless." He stretches, letting out a long yawn. It's the first time I've seen him so . . . casual. Something is very wrong here. "You started this war, Karalevine. You wanted it. You fought for it. You demanded it with all your fury and tenacity. You are the reason I am as close as ever to losing my throne. Someone must pay the price for that."

Before I can say one word, Malakyte waves his hand casually, and two SSPARROWs leave the room hurriedly. When they return a few moments later, I fall to my knees in utter horror.

"Malakyte, what have you done?"

CHAPTER 63

FAMILIES OF CONVICTED REBELS WILL BE IMMEDIATELY
STRIPPED OF ALL CATO CREDITS, THEIR HOMES AND ASSETS
SEIZED BY ARIANYTE, AND ALL ADULTS SENT TO THE TRIBUTE
CAMPS. ANY JUNIOR CITIZEN UNDER THE AGE OF EIGHTEEN
WILL BECOME WARDS OF ARIANYTE AND RAISED BY
THE OCCUPATION.

At first, I'm merely confused. The sight before my eyes hasn't fully connected to my brain in such a way that I can accept what's happening.

Several SSPARROWs haul in a ten-by-ten-foot giant cube made of some type of clear material, whether that be glass or plastic or another alien substance, I don't know. It's so huge it was wheeled in on a flat dolly contraption. For all intents and purposes, it's a glass prison. One big enough for the average adult to stand tall and fit at least a half a dozen people inside.

But fuck the cube. It's who's inside that I care about.

Jance.

Ardelle.

Ahren.

Saris.

Sylo.

They're all trapped inside that cube.

Prisoners.

I see them shouting and slamming their fists against their confinement, but all I hear are hollow thuds.

Having no sense of self-control whatsoever, I charge at Malakyte as he sits on his token throne. I don't make it to him, of course, before one of his sky-rats wrestles me to a stop.

I curse at him with feral screams. "I will fucking kill you this time, Malakyte. I mean it. Let them go! Now!"

The prince merely smiles at me, sly as a cat.

I slump, only held up by the sky-rat's grip on me. I glance again at my screaming friends trapped inside the muffled cube. Realization clamors in my head like blaring alarm bells.

Someone is missing.

"Where the hell is Trinity? What did you do to her? Tell me what you've done to her."

Fear and anger blast through me, panic building. Something isn't right. If they felt so much malice, so much resentment and animosity for me that they'd straight-up leave me, I'd see that emotion on all their faces. I don't see a glimmer of that when I look at Jance or Ardelle, not even Sylo, who stares back at me with worry and sadness and panic but not hatred. Not even close. This picture is painted wrong, and I'm terrified to know why.

"Where is she?" I yell again, star mark coming to light. A pain builds in my stomach, anxiety ravaging it.

"I wouldn't use that crystal if I were you." Malakyte straightens his jacket, black as night and made of the finest, most luxurious fabrics. "If you blast even the smallest amount of that magic in this space, say goodbye to yourself and all your friends because we're in space, my darling Karalevine. And things are a bit more flammable up here than they are where you come from. Shut that crystal down, right now."

Shit. He's right.

"Bring out Miss Monterey," he tells a SSPARROW, who nods and leaves the room.

I'm clenching my teeth hard. "I swear, if you hurt her, I'm going to—"

Malakyte points past my shoulders, interrupting me. "See for yourself."

Stalking through the throne room's main entrance is Trinity. She's dressed in tight army-green pants, worn leather boots, and a black-and-orange jacket. Her braids are wrapped tightly on top of her head in a large bun. I see no bruises, cuts, or swelling, so she hasn't been tortured. Thank the stars.

Shaking the SSPARROW off, I run to her, wrapping my arms around her tightly as I take in her spicy scent. Something familiar and safe.

"I'm so glad you're okay." I breathe as I release her, but I notice she doesn't hug me back. The coldness in her Tawny Brown eyes instantly makes me fear she's already been Reconditioned.

Yet, Trinity cannot meet my eyes full-on, and her body language is fidgety.

My head whips to Malakyte, who's now across the throne room from me. "What's going on?" I ask, turning back to Trinity.

Narasteé snickers from across the room, and Pacey lets out a sound that echoes it. I try to breathe, but something tightens in my throat. Malakyte's throne looms over me. And in the middle of this suffocation, Trinity refuses to meet my eyes.

"Trinity?" I demand, but the tightness in my throat makes it sound much more pitiful than I intend.

Before my friend can reply, another SSPARROW enters the throne room with a woman I've never seen. She's possibly in her fifties, and her years of hard labor have grayed her hair, wrinkled her face, and bent her fingers at odd angles. Her skin tone is a match to Trinity's, dark and cool, but far more aged and marred with time.

Trinity gasps as she sees the woman, and I immediately know who she is. As Trinity dashes to her, the sinking feeling in my gut transforms into a full-on pounding in my ears.

This is Trinity's mother, Martha.

Tears streak both cheeks of mother and daughter, and after what Trinity had to witness with her father, I am happy for her. Although, I know—*I know*—this reunion is not without immense cost. Just what did Trinity sacrifice for her mother's freedom?

After a few more moments of their reunion, they both stand, holding onto each other for dear life. Trinity faces Malakyte. "So, we're good, then? Can we go?"

I look from them to him, wondering how this has even been arranged.

Sighing, Malakyte flicks his wrist nonchalantly. "I am a man of my word. A deal is a deal. You are free to leave back to Earth."

"What deal?" I snap before Trinity and Martha can even take a step towards the door. "Trinity, *what did you do?*"

Her eyes are full of genuine sorrow as she looks at me, and my body shakes. Trembles with so much ire that keeping the lid on my powers is an actual fight.

"I'm sorry, girl. I'm so sorry. I didn't have a choice."

"What do you mean?" My voice cracks, tears manifesting in place of my crystal's power.

I haven't seen Trinity cry in years, but she does now. "Right after our attempt on the Azurite, I was stolen off the streets. I fought, Kara, I did. I refused to give up anything, and I was willing to die for the cause, for the Rebel's Song . . . until Malakyte said he could free my mother. Then it just . . . changed. I was given a job . . . get you to him." She nods to Malakyte.

And it clicks together like a terrible puzzle piece. "The Titan Games were your idea . . ." I whisper. "You knew Malakyte was in the bar that night, too. That's why you blew me off when I told you I saw him."

She doesn't deny a word of it. "Malakyte didn't know about my plans for the games, so I snuck him in the club through the back. He'd see that I was bringing you to him. I did it this way so, at the very least, Earth would have a chance at stopping him. I . . . I didn't want to sell them out, too."

"Oh, you sold them out alright! Did you not hear his crazy bitch of a sister and her plans to have her soldiers come in and take over the whole planet? Fuck, Trinity!" I point to Selenyte, the looks of utmost satisfaction on hers, Naresteé's, and Malakyte's faces.

"What did you do?" I demand again.

As Trinity's chin quivers, her eyes glide behind me, to the others. "After you went up to compete in the second game, the others . . . they were taken right then. They never came back. Those who remained behind were taken when I told Arianyte where they'd be. I had to, Kara. I had no choice. I'm sorry."

"So, you traded them for her?" There's no attempt to keep the venom out of my words.

Trinity gives me that face—the same one Geonni would give when he knew he was wrong but could never admit it.

"Just admit you sold us all out!" I yell. "You sold *me* out. You sold out your father's principles. All he worked for, all that *we* worked for. You sold out each person in that bar who cheered for you, every rebel, each of their families, and all the Terrans on this planet. You've doomed them all, Trinity."

Trinity stutters some but ultimately relents. "I'm sorry. I . . . I just—I couldn't say no. She's my mom and—"

"And he's my father!" I scream at her, pointing at Jance as my voice cracks with rage. "Who was typing on the lens? Why did you make it seem like they left me? That's—"

Malakyte jumps in. "I insisted on it. My reasons are my reasons."

Sick motherfucker.

"Get the fuck away from me." I step back, even though I want to jump across the space and strangle the girl I thought was my friend—my sister. And my resentment burns so hot that I want to set this ship ablaze and take everything down with me.

"I hope having your mom back is worth ruining the world. Your father would be so proud."

Even in my volatile anger, I regret saying it.

My friend stares at me, pain etched into her every movement, from the pinching in her brows to the stiff way she turns and collects her mother, who looks at me with nothing other than pure sadness. Together, they latch arms and walk toward the door.

I can't wait for them to be out of my sight until a thought snaps into my mind so fast there's no stopping myself.

"Trinity!" I call out, and she stops right before the door. My heart slams against my ribs, and I have to swallow all my pride. "Take care of my dog. Don't let her go back to the streets."

Narestée snorts. Trinity merely nods softly. Then mother and daughter are gone.

Leaving us with the fallout of their freedom.

This all makes so much more sense now. Ardelle, Jance—the rest of them—they never actually abandoned me. And I believed it so easily . . . I never even questioned if it were true or not . . .

Malakyte chuckles softly when he says, "I could blow their ship up on the way down to Earth, get you some payback, if you'd like?"

I snarl at him. "Leave them be." For all Trinity has done, for how much I hate her guts right now—no. Because I'd do the same thing if it were Jance. I'd do anything to keep him safe. I just can't believe I fell for her ruse. Plus, if we don't make it down from this ship, Earth will still need the leader of the Resistance.

When I finally face my body towards Malakyte, still sitting on his throne over his so-called subjects, he grins with fire in those Coal-Black eyes. They twinkle like a cat who just caught his mouse.

"What do you want, Malakyte?" I ask dully, trying to quickly and efficiently come up with some sort of plan to save everyone. I'm too ashamed to meet Gavrielle's eyes this time.

"Nobody has to die," I add, hoping I can convince him to spare them. "We can still work this out."

"Perhaps they don't, but somebody must pay the price."

My chest tightens at his words, and I shake my head. "I'll pay it. It was all me anyway, just like you said. I fired up the Terrans and spooked your council, it's *my fault*. I'll do whatever you want."

From the window behind Malakyte's throne, a giant burst of light draws my eyes to it, and we all shift in that direction. Malakyte rises and walks to the floor-to-ceiling window as hundreds of spaceships begin zapping into Earth's orbit through some type of warping technology. I turn towards the others in the cube, horrified. I didn't think Selenyte's forces would come this quickly.

"Looks like your fleet has finally arrived, sister." Malakyte's voice is cool yet displeased. "Right on time."

The prince flags a soldier, who then wordlessly walks over to the prison, where he begins typing on some digital interface on the outside of the cube. Seconds later, a thick red gas starts to fill it.

I spin back to Malakyte. "What are you doing to them?" I demand, watching as the others try to avoid the red cloud, but they can't escape it.

They'll never escape it.

CHAPTER 64

UNDERGROUND REVOLUTION:

GO DEEP, REBELS, UNDERGROUND DEEP. CREATE SECRET NETWORKS, HIDDEN LAIRS, AND REBEL HUBS THAT'D MAKE BIGFOOT PROUD. STAY LOW, STAY QUIET, AND KEEP THE SQUID GOONS GUESSING. THEY WON'T KNOW WHAT HIT 'EM.

They're choking—they're dying.

This situation is rapidly coming apart at the seams, and through the pounding of blood in my ears, I hear the two ice-cold siblings arguing by the window.

"Give it to me," he demands, holding his hand out impatiently. Selenyte clenches a device in her cold hands, but she keeps a firm grip on it as she holds it tightly to her chest. It's some communication apparatus like a Dezlar, probably to communicate with all those ships entering the Aurora System. Malakyte grasps her wrist roughly, but she refuses to let go of it.

"Give it to me," he repeats maliciously.

She tries to yank her wrist from his grasp and succeeds, turning around, but Malakyte is right on her.

This is ridiculous.

"Hey!" I yell at the two of them—more so Malakyte—but there's no acknowledgment at all. Gaping at the siblings as they fight and bicker and snarl over the communications device, I stand there wide mouthed.

I turn back to the cube and gasp at how fast it has filled with the smoke, the ones inside being devoured by the color Killer Crimson. I can still see them within, but they're just dark shapes. I can hardly tell my father's broad shoulders from Ardelle's, and Saris's slight frame is getting lost amongst the others.

What is it doing to them? How much time do they have left in there?

"Malakyte!" I yell, him and his sister in a practical physical brawl over by the window, Selenyte's warships a fitting backdrop for the two.

My chest begins to burn, panic clawing up my throat.

What do I do? How do I get everyone out of this?

I close my eyes and take a deep breath through my nose. *Remember why you came here in the first place. Pacey.*

My eyes snap open, an idea bursting to the front of my mind.

I find Gavrielle's eyes, hoping to the damn stars he gave me what I think he gave me.

He's already watching me. Gavrielle nods, almost imperceptible.

Do it, his eyes tell me. *Do it, now.*

I grip the thin glass orb hard enough to crack it slightly. It's now or never.

Pivoting at my waist, I turn my upper body and chuck the orb directly at Pacey Dawson's face.

CHAPTER 65

Pacey's shriek is accompanied by Naresteé's gasp, but neither are quick enough to prevent the orb from hitting Pacey directly in the forehead.

"You crazy little bitch!" Naresteé seethes at me as a small white cloud envelopes Pacey's entire face, causing her to cough uncontrollably.

I don't waste a single second of time.

My body launches for the cube, and I know I'm being chased the moment I move towards it.

I manage to slink away and dodge most of the SSPARROWs, familiar with how they move, their metal bodies simply too slow to catch me. One manages to wrap his hand around my hair and pulls me back, but I donkey kick him in the gut, and he flies backwards.

Keep going, I push myself, the cube mere feet away.

The soldier who initiated the gas stands in wait for me as I make it to him, and we immediately begin fighting for the prison's controls.

I duck and dodge him easily, but it's getting him down that's difficult. I'm weak, my fight with Selenyte barely a half hour ago, and I curse myself when I see an opportunity to kick, but I missed it.

Pacey starts screaming, the sounds echoing through the throne room.

Another SSPARROW takes the slight distraction as his opening and pounces on me from behind, my body thrust into the soldier I'm currently going toe-to-toe with.

They throw me alongside the cube's walls, the sound a hollow thud as my front is slammed into it. One of the bodies from inside bangs against the wall, but they're just a silhouette.

The two soldiers seize my body and drag me away from the box, and my cheeks heat with the shame of my failure. They hold me tightly as they force me to my knees before Malakyte's throne.

The prince and princess both gaze at me with surprise on their faces. My distraction caused their spat to cease, but that doesn't stop Malakyte from taking the opportunity to pluck the device from Selenyte's hand. She hisses at him as he whips around and stuffs it into his pocket, satisfaction plastered all over his face.

"What is that?" Pacey shrieks, pointing at nothing. She runs past the pillars and over to the room's corner and out of sight for a moment, only to return with her sickle in hand, ready for battle. Naresteé tries to calm her, but it does the opposite.

"You get away from me!" Pacey cries, her scythe between her and Naresteé.

"Pacey, you must be hallucinating. You're fine."

Pacey lowers her weapon.

Is this going to work like it did on Gav? I have no idea how long it'll take to bring her memories back, if they come back at all.

Naresteé tries to come at me, but Pacey cries out.

"Don't leave me!"

Selenyte comes for her brother once more.

I try to fight the SSPARROWs again, causing both to tumble to the floor with me.

It's madness in here.

"Enough!" Malakyte's voice booms, and even I can hear the fury on the edge of his tone.

Everybody freezes, including me.

"Naresteé." Malakyte points to Pacey. "Deal with her."

She obeys without a word, returning to Pacey and hushing her with soft words as she presses Pacey's face into her chest. Naresteé doesn't take her eyes from me for one second.

Malakyte snarls at his sister, and she backs off. Leaving the window, he walks up to me and orders his two soldiers away. I refuse to remain on my knees before him, so I stand on trepidatious legs.

"You're just full of it tonight, aren't you? You were almost able to free them. I'm actually a bit impressed. Although, I can't decide if I like it or if I hate it."

I ignore him. "What is happening inside that box? What are you doing to them? Tell me right now."

Smiling victoriously, Malakyte flaunts the communication device he wrangled from Selenyte. She fumes beside him, eyes practically daggers. "To commemorate the last Titan Games finale, I want to offer you a choice. I promise I won't partake in another fake-out this time, as fun as those are. See, with this device, I can order those ships back from whence they've come, and you can liberate Earth and all its people like you promised. All you need to do is let the people in that box succumb to the poison now coursing through their veins. Or you can save those you love so dearly, your precious Starseeds and Ringers, but in doing so, you doom the people of Earth to a very bloody takeover. I'd choose quickly. That gas will kill them in less than ten minutes."

My chin quivers as I try to form a response, but I cannot. All I can see within my mind is the moment Malakyte made me choose between Jance and Geonni under the arena, how he tricked me and shot the opposite person. He says he won't do that again, but can I believe him? Even if he does keep his word, how am I supposed to pick? The lives and freedom of everyone on Earth or the ones I love most . . .

How am I supposed to make a choice like that?

"The question you need to ask, dear Karalevine, is this," Malakyte says, picking at his nails. He looks up from his fingers to stare directly into my soul, "are your loved ones worth ruining the world for?"

The same words I spoke to Trinity.

"Are you a selfish rebel, or are you truly Earth's valiant hero? Do you harbor righteous dreams, or do you yield to the temptation of darkness, Karalevine?"

One by one, my friends and family fall to their knees.

One by one, alien spacecrafts arrive within orbit.

Am I good or am I bad? That is what it truly comes down to, isn't it?

CHAPTER 66

"They're dying," Malakyte informs me, like I need reminding.

Five lives or billions?

Is one choice morally good and the other ethically immoral? Is it that black and white? What option makes me a hero and which makes me a villain? Does sacrificing billions of lives make me evil? If I were standing on Earth right now, I'd say yes, one hundred percent yes.

So, who do I want to be? The hero or the villain? A teammate or a lonesome savior? What are those trapped in the box thinking? Do they think forfeiting their lives for the greater good is the ultimate sacrifice for me? Or do they see it as the greatest betrayal? What is the *right* choice?

What does this choice make *me* in the end?

Malakyte wants to know if I'm inherently wicked like him or a decent person like my other Starseeds and Ringers. He's forcing me to confront who I am at my core. And, truthfully, I don't know. All I can do is follow my heart and hope the people who love me forgive me in the end.

I hear my father's voice again in the back of my mind, as if he never left me—which he hadn't.

You know exactly what to do, kid.

I grasp his ring, desperately trying to find his dark head of hair through the smokey color Bloody Night.

The choice is agonizingly obvious.

"I've decided." I attempt to hold my head high, even though shame is beating it down. Shame and pain and more heartbreak than I thought I could ever bear in one day. "Send the ships away. Now."

I can barely pry the words from my throat, but my eyes never leave those I love as I fail them in the ultimate way. The huge part of me hopes Malakyte plays the same trick on me as last time. I hope he saves my father's life again.

But I don't think he's going to.

I tumble to my knees, the weight of it all hitting me.

"Send the ships away!" I scream, the shout echoing off the room's pillars and walls. My crystal lights up the room, and I'm so close to the edge I could slip and blow it all away at any moment. "Or I'll destroy you all right here and now, I swear it." Let's hope he believes it because the only strength that remains is the grotesque vehemence I have for him, and it's the one thing keeping me from completely losing my shit.

My blood pressure drops, and I feel how weak my body has become. I have to watch this . . . watch them all die. No. No, I can't. I can't . . .

Pacey screams, either from watching her brother slowly die or from some hallucination even worse than real life. I can't tell. It's all so horrible.

Malakyte calls on Selenyte's device, and I hear him say the words. But until the fleet is fully gone, I won't believe I made the right decision. The choice I hope they'd want me to make . . .

Selenyte begins seething at her brother, yelling and jumping on him to try and grab the device. Malakyte shoves her away, and she takes offense to the action. She approaches him one more time and slaps the prince straight across the face, the sound echoing in the silence. Selenyte storms off in a fit of snarls and fuming huffs. The sounds of shattering items follow in her wake. Seconds later, a door that I cannot see slams, making me jump. There must be other doors that lead in and out of this room that I don't know about.

I couldn't care less about how upset the princess is, and I curl into a small ball on the throne floor. The red cube sits looming and haunting in my peripheral, and all I can think of is how much they're suffering in there and how I led them straight to their deaths. I close my eyes, cover my head in my hands.

"Congratulations, Karalevine," Malakyte's voice taunts. "You're a far better person than I expected. The people of Earth will call you their hero, after all."

If they know what's good for them, they better never call be that word because all I am is someone who gets their friends and family killed. That's no hero, even if I am sacrificing them to save the world.

"I hope you're disappointed," I tell him, knowing he likes the darkness in me better.

But before I can say or act further, I'm suddenly grabbed, captured from behind by cold, glacial arms in a vise-like grip. My first thought is Malakyte, but when my eyes fly open, he still stands in front of me.

Then a pointed tip of equally icy steel is held over my chest.

Malakyte's eyes go wide with what I swear is pure fear, and in an instant, an even greater dread freezes me, locking me in a prison of my own body.

As if I were made of ice.

Selenyte Ardeen has me by the throat, and her vow rings in my ear like a wicked bell, a curse promising to burn my entire world asunder.

"If I'm not getting Earth back, then I'm taking this crystal if it's the last thing I do."

CHAPTER 67

TERRANS CONVICTED OF REBELLION OR LEADING RESISTANCE MOVEMENTS WILL ENDURE PUBLIC MUTILATION OR EXECUTION AS A PERMANENT REMINDER OF THEIR DEFIANCE AGAINST ARIANYTE.

Maybe this is my punishment for all the terrible choices I've made. How I let my rage rule me. Perhaps I deserve to die in front of my family.

Gavrielle remains unnaturally still in the corner of the throne room, seemingly unaffected by Selenyte's threat. But I see him, slowly—so unbelievably slowly—move towards me. I don't think he'll get to me in time.

Pacey breaks free of Naresteé and begins swinging her scythe around at nothing, Naresteé attempting to grab it from her.

Thuds from the prison are getting louder, more panicked . . . because they're dying.

The throne room has been thrown into chaos.

Selenyte does not tremble as she grips the dagger in one hand and holds me around the throat with her other.

"Sister," Malakyte says calmly, holding his hands towards her, palms up. He looks like a completely different person, all his fun and games ending the moment my life began teetering on the edge of a blade. "There is no need for these theatrics. Let Karalevine go. I'm certain you and I can come up with something to occupy your time that doesn't involve these insignificant Terrans. They're beneath you. I understand you're upset about the warships, but you lost this game all on your own."

The prince's new mask is unlike any of the others I have ever seen him portray. The softness that replaces the hard, arrogant cruelty from mere moments before is so believable it's jarring. Is he actually scared of losing me?

Selenyte adjusts her hold on the dagger and backs away from her brother. Each step he takes, she retreats two more. "I'm sick of her ruling your life, Mal. Let me end this once and for all before she ruins this empire for good this time. She means to end us. The girl has been screaming it from the rooftops. And why would you ever let *her* decide whether or not *my* ships remain? This was my plan, and I bested you. She doesn't get to rip it all away from me, and neither do you."

"Malakyte," a voice hisses from the corner of the room, having somewhat gained control of Pacey again. "Let it happen. Let us be done with this."

She would.

Bitch.

"Stop!" Malakyte's voice booms over his throne like he all but rules the galaxy already. "My Star will not be harmed. Now, Selenyte, as your brother and future king, I'm demanding you release her."

Gav has left my field of vision, meaning he's already moved behind me.

"Selenyte," Malakyte tries reaching for us again. "What do you want? I'll give you whatever you want."

"I want her crystal." I don't see much room to budge there.

Malakyte's face is distorted in pain. He'll clearly choose her over me. That's his sister, after all.

"You can have anything but that," Malakyte says, his voice teetering on shaky. "She cannot survive without it." I almost laugh. Of course, Trinity lied about Pacey's surgery, too, hadn't she? Malakyte just confirmed it.

I cry out as Selenyte's dagger dives deeper into my skin. The blood is already dripping at my feet. My heart thrashes under the sharp Arianyte steel as if it knows how close to death it truly is. Unable to help it, my crystal lights up beneath the blade, and this makes Selenyte laugh.

"You're going to soil yourself, aren't you, little girl? Pathetic Terran trash. I do not know what you see in her, big brother."

Silence.

"How about this," Selenyte continues when her brother doesn't play her wicked game. "If you love her so much, Mal, then give up the one thing you want more than her. Give up your throne. Give it to me, and I'll let her live."

The squinting of Malakyte's eyes makes me wonder if Selenyte has been playing him this entire time. I doubt she cares about her opportunity at torturing the Terrans and Earth. My Elendril crystal likely doesn't entice her as much as she claims. The real prize for her is the throne. Exactly what she's been conspiring to obtain all along. Everything with me, the whole Mistress façade, this Council of Dipshits or whatever they're called. Selenyte had one sole goal: the Arianyte Throne. And Malakyte, for all his plotting and scheming, is on the edge of giving it to her.

The silence of his contemplation goes on and on for what feels like hours.

"Well, big brother? Which appeals to you more? Power or love?"

Power or love. Life's most seductive vices. What people fight for, live for, and most importantly—what they kill for.

I lock eyes with my villain, wondering if this is the moment he'll finally do what bad guys do—let me die. Although, the look he gives me blasts away all the walls he's built up. I see him, the real him, in this brief flash between life and death, and we fuse together through that fried ribbon of connection that managed to survive all this insanity. I can see his crystal lit up underneath his clothing, his emotions detonating.

But I know pity when I see it, and in those onyx eyes, that's what I see. In the end, power always wins over love . . . it's why it's at the root of all evil.

Knowing I have mere seconds left to try and survive this, I try one last attempt at survival. With all the strength left in my body, I elbow Selenyte right in her ribs. With that, I take hold of the arm locked around my throat—and pull. I drop all my weight, falling to my knees and letting gravity do its thing. But Selenyte is so strong and clamps me securely to her front. Her grip is like iron frozen in ice. Malakyte uses the scuffle and makes a dash towards us, and he manages to get close enough to grab me. I gasp despite myself, reaching out for him. I feel the coldness of his fingertips, but Selenyte succeeds in keeping me out of her brother's grasp, ripping us apart.

Until we back up against something hard.

I can tell she doesn't expect it by the tiny squeal that escapes her throat, her breath cold on my ear. I know it's Gavrielle.

Hope flares.

That is until I see a black metallic SSPARROW helmet dropping to the ornate floor at my feet. A soldier? I feel a strong body grabbing onto the princess roughly, and I crank my neck backwards, meeting the eyes of the last person in the world I expected to see.

Deimos clasps onto Selenyte's wrist with the metal hand of the SSPARROW uniform, drawing the blade out from my chest. She struggles against him. A hiss roils from her throat.

Deimos purrs in her ear, "The only person who's going to rip that crystal out of her heart, is *me*."

CHAPTER 68

After all we've been through since the carnival, was it all just a play to get my crystal?

To be closer to Zariya, I have no doubt.

"Remove your hand from me, you cretin!" Selenyte shrieks and slams her elbow into Deimos.

This distraction is my one chance. I clench my teeth and try to twist from her hold a second time. I get loose but then she rips me back into her death grip. The three of us flail around like fish out of water, all trying to keep hold and also get free of one another.

I see a flash of movement straight ahead of me. It's nothing but a black blur where Malakyte was standing, but all three of us are thrust backwards by some forceful wind, Selenyte's stiff arms pulling me on top of her.

We fall onto the cold, hard tile. I land directly on Selenyte, who lands on Deimos, who grunts loudly from taking both our weights.

Selenyte releases the dagger at my breast, and it falls directly into my lap. I take it. My hands tremble as I shift my body to face them both, knife ready for attack.

I raise the dagger to Selenyte but stop dead in my tracks, dagger glinting off the cyan lights, frozen in midair.

A matte black spike, thin and metal, protrudes from the very center of Selenyte's forehead. A single drop of dark-blue blood slowly cascading down her flawless face, like a porcelain doll with a crack in its veneer. Those perfect full lips are parted in a shocked

O, no doubt having seen her brother's blade coming for her far too late to be able to dodge it. It sits buried in her brain.

My head whips back to look at Malakyte, whose body is still angled in his throwing position. His face is stunned, body stiff and still. He threw this dagger straight across the room, splitting his sister's skull wide open.

Selenyte Ardeen is dead.

Just like that.

"Make one move towards my Star, and my next blade will bury itself in that lackluster brain of yours, Deimos." Malakyte's face is drenched in shadow, yet his voice booms like a king's.

The entire throne room is hushed in stunned silence. Even Pacey's hallucination-fueled cries have ceased.

He . . . he killed his own sister.

He killed her for me.

Just like that.

Fuck.

Holy *fuck*.

What will the consequences of this act be, I wonder? The murder of the princess of Arianyte will reach the ears of the king and queen at some point, whether that news will be the truth. That's another question altogether. My bones quiver at the thought of the royals arriving here on a rampage to find their daughter's killer.

When I look at Deimos, I see the same look of utter astonishment that I'm feeling. There's no malice or bloodlust, and I feel that Deimos was never intending to kill me. He merely has a flair for the dramatic, per usual.

Gavrielle stands several paces behind the three of us, visibly appalled by the prince's actions.

I'm lifted to my feet by cold, strong arms and dragged away from Selenyte and Deimos. Then Malakyte charges at Deimos, ripping him out from under his sister's body and pinning him to the floor by his neck.

"Detain this impostor," Malakyte seethes, his soldiers following suit without hesitation or question. Two SSPARROW come and take Deimos from Malakyte, and Selenyte's body sits sprawled out on the throne floor. Deimos struggles against the soldiers, but they don't budge. I really hope Malakyte didn't notice what Gavrielle was doing, and if he did, hopefully he thinks it was for the prince's best interests, not mine. Gav doesn't seem to want his cover blown just yet.

Malakyte's eyes are a volcano, a tsunami, a roaring star—all wrapped into those pools of darkness. He's both in agony and flooded with relief.

I gape when he returns to my side.

"Do you not understand when I told you how much I loved you, Kara?" he whispers so only I can hear. Love . . . "I'll kill anyone to protect you, protect our throne, and I'll do it again and again, until the end of time or until there is no one left for me to destroy. Until not a soul was left in this ratchet Universe but the two of us."

When had he—

Oh, I remember . . . but that vision of him in the maze's reflection, that was just an illusion from the gas. No, it couldn't have been, not if he's referencing it now.

And though I am thoroughly repulsed by his actions—the depth of darkness that must reside within him that allowed him the fortitude to kill his own sister—I am also not entirely as disgusted as I should be. He pushes me away only to draw me back in again, as beautiful and deadly as the ocean itself. As dark, as deep, as mysterious.

Having someone willing to kill for you is not something you get every day, not by a space mile. He *killed* her.

For me . . .

But if he's capable of killing his own sister, his own flesh and blood, he's capable of *anything*.

It utterly and completely terrifies me because now I know that he'll do absolutely anything to make me his, and I don't have a chance in hell at stopping him.

CHAPTER 69

Time is ticking for the others, and I've got to use this moment to my advantage while his adrenaline is pumping and he's still in shock. If I can somehow save the ones I love, get them out of that box and away from the poison slowly killing them, then I'll try anything—exploit any weakness or circumstance.

"Malakyte," I place my hands on his. Gently, cautiously, I anchor him back to reality. "It's okay. I'm here. You saved me."

He looks so vulnerable as he gazes upon me, eyes awash with so much guilt and pain I had no idea he was even capable of feeling. We stand close to each other, close enough that nobody else can hear when I say, "It's going to be okay."

Malakyte seems to steady himself, coming back into his cold, calculated persona, aware there are many others in this room he cannot allow to see the true him. To see the pain he's experiencing.

I allow him to brush my hair off my shoulders and lightly graze over my chest, where his sister had cut and almost killed me.

"Please," I beg him, voice so quiet and soft and vulnerable. I take his cold face in my hands. "Please, don't kill them. Just let them go. I'm here, and I'll stay. We can be together, just . . . stop the bloodshed. Enough people have died because of us. My father is in there. If you do this—if you kill him—I will never be able to forgive you and there's no chance we could ever reconcile. Let them walk away, and I'll let everything from the past go . . . I will go with you and be with you, no questions asked. I like you. You know that I do. I can forget Ardelle and we can be together. We can rule and be together. Just, please, Malakyte, don't do this to me."

His eyes glide to the floor, where he teeters back and forth from being present with me and off in his own world. He's struggling.

I pity him.

"You don't have to be a monster, Malakyte," I say. "You don't have to be like her. You're better than her. You're a better person. I can tell by how you've treated the people of Earth. You treated them way better than she was going to. I see that now."

It kills me, but I have to say it. I must make him believe me. For them.

"Please," I echo, begging him with my eyes. "I'll do anything, Malakyte."

He's struggling to hold eye contact, something I've never seen him tussle with before. Does he regret what he did? Does he wish he had thought it through more?

When he looks back up at me, those dark eyes are as hard as steel. The Malakyte I've always known has finally returned.

"Anything?" he asks, that devilish, terrifying smirk forming on his dark lips.

My body is beginning to heat, from fear, from anticipation—I can't tell.

Say yes, I order myself. *Do whatever he wants. Save them.*

"Yes, Malakyte. Anything."

That smirk becomes a full-on grin.

"Kiss me."

CHAPTER 70

"Kiss you?"

Malakyte's eyes trail down my body, tracing every single curve, scar, dip, and valley. "Yes. Kiss me like I know you've wanted to since the moment we first met. Kiss me like I'm the last drop of water in a parched galaxy. Kiss me, Karalevine, like you mean it—like you want it. And let him watch, the way he made me watch."

Ardelle will have to be living to watch. It's going to hurt him, possibly break his heart—but if it means getting him out of here alive, I'll shatter his heart to keep it beating.

It's ironic that Malakyte wants Ardelle to suffer for that night at the ball, where Malakyte saw the two of us kissing. It was me who wanted Malakyte to watch, not Ardelle. It was me who chose to make Malakyte jealous . . . I shouldn't have been so vindictive. I shouldn't have poked the bear. Because now he's awake, and he's the one hungry for vengeance now.

"Stop the gas right now, and I will. And you'll let them go? Let them live, not go after them, not Recondition them, they'll leave and get back to Earth safe. No wanted status, no being hunted. They get to go back to Jance's house, and they're free from you and Arianyte. They keep their crystals until they die naturally and then you can have them back. You must keep your word, Malakyte."

Malakyte takes a minute to ponder my conditions, eyeing me suspiciously.

"Sure, Karalevine. Yes to all of it." His eyes are already looking at me with heady desire. I swallow, a tension beginning to bloom in my chest. Is this really going to happen? Right here, in front of everyone?

Without a word, Malakyte walks over to the cube and begins tapping on the interface. My heart pounds. The gas quickly seeps from the box and gets sucked out through some duct in the ceiling. The sound of their coughing becomes audible now, but it's a terrible clatter in my ears. Slowly, the opaque red box reveals the figures within, and my chest explodes with relief to see they're still alive.

Malakyte walks back to me, and I'm slightly disappointed he didn't let them out. But they're no longer in immediate danger, so I suppose that's better than nothing.

Can I trust his word to truly let them go? Stars know I can't.

I need a backup plan.

The prince stands before me, an ingenious smirk upon his lips.

"Okay," I manage to chirp out, throat tight with a buzzing, nervous energy.

Stars, help me. I'm actually going to do this. Kiss Malakyte . . .

"Okay," he echoes, voice much more confident than mine.

We gaze at each other for a long, long time. Each daring the other to go first, to cross this previously uncrossable line.

Malakyte moves a tiny bit closer.

My body trembles. My knees quake.

It's just a kiss, dammit.

But is that what I'm nervous about? Am I afraid, or am I excited?

Stars . . .

The ice wafts from his face as he bends and whispers tenderly in my ear, "I can smell your desire, Karalevine."

Fuck, the way he says my name just now . . . it's more than desire.

No. He's wrong . . . that's not what I'm feeling. Right?

Do it, I hiss at myself. *Don't be a coward. It's just a kiss.*

But this is Malakyte Ardeen, the prince of the Arianyte Empire. He isn't just anything.

And a mere peck on the lips will not satiate his appetite for me. I have to make it appear real, give him everything and more if I'm going to save them all.

My heart is a ravenous beast, repelled and attracted all at once. I have a beautiful monster before me, honed with cruel vitriol, brandished in the pits of a devious hell, and wrapped in a gorgeous bow of cold, hard grace and refinement.

His lips graze mine like the frosty touch of death itself, seconds away from drawing my soul straight from my lips in what's either going to be the worst kiss of my life or the very best.

As our lips finally meet, I ravish Malakyte Ardeen to his very core, my own exploding with the icy sensation of him. Burning with the fire of a thousand stars, I hold nothing back. It's like no other bliss I've known—a cruel, devious paradise.

Malakyte tastes like a crisp winter's morning. Clean and bright with citrus and shadow. My body betrays me because, as his cold tongue enters my mouth, I bloom and explode from within, the heat ravenous in all the right places. It shouldn't feel this good to kiss him, to desire him and want more of him even as he wraps his arms around me, bringing me in close. He should repulse me, after all he has done. And yet . . . he doesn't.

Our kiss is ice, and it is fire. It is danger, and it is pleasure, and it is hotter than I ever could have imagined. I do not fake-kiss him like I had planned. It's impossible. I'm kissing him for real, my body not allowing me to do it any other way.

A moan escapes my lips, and it causes him to shift under me, pressing his front in between my legs, so he makes sure I feel all of him in a way I never expected to. The fucking prince of Arianyte is as hard as a rock beneath my lips and by the stars if it doesn't make me feel all the more powerful for it.

He slowly—so painfully slowly—cups both his hands around my face. And it's this gentle, kind, sweet touch that confuses me more than anything else. For the first time in all this, I understand why Zariya fell in love with him, even though somewhere in the recesses of my mind, she's screaming at me to stop.

But I can't stop.

Not even with the gasps in the room, the displays of disgust and the shouts to stop on both sides. Neither of us cares, nor can neither of us end this moment.

Yet, when the guilt finally hits me, it isn't Ardelle who I initially think of. It's Gavrielle . . . Knowing that he's watching this and just tried to kiss me during the last game, but I denied him. Perhaps I'm breaking his heart tonight, too.

My star is fully lit up when finally—*finally*—I break our kiss.

My lips are swollen as we part, but we remain just as close, not quite ready to release each other yet. This moment is finite. It's fleeting as soon as it began, and I hate myself so fucking much for enjoying it. I wonder how long he's waited for that kiss . . . I wonder if he's thinking of Zariya? I wonder why that makes me feel a tiny bit jealous of her.

His hands move from my face to my shoulders, so tenderly it makes me want to cry. The soft touch is such a contrast to what and who I know him to be. If only . . . he wasn't such a bad person. If only he was better . . . if only he could be redeemed. If only, if only, if only . . . the story of my life.

And I can't live on "if only" any more than I can live on a planet without oxygen. I cannot trust him to keep his word. He's never going to let them go. Their freedom will always be his bargaining chip, constantly hanging over me. I'm prepared to take the punishment for this. I just hope to the stars the risk is worth it.

Because, unlike me, Malakyte will always choose his darker nature over his good. He doesn't care whether he's a good person or a bad one. He'll kill his own flesh and blood to obtain or keep what he wants most.

So, I thrust my plan in motion—praying to the stars it works.

Using my crystal's energy—revived from Malakyte's kiss—I shoot at the cube prison without ever taking my eyes off the prince. My crystal zaps the prison walls, completely ricocheting right off it. The fear that it'll blow up the entire Azurite like Malakyte suggested earlier brings the sexual tension down a bit but hardly.

Yet, Malakyte's gaze doesn't stray when the thin, jagged lines of antimatter bounce off and annihilate parts of his throne room. Doesn't look pissed at me or angry or anything other than completely and utterly fixated on me.

"You're such a bad girl, Karalevine," he says to me slowly, voice low and deep and fuck if I wish he'd kiss me again, the stupid motherfucker. "And stars, does it make me love you even more. But, ultimately, I need to teach you a lesson I failed to drill in last time we butted heads like this. That you don't fuck with me and get away with it."

CHAPTER 71

NEVER LOSE HOPE:

ABOVE ALL, REBELS, NEVER LOSE HOPE. WHEN THE FIGHT GETS TOUGH, THE UNIVERSE THROWS CURVEBALLS, AND THE ODDS SEEM INSURMOUNTABLE, KEEP THAT REBEL FIRE BURNING. BELIEVE IN THE POWER OF FREEDOM FOR ALL TERRAN PEOPLES, AND LET IT FUEL YOUR EVERY STEP.

When I look over to the prison, I see that it's charred and smoking but regrettably intact.

"I had that prison made specifically to withstand you, dear Karalevine. So, unfortunately, your attempt was nothing but futile. Shame. I so wanted to free them, after that kiss."

I grind my teeth into a snarl. Of course he'd go back on his word. It's what he does.

"Don't look at me like that, not after what we just shared. You'll be fine without them, in time. I promise. All you need is me. And believe it or not, I'm wholly disappointed in you. You clearly don't trust me, which means you have no intention of actually coming with me willingly. You'll fight me, tooth and nail. I know you enough to know you will do everything in your power to destroy me, and I cannot have that type of vitriol by my side, especially seated on my throne. You're the one who just proved they cannot be trusted. Again. Don't you ever learn your lesson?"

Is that why I'm here?

All so he could teach me a lesson in how never to defy him.

Was this entire thing—him getting ahold of me, his deal with Trinity and him Reconditioning Pacey—all moves in this twisted game of chess none of us knew we were playing? While we were playing the Titan Games, Malakyte was playing a game all his own.

And we're nothing but pawns.

I look to Malakyte now and see him for who he truly is.

What he truly is.

My monster.

My demon.

My villain.

My curse.

Seems like I'm collecting a lot of curses recently. Even with the taste of him on my tongue, the desire pooling within my body, I see Malakyte in all his cruel, destructive glory. He's evil . . . evil in the way a genius is creative. Brutal yet giving, distant yet vulnerable, beautiful yet horrifying. He's never going to change. A by-product of a screwed-up family who failed him. I can't . . . I can't save him.

Stars know if I can save myself and the others *from* him.

Malakyte notices it—he sees the fury in my eyes—he knows that I've figured out a portion of his game.

And it's not good for me—or the others.

"Take the prisoners out of here, torture them however you'd like," Malakyte tells his SSPARROWs, and my eyes go wide.

"Are you fucking kidding me, no—no!" I roar, practically commanding them myself.

As one of the SSPARROWs takes a step towards the cube, I chuck Selenyte's dagger, and it hits the soldier directly in the neck, precisely in the armor's opening. Stupidly, he rips it from his neck, likely forgetting that'll only kill him faster. The blade clanks to the floor, his body following seconds later. "You'll all die before you touch them," I seethe, and none of the other soldiers are stupid enough to move. I have no mercy for anyone who's going to torture my friends, but all I hear is *Killer of Worlds* in my head on repeat.

"Naresteé," Malakyte says without looking away from me, and I swear, shadows dance around him. "It's time."

I risk glancing over to Naresteé, who's sitting on the floor with Pacey, who's now quiet in her arms.

Whatever he is planning on doing, I cannot let him.

Naresteé crosses the throne room, and I hear Gavrielle's voice cry out, echoing against the freezing vise Malakyte has me locked in.

Gav charges for me, finally breaking character. To be my shield, my defender, my protector. *I shouldn't need saving*, I think to myself.

With a flick of his wrist, five of Malakyte's soldiers have Gavrielle down on the ground before he even gets halfway to me.

Deimos struggles against his soldiers, but they hold him tightly.

One good thing is, all the SSPARROWs are now either otherwise occupied or dead.

"Malakyte," I whisper, stepping away slowly as he and Naresteé being to approach me. "Please, don't. Just let them go, and I'll do whatever you want." I try again, but I don't know what else to say. "You don't have to do this." My eyes plead with him, beg him.

Reaching me, he bends down to my ears, the coldness of his breath sending shivers along my spine, both of fear and of the memory of the kiss we just shared. "I would have, had you not ruined our moment together by trying to free them. You don't have trust in me, which means I cannot trust you to behave yourself. Besides, you should worry much more about your own memories, Karalevine."

I jerk away, pulling against him, but he holds our bodies firmly together. His gentle temperament is all gone by the time Naresteé reaches us. The two of them force me down to the ground, even though I fight them. Once they've coerced my back to the floor, Malakyte straddles my waist and uses his body weight to pin me. Naresteé holds my shoulders to the cold stone tiles.

I scream.

"Get off of her!" Ardelle roars.

How can the man who just kissed me like I've never been kissed, who touched me so gently, be this cruel?

I finally hear my father's voice out there somewhere, panic-fueled and dripping with fury.

"Malakyte, stop this! She's a child!"

The icy prince does no such thing, of course. Instead, he takes my wrists and pins them over my ears, looking down on me from above. He's put me in my place. "Technically, she's an adult now."

Pinned here, it hits me that this whole time I thought I was some sort of hero, despite struggling with my dark side. But I'm not strong—I'm weak. Just a bombastic, wannabe savior. What a blow to my identity. Because what does it matter if you lose, in the end? I'm nothing but a fraud, and I did this all to myself.

Don't give up, a voice inside tells me.

But I want to, I argue back. I want to stop fighting so badly. Everything I do is wrong. Everything I do hurts the people I love.

I close my eyes against Malakyte's body above me like this. No, he doesn't get to treat me this way. He hasn't earned his right to touch me or force me down in this violent way. Nobody could convince me that he doesn't see how violating this is, but he's not paying attention to how I feel. Gav would see, so would Ardelle . . . but he's not like Gav and Ardelle. He doesn't care if he hurts me.

The pain of that realization alone is enough for my crystal's magic to surge. Both Malakyte's and Naresteé's eyes widen when they see my star light up. Their gasps come second. I send Naresteé flying across the room with a quick jolt. But for Malakyte, I reserve something special.

I shock Malakyte's hands, causing him to release my wrists. He still sits atop my waist. I create a ball of antimatter between my palms, allowing it to grow bigger and bigger until it's the size of a melon, at least.

"Karalevine." My name is a warning on his lips and I see the fear in his eyes. "You'll kill us all with that. Do not release it here. Your father will be killed."

"Don't use my dad as a bargaining chip, you weaselly piece of shit," I sneer as I shove my antimatter directly into his chest—into his crystal.

Malakyte screams.

I don't let up. I pound and pound and pound my crystal into his. I must destroy it. I have to obliterate his Elendril crystal in order to prevent it from bringing him back to life again.

Naresteé screams somewhere in the distance, ordering the SSPARROWs to abandon their hostages and to stop me.

They're too afraid to move.

The light from my crystal is near blinding, and all I can see is Malakyte's inky-black hair whipping from behind him as if he were in a hurricane, but he's still alive and trying to push past my power. I must dig deeper—find more power, use every ounce of it I have left. But instead, my antimatter is getting smaller. No, no, it's not enough. I need more. I need to obliterate his crystal.

The fear alone causes another swell in my crystal, but it's the last bit that I can muster, and I know it's about to dry up and cease completely. The final push blasts Malakyte's body off me, throwing him all the way to the opposite side of the room. He hits his throne hard, whacking it and landing at a very unnatural angle. He's smoking, his clothing charred and burned away. He doesn't seem to be moving at all.

"What have you done, you fucking bitch!" Naresteé screams, fury like nothing else I've seen from her. She rises, ready to come and kill me, but then Pacey lunges for her.

"Stop!" Pacey cries. "She'll kill you, too! Don't!"

The hallucination gas doesn't appear to have worked on her yet, and I don't know if it's going to. Naresteé looks hesitant, unsure of whether to come at me or remain where she is.

But this isn't over—not yet.

I don't waste a single precious moment.

I jump to my feet and dash towards the others in their prison. My body slams into the cube, bouncing off it. They all shout at me as I begin pressing the electronic panel, trying to figure out how to unlock them.

It's a foreign alien interface, one I don't understand as my fingers tap along the smooth surface—trembling. Where the fuck is the unlock button, dammit?

I try to read it, try to ignore their shouting and pleas for haste. Try to forget my fearful uncertainty if Malakyte is actually dead or not, if Naresteé and the SSPARROWs will come for me out of vengeance.

The voices within the prison cube get louder and more insistent.

My heart is like a runaway train, and I can hardly feel my body.

I slam my finger into the screen. Nothing happens. My sweat is causing it not to function. I press it again and again, and it finally goes. Then I see the basic interface. Lock and unlock. There it is!

Unlock.

They're free!

No, wait . . .

Nothing is happening. Is it my finger again? Or is it merely taking time to unlock? I slam down on the screen, pushing it over and over.

"Kara, watch out!"

I'm clobbered from the side. My head hits the floor with a crack so hard, so loud, that I swear I hear it echo as I'm dragged into an eternal blackness.

CHAPTER 72

My eyes flutter open, and I remember only the shadow and endless dark.

That is, until my head begins to pound like nothing I've ever known.

There's a wetness around my ear. It's got to be blood.

Stars, my head . . .

The others!

I try to rise, but I'm shoved down on my back. Such cold hands . . .

The ringing in my ears is out of control.

When I open my eyes, I see the stars on the window ceiling, the beautiful vastness of space sprawled out before me. Endless as a dream and as dark as a nightmare.

My body is lifted by the collar of my uniform, an icy cold breath wakes me from my hazy slumber. "Nice try, but if you want to kill me, you're going to need to take off my head."

Malakyte drops me back to the cold, hard floor.

I cough in pain as my lungs burn. My eyes are hardly able to focus on him at all. Fuck . . . My crystal wasn't strong enough . . .

If I were at full strength, then maybe I could've done it, but I failed *again*.

Malakyte's hazy form disappears from my line of sight, only to be replaced by something else. I see glowing. A beautiful set of radiant yellow orbs. They're fuzzy, growing from large to small, blurry to even more unfocused.

But what I can make out, above those two yellow orbs, is a set of horns.

Narosteé . . . she's above me now, looking down upon me with her glowing yellow eyes . . .

How odd. Why would her eyes be glowing like she has a crystal? Silly, she doesn't have one. That's Malakyte's crystal—the yellow one.

I blink. My vision clears more, but I'm transfixed upon those eyes. The pupils are definitely glowing yellow, surrounded by Ruby Red irises that are chilling and vile. A monster made flesh and bone, a demon unto this world. That's what Narosteé is.

So, how can she be using Malakyte's crystal if she—

The answer comes to me all too late, my muddled thoughts so completely useless.

How had none of us suspected it? How had we not questioned *who*, at the very least?

Who was Malakyte's Ringer?

Well, we know now.

But wouldn't I have seen the mark upon her hand?

Perhaps not, not with the stippling along her skin. It likely blended right into the oddly textured pattern she naturally has.

Fucking stupid to not have known or seen it.

Now she's got me in her clutches. I can sense it. Feel her magic seeping into me like a poisonous sludge. It sinks into all of me, parts I shudder at allowing her dark soul to touch. Yet, she blasts her way in, past all defenses and walls built around my mental shields. She barrels in deeper and deeper and deeper. Fear plunges its way behind the devastating route her magic takes within me— within my mind. A soul-crushing type of horror, one that leaves me breathless and immovable. Hopeless and cold and tragically small. I can't even scream.

"Don't be frightened," her sweet voice says to me, like a mother easing her child back to bed after a nightmare. *"It'll all be over soon. Soon, you won't feel any of that fear. Any pain or loss or anger. Soon, all that vindictive hate you have within will be gone."*

"No . . ." I beg, but barely—the sound hardly a whimper.

Is this the cost of vengeance? When the stakes in poker are raised, it's time to double down or fold . . . I've been relentlessly doubling down for quite a while, and now that it's time to pay up, I am not prepared for the price demanded of me.

I feel Malakyte move my limp body, laying me against his chest. He takes ahold of my hand, lacing his cold fingers through mine. Out of pure terror, I squeeze back—tighter than a vise.

Narestee's hand cups my cheek as she caresses it softly and tenderly.

My instincts scream at me. Why are they touching me like this? It's all wrong . . . No! Don't give into her!

Don't give in!

That's right. I have to keep fighting.

No matter how much it hurts.

Somewhere deep inside me, the hero that I wish I could be, sparks back to life. I kick Narestee, elbow Malakyte in the chest, and pull myself away with what little strength I have left.

They don't follow or try to prevent me from crawling towards the cube and the others. My head still rings and explodes with pain so severe I can't even stand. So, I drag myself instead. I see my loved ones inside their confining little pocket of Hell. Unable to help, unable to stop whatever Malakyte and Narestee are trying to do to me.

But it's my fault this is happening. It's all my fault . . .

What have I done?

I'm such a fool. Such a foolish, stupid girl. I thought I could barrel in here and bring Arianyte down or at least make things right again by saving Pacey. Instead, I made everything ten times worse. I'm not a warrior for justice. I'm not anyone's savior. I got Pacey Reconditioned. It's my fault Jance and the others are now captured. Now, the one man I want to kill so badly has me exactly where he wants me, and I was too much of a hot-headed brat to see it coming. The darkness in my soul brought me straight here, and he's going to win because of it. And if he wins, then that means we . . . Oh, stars. My bones quake with the certainty that we're going to *lose*.

Lose this fight with Malakyte.

Lose the battle for Earth's freedom.

Lose everyone I love.

I learned my lesson too late. I tried to be a good person, to do all the right things and not let my darkness and anger and emotions control me, but when I finally realized the error of my ways, it was just too late. And now we've lost.

We've lost . . .

The words hit me harder than my skull cracking against the stone floor.

We're going to lose, and he's going to win . . . I thought I was prepared for him, but I could never truly prepare for Malakyte Ardeen.

When I finally make it to the others, I can hear them a bit better. Ardelle is squatted down as low as he can get, Jance on his knees, their faces masks of terror and agony. I wrench myself up to a sitting position, leaning against the prison wall.

"Darling, run. Forget us and go. Run from here. Get out now." That's Jance . . . my father's voice.

Then I hear Ardelle say, "Thumbelina! Don't give into it! Thumbelina!"

Thumbelina . . .

Thumbelina . . . ?

What an odd name for a person.

I've never heard that name before. Who's Thumbelina? Who the hell is he talking to?

In fact, how did we meet again? I know them. I know their faces and names, but for some reason I'm having a hard time placing how we know each other . . . They are . . . They are important, though. Jance is important. So is Ardelle.

I notice my reflection in the material of the cube.

Notice my eyes are glowing bright yellow.

And then that fear, that soul-crushing dread, latches itself to me . . . and it will not let go.

My body begins to hyperventilate, panic overwhelming my system, and I can't breathe. My breaths are loud and wheezing, head dizzy, and I wobble, barely catching myself on the side of the cube.

No . . . no. This isn't happening to me.

"Babe! Look at me!"

"Kara! Kara, focus," Jance says, and I look up to see him. There's a collar strapped to his neck, around all their necks, but why? Why does that make me feel so much pain?

I'm losing my grip, losing my control and my sanity all at once. My body rocks back and forth, eyes wide as they bounce around the room. I want to escape, but I'm not sure where I am or how to get out. How did I get here? What is this place? I don't know. I don't know!

My palms cover my eyes. What's happening to me?

"Kara, darling, just breathe and stay calm for me." Jance's deep voice is like a lifesaver being thrown to me while drowning at sea. "Focus on me now, just you and me."

But he can't save me. Nobody can . . .

I jump up, needing the safety of his arms, but I bonk the barrier between us—forgetting it was there.

"Don't let him do this to me. I don't want to forget. I don't wanna go," I beg, clawing at the cube's walls. I'm dripping in sweat, and I feel like I'm having an out-of-body experience or on a terror-fueled nightmare I cannot wake from.

"Don't make me."

"Look in my eyes," Jance tells me, and I'm shaking my head like that'll somehow make this stop.

"I'm going to forget you. I'm going to forget everyone, and I don't want to. Don't let him do this to me, Daddy, please. I don't want to forget you."

I break. I sob and I scream and pull my hair because my mind is like quicksand, and it's dragging me down. I can't stop it. I've never known such agonizing terror.

"You're not going to forget me, baby, you won't. It's going to be okay," he says, but the tears in his eyes say otherwise.

"Stop this, you sociopath!" the woman in the box shrieks, but I've forgotten her name already . . . I . . . I don't remember her. It doesn't matter. I can hardly hear her over my own cries and whimpering. I curl over myself, face buried into the cube's wall. Jance keeps saying things to me, but my rasping breaths are blocking out his words.

"You motherfucker!" the tattooed boy howls, practically throwing his entire body into the prison's wall, the sound nothing but a hollowed thud, and even though the material does crack, it doesn't break.

"I love you, Kara. I love you, and I promise I'm going to fix this. I promise. I'm so sorry, baby, I failed you, I'm so sorry . . ." the dark-haired man tells me, and I gasp because I've forgotten his name. My eyes go wide, and I search my mind for it, desperately digging into the trenches of my memories, only to be swallowed up by darkness.

I clasp my hands over my mouth in horror, but it doesn't stifle the primal wail that crawls up my throat like a demon ascending from Hell—unstoppable and horrific. He sees it . . . He knows I've forgotten a vital piece of him, and he cannot hold in his emotion. I don't think I've ever seen a grown man cry like this . . .

Jance!

My memory battles against what's being done to it, retrieving his name for me one last time. That's him . . . my father.

"Jance . . ." I whimper, "I'm so sorry. This is all my fault."

In a desperate, frenzied hysteria, I see a bloody dagger sitting on the floor beside me and grab hold of it. I wipe the blood away

and quickly carve two letters into my forearm, and the room collectively cries at me to stop. J for Jance. F for father. So, no matter what, I won't forget.

I drop the dagger with a hollow clank. Gripping onto the ring necklace, I say his name over and over and over again. I will not forget him this time!

Jance is my father. Jance is my father. Jance is my father.

Jance. Jance. Jance.

Jance.

Jance.

Jance . . .

What was I thinking of? It was something important . . . Dammit, what was it? *What was it?*

The tattooed boy falls to his knees, trapped behind plastic, but it might as well be a whole other planet.

I've forgotten his name, too. But I love him . . . I love him.

"Kara . . ." he whispers, tears falling and face anguished, and the way he says my name hurts somewhere deep inside, but I can't recall why.

A scuffle of bodies from behind me steals my attention, a voice crying out for me. I turn to see who it is, and I'm so confused. This person looks exactly the way Gavrielle would look at this age.

He's alive? I didn't kill him at the orphanage? But, but how? Why is he here? He looks so upset, so anguished. Everyone does . . .

"I promise I will free you from this!" He cries to me, several soldiers beating and slamming and pinning him down, but still, he fights to get to me. "I will free you! I will bring you back!"

What is he talking about?

Footsteps clank out from behind me, soft but assured, and I know it's him before his icy hands lift me up and pull me away from those I love.

I scream, I cry, and I claw for them.

I scream for the people within the clear box. I cry for the man fighting soldiers just to reach me . . . And I claw at Malakyte.

He sits us down ten feet away from the cube. "This will all be over soon, I promise." His voice is soft, calm, gentle as he holds me in his lap.

"Please, Malakyte," I beg, I cry. "Stop. Stop! I'm scared. Don't do this to me. Please. I'm so scared. Please! I'll be good, I promise. Malakyte! Malakyte, PLEASE!"

I don't want to lose all of them. I don't want to lose who I am now. If I go back to the girl I used to be, that bitter and lonely vengeful girl, I'm going to lose every ounce of progress I've made. Even if I didn't grow fast enough, I still changed for the better because of them because of . . . because of . . .

Malakyte pets the back of my head softly, as I beg like I've never begged in my entire life for anything, my pride all but shattered.

"I'm so sorry for this," he says as he wipes my tears from my cheeks tenderly, his voice sincere. "I know you're frightened, and I'm here for you. I won't leave you to suffer this alone, even if you did just try to kill me. And you won't forget me. That, I can assure. It'll all be over soon. I take no pleasure in your suffering, contrary to what you may think of me. However, this was the only way. It's the only way we can be together."

"*Please . . .*"

"I'm sorry, Karalevine, don't say that I didn't try to warn you. There are no more bargains to be made. We both know neither of us can keep our word to each other. Hopefully, once this is over, we can start fresh and be better people to one another."

Holding me tightly, he wouldn't let me go anywhere, even if I wanted to. I feel my memories slipping away, like smoke in my hands disappearing into an empty night.

"Don't take him from me," I bargain, pleading not to lose that one thing. But I have forgotten who he is. Is he my lover or someone else I care about? I don't remember, I just know I cannot lose *him*. "Don't take him away."

"If you're a good girl, then I'll let you two remain together," he says. I'm not sure who he is talking about. All that remains is fear, looming underneath my empty thoughts. I hold on to Malakyte Ardeen for dear life, even though that fear clings to him as well.

I can say for certain that I am not prepared for the price of vengeance. The cost is far too high . . .

Malakyte whispers in my ear and holds me tight. I want to run away from him, but he's the only one helping me . . . the only person trying to get the sickening dread to stop.

My world is crumbling down to this tiny moment, where I'm confused and not understanding my own feelings. There's no "why" behind anything. Why am I feeling pain and worry for people I cannot name? Why are they here and why are they trapped and what is going on?

Then I hear a sound, one like beeping and mechanical noises, almost like gears turning. It breaks me out of this horror-filled loop of unanswered questions.

That girl . . . I know her . . . She stands at the cube prison with a giant scythe tied to her back. The keypad flashes red, and the walls of the cube slowly open from the bottom. She glares down at Malakyte and Naresteé with a cruel, angry expression on her face.

"You people . . ." she rasps, so much anger in her voice. "You sick, disgusting people. And you!"

The girl points to Naresteé, whose eyes are wide with confusion and fear.

"You will not get away with this!" The girl snarls, "Not with what you've done to me. For what you took from me and for what you tried to replace in my heart." She covers her heart with her hand, pain etched into her beautiful features.

"How are you remembering?" Naresteé asks.

Elation fills me, and through my tears, I smile, even though I don't know why.

"Let her go! Let her mind go!" is her only answer.

My head feels a little emptier.

The boy with the tattoos forces the walls of the cube up faster, pushing his way out.

"Sir!" A SSPARROW shouts. The ones holding down the other two extras on the other side of the room. "What do you want us to do?"

Malakyte yells, voice loud in my ear, "Let them flee. They will be caught eventually. Keep away whoever is foolish enough to try and keep me from my Star."

"I'll kill you!" the tattooed one shouts, launching himself towards me. He charges for us, but he's met with a barrage of metal soldiers. They fight him instantly. Malakyte scoots us further away, keeping hold of me to the point I cannot get free.

"Get the fuck out of here!" someone yells, and I look over to see who. He's a green extraterrestrial. and I know him, *I know him*, but . . .

"Sylo, take my sister and the others and run! Pacey, go!"

"No!" she shouts back as a tan-skinned boy I can't remember grabs her shoulders. "I am not leaving her!"

A broad man with dark hair plows his way through the soldiers and manages to make it to Malakyte and me. Instinct drives me to go to this man. I squirm in Malakyte's arms, kicking and slapping and scratching. He won't let me go! My magic fires all over the place, uncontrollably shattering everything in its wake. I've lost all control of it.

"One of you, get me a collar now!" Malakyte yells.

The man is close to us, and I force my magic away from him. But then he stops suddenly, like he's been hit by an invisible brick wall. His eyes . . . they're glowing yellow.

Fear strikes me cold again, and even though I cannot remember why, I *know* this isn't a good thing—it's a terrible thing.

"No!" I scream, and it's so bloodcurdling it gives me goose bumps. "Stop! Stop it! Leave him alone!"

The tattooed boy is slammed to the ground by soldiers, the other people now running for the throne room door. They're close enough to escape. The SSPARROWs aren't chasing them. They're too occupied with the two men before Malakyte and I. Who are they? Why can't I remember who they are?

The others run, and I can't see them anymore. Thank goodness . . . thank goodness they can get away. This is a bad place . . .

The younger one plows past the soldiers fighting him, feral and savagely battling his way to me, despite all the metal bodies that pummel him. He's hauling them across the floor by his elbows as he claws inch by inch towards me on his stomach. He gets near, and I manage to slither out of Malakyte's grasp temporarily—my magic ceasing once I do. His arms wrap around my legs, and I slip, my chest hitting the hard ground. Malakyte's cold hands grip my waist now, dragging me back to him. I reach for this other person, his hand outstretched for me. I know him. I *know* him. He reaches and reaches, and I try to clasp his hand. We're so close, only an inch apart . . .

Cold arms seize my body. I'm lifted into the air high above the battle taking place below.

Malakyte is carrying me away . . .

I scream, the fear unrelenting. The horror a palpable presence entering the room as if it were a god. Here to wash the mess I've created by utterly changing the dynamic of everything I've known. Coming to wipe the slate clean with annihilation.

Yet, in all the chaos, a sweet voice rings within my mind, a soft caress. *Don't fear, my darling. Soon, you'll be safe and warm and more loved than you can ever imagine. Those people before you don't love you.*

Yes, they do!

Sweet girl, don't you remember? Don't you remember how awfully they treated you when you came to live with them? How they shunned you, bullied you, dismissed you? If you could see it again, you would agree. Let me remind you how they treated you and how much they despise you.

I'm not sure who she's talking about until I'm zapped into another time and place. The room I was just in vanishes as I watch over and over the scenes I must have forgotten. Like how cruel everyone was on my first night there. I remember Jance and everyone—I can't believe I had just forgotten them. I remember how Jance made me sleep alone in the basement of his mansion and the cruelty of this man. Then, I remember how Pacey sneered at me and judged me:

"My stars, you're pitiful. Worse than a withering house plant stuck in its pot . . . I won't be caught dead with you, especially dressed in those rags."

Spoiled rich *bitch*.

And then it hurt so much when Jance was training me that one night when he wouldn't stop pinning me down, even when I ask him to stop. I told him about the abuse that happened to me when I was younger and how I was triggered by him, and he was so heartless about it. I relive it all.

"What is your problem?" His voice bites cold and slick with disdain. "Oh, what? Did some man touch you or something? Get over it. I don't train weak little girls who can't handle their emotions."

I remember how much those words broke my heart. He's a terrible person. How had I forgotten that?

"Get off me," I beg, all strength in my voice whittled down to a pathetic whimper.

"No."

The memories are all returning to me like rapid-fire. I had forgotten them, and now I'm remembering them again, and they're terrible. Why was I trying to save these people? They're awful! They were just using me, like everyone always uses me, then throws me away.

Now, I'm remembering when I gave Ardelle his tattoo. I wanted to kiss him that night . . . I thought, maybe he liked me, too. But now I recall, he was just using me.

"This tattoo isn't all that great," he says, looking at it in the mirror, face disinterested. "The other ones I have are better. Whatever. You can go now."

He would never like me in return. I don't even know why I liked him in the first place. He was always so mean to me. He didn't treat me the way Malakyte has always treated me. Malakyte . . . he saw me. He sees me, all of me, and that's all I truly want.

I'm alone in a dark room now, the memories of the others replaced with this dark void that I now stand in. The pain of what I just remembered weighs heavy on my heart. Yet, this place, this bleak, endless void—is awful. I can feel myself in it, as if I'm residing within my own mind, inside that darkness that is and has always been *me*.

This darkness is me. It's the me that I hate, the me that I cannot escape from because there's no separating the two. It's the monster within me that I can never be free of. All the pain and rage lives here, too. I feel it all. All the horrible memories of my past linger in this place, and they've come back to torture me into madness.

"I can make it better," a sweet voice promises. I look, and from out of that deep darkness comes a figure.

A figure with horns.

"I can make all these terrible memories go away. You won't have to feel this pain or this darkness ever again. You'll feel only love, only warmth, and only freedom."

My immediate reaction is to recoil, her form terrifying and scary.

But her voice is so sweet and kind.

The two don't match.

Her finger points to the left, where I see the manifestation of my nine-year-old self. She's in that house, in that bedroom—with *him*. Not the first monster I'd face but by far the very worst. He walks into that room, the sound of his belt coming undone. He crawls onto my bed. He crawls onto *me*.

"Stop it," I whisper. "Stop it!"

I don't want to see this again.

Thankfully, it vanishes in a puff of smoke, but the memories and pain remain.

A pale hand reaches out for me, almost lovingly. When I turn, Malakyte is standing in the horned woman's place. "Do not be afraid, sweet girl. I am your best friend, your only friend. I want only what is best for you."

I want so badly for a friend. One who's nice and doesn't hurt me.

He says, "I know, I want a friend who's good to me, too. Let me be that for you."

I want that, but a small part of me out there in the dark somewhere cries and beats against it, begging me to say no.

"Don't cry." He wipes my tears, and I gaze into his eyes. "Do you want me to make everything better? Do you want to be free from the pain that's shackled you all your life? The abandonment, the abuse, the trauma that man in that bedroom caused you. I can even take away all the horrific things the other Starseeds and Ringers have done to you. All of it can be erased. Those people who hurt you will never do so again."

All my life, I've suffered. Like I've been destined and cursed to suffer. I'm sick and fucking tired of it.

"Yes," I say. "I don't want to feel this way anymore."

He smiles at me, and my chest blooms with trepidation. Am I doing the right thing? Or . . .

"That's good." His voice is like sweet milk and honey. "Now, just say this one sentence for me, one simple sen—"

"*No!*" a voice rings out within my mind, somewhere so far away. "*Run Kara! Run away from him!*"

It sounds like a young boy's voice, but it's fleeting . . .

"Say this simple phrase, 'I forfeit my subconscious protection.'"

I open my mouth, but something in me hesitates.

He only smiles at me patiently.

"I forfeit my subconscious protection," he repeats. That's not too hard to say. I can do this one thing to find freedom from pain.

My heart thrashes, teetering on indecision. I don't want to hurt anymore.

"I forfeit my subconscious protection," I say, and immediately, Malakyte vanishes, and I'm alone once again in the darkness.

Giant walls explode from the floor. One bursts in front of me. Another blasts from behind. It's only then that I realize I'm trapped. Trapped inside a prison. A jail within my mind, within my soul.

I'm trapped . . . I'm trapped . . .

I'm trapped!

A voice pings out within the darkness, different from the one before it, like a hiss from a snake.

One word, one name.

Malakyte.

What has he done to me?

I'll never know because the darkness closes in and before I can even scream my memories are obliterated.

CHAPTER 74

The shouts from the throne room fade away as Karalevine and I leave through the side door. My soldiers will take care of this farce. She'll calm down and forget what just happened any minute now.

"Don't cry, my sweet Karalevine. I'm here for you. Hush now. It's going to be fine. You're going to be just fine."

Seeing her so upset, I wince as my chest physically aches. Her cries pain me more than I can admit. I hurt knowing the fear she's experiencing and find solace that she'll forget that terror. Even so, a lump grows in my throat when I think of how to explain myself to her.

"I am sorry, Kara. Please, forgive me for this. It wasn't how I wanted this to happen between us. But I'm a weak, pathetic man, and I do not deserve you. It's just that . . . I cannot bear to live without you a moment longer. I'll play the role you cast me in to perfection. If it means in the end, you can be mine again. You loathed me so much you never would have been mine otherwise."

Although, I doubt she'd believe any of that. I'm lacking confidence that she'll see this as an act of my love. The only way we can be together is if I take her memories back to before last year's Titan Games. Before she fell for that Terran trash, Ardelle.

She's far too good for a lowlife Terran like him. She deserves a prince. An emperor. She deserves to be empress, by my side.

And so she shall.

This was the only way I could guarantee she doesn't destroy my empire while sitting by my side. Her attempt on my life was proof of that, proof I made the right call. This truly was the only way . . . she'd never be loyal to me otherwise, no matter how badly I wished for it.

Karalevine goes limp in my arms, out like a light. Naresteé's Ringer magic has hit its peak. She must have gotten deep within Karalevine's subconscious, just as planned. The true reason Naresteé spent so much time with Miss Dawson. That's how we knew which crack to slither through to fully ensure the new memories stick. The whole ruse with the Starseeds abandoning her was all for this moment. I'm pleased that it worked.

She's mine now. She'll be mine forever.

Finally.

She looks so peaceful, so adorable, as she sleeps in my arms. She's beautiful, even though her body is beaten, bloodied, and bruised. These Titan Games were certainly hard on her. I must tend to these wounds, including this head wound I accidentally gave her, and after that she will be put to bed. To sleep for a few days, while her memories reset into the narrative I have crafted for her through my Ringer's magic.

Then and only then will she wake as the woman I've always wished her to be.

Similar to how the old Zariya was.

She will not fight me, will not hate me, and she will not desire anyone else but me. The scent of that imbecilic, posturing fool Ardelle is all over her. I scented it the moment I got close enough to her. I'll have to rectify that little hindrance. My doctors will make sure she doesn't conceive. Assuring we don't have a repeat of last time. Zariya's little love child with Erodis will never happen here. The only child Karalevine will bear will be my own. When the time is right, she'll have only my scent on her. No other man will ever touch her again. She'll only desire me and me alone. I will never have to share her again.

I cannot help but smile ear to ear, victory finally at hand.

How can this not be proof of my love?

All of this, all my planning and scheming, it was all for her.

For us.

CHAPTER 75

THE TERRAN POPULATION OF EARTH HAS OFFICIALLY DECLARED WAR UPON THE ARIANYTE EMPIRE. IN DOING SO, ARIANYTE HAS INITIATED "THE STABILIZATION PROTOCOL," AS OUTLINED IN THE DEVOURING ACCORDS. ANY TERRAN WHO REFUSES ANY, AND ALL DEMANDS FROM ARIANYTE OFFICIALS OR SSPARROW ENFORCEMENT WILL BE IMMEDIATELY DETAINED, IMPRISONED, OR EXECUTED ON SIGHT. DEADLY FORCE WILL BE USED TO ANNIHILATE ANY TERRAN WHO ACTIVELY ENGAGES OR SUPPORTS THE REBEL AGENDA OR WHO REFUSES TO COMPLY WITH ARIANYTE RULE OF LAW. ALL TRANSPORT FROM AURORA BASES, OUTPOSTS, AND BEYOND THE SOLAR SYSTEM ARE HEREBY GROUNDED UNTIL FURTHER NOTICE. ALL ARIANYTE SERVICES ARE HERBY SUSPENDED UNTIL FURTHER NOTICE.

KARALEVINE RUZZ
THREE WEEKS LATER

My eyes open to a spectacular view.

As I lay on my side in the comfortable bed, lids still heavy and mind drowsy from a good night's sleep, I wake to a view of planet Earth, spinning silently on its axis. The roof of our bedroom is a tray ceiling with a glass cutout, giving us a gorgeous scene of the stars beyond the Azurite. The lighting is dim, a soft orange glow all along the royal suite, but it's enough to see the outline of our chairs and seating area. It is cold, however. But when I look back up to the ceiling and see the stars, I smile. It's the view I've woken to for months now, since Malakyte brought me onto the Azurite after Deimos and the Resistance threatened not only him but us as well. Geonni and Deimos almost killed me at the last Titan Games finale, the arena being destroyed because of them. There hasn't been any Titan Games since, both Deimos and the rebel leaders in the wind. The rebels, those who used to be my family, forsaking me. I often felt hurt when thinking of them, of Geonni and Trinity, but I can't think of either of them anymore. They're nothing, they're down there fighting a losing battle. And one day, I'll fight defiantly against them, but not today. This day, I am comfortable and happy and in love.

When chilly arms wrap around me, I turn to my side and try not to squirm.

"What?" he asks, voice rough but soft as he cuddles up behind me.

"I just . . ." I begin, not knowing how to describe the sensation of his cold body pressed up against mine. "I just figured I'd be used to how cold you feel after all this time."

He makes a contemplative sound with his throat and kisses the back of my neck with those cold, attentive lips.

"You will," he finally confirms, and I have no doubt. "I, on the other hand, am obsessed with how warm you are. I wish we could be the same temperature. I wish I didn't make you shiver."

In turn, I make a similar sound to the one he just made. I don't mind it, I really don't. If I get to be loved by him, I'll deal with his icy cold skin.

"These last few months have been the happiest of my life, so a bit of shivering can be tolerated, I suppose. If you're nice to me, that is."

His chuckle vibrates against my back, his body flush to mine.

"Aren't I always nice to you, Karalevine? Have I not given you the world?"

Here we go again, him fishing for compliments.

"You know that I'm happy" is all I need to say. "Although, I do wish we could find the other Starseeds, and their Ringers. They'd be a huge help in the fight against Deimos and the rebels."

I shift, turning to face him.

"Let's go back down there. Let's find them. Deimos will never stop, and Geonni . . . he's slick. He'll never stop trying to bring us down. We have to stop him, too. I'm going stir crazy being kept up here. I'm your Star, I'm supposed to be fighting for you. Let me. After he betrayed and abandoned me, I want to get even."

Like a gnawing itch I couldn't scratch, finding the others who hold the Elendril crystals has become an obsession for me. It's the only way to fight Deimos and Geonni. "You only have Jance and I. That's only one single pair. The other Starseeds and Ringers could be with Geonni for all we know. Your goal was to bring all of us together, right? Then, let's do that so we can stop Deimos and Geonni, save the Earth from their terrorism before they do something they can't take back. Plus, you know I need to get back down there and keep searching for Gavrielle. You promised me we'd find him after all these years of us being apart."

"In time." He sighs, and I can tell that's the end of that conversation. "Besides, the future empress of Arianyte has far more pressing concerns than worrying about a silly rebellion now, doesn't she?"

Stars, I don't hate the way that sounds.

And I smile, full and genuine.

Empress.

Empress of Arianyte.

The power and prestige that title brings. It's toe-curling.

"It sure has a ring to it, doesn't it?" I say, unable to keep the slight tremble from my voice at the implications of the words. "It still intimidates me."

Malakyte stretches and sits up, turning to gaze down at me affectionately.

"The galaxy will adore you."

"What about your parents?" I ask, "Do you think they've gotten word of your sister's death yet?"

He's quiet for a long moment. "Ultimately, they'll come. When that happens, they'll meet you, and we will cement our arrangement and rule. Let me deal with them regarding Selenyte. They'll be in grief, since her murderer is still at large."

"I can investigate it further," I suggest, but I already know he's going to shut me down—again.

As if I'm a psychic, his head tilts the way it always does when he tells me no. "I have the best investigators on it. They'll bring her killer to justice; I am certain of it."

"They're not better than me," I say playfully, but on the inside, I'm dead serious.

He reaches for me and cups my chin in his hand, a slightly cold spindle crawling up my spine. "Of this I have no doubt. I need you with me and safe. There are those that wish to take you from me. I will not allow them access to hurt you. Future empress of Arianyte."

I smile up at him, knowing we will only go in circles if this continues. "Of course, future emperor of Arianyte. Did you ever expect to be here, like this? I mean, I know when we first met, I never would have thought . . ." Something tickles within my mind, but it fades away just as quickly. "Yeah, sorry. I just never thought this was how my life would turn out. Do you ever feel that way?"

It's his turn to beam, both sets of lengthened canines on full display.

I wish this moment would last forever.

Malakyte takes my hand and kisses the back of it as he tells me, "I always knew you'd choose me in the end."

EPILOGUE

GAVRIELLE ABRAXAS

The Azurite is a colossal place, there are many nooks and crannies in which to hide. These past weeks have been full of watching and hiding and running. Although, I remind myself I am lucky to have gotten out of that throne room with my life and my memories intact.

Some hadn't.

Including her.

No matter which location I choose to rest my head, her screams echo through my mind. It almost broke me the moment she screamed for Malakyte to spare the memory of her father . . .

Having to watch her experience her memories shattering before her eyes . . . that had broken me.

It's why I'm on a mission to rescue her, to save her from this living nightmare. I promised her that I would, even if she no longer recalls the vow. I know there's a way, because she brought me back from the dark abyss of Naresteé's Ringer magic—Pacey, too. She found me, and she brought me home.

It's my turn to do the same.

I take my time as I stealthily walk past the engine room. The space clouded in red light and steam. The workers down here are exhausted, underpaid, or Tributes, so they turn a blind eye to my presence—our presence. I don't need to use my magic to hide myself as I sneak through. We've been here for a few days now, and that's already too long to be safe. We'll have to leave tomorrow, find a new nook to hide in for a couple of days. The process on repeat. It's the only way we can hope to survive in the underbellies of this fleet. Because the prince is patient, cunning, he likes his prey to come to him, but that doesn't mean he isn't hunting us, as well. He's privy to the fact we lurk within his Azurite, and he knows we're going to come for his bride.

When I open the heavy metal door to our makeshift cabin room, I close it, assuring not a single person is in sight, just to be safe.

The voice that greets me lies on his bed of blankets, stinking like a rat in the sewage halls. "Why the long face?"

"Deimos, you're a treat, as always."

He sits up flamboyantly, as he does. The man is . . . odd. Yet, he, the Terran girl named Pacey, and I have been hiding together for a while. It's safer to separate into duos or trios, drawing less attention to us. Every couple of weeks, we alternate. That way, no one group looks the same—again, to be safe.

"Any news?" he asks, and I see that hope flash in his eyes, hope I'm struggling to hold on to myself. Pacey looks up from her small, makeshift bed made of dull blankets, her large eyes haunting each time she glares up at me.

I cannot lie to them. "The rebels within the Azurite say she doesn't leave the prince's side. It's rare he leaves her alone. They appear to be basking in their new romantic love for each other."

That latter fact boils my blood, although I do not show it.

Deimos growls and hisses at my words. I hate this more than he knows. Pacey, with her knees held up to her chest, merely ducks her head between them.

"That sick bastard," Deimos seethes. "He scrambled her mind, so she believes she's in love with him. Jupiter's rings. He's a madman. And the other one? Pretty boy—her brother?" He nods his head towards Pacey.

"I was finally able to find him," I say, eyes looking down at the bottles of water and small bits of food we've managed to collect.

Pacey's head jolts back up at me, but she's not hopeful.

"And?" Deimos presses impatiently, but my eyes never leave the Earth girl's.

I sigh, not the least bit overjoyed to deliver the news to my Starseed companions. "His memories have not been altered, from what I was able to glean. Malakyte has him down in the fighting pits, fighting nearly all day, every day. When he's not in the pits, he's . . . with the SSPARROWs. He's collared, obviously. It's bad. For whatever reason, Malakyte seemed to keep his memories intact and threw him down there to punish him, making him watch as Malakyte flaunts Kara around like she's his new prize. So, Ardelle will always know what happened to the woman he loves. That he couldn't save her in the end. That's what it appears to look like, anyway. I cannot be sure of the prince's motives."

Pacey begins crying. The Azurite is always echoing with the sounds of her heartbreak.

For the first time since meeting him, my alien comrade is stunned into silence, the skin around his wide eyes growing more sunken in and wrinkled as the days go by.

"Holy fuck . . . not even I would think of something that sick." He shakes his head, scratching his long, extended ear. "Pretty boy doesn't deserve this. None of them do. What of the Ringer?"

He means Jance, Kara's father. This, at least, isn't as terrible. "His memories have been wiped, it seems, and he's acting as Kara's personal guard. He's not permitted off the ship, but at least they're together in some weird, sick way."

Deimos merely shrugs. Like I said, not terrible. Could be worse. Jance could be Ardelle.

"How are we going to save them?" Pacey mumbles dully, her chin resting on the top of her knees. "How are we going to stop him?"

With everything in my chest, I wish I knew the answer to those plaguing thoughts of hers.

I lean against the cold metal door, sighing deeply and doing all I can to keep the hopelessness from creeping in.

"Kara wouldn't give up. She'd find a way. Just like she found a way to free us from our mental prison. Our shackles seemed unbreakable, too, and she all but started a revolution to free us from those bindings. Earth is in shambles down there. They know Arianyte has taken her captive and war has begun. She did that for us. No matter what we must do, we will find a way."

Deimos raises a white brow at me when he asks, "You love her, don't you?"

I do not hesitate to answer. "I've always loved her."

"Malakyte isn't going to let her go without one hell of a battle," Deimos challenges. "Now that he has her, the only way to get her back is to kill him. We had a solid plan to stop him last time. Look where it landed us."

"Yes, we failed," I agree, rubbing the stubble growing along my chin. I include myself in this because I was also amongst the ones who failed that night. "However, we're going to be smarter, swifter, and a hell of a lot crueler this time around. I'll cross any line, lie and cheat and steal and kill and fuck whoever I must to get her back. That is how we'll stop him and save them all."

Pacey seems slightly more hopeful, a flash of optimism twinkling in those large sad eyes.

For the first time since fleeing the throne room together, Deimos's mouth lifts into what I can only call a smile. "I like you, muscles. I see why you're my Ringer, after all."

I smirk in return, if only an ounce.

I'm coming for you, Kara, no matter what. I'm coming.

More by Arabella

Did you love The Mark of Dreams and Darkness and seriously can't wait for book 3, The Mark of Shadows and Starlight? Well, you're in luck, because by clicking the link below and signing up for the Arabella's Army newsletter you can get access to exclusive scenes from Malakyte's POV. Does his obsession with Kara sound romantic, or straight up stalkerish? Well, just wait till you see this special scene, revealing a huge secret to Kara's past that you can't get anywhere else. The Mark of Shadows and Starlight is coming fall 2024

Want to show Arabella some love? Please consider leaving a review on your favorite bookish platform like Amazon, Goodreads, Barnes and Noble, and wherever you like to leave your reviews. Reviews help Arabella tune to her reader's needs and desires, and reviews are always greatly appreciated. Don't forget to tag Arabella on social media if you loved this book, took a picture of the novel, or draw art inspired by this story.

Links to all your favorite review platforms are included in the QR code's link below.

ACKNOWLEDGMENTS

Writing book two was an entirely different process than writing book one. It's incredible to think I took nearly four years to write one book yet managed to write my second book—completed and ready to publish—in just one year. A lot had to happen for *The Mark of Chaos and Creation* to come together in the end. That book is so special to me, and I don't know if any of my future books, even this one, will ever quite mean what Chaos and Creation has meant to me. That being said, writing *The Mark of Dreams and Darkness* truly made me feel like a real author. I'd like to think that becoming a storyteller is what happened with this book. That, if you've made it this far, I did my job and entertained you long enough to finish the book and hopefully are excited to read the next installment.

My goal has always been to become a storyteller that tells you, the reader, an amazing and engaging story. One that you, hopefully, cannot put down and relate to deep enough to tell your best friend about. A story that goes beyond paper and ink and infiltrates your heart, perhaps heals you in some small way and leaves you better for it. I know I'm capable of that, but because I'm a real author now, I question myself incessantly. I've grown so much between books one and two, and I hope if you've followed me on my journey that you see that growth and appreciate my commitment to becoming a better writer with each and every book I write. That will always be my commitment to my readers, that no matter what, I'll always try to improve and do better, book after book. Not many people write their first books, and even less write that book's sequel. So, book two truly made it feel all more real. That I'm actually doing this author thing. And that's incredible because it's my dream to be an author, and I hope I can continue to do it for a long time. Without readers like yourself, I wouldn't be able to do this job. You are who I do this for. I want to share with others my passion for storytelling and use it to entertain, heal, and make people laugh and cry because that's what a good storyteller does. That's what a good author does, and I feel like I'm becoming that now. It's incredible to experience, and I couldn't do it without you.

Speaking of those who I couldn't do this without, I'd like to thank the amazing team of professionals that I've got behind me. Without them, there would be no way this book or this series would ever have gotten off the ground, let alone become as successful as it has been. From the outline to the final storytelling pass, the amazing team at Writer Therapy has been an insurmountable portion of this book and is the story's backbone. Chersti Nieveen, Andraea Jones, Tanner Perkes, and Ben Stapley all worked so hard, so diligently, so thoroughly on this book that it wouldn't even come close to sparkling as brightly had they not put all their hard work and dedication into it. The book not only is one hundred times better than it otherwise would have been, but probably more importantly, I am a better author because of them. I learned so much more about storytelling and writing, psychology and marketing, what works and what doesn't. I could go on and on. That is the staple of a truly amazing editor, where they make the author a better writer at the end of the process. To me, that's something that goes beyond one single edit on one single book. Having a team of editors who are so passionate about this book and this entire series is worth more than gold, and I am so lucky to have them by my side.

Second, my copy editor Samantha Pico at Miss Eloquent Edits has painstakingly polished and refined this book on multiple levels. From the sentences and grammar to the beautiful formatting, Samantha has made this book look and feel as professional and beautiful as any New York Times bestseller, and I couldn't be more grateful for her talent, patience, and friendship. I am beyond honored to have you on my team.

Next, another person I couldn't have done this without is Stefanie Saw at Seventhstar Art Services, who designed my beautiful and gorgeous cover and hardcover design. A special shout-out to Florian Cavenel for his amazing artistry of the scythe on this cover. The two of you are such an amazing team, and you never disappoint me when it comes to the beauty and stunning nature of my covers. The compliments and eyeballs my book gets purely based on this cover has been astonishing. We won Best Indie Book Cover for *The Mark of Chaos and Creation*, and I have no doubt we'll win another award for this book, as well. You're so very talented, the both of you, and I am thrilled beyond measure that I get to work with such amazing artists like yourselves.

For my special hardcover edition, I'd like to thank Jen Houser at Painted Wings Publishing for her amazing talent with the inked edges and interior border. I've never seen anyone else do this, and it's truly a mix of genius and artistry my brain will never be able to comprehend. It's so cool, and this special edition is special because of you. I'm so very happy our paths have crossed and I have the opportunity to work with you.

Finally, as a little future acknowledgment, I wanted to thank Nikki Grey for her amazing audio narration that'll follow publication at a future date. Her performance in Chaos and Creation was truly fantastic, and I know she's going to absolutely kill it in Dreams and Darkness. I look forward to working with you again and hearing my characters come to life. It's truly one of the best parts of this job, and I'm so grateful you are my Kara, because you embody all of who she is exactly as I see her. You bring her and all the other characters to life in a way very few narrators can. You're so very talented, and I am so very lucky to have you.

And because us authors never get here alone, my family is next on the list of people I have to thank. My mom, dad, and sister have been such amazing supporters in more ways than one. I'd never be able to do this without them. Being an author is amazing, but sometimes, it's incredibly hard. There are days I don't believe in myself, times I want to quit, and moments where I don't think I have what it takes. Without my family's constant and unyielding support, I wouldn't be here. I wouldn't have the guts to put my books out into the world. Knowing that you have people who believe in you is half the battle. My sister Sabrina is my constant companion at cons and events, and I couldn't do them without you. You're the best big sis. And, Mom, I know you're my biggest fan, and I wouldn't have it be anyone else.

I also have so many great friends who've been supportive of my books. I was so thrilled to see how many people bought and read and supported me, so it was very humbling to have your support. For all your shares, reviews, comments, encouragements, videos, tags… thank you so much for hyping me up and making me feel like I can do this. I need you more than I can say, and my gratitude is simply overwhelming.

And I couldn't write an acknowledgment without thanking Arabella's Army. All my readers, supporters, and fans. The ones who buy my books. I've saved the best for last. Chaos and Creation didn't blow up overnight. It's been a slow, steady climb that I hope will only continue to keep growing and reaching more and more of you. All the videos, comments, tags, posts, hashtags, emails/ DMs, beta readers, ARC readers, street team—all of you are what makes me successful. You're the ones who share my books, tell your friends, and make this possible for me to continue writing. For those who show up at events just to see me—thank you so much for your dedication and passion for this series. For all my Malakyte-lovin' girlies—you know who you are—I see you! All of you in Arabella's Army mean so much to me. I love you guys. I truly do. Thank you for being my reader. I hope my books give you what you need, even if it wasn't exactly what you asked for. Thank you for experiencing this wild ride with me, for sharing and posting and recommending these books to those you think will love it. Thank you for taking a chance on something different, something that's outside the box but just as spectacular. It takes courage to go off the beaten path sometimes, so thank you for being a loyal soldier in my army. The amount of love and support for me and this series has been so humbling and beautiful.

Thank you for reading this book. Book three will be coming next year, with all the spicy drama and action you've come to love from me. In the meantime, use the following hashtags to post, make TikToks, to share and let the world know what you thought of this second installment. Do not forget to leave a review on Amazon, Goodreads, or Barnes and Noble—multiple platforms are totally okay! Just copy/paste your review into each platform—it helps so very much.

#SaveKaraSaga
#TheMarkofCreationChronicles
#TheMarkofChaosandCreation
#TheMarkofDreamsandDarkness
#ArabellasArmy
#ArabellaK.Federico

About The Author

Arabella is a loving dog mom who enjoys art, roller skating, good TV shows and movies, and all things fantasy and supernatural. When she isn't writing she's often drawing character portraits, making content on her social media accounts, and helping other aspiring writers realize the dream of becoming a published author. Arabella loves to inspire and teach the craft of writing to others and finds fulfillment in sharing her knowledge to the world in hopes she can give back to those who taught her along the way.

You can find Arabella on social media by searching Arabella K. Federico or by visiting https://www.ArabellaKFederico.com. Arabella has a reader's only private Facebook group where there's special artwork and one-on-one access to Arabella all throughout the year. You can find the Facebook group by searching Arabella's Army on Facebook.